T0354776

JOURNEY
OF A
BLACK MAN

JOURNEY
OF A
BLACK MAN

PRINCE OLUGBENGA ADEGBUYI OREBANWO

JOURNEY OF A BLACK MAN

iUniverse books may be ordered through booksellers or by contacting:

iUniverse
1663 Liberty Drive
Bloomington, IN 47403
www.iuniverse.com
1-800-Authors (1-800-288-4677)

ISBN: 978-1-5320-0069-0 (sc)
ISBN: 978-1-5320-0070-6 (e)

Library of Congress Control Number: 2016909790

Print information available on the last page.

iUniverse rev. date: 08/11/2016

Martin Luther King, Nelson Mandelanism, Empower My Obama Movement, Peace, Agile, Reconciliatory

Peace: Embraces Martin Luther King life and ideology.
Agile: Symbolism of people worldwide that have, and are standing for humanity, democracy and love.
Reconciliatory: Embraces Nelson Mandela ideology of reconciliation amiss hostility.

Voice of an African Boy
I am **BLIND!!** Of the future, for there is **HUMAN MAZE!** everywhere I look, and try, and gaze at the **future horizon!!!**.
Look! Look!! And stretch your thought, beyond **now!** But see! Only within the horizon of **hopeless! And suffering! And lack! And poverty!** Search and gaze inward at **then!!**
To render the **view of now**, perhaps the **MAZE!** could fade, yes! make **MOCKERY** of my plight, "get **EDUCATED** they preached!
And your **SHOES ECHOE SUCCESS!** to the hearing of him, reluctant to study hard."
Tough, hard, hunger, passed **WAEC! GCE! JAMB!** and **monsters** of **ACAMEDIC FEAR!!** defeated.
I beat my chest for **BACHELORS, and, MASTERS** in **SCIENCE, ENGINEERING, HUMANITY, and PHD** in all phase of human endeavors, only to see this **MAZE!!!** And blank horizon, always in control, **monsters of greed, and corruption here and there, my VIEWS!!!**

How amazing? This ugly monster now so popular above any face I see.
It's name common in every tongue, **WHY?** And **HOW?**
Now this my **local creature** is known global, and "**Opera Winfrey**" comments "**they call you 'Mungun' '419'.**"

GOLD, SILVER, DIAMOND, PETROLEUM, MINES, and MORE, NORTH, SOUTH, the SOIL rich!! Feed and nurture us in past.
Why? We with pride! Supplied raw materials and resources to the world.
But **now, more scavengers to feed is my view!!**

This monster prosper! only prosper!! and only prosper!!!

(BBC News Africa, www.bbc.com/news/world-africa-26270561, 20 February 2014: Nigeria central bank head Lamido Sanusi ousted by the president for "financial reckless and misconduct." Mr. Sanusi caused shock waves in Nigeria when he alleged that $20bn (£12b) in oil revenue had gone missing......).

How? Where this monster originate?

BACKWARD search! rewind the scene of life, to past horizon, "EFCC to probe Babangida's asset in France, Tuesday, 30 Jan 07 http://www. effcnigeria.org/index.php?option=com_content&task=view&IT..." "French paper put the overall worth of IBB at #450 billion (EFCC, 2007). ---- recently, indications emerged that the EFCC had made a breakthrough in its bid to probe IBB over alleged mismanagement (better refers as 'steady') of more than $12m oil windfall--- during the 1991 Gulf war, code-name 'Operation Desert Storm' ---".

"According to post Abacha governmental sources, some $3 to $4 billion in foreign assets have been traced to Abacha family and their representatives" Encyclopedia Britannica, 2007: online. IT press release, London, 25 March...; Abacha family in 2002 accepted to return $1.2 billion that was taken from the Central bank, The World watch Institute (2003); the names of Sani Abacha and his widow Maryam, (see Nigeria recovers Abacha's cash BBC news retrieved on 2006-10-21), are often used in 419 scams; he is identified in scam letters as the source for money that does not exist, (see 'Who wants to be a millionaire? - an online collection of Nigeria scam mails;

- all cited' Corruption Allegation, at http://encyclopedia.org/wiki/ San_Abacha(07/02/2007). ---")

"--- indication that suggest President Obasanjo as probably corrupt during his tenure was Library Launch at Abeokuta, Ogun state Nigeria that is the Obasanjo. President Library (OPL) project. ---". "Corruption started during the Shagari administration, Nuhu Ribadu chairman of the Economic and Finance Crimes Commission (EFCC), accused his regime of introducing corruption in Nigeria's body politics. ---" "http://www.academia. edu/155571/Polical_Corruption_Ctritica_Governac_Prolem_facing_the Nigeria state; Corporative ---" by Brian-Vincent Ikejiaku.

"The Second Republic, under President Shehu Shagari, witnessed a resurgence of corruption.

The Shagari administration was marked by spectacular government corruption, as the President did nothing to stop the looting of public funds by elected officials. Corruption among the political leaders was amplified due to greater availability of funds. It was claimed that over $16 billion in oil revenues were lost between 1979 and 1983 during the reign of President Shehu Shagari.....

(Dash, 1983)....

No politician symbolised the graft and avarice under Shagari's government more than his combative Transport Minister, Alhaji Umaru Dikko, who was alleged to have mismanaged about N4 billion of public fund meant for the importation of rice."

"http://www.unh.edu/nigerianstudies/articles/Issue2/Political_leadership.pdf" --- by Michael M. Ogbeidi

"General Yakubu Gowon ruled the country at a time Nigeria experienced an unprecedented wealth from the oil boom of the 1970s. Apart from the mismanagement of the economy, the Gowon regime was enmeshed in deep-seated corruption. By 1974, reports of unaccountable wealth of Gowon's military governors and other public office holders had become the crux of discussion in the various Nigerian dailies.

The Federal Assets Investigation Panel of 1975 found ten of the twelve state military governors in the Gowon regime guilty of corruption. The guilty persons were dismissed from the military services with ignominy. They were also forced to give up ill-acquired properties considered to be in excess of their earnings (M. O. Maduagwu quoted in Gboyega, 1996: 3)."

"http://www.unh.edu/nigerianstudies/articles/Issue2/Political_leadership.pdf" --- by Michael M. Ogbeidi"

"In the same vein, the Belgore Commission of Inquiry was established to investigate the 'Cement Armada'. The Commission indicted the Gowon government of inflating contracts for cement on behalf of the Ministry of Defence for private profit at a great cost to the government. In its Commission noted that the Ministry of Defence needed only 2.9 million tons of cement at a cost of N52 million as against the 16 million metric tons of cement, it ordered, at a cost of N557 million (Afolabi, 1993)." "http://www.unh.edu/nigerianstudies/articles/Issue2/Political_leadership. pdf" --- by Michael M. Ogbeidi"

"The General Aguiyi Thomas Ironsi military government that replaced the sacked civilian regime instituted a series of commissions of inquiry to investigate the activities of some government parastatals and to probe the widespread corruption that characterised the public service sector of the deposed regime. The report on the parastatals, especially the Nigeria Railway Corporation, Nigeria Ports Authority, and the defunct Electricity Corporation of Nigeria and Nigeria Airways, revealed that a number of ministers formed companies and used their influence to secure contracts. Moreover, they were found guilty of misappropriation of funds as well as disregarding laid down procedures in the award of contracts by parastatals under their Ministries (Okonkwo, 2007)." "http://www.unh.edu/nigerianstudies/articles/Issue2/Political_leadership. pdf" --- by Michael M. Ogbeidi"

"The First Republic under the leadership of Sir Abubakar Tafawa Balewa, the Prime Minister, and Nnamdi Azikwe, the President, was marked by widespread corruption. Government officials looted public funds with impunity. Federal Representative and Ministers flaunted their wealth with reckless abandon. In fact, it appeared there were no men of good character in the political leadership of the First Republic. Politically, the thinking of the First Republic Nigerian leadership class was based on politics for material gain; making money and living well." "http://www.unh.edu/nigerianstudies/articles/Issue2/Political_leadership. pdf" --- by Michael M. Ogbeidi"

Whoa! With "**Nigeria**" political foundation bad and her **first** "**British**" **educated elite turned** politicians! **Inherit** corrupt style of administration!! Evident! Historically!! **OH!!!**

"......... In 1956, the Foster-Sutton Tribunal investigated the Premier of the Eastern Region, Nnamdi Azikiwe for his involvement in the affairs of

African Continental Bank (ACB). Under the code of conduct for ministers, a government officer was required to relinquish his holdings in private business when he assumed public office. The Foster-Sutton Tribunal felt that Zik did not severe his connections to the bank when he became a Minister. The Tribunal believed that Zik continued to use his influence to further the interests of ACB.

Zik, his family, and the Zik Group of Companies were the principal shareholders of the African Continental Bank. ACB loaned over L163, 000 to the Zik Group of Companies at low interest. The Zik group did not have to repay the loans until 1971. ACB was a distressed bank. The new registrar of banks in 1952 refused to grant ACB a license. Attempts to find partners for the bank in Britain failed because of the insolvency of the bank......."

"Corruption in Nigeria: A Historical Perspective (1947-2002) (Part 1 of 2)"
"http://africaunchained.blogspot.com/2007/09/corruption-in-nigeria-historical.html"
By Rina Okonkwo

"....Obafemi Awolowo, the first premier of the Western Region, was found guilty of corruption by the Coker Commission in 1962. In 1954, the Western Region Marketing Board had L6.2 million. By May 1962, it had to exist on overdrafts amounting to over L2.5 million. A loan of L6.7 million was made to the National Investment and Properties Co., Ltd. for building projects out of which only L500, 000 was ever re-paid. The Western Region Finance Corporation and the West Nigeria Development Corporation also received loans of millions of pounds, which were never re-paid. The Coker Commission found Awolowo responsible for the all the ills of the Western Region Marketing Board, and Awolowo "without a doubt has failed to adhere to the standards of conduct which are required for persons holding such a post."9........"

"Corruption in Nigeria: A Historical Perspective (1947-2002) (Part 1 of 2)"
"http://africaunchained.blogspot.com/2007/09/corruption-in-nigeria-historical.html"
By Rina Okonkwo

African Prince,
March 3, 2014.

CHAPTER 1

The African Boy in United State Of America!!!,

Who Am I?

"Congratulations!" echo here and there from everybody that I know. I appears to be more popular than what my imagination could have made me. It seems I should be able to get any lady to agree to marry me just by asking her and without her giving it any thought. This wouldn't have been possible, yesterday, before I got the "Big Brown Envelope" from the American Embassy, which confirmed that I had won the American immigration visa lottery and won the "Green Card" that would allow me into the USA. Prince Adegboke a light weight man of about 5feet 8inch in height sat on a chair made of timber on the balcony of the third floor of a four story building while he thought. And his mother, a woman in her late fifties, wearing a buba ati iro (top and rapper) dress made with ankara (African cotton fabric) called him from her room which is on the same floor of the house.

"Adegoke! Adegoke! Where have you been? Are you now telling everybody your plans, and when you are leaving for the airport? Prophet Ajakaye prophesized that you should keep your travelling plans secrete and not to tell anybody."

Then he got up from the sit and walk to her room which is the first of the three room flat that she and his four siblings live and he responds

"No, Mama Adegoke, why do you always think that I need any of these fake prophets' prophecy before I can make decision about my life? I have

1

not being telling anybody but Chief Tairu, whom God use in making me to played the lottery."

"Adegoke, let me pray for you before you get into the plaine to America, because as your mother, I have to protect you with my prayer even if you think you are grown up. I want you to know that a child would always be a baby in the sight of his parent, irrespective of his age." Reluctantly, Prince Adegoke kneels down in the front of his mother, and she took out a small wooden cross from her Bible and prays for him.

"Bye bye, boda mi (my brother),"

he was greeted by his siblings. Shaking hands with his brothers and sisters, and prostrates for his mother, Prince Adegoke bides them "good bye" as he went to the airport terminal to board the plaine for the journey to the USA. In the plaine, he thinks, I wonder why my mother and every of my people in Nigeria are so afraid over everything they do, always full of suspicious minds and see everyone as potential enemy?

Whereas, from my observation, the people of the Western world (the white) have learn to do things together without the fear that every of his neighbor would use witchcraft to affect his progress in life.

Several years later, he was having conversation with his friend Kunle:

"I have being in Texas for about 13 years and it is obvious that life is far tough and difficult for black people when compared with the white. We the black people are being looked down on by the white, and considered and treated as if we are not human being. Kunle did you know that I faced a lot of discrimination in the USA Navy? And I was made to do all the dirty works and especially those which the white boys would reject. Obi1, I would be called and ordered to man posts that were extremely hot and difficult for the excuse that I am from Africa and after all strong. Inspite the order of the Captain Stanburger of my US Navy destroyer ship, that such posts or duties should be evenly assigned so as to ensured that not only me, Petty Officer Adegoke would be made to take such duties alone."

"Adegoke!" "Yes you are correct we never knew that we from Africa are considered less human, not until we get here. I remembered on my first job at a nursing home, I was asked by an African American lady that do you people sleep on the tree? Because that is what they tell us that the people in Africa are like Chimpanzees and primitives."

"Kunle!" "You remember the court's verdict of which the judge announced: 'I found you guilty as charge for public intoxication and she continued though as a judge in this court with more than 3 years experience, I found you Adegoke Banwo facilitating for standing up and defending yourself on this matter, and your evidence is quite convincing that the police men did not give your mental health the necessary serious consideration, but unfortunate, you have to take the guilty verdict.'"

"Adegoke!" "We all know that a black person does not have right for justice in this country. Black people would not be able to get good job, even though he/she may be very well qualified for the job."

"Yes, of course, people of my race cannot get a company for internship in Engineering in the University of Texas, while the white students are given opportunity for co-ops from their high school till they graduate in the university."

"Are you just realizing that you are giving the 'Green Card Visa' irrespective of your qualification, just to come and do the dirty work, which the white people are rejecting? Go to all these big building offices, you will found the white people working as administrators and managers, and if you look and observed them they do not put in much serious work when compared to the people engage in the blue collar jobs who are always sweating it out and with far lesser pay."

"Kunle!" "Do you realize that whenever there is a resection, or the economy is slow, the black people are always made to suffer the consequences of it."

"Yes Adegoke!" "Even in Engineering, with the advancement in programming, the white people are now making themselves managers in the Engineering fields without having the experience or knowledge of simple Algebra. Since it now so easy to do so because all the data could be program using software programming languages which is now easily contracted out of USA to place like Indians and other Asia countries. And whenever the artificial resection takes place, or the economy is slow, guess what happen? The black engineers are the first people to be sack, but only to be re-employed with lesser pay or reduced and no incentives."

"But, Kunle!" "Why are we black people treated so low, and in fact being subject of hatred by the white, even though there is abolition of slave trade and the various effort by some good white and black people to create equal opportunity for all God's creation. It is surprising that you still found people trying, throwing, and confronting we black people with white supremacy every now and then?"

"Adegoke!" "You should be able to answer the question, are you not from the Royal home? After all you are Prince Adegoke of the Ijebuland in Nigeria. You should be able to prove if you're inferior to the Royal Princes and the kings in Europe."

"Thanks for the mockery, but in fact, you're quite in order! I would have to investigate by researching into our history to know who we the black people are, and how we found ourselves in this race inferiority mess?"

However the following month Adegoke told Kunle after the end of a Sunday morning church service at at The People Baptist Church car park that "Kunle!" "I have purchased my flight ticket to Nigeria, and I would be leaving on May 13, 2015, since our conversation last month, I have given a serious thought of how far our people have been suffering over this race issues and the spirit of the Awujale (Emperor of the Ijebuland) in me is compelling me to do something about it."

"Adegoke!" "Is it because of what I said? I don't mean to hurt your feelings at all. I was only joking."

"Kunle!" "You don't have to worry. It time for something to be done about it. May be that is why God made us to have the conversation."

Thereafter they entered into their cars and said good bye to each other, and Kunle drove his car away from the church premises. And Adegboke remains in his car, listening to an hip pop music while he wait for a member of the church that needs a ride home.

Now in Nigeria:

"Welcome home! American boy! What have you brought for us in Nigeria? Mama Adegoke congratulations, he arrived back save, and more healthy."

"Yes Adesola!" "Your brother looks very radiant and big, he must have been feeding very well in America."

Princess Adesola, Prince Adegoke's sister, a beautiful slim stature lady in her mid twenties of about 5feet 8inch tall ran towards him and embraced him and said:

"Broda mi!" "Ki le mu bo fun wa!" ("My brother!" "what have brought for us!") "Since over five years now we have not seen you, you must not tell me that you did not bring American things for us, otherwise we would have you send back to the USA."

"Mama Adegoke!" "Please help me to explain to these police officers, who are 'shouting waitin you carry' when they don't have any touch light in their hands, that I only come home in a hurry with a message for the Awujale Oba Adetona, because I am being compel to come and see what can be done to improve our economy and business here in Nigeria."

Mama Adegoke responds,

"but, you should have realized that it would have been wrong of you to come home without bringing gifts for people at home, not to talk you did not even remember to bring gift for me your mother."

"I know mama Adegoke that you are the number one police officer, that would always want to get bribes every time, and by the way where is your touch light? Because without having one in hand, that makes you a fake police man, so I have nothing to give you."

"Adegoke!" "Please make sure you buy or get some money as gift for my sisters and aunty in Ijebu-Ode, since you have not seen them for a long time, even if it is small it is better than meeting them empty handed. And before you leave come inside your room so that I can talk to you privately."

"Yes mama Adegoke, here I am."

And his mother said:

"You remember the prophecy that Prophet Ojo said that you should not shake peoples' hand when you get to Ijebu-Ode. I beg you in Jesus name please listen and do as you are told, because I am your mother, I should know best how to protect you against evil people and witchcraft."

"OK, I have heard you and don't worry yourself over nothing, and beside I have told you to stop letting these fake prophets continue telling you lies as prophecies. They are just tying in getting the little money you have, and they are only succeeding by creating unnecessary fear in you instead of faith."

"Welcome to Ijebu-Ode Unfila, Unbata"

(nicknames given me when I was months old) my cousin Adeshina Salami a slightly built man in early sixties smiling, raise me up as I was about to prostrate to greet him and he said.

"Omo America!" "Ko le do bale, di de!" ("You are now an American so no need for you to prostrate!") "How is my Aunty? (which he meant Cousin). How is your journey from the US? You said you want to see the Awujale Oba (Emperor) Adetona. I should be able to take you to his palace, but he may not give you the excepted audience because he is now old, so I would suggest we tell the Oba (king) Kasali of Itele, the Kabiyesi (the Unquestionable one) of your mission and he would be able to get it done or bring the Awujale Oba (Emperor) Sikiru Adetona on board."

"OK, broda mi Shina (my cousin Shina), we would go to the Oba Kasali."

Then after about one and half driving on the bad roads, for a journey that should not have taken more than 20 munites. We arrived at the Itele town.

"Kabiyesi o! Kabiyesi o!"

I greet the Oba Itele, an elderly man in his eighties siting on a mahogany chair at the porch of his mansion constructed in the middle of well hedge compound that is of about ten hectare land, stretching in prostration on the ground at his front because that is the proper manner of greeting an Oba in Yorubaland, where we the Ijebus are prominent.

"Kabiyesi! I Prince Adegoke, a great grandson of the Awujale Oba (Emperor) Sotejoye of Ijebuland, and the Awujale Oba (Emperor) Afesojoye Anikilaya of Ijebuland, came fromTexas in USA, and wants to know our history right from Noah, so that we can have a true information about our race, and also make a movie of it like other races."

"Welcome my child Adegoke!" "I am pleased with you and your mission. I shall be willing to assist you with your request and mission. In fact, I want you to meet Prince Adewale, who I believe has a similar motive like yours and I think you can work together with him."

Then the Kabiyesi told one of his attendant to bring him some books and other literature to read while we awaited the arrival of Prince Adewale. Afterward we had discussions about the nature of things in the country and about electrical power generation, because he is also an electrical engineer. Later I excused myself from his presence so he could attend to other people, and discuss with them issues concerning Itele town. Then the next morning the Oba Kasali released some literature to us and we were exposed to a transcript of the oral narratives of our history that had been given by our ancestors:

Yoruba's Ancestors account of creation of the Earth by GOD

We are told by our ancestors that we are strongly grounded in the belief that a mighty, mysterious, mythical and unquestionable being, who is in the heavens far far-away from the earth, who is called the Lord of the Heaven, **OLORUN, OLORUN-ELEDUMARE**, who was self derivable through whom all things were made from time immemorial, he is the manifested and unseen **GOD** who is in everywhere and who knew everything from the past, the present and well into the future. This is the believe on which the faith of our forefathers in the Ifa (Yoruba oracle) is vested. As we know by our ancestors, that **OLORUN** (God) in heaven created the higher divinities we refer to as the Angels, and then the lower divinities or deities called the Orisas (gods), to assist **GOD** in the discharge of his wishes. And these deities numbering some 201, or up to 1700, as to some claims, **OLORUN** create and all things as to his delight. According to the Ifa (Oracle) the heaven existed above and encircling a formless waste and watery void called Ibu omi, before **OLORUN** creates the deities to assist him in creation. Thereafter, **OLORUN** create man in his own image from clay. (Genesis 2 verse 7, Quran 6 verses 2, 21 and 23). Then **OLORUN** told all the deities to close their eyes and cover their face with their hands, and all the deities did except for Orunmila whose eyes were open and was able to see through the space in his fingers. So **OLORUN** told him to join him as a living witness and Orunmila assist and actually mold the eyes and ears of the new creature whom they called **Adamaha** (Adam). Thus, Orunmila became second in command to **OLORUN**, because of his role Orunmia is also called Eleri Orisa, Eleri Ipin (God own witness) by our ancestors. After, there was the time when the heaven become overpopulated, and **OLORUN** decided on his own hidden agenda to create a new firmament for the deities and man, so as to separate himself (**OLORUN**) from them and only communicate in spirit thereafter. Then **OLORUN** instruct the Orisas and man to take all the materials needed from the heaven and sent them out through a tunnel connecting the heaven to the formless waste and watery void that is referred to as Ibu Omi (Body of water) in Ifa (Oracle) also see (Genesis 1: 1).

However, Orumila being the last to leave heaven, took with him snails shells containing sand. Other deities like Ogun took iron, thus he is being referred to as the deity for iron smith work and all metal works, and all these deities are known today to represent different use of materials in relation to employment and relative to the materials they took with them from the heaven. Then Orunmila poured out the sand to form a whorl of the earth; the Pangae-Laurasia complex according geomorphologists. Then to determine its suitability and strength of this whorl of the earth, a chameleon was made to thread on it and a hen (bird) followed which scatter the sand on it that create the continents which were joined together as a clump called the Pangae and Laurasia continents. According to our ancestors, the location that is referred to by scientist as "Pangaea" was likely the location of the first settlement on the earth, called the "Atlantis" and it is at the point where the present West African coast was conjoined with the eastern coastline of the South American continent. Then after they had settle down, the other deities become jealous of Orunmila, and maltreated him, they denied him of the materials and resources that are due to him. And there was quarrel among the deities which result into riotous situation and disorder. So Orunmila complained to **OLORUN** and **OLORUN** gave him the permission to return to the heaven with his followers. Then after, **OLORUN-ELEDUMARE** (God Almighty) open the dam in the heaven and flood the newly created earth, that is the Atlantis in Pangae. And the flooding and drowning of all the other deities and their followers on the earth. Thus, result in the sinking of the continent of Atlantis, during the **Ice Age** which lead to the creation of the **Atlantic Ocean** at the time when giants inhabited the earth with man, according to Genesis 6, 7. This event can be considered as synonymous to the events of the eviction of man out of the **Garden of Eden.** However, the Ifa made us to know that it took **OLORUN** seven generations to repopulate the earth again, but instead of sending people all out together at once through the connecting tunnel, they were returned back one at a time. The journey from the heaven to the earth was routed through seven hills in the heaven before the boundary, the Hades or the grey zone for fear, which is before the Erebus or the dark or the black zone which is synonymous to the womb or pregnancy. And more..... The work of nature creation was done by the deities (gods) the Ogun (metal), built roads. the Orunmila, build houses, farmlands and the introduction of the oral hygienic habit of chewing sticks that result in the Yoruba tradition and culture of oral hygiene of chewing sticks and rising with water in the morning before eating. Eventually some wicked deities came to the earth from the heaven such as Iku (Death), Ogun (wars and strife), Sango (contravention of nature), Sopanna (epidemics), and more. These have such destructive effect, and cause the seeds of distrust, hatred, wars, fighting, and commotion over the earth.

Then Adamah (Adam) great grandchildren became very prominent farmers, craftsmen, builders, sorcerers who are gifted by **OLORUN** with great magical powers and witchcraft that enable them to create a wonderful society. However, among them was Nuhabi (Noah Gensis 6,7,8,9) who was a great statesman in Ife (one of the Atlantis cities). He was very rich and a strong believer in monotheism which is the worship of **OLORUN-ELEDUMARE** only, while others where worshiping the fallen deities (angels) and Esu (The Devil), who was the supreme commander of the deities, and he became arrogant to **OLORUN** after the creation of Adamah (Adam), and seeing the glory with **OLORUN's** future plans and prominence of the descendants of Adamah on the Ile-Aye (Earth), Esu became jealous, and tricked Adamah who fell, and worship the Esu. But **OLORUN,** have to accept the argument of Esu at the throne of mercy that Adamah had failed in obeying **OLORUN-ELEDUMARE** since he had obeyed him Esu, and thus by the spiritual laws and principle of the heaven beings, Adamah has become his Esu's subject. Then **OLORUN** send Adamah out of Ogba-ajala (The Garden of Eden) see Gensis 3: 1-24. And Esu with the help of some bad deities like Iku (Death), Soponna (Epidemics), and others continue in making the lifes of Adamah descendants to be difficult. So **OLORUN-ELEDUMARE** send Esu and his evil supporters away from the heavens and they become the fallen angels see Genesis 6: 1-4. Then these deities' grandchildren eventually settled among Adamah's descendants, intermarried with them to produce more powerful and sinful people in cities and towns of Atlantis. They understand the sorcery, witchcraft, magical powers of the Heaven's work and nature, together with **OLORUN-ELEDUMARE** divine ways of using nature and the forces of nature in making things happen at his will. Such as man travelling in the time dimensional space, the use of the stars and the galaxies to predicts nature, seasons, make rain to fall suddenly, produce storm, and more. Omo-Adamah (Adam's descendants) can pronounce curse on anything, even on nature and eventually, due to greed and envy, they start cursing each other, lording over others, enslaving themselves by raiding of farmlands, forcing bribes, and unfavorable interest rates on loans over each other. Then the Atlantis become polluted with evil vices, such as homosexuality, and killing of fellow Omo-Adamah and the worship of their passed heros as gods become so prominent. Thus Esu's evil plot become very successful to the extent that it was able to deceived them that it is the better alternative god to **OLORUN-ELEDUMARE.** Then Omo-Adamah (people) build high alters of worship for Esu and ask from it permission every day in every situation before doing any thing, which is not suppose to be, because **OLORUN-ELEDUMARE** has never make or demand, or placed such burden on them. However, Esu (Devil) creates fear and distrust among them, such that they start disliking each other. The usual worship of **OLORUN-ELEDUMARE** with sacrifice of thanks giving for good farm season with crops and fruits by the farmers and animals by hunters and nomadic, was made complicated by the Esu, who deceived them that such sacrifice should be made to it alone and it should be done every day, with yams, palm wine, palm oil, palm leaves, animal bloods and more. These sins of worshiping of their past heroes and ancestors in the form of idols (wooden and metal images) cause envy among them, which become things of personal pride and result into unnecessary rivalry of whose idol is more superior and powerful over the other and result into pronouncing curses and evil words on each other. That brought the diseases, the famine, and the draught on the earth.

However, Esu and his fallen deities took the glory in this and more, by making Omo-Adamah (Adam's descendants) to become afraid of **OLORUN-ELEDUMARE**, and thinking **OLORUN** is the cause of all these problems, which made them to withdraw away from **OLORUN,** and more towards Esu, which denied them of **OLORUN-ELEDUMARE's** mercy and protection over them and the earth. Thereafter, there was a great famine in Ife such that the animals were almost finished, and food become so scarce. However, Esu told the prominent Omo-Adamah (Adam descendants) that it is the solution to their problems, and that the problems was because of the human being among them that would not worship their idols, so they should kill, eat and sacrificed the weak Omo-Adamahs, and those found guilty of not worshipping him and their gods at a very big alter that should be build to honor him. Then Omo-Adamah did as Esu commanded them, which made **OLORUN-ELEDUMARE** to destroyed them but preserved Nuhabi (Noah) and his family, who **OLORUN** had told to build a big ship to house all different kinds of animals in the land, the birds, other creatures, and his family, and **OLORUN-ELEDUMARE** destroyed the Atlantis with rain and flood. Then after, when **OLORUN-ELEDUMARE** anger had stop, he landed the ship on a mountain in the present middle east see Genesis 7, 8: 1-4.

However, Nuhabi descendants who are grandchildren of Ham settled in the land of the present Ethiopia and Egypt by the Nile valley because it is fertile. And they are people of black color or better described brownish in appearance, with curly hair, they speak Yoruba language, and continue with the worship of Ifa (Oracle), they began agro-culture site and civilization. But since Esu (Devil) is still given equal access in the Heaven's court before **OLORUN-ELEDUMARE** (God Almighty), Esu was able to have interaction among them. So there come a time when Lamurudu, a man who was synonymous with Nimrod, Noah's great grandson, (Genesis 11 verse 1-9) decide to recreate the link between Ile-Aye (Earth) and the Heaven. Then Lamurudu called the prominent Nuhabi's descendant and discussed with them about the ways to connect back to **OLORUN-ELEDUMARE** in the heaven since they had looked without success for the magical rope that link their ancestors to the heaven, that Nuhabi had told them about. And whenever they had consult the Ifa, the message would be twisted by the Esu, who had polluted the minds of the Ifa priests and always changed the Odu Ifa (Oracle divine tools) which gave them wrong messages about how to get back to **OLORUN-ELEDUMARE.** And Esu still continue in making itself appears as the main link they need to reach **OLORUN-ELEDUMARE.** Then on one of such days, Esu told the Ifa priests to informed Lamurudu to construct a very big and tall tower to reach the heavens so as to get to **OLORUN-ELEDUMARE,** since **OLORUN** refused to communicate with them. And Esu, informed them that, they could do so with it's help, and that with their united in faith, and working together in unity, it would lead them to the main heaven, confront **OLORUN-ELEDUMARE** and make itself Esu the supreme lord in the heaven. However, Lamurudu and his fellow human being like the ideal, since they really need to communicate with **OLORUN-ELEDUMARE,** so there was a great celebrations with killing of animals for sacrifice, musicians, magicians and more. Then Lamurudun ordered the construction of a very big and tall buiding which was already so high into the sky and approaching the heavens. But when **OLORUN-ELEDUMARE** saw the efforts of the descendants of Nuhabi (Noah), he said

"I have to pity the children of Nuhabi, and seeing their faith and ability to work together, there is nothing they cannot achieve in as much they work together in faith and unity."

However since the Esu is still using them, and **OLORUN-ELEDUMARE** knowing that it's dangerous for them to remain unified under the leadership of Esu. Then **OLORUN-ELEDUMARE** ordered Orunmila, (the arch angel) and other angels to into the miss of the Nuhabi descendants and bring about the spirit of confusion with different tongues and languages (Genesis 11: 1-8.) Thus the Nuhabis are now separated according to the land of each of their settlement based on continents according to the three tribes of the great grandchildren of Nuhabi, of which Ham settled in the African continent, Japhethites in the continent above Mediterranean sea, and Shem in the Arabian land.

The Oba (King) Oduduwa

Many generation had past, and the descendant of Ham have spread to Ethiopia and Egypt and under the leadership of Oba Oduduwa, who our ancestor said parent us, the present Yorubas, Ijebu and Ishekiri. He was said to be a high Priest-king of Ifa (Oracle), who had came from the remnant of the Atlantis city (Ife) to Ethiopia and Egypt and became the ruler before the Pharaoh Akhenaton, and helped the development of the monotheistic faith of Horus/Horise/Orisa/Orise out of the worship of Ifa, which is the worship of the **OLORUN-ELEDUMARE** (God Almighty) as the Orisa

13

Oke (the God in Heaven), this brought stability and prosperity to people in Egypt-Ethiopia, and they were able to build a strong wall city. Thereafter, people of other race mostly of the Edomites and the Mulattos came, and dwell in the city, they brought with them more other gods, which result to confusion and hatred. However, Oduduwa could not tolerate what was going on so as the Priest-king of Orisa Oke, he did not want to curse and wage war on the city he had build and more so the Mulattos are mixed race of Ham and Edomites (Present North Africans, Greece and Italians). So he left (abjugate) as the Oba (Emperor) and settled in Ile-Ife with some people, of which his son Oranyan was the prominent, and Oranyan had many wives and children, but Uku Ogewu the parent ancestor of the Jebu/Jebusite remain as the Oba (Emperor). Then when Oba Oduduwa got to Ife (Land of choice) also known as Atlantis. He met a large settlement of people that look little bit different from them, they are more shorter with bigger head, more darker in completion with more broad nose, but still speak almost similar accent and they were called Agbomiragun (Aborigine). Moreover after several confrontation and wars, Oba Oduduwa subdued them and rule over them at Ile-Ibinu/Ibini (place of anger because Oba Oduduwa left the land in anger). Then Omo Oba (Prince) Oranyan became the ruler with the title Omo Oba/Omoloba (Grand Prince). This settlement became the first big settlemt and city/kingdom which become the Ibini empire as named by the Portuguese in the 14th century. However, the descendants of Oranyan become the Olus (Lords/Kings) in West Africa and West of Nigeria. The Uku Omoloba Ibini the Oba of Ibini, the descendant of Uku Ogewu, Ajogun, Ogborogunda also known as the Oba (Emperor) Obanta and the Awujale of Ijebuland, Olu Owu Olowu, Olu Popo, Olu Sabe, Olu Oyo/Olunioyo the Alafin Oyo, Olu Ara Alara, Olu Ajero, Olu Ila, Olu Ilesa Owa Obokun, Olu Ikole Elekole, Olu Ado Ewi, Owoni Ooni Ile Ife, Olu Owo Olowo, Olu Akure Deji, Olu Ketu Alaketu, Olu Ake Alakebode, Olu Ondo Osemawe, are the orginal descentants of the Oba (Emperor) of Ethiopia and Egypt

However, after many generations, the descendants of Nuhabi (Noah) have been scattered in the continents separated by the seas, and they continue to be deceived by the Esu (Devil) and his fellow evil deities. Moreover, **OLORUN-ELEDUMARE** have mercy on Omo-Adamah

(Adam descendants) and seeing how they have fallen to the manipulation of their enemy Esu, **OLORUN-ELEDUMARE** decided to make a refined Omo-Adamah race from Abraham, whom he told to go to Egypt during a farmine, where he met a beautiful woman Ewadunni, who was a descendant of Cush that was the Pharaoh of Egypt then. Abraham who fear **OLORUN-ELEDUMARE** and was very successful man with excellent character, and which made Lamurudu's great grandson to give his sister to Abraham to have as concubine, in order to serve as a symbol of alliance between them, and to prevent Abraham from attacking them during his stay in Egypt. Then **OLORUN-ELEDUMARE** made Abraham to become very great and promise him and also teach him the secret of being rich when **OLORUN-ELEDUMARE** told him to pay tax in the measure of tent of his supplus or gain in each season to Melchizedek, a Salem High Priest and king of Salem. Thereafter Abraham became highly blessed in Salem Genesis 14: 18-20. Mainwhile after some seasons Abraham return back to the lands of his sojourning and he took Ewadunni with him, but because of rivalry between her and other Abraham's concubines and especially Sarah, Abraham's wife. Ewadunni stayed in the land of Cannan. However, descendant of Abraham through her become the Jebus that eventually become big nation, powerful land cultivator, caravan, that trade in cloths, spies, dyes, Camels, Sheep, goats, rams and more. The Jebus build the strong walled city called Jebusalem, which become the present day Jerusalem see Genesis 10: 16. Then after many generations, the descendants of Abraham have become so many and they continue in the evil ways of life of their neighbors, and the influence of Esu (Devil), also become great among them that **OLORUN-ELEDUMARE** cursed their land with famine, but took only Abraham's descendants through Jacob, his children with their slaves, and live stocks to Egypt see Genesis 50: 1-end.

Moreover, about 2000-1500 BC, after the Hykos invasion, the Jebus also kwon as Jebusites (Jebusalem) are strong warriors, and good with the swords, machetes, catapults, Ofa (arrows), archers, and more of weapons for battles. Their fame become well kwon, and they even defeated the Greek aggression and expansion, because of their excellent skillful horse warlord, and mask men. However, during the Israel's exodus back to the lands which Abraham had sojourned, that **OLORUN-ELEDUMARE** had promise Abraham's descendants, the Jebus coexist peacefully with their cousin the Isrealites in Jebusalem, since **OLORUN-ELEDUMARE** had purposely preserved the Jebusites so as to teach the Israelites the art of warfare, Joshua 1:21. Genesis 10: 16. Then after many generations, the Jebusites and the Israelites had become so many and had intermarried see Judges 1: 21, Juges 21 and they had both forgotten about **OLORUN-ELEDUMARE** and full of the sins of worshiping Esu (Devil), and their ancestors, with other deities, together with human sacrifices, so this made **OLORUN-ELEDUMARE** to forsake them. However, after, the Jebusite become more peaceful see Judges 21: 20-25 that the land become too small to accomondate the Jebus and the Benjamite, Judians that dwell there which lead to conflict about land for their use and expansion. Mainwhile, this trouble continue until the time of King David who defeated Jebusalem and changed the name of the city to Jerusalem Psalm 7, 1 Chronicle 11: 4, during the time of Alare (Araunah/Alara) 1 Chronicles 21:14-30 and 1 Chronicle 22; 1-19, who had reign as king over the Jebus in Jebusalem. The narration in 1 Chronicles 21:14-30 and 1 Chronicle 22; 1-19 shows that the land of Jebusite is very dear to **OLORUN-ELEDUMARE** (God) that **OLORUN-ELEDUMARE** choose it as the place for the temple which King David build at the land of Alare (Araunah/Alara) King of Jebusite whom because **OLORUN-ELEDUMARE** had mercy on and Jebu people stop the plague on Isreal which **OLORUN-ELEDUMARE** used because of the sin of King David of counting the fighting men of Isreal.

The First Leg of the Jebusites Sojourn out of Canan

King Alare (Araunah/Alara) left Jebusalem with his children and the Jebus to the Owodaiye in Sheba country which is by the coast of Southern Sudan at the present Ethiopia tip of Arabian peninsula bounded in the North by Nubian at the Western of Tigre. After the Angel of the Lord stop the killing of the army of king David at the front of Jebusalem, because king David had ordered a census of his military strength to be taken so as planned the attack on Jebusalem which **OLORUN-ELEDUMARE** had promised him. (See 2 Samuel 24:1-16)

Thereafter king Alare/Araunah became a very strong king and from there he launched attack and crushed Sudan, which was a Yoruba country but had fell to the Greek and then fought his way to Egypt, conquer the Napata after thirty years of wars. He put a strong front against the invasion and aggression of descendants of the notorious Alexander the Great, the king of Macedonia.

Then some of the Jebus in Meroe migrate from Sudan into East Africa to form cities like Jebusaga, Jebuduli. The migration of the Jebus lead by Oluiwa a great grand son of Alare in about 1250 - 1450 is also reflect in National Park in Tanzania called the Liuwa Plain. The path of Oluiwa migration follow through hills and valleys in Chad and Niger Bornu and Yarraddh in Kordofan West Sudan

Bilquis Sungbo of Eredo in Ijebu-Ode (known as the Queen of Sheba in Ethiopia)

Moreover, king Alare saw a very beautiful woman called Esiwu on his arrival at entrance of the city of Sheba, who had been very nice and shows lot of cares for king Alare's warriors that had arrived ahead of king Alare. Esiwu was a princess, and a daughter of king Sahiha, who the Arabian fighters had killed when they invade Sheba in search of precious metals. And Princess Esiwu had instructed her attendance to take good care of the warriors' horses and house them. Then when king Alare got to Sheba, Agbegba, king Alare's Chief military General, told king Alare how Princess Esiwu had been kind to them so, king Alare went to meet her at her secrete dwelling place which was a cave house, that was full of male, female servants and maids. But her senior maid while she was on her kneels at the front of him said to king Alare

"my mistress is not in position to come out to see my Lord."

Looking down so as to prevent eye contact with him she and add,

"the princess would not want to be disturb because she is mourning her dead parents and brother."

17

But king Alare who cannot stand being address by a servant, got very annoyed, and shout in loud voice,

"who is she to disobey my command",

and walk pass her, but before he walk into the inner chamber, Princess Esiwu who was almost at the entrance of the inner chamber ran out and greet him. And when he saw her beauty and noticed that she was of royal blood, because of her dress that was a very rich robes. He extends his left hand to her and invite her to sit by his side while she explained that she had came to hide and took refuge in the royal cave build by her great grandfather because of the Arabian invaders.

Then king Alare called Agbegba, and ordered

"get some Ojas (military Servants) to spy on the invaders and bring report of their positions, strengths, and weakness."

Then the third day after the Ojas's report, king Alare ordered

"The flutes for the call of war shall be blown"

and he lead the attack on the palace and rescued the workers in the mines, and king Alare took Princess Esiwu as a wife. However, some years later, after king Alare had left Sheba for the invasion of Egypt, Princess Ewisu gave birth to their only child, the Bliquis Sungbo also known as the Queen of Sheba.

But king Alare died after two years of his reign, and thus the Ijebus are called "Ijebu omo Alare" (Ijebus the descendants of Alare/Alara). However, the descendants of king Alara established the 25th to the 27th Dynasty of Pharaoh in Egypt. And after ruling for almost two Hundred years, the Jebus were defeated and driven back into Sudan, because the Persians (Semites) assisted the Egyptians of the upper Nile who are Mullatos.

Then Oba Obirin (Queen) Bliquis also known as the Queen of Sheba became a very strong and powerful ruler of Sheba in Ethiopia, and her fame was well known throughout the region, because the strong warriors that her mother helped had been nice and very loyal to her. She made Sheba and Ethiopia to become a strong allied with her beauty and charm, which she used effectively in bringing the strong and powerful men who were also influential Princes to Sheba, and Sheba became a very popular female shrine where sojourners and merchants took rest. Mainwhile the female entertainments and dancers attract visitors from all over the Arabian region, Egypt, Ethiopia and Sheba, and eventually, when king Solomon became very famous, and Oba Obirin Bliquis visit Jerusalem to witness his fame, and the splendor of king Solomon. (1 Kings 10:) king Solomon became entice by her beauty, and of her famine courtesy to the extent that he proposed to her for marriage. But because she was overwhelm with the affairs of Sheba and the female shrine prosperity depends on her supervision and management. And also the Shebas' Ojas (ministers) and priest advised her not to marry king Solomon, so she left Jerusalem and return back to Sheba, and she became pregnant when she return to Sheba. However, she and her son would always visit king Solomon in Jerusalem, but after she had tried without success to make king Solomon pronounced their son as the successor to the throne of Jerusalem after Solomon. Then their son called Marigbaki, who was about 24 years, became restless, and after seeing his father who was so powerful as a king, Marigbaki now wants such power, and influence in Sheba. And Marigbaki, who was being influenced by some powerful Princes in the Arabian region who were not being favored by Oba Obirin Bliquis's (the Queen of Sheba) relationship with king Solomon, to become the king of Sheba instead of his mother. In fact, one of the Arabian Prince told Marigbaki

"since you are now above 21 years old, you should be able to lead the army of Sheba to war, and I will encouraged you to make public display of yourelf as a king with the ceremonial crown at a public banquet in Sheba."

So Marigbaki took the crown and put it on his head and also put on the robe of the throne of Sheba without asking his mother for permission. And he made such a public displayed of himself as the king of Sheba, to the delight of those powerful princes and kings of the Arabian regions who encouraged him so as to annoyed the Queen of Sheba, who was the head of the military, and the head of the priests of the gods of Sheba. Thereafter there was confusion among the military ranks of Sheba about who was in charge; being the young prince who was acting as the king, with the influence of the princes and kings who have always been strong enemy of Sheba, or the Oba Obirin Bliquis who was the actual legitimate ruler, but have lost the crown and throne to her son. However, the priests of Sheba and the warriors of Sheba, that were not among the official guards to the Oba Obirin Bliquis had made a plan to attack Marigbaki, with the argument that his self declaration as a king was a coup de tact, which is not accepted in Sheba, because by the Yoruba culture, there cannot be two commander in chiefs of the country military force. Then when the Oba Obirin Bliquis heard of these, she order all the military chiefs in the country of Sheba to report to her at the refuge cave. And since some of the strong warriors of Alare which all the warriors feared were still her guards, so all the warriors obey her command. Then the Oba Obirin Bliquis made the military to remain under the command of her son Marigbaki and she left Sheba with her most loyal guards and maids with the entourage of Olu (Lord/Prince) Olu-Iwa back on the journey to Ife. Thereafter the Oba Obirin Bliquis eventually made her place of settlement in Eredo in Ijebu-Ode.

However, the Olu Olu-Iwa who was a grandson of Alare lead the Jebus and they migrated deep into Sudan to form the kingdom of Meroe. But after some time the land was no more big enough for the cultivation and the way of lifes of the Jebus, so they migrated to the land of their Ethiopian cousin and later, the Oba Olu-Iwa consulted the Ifa priest and was told the Jebus have to migrate back to Ife (Atlantis) where king Alare had always want them to go. Then the migrant where referred to as Irun or Igba, which the Ijebu called Irunmale or Igbamale. Using "Ahmed Osman in his book 'Jesus in the House of the Pharaohs' PP 144 - 148. He cites the name Urusalim which was used in the 'Tell Amarna letters to describe palestinian Jerusalem'. Urusalem means to establish (uru from yarah) and peace (shalom or salam)." This shows similarity in the word Irumale (Urusalem) which in Ijebu (Jebu) means people of Ijebu (Jebu). And when Oba Olu-Iwa got to Imorere in Ile Ife where he met the descendants of the king Oduduwa who were his cousins and the Ora-nfe descendants, they settled away from their location in a place called Oke-Agonun which is still in Ile Ife till today. However, the land was good for cultivation and animal husbandry, and though the Oba Olu-Iwa descendants, the king Oduduwa descentants and those of Oranfe all lived in peace among each other. But, after some seasons, the Oba Olu-Iwa descendants were getting stronger and bigger and the land was no longer big enough for them. Then Oba (king) Olu-Iwa descendants migrate, but they were send away by the descendants of the Oba Oduduwa and those of Oranfe with festivities and singing:

"Ijebu maize ripened in the farm
when they changed their style,
they said none must go to Oke Agonun,
But I will visit Oke Agonun tommorrow.
The Ijebu maize rippened in their farm,
I will harvest."

The Oba Olu-Iwa's prominent followers that are warriors and keep the migration safe were:

1. The Ogbeni Oja (Valient among the Oja)
2. Oja Eginrin often referred to as Jaginrin
3. Some other smaller Oja Called Ogidigbo

These were the administrators that help in keeping peace among the people. When they settled at Ijebuland, However, Oba Olu-Iwa and the community leaders attempt to shift a river course that always affect their settlement and have being overflowing it's bank, destroying crops, their property, and also kill people without success.

Mainwhile, the order of leadership after the Oba Olu-Iwa were:

1. The king Olu-Iwa three sons who were controllers and overseers of three important settlement:
    i. Atosin, who was the ruler over the settlement of Ibu Omi (lagoon)
    ii. Owusin, who lived up land of Ibu Omi
    iii. Olomojobi who lived near Atosin.

21

There were significant Chiefs who helped in administrative functions call the Oja. The less significant among them were called Ogidigbo and have their sit under Eginrin. The most significant minister (chief) was called the Ogbeni who was constant companion to Oba Olu-Iwa and always sat with him in the council. Next to the Oja in rank were the Otus who were in charge of rituals and spiritual sacrifices to appease the gods for the settlement. After the death of the Oba Olu-Iwa, the Ogbeni Oja decided to cast lots (Ifa) on which of the Oba Olu-Iwa's children would succeed him, and it fell on the first daughter of the Oba Olu-Iwa named Oba Obirin (Queen) Ore Alaanu who the people sing praise:

"Ore ye-ye O!
Ore Alaanu O!
Ore Obu!
Ore Oke!"

meaning:

"Ore, the kind mother!
Princeless commodity in the market"

Also attempt were made by the Oba Obirin Ore Alaanu and other successors after her to shift the course of the river but without success.

The Second Leg of the Jebusites Sojourn out of canaan

After the Oba Olu-Iwa had settled in Ijebuland, Arisu and his younger brother Aruseni who had followed the Oba Olu-Iwa to Wode (Wadai) (see Wadi of Egypt 2 Kings 24:7) in Sudan and migrate to Ijebuland. However, Arisu a descendants Mojo, Onile-ere also called Ajebu, Olode, Liworo, Ayegun who were their head ministers. Followed the path of the Oba Olu-Iwa to the land of Orai (Ile Ife) and they were received by the descendants of the Oba Oduduwa and the Oranfe, but they left for the settlement of their most close cousin the Oba Olu-Iwa at the Ijebuland. And when they got there, they discovered that the Oba Olu-Iwa was already diseased. However, Arisu settled and become the Oba (King) of Ijasi, Ode the

Olode, Mojo, Onile-ere also known as Ajebu was given the land by the sea (Ibu Omi) where the Oba Olu-Iwa had put his son Prince Atosin to be in charge. Oba Monigbuwa who was the king there and he allowed Ajebu to dwell in Ibu (arround the water) and Olode to dwell in the open (dry land) and the combination of their dwelling result to the city known as Ajebu Ode which is referred to as the Ijebu-Ode. However, the Oba (king) Monigbuwa in attempt to find the solution of shifting the course of the river that is usually over flooding and killing people. Summoned an Ifa priest called Leguru to inquire about how to shift the base of the river so that Ijebus would be able to make use of the land and stop the river from over flooding. Then the Ifa (Oracle) revealed that the Oba Monigbuwa had to make sacrifices of various things and that he would have to performed rituals and appeasement to draw out the female water spirits from the sea.

These are the female spirits from the sea, that later become deities worshipped in Ijebuland today.

1. Omi-tutu
2. Yeye
3. Yemule
4. Yemoji
5. Ololo
6. Okiyan
7. Uren Ataba
8. Mojalake
9. Oluweri and others.

After the calling out of these spirits, Leguru told Oba Monigbuwa that the lot (Ifa Oracle) had choosen him as the sacrifical lamb or animal of bargain, However, the news brought great sadness to Oba Monigbuwa, and he tried to look for other ways to appease the gods. But the gods insist on the Leguru, because of his stubbornness, and his arrongancy for performing the rituals that displayed their female companions from the seas. However, on continuous intervention of Ajebu and Olode, the Oba Monigbuwa gave the consent for Leguru to go ahead with the ritual after the Oba Monigbuwa had asked Luguru what is to be done for you, for this big favor you are about to do for my people of Ijebuland. And Leguru answered; as I am going to flow with the river, don't maltreat my children (people). If anyone has offend you or commits a crime, and if he succeeds in running to my house don't touch him.

Then Leguru request the king to present all the items that he had requested for the ritual that would accompanied him, and the Oba Monigbuwa present the items, so after Leguru had performed the rituals. He told them to spread the eni egba (mat made from cane) on the water for him and also request that a white pieces of cloth be spread on it. Then Leguru wrapped himself with white cloth and sat on the mat. He placed his objects of Ifa divination on the mat, started to knock on his Ifa tray and continue shacking his Ifa tool profusely. As he was knocking it, he started recitation of incantations, gradually the water shift base and started flowing out. However, the place where the large expanse of water finally stopped is now called Osa (Lagoon). and Leguru honor he is mentioned in Porogun till today.

Mainwhile as Leguru on top of the Lagoon flows away, a dry land emerged and the second set of settlers began to clear the environment and build their homes. First they prepared an accommodation for the deity of Alare (whom the Ijebus called the overseers of the universe). They term Alare god as someone we cannot be seen but, who sees us (God) whom they believe has control over all things on land and in the universe. The Ijebu faith in the Alare that makes people of other ethnic groups to refer to the Ijebu as "Ijebu Omo Alare" (Ijebus the descendants of Alare).

Then Ajebu locate his settlement as was predicted, in where the Lagoon was formerly located, which is called the land of Ajebu or the forest of Ajebu in Ijebu-Ode till today.

Ode, popularly called the Olode, established his own settlement in the open land where people easily visited him to commiserate with him for his backache. Olode was a misterious person, who when visited in the morning was seen to be in great back pain. But when visited in the evening, he would be hale and healthy. This made the neighboring communities to Ijebu-Ode to make comment:

"How is the back of Ode?"

And there would be response from an Ijebu-Ode person, that "the back of Ode is healed (good)."

However, Ayegun choose to settle arround an Odan (shade) tree called Aba, which gives a settlement there at Aba, called Imuaba. Alado and Isendo settled near an Ipa tree, which is a place arround the site of Obanta and the area is called Imupa in Ijebu-Ode till date. Mainwhile, Laguru lagoon continue to retrieved the land to where the Olososa chose to settle and is named Osasa near Ijebu-Ode. Thereafter the first the second groups of migrants had established their communities around the main town of Ijebu-Ode, and other groups went out to establish their settlements at the outskirts. Mainwhile the three important settlement that first emerge from Leguru lagoon route outskirts of Ijebu-Ode are: Ale Okun, Ale Musin and Ale Remo (Okun land, Musin and Remo land).

Then as Leguru drifted with the large body of water he reached the first kingdom of Alara that lies along the path of the flooring lagoon which Leguru was travelling, where the Lagoon had swept away the kingdom of Alara. Also the Lagoon inside the community, wipe by the flood is referred as Osa L'oko (Lagoon in the forest) till today. However, Laguru further left a wonderful sign in the land, which is called Olugbodere, where people do hear echoes of Leguru's Ifa divination from the bottom of the lagoon. Where the Ifa celebration is observed every five days. And he went further and got to a place called Alara, where the Kings and market leaders meet annualy. Thereafter, Leguru continue to the place he named the land of Abowada, then to Agoro, which is also known as Igbo Bini, the domian of the Oba of Benin. And Leguru passed through the land called Igbo and moved to Abolawo near the land of the Itsekiri. However, at Abolawo Leguru gave birth to a son called Olu. Mainwhile, Olu gave birth to Agoro, the father of Orunfemi. And Agoro always accompanied his grandfather Leguru whenever he carries out Ifa divination in different places. Then Agoro later found a market which he named Iparamo, where Leguru died and was buried.

Thereafter some years later, there was a conflict between Leguru descendants and people of Abolawo, over who was to be the head of the spiritual Ifa worship place where Leguru died and Olu defeat them. Then, Olu descendants, Asogbon and their followers left Abolawo, for another place where Leguru had also left a sign when he passed through. And they met a ruler whose name was Olugbo, who was of the linage of the Oba of Benin, and he had migrated to the land, and he gave his daughter called Adele to Agoro, whose descendants settle in the Imiwen-Olugbo land which they name Ode-Imiwen now Mahin. The descendants of Leguru in this region are called the Ilaje, and they watch over the sea for the Awujale till today.

CHAPTER 2

The Dynasty of Oba Awujale (Emperor) of Ijebuland

Olu (Prince/Lord) Ogboroganda the great grandchild of Oku Ogewu, Ajogun, who was one of the Priest-King Oduduwa great grandson. And who's mother was a great granddaughter of the Alare, a Jebusite King. However, Olu Ogboroganda become a very prominent king in Ethiopia, but his reign was shorten by internal turmoil among his cousins and princes who were always fighting over the right of who to rule over different parts of the Arabian cities. Then Oba (King) Ogboroganda decided to concentrate his military campaign away from Ethiopia, but on the plead of his mother, he went to defend his cousin in Egypt against the Arabian aggressions. However, the military campaign result to serious fight in Egypt and Ethiopia-Sudan in which Oba (King) Ogboriganda military might, with his efficient horsemen warriors and skilful Nubian archers of the kingdom of Meroe, reputed as pupil smitters as they rendered blind most of the Arab horsemen by shooting them with arrows between the eyes. Moreover, the Islamic literature referred to them as the Lintui or the Sentui meaning the pupil smitters. Then the fighters and the warriors princes all agreed to made Olu (Prince/Lord) Ogboroganda the Pharaoh (Emperor) so as to unite them and they become a strong front against the invasion and aggression of descendants of the notorious Alexander the Great, the king of Macedonia.

Thereafter, the Oba (Emperor/Pharaoh) Ogborogbanda ordered the rebuild of the wall of the city of Pharaoh, and organized the training of chariot fighters and archers. These boost the moral of the fighters and they become very strong under the leadership of the young the Oba (Emperor/

Pharaoh) Ogborogbanda, who was very popular among ladies, kings and princes of importance cities and countries around.

Thereafter, the Oba (Emperor/Pharaoh) Ogboroganda's interest was shift to the land, Ife were his great grandfather the Oba Oduduwa had migrated to. And when he could no more stand the jealousy, that cause continuous divisions among his cousins, and the princes who's main ambition of becoming the Pharaoh continue to affect the unity and peaceful ruling of the city of Pharaoh. Then the Oba (Emperor/Pharaoh) Ogboroganda agreed with his chief Generals that they would have to migrate to Ife after the end of the war campaigns against the descendants of the Alexander the Great. Then it became known that the descendants of the Alexander the Great had been defeated, and the king of Macedonia had turn back from the attack of Egypt and face India since the fighters of the Oba (Emperor/Pharaoh) Ogboroganda made it difficult for him to penetrate into Egypt because of the strong resistance that was put in place at the Egypt-Sudan by the archers.

However, the peace that followed after the defeat of the Alexander the Great descendants, made the Oba (Emperor/Pharaoh) Ogboroganda to become popular, but the more older princes that had influence over the other parts of Egypt made it difficult for the Oba (Emperor/Pharaoh) Ogboroganda to be able to rule the city of Pharaoh. And Arabs took advantage of this weakness, and caused more division in the leadership of Egypt. They were able to weaken the kingdom of Meroe, so a parallel king was installed in the upper part of the Nile in Egypt that are Mullatos. Also the Oba (Emperor/Pharaoh) Ogboroganda's mother was murdered by one of her maid on the order of the Northern king.

Then the Oba (Emperor/Pharaoh) Ogboroganda on the advice of an influential Jebu princes and his chief Generals, accept that they should leave Egypt for Ife. But the Oba (Emperor/Pharaoh) Ogboroganda brother Olu (Prince/Lord) Olugbolu, who was also the most leading general made a secret attack on the Pharaoh of the upper Nile and killed him and the princes who had collaborate with him in the murder of his mother. But the Oba (Emperor/Pharaoh) Ogboroganda ordered his second most chief

General to go to the upper Nile with his mother's scarf to his warrior brother and persuade him to stop the killing of their cousins, because his mother would not want that to continue. Then Olu Olugbolu listened to the chief warrior, who he also had a great respect for, because they are cousins, However, Olu (Princes/Lords) Olugbolu cried when he took his mother's scarf from him. Then he ordered his generals to put a stop to the onslaught of the princes and warriors in the upper Nile. Thereafter, the army of the Oba (Emperor/Pharaoh) Ogboroganda follow Olu Olugbolu back to the Southern Egypt. And when the Oba (Emperor/Pharaoh) Ogboroganda saw his brother, Olu Olugbolu, they both wept and buried their mother. Then after the funeral, the Oba (Emperor/Pharaoh) Ogboroganda ordered the trumpet to be blown for the Yorubas, the Ifa priests and worshipers to move out of Egypt-Ethiopia and Sudan to the entourage and migration to the Atlantis known to them as the Ife meaning the place of our choice (present West Africa to Central Africa).

Then when the Oba (Emperor/Pharaoh) Ogboroganda and his followers got to Ile Ife the land of the Oba Oduduwa's first settlement, and discovered that the Oba (king) Olu-Iwa descendants had settled in Ijebu-Ode. The Oba (Emperor/Pharaoh) Ogboroganda ordered

"we shall continue on our journey to Ijebu-Ode where our people are."

However, when they got to Ijebu-Ode, the city wall gates were locked, and there was a great panic and the people were ready to protect their land against the large and mighty strong horse men warriors approaching them. So the Oba (Emperor/Pharaoh) Ogboroganda ordered

"the army shall surround the city wall, and do not to attack Ijebu-Ode."

Then he look at his brother Olugbolu and add

"some Ojas (War Ministers) shall meet with their leaders with the royal staff of my great grandfather the Oba Alare and shall display my military might for our cousins in Ijebu-Ode for them to see and they can know that I the Oba Ogboroganda is here for peaceful settlement among my people and the descendants of the Oba Oduduwa and that of the Oba Alare."

And he ordered

"non of you the most senior of the Ojas shall receive any of the city's hospitality, but you are to demand that the Ijebu-Ode leaders and princes to come and meet me for discussion and pay their homage as the custom and the tradition of our ancestors demand since I am the surviving elder and the Oba awon Oba, Alaye luwa eni ti o je ogun Oba Alare (the king of kings that inherit the staff of authority of the king Alare)."

Then he walk to front of the warchiefs and add

"I am sure that my cousins would not failed to recognized that the owner of this staff of authority is the most senior among the royal descendants of the Oba (Emperor) Alare."

However, Olu Olugbolu said

"can you the Oba permit your servant to lead the warriors so as to ensure that our inheritance interest shall be well represented in the discussion and to ensured that your people would not engage in unnecessary war?"

Then the Oba (Emperor/Pharaoh) Ogboroganda and his brother Olu Adegbole after serious private discussions aggreed that Olu Olugbolu shall lead the warriors.

Thereafter the gate was attacked at night and after some serious fighting, Olu Olugbolu's warriors gain control of the fight and they push their offensive attack into the city and after the third day, when the warriors at Ijebu-Ode heard that Olu Olugbolu would not to kill the captured Ijebu-Ode warriors, but explained to them that we were cousins and both were descendants of the Oba Alare. And the leading warriors of the Ijebuland that were not slave knew of the Oba Alare, and they checked the marks on the face of the warriors they had killed and those captured and saw that a lot of them had the same three marks on their face just like they do. Then the warriors report their observations and what the captured warriors said to their Omo Obas (princes) and Obas (kings).

However, the Olus (Princes/Lords) call for a meeting of the Olus (Lords) and other relevant leaders and discussed the issue. Then, the Oba (king) Oshiguwa of Ijasi who is the leading Olu (Lord), summoned the Ifa priest to consult the Ifa of Odusola.

Then Odusola said

"Kabiyesi o!" "Kabiyesi o!"

Odusola, prostrates before the king's throne and sat on his mat and start the Ifa consultation. And said;

"the Ifa (Oracle) show peace and progress for the coming of the king to the Ijebuland, and added these people that are warriors that are without the three marks on their face are slaves warriors, but the warriors that have the same three face marks as our own are our cousins from Egypt and Wadai."

Then the Oba (king) Oshiguwa thank Odusola, when he was leaving the palace, and the Oba (King) Oshiguwa, breath deep and said:

"Omode so si ni lelu o tun fi iyo si, iso ni yi ko se gbemi, be pelu iyo ko se tu da nu (A child messed right into a person's mouth, and at the same time feed the person a sweetly meal. It not easy to consume stinking mess, but you still want to consume the sweetly meal) who would hear of his death warrant or sentence that should not feel disturbed?"

And add after serious thought,

"but on the other hand, the Ifa of Odusola, now informed us that these invaders are our cousins, and the Oba (Emprior/Pharaoh) outside is also going to bring peace and progress to us."

Then he realized that that people where still prostrating on ground, and said

"why are we being afraid, and worried over nothing?"

And smiling, the chiefs sensing that his words are now more friendly, said

"Kabiyesi o!" Kabiyesi o!" "Thanks for being thoughtful."

And they got up and sat on their various positions in the palace.

Then the Oba (King) Oshiguwa, summoned the Ijebuland chief minister of war, and ordered

"a horse man shall carry a white cloth which is attached on the top of long stick and ride to the front of the campaign so as to inform the invaders that we mean peace."

So the Chief Minister of war instructs a warrior to carry out the Oba (King) Oshiguwa's order and when the warriors of Olu Olugbolu saw the horse man with the white flag approaching them, they informed him, and he ordered his army

"hold your attacks."

Then when the warriors were closeby he add

"the gods of our father Alare is now in charge because our cousins have seen that we mean peace too."

Then he face his warchiefs and order

"a horse man warrior shall approach the warriors coming with the Oba Alare's staff of authority as the main Oba (Emperor/Pharaoh), and tell the warriors that we are cousins, of the Jebusite tribe too and we are of the same blood relation of the Oba Alare. We shall come into the city and talk with their Olu (Lord/Blood linage of the Emprior) to give the message of Oba (Emperor/Pharaoh) Ogboroganda, Oba to wa ni ta (The Emperor/ Pharaoh is outside the city wall)."

However, when the two leading warriors met and exchanged information, on hearing of the Oba (Emperor/Pharaoh) Ogboroganda's name the

Ijebuland warriors, and couple with the word, blood relation of the Oba Alare, became more fearful, and they rushed back into the city and said

"Oba ni o!" "Ni ta o!" ("He is Emperor/Pharaoh!" He is outside!") "Oba Ogboroganda, Oba ni ta!" ("Emperor is outside!").

Then when the news of what the warriors had brought spread to the people, in the city they became very afraid, saying

"who can stand the Oba Ogboroganda, who is the most dreadful of all Ijebu warriors ever known!" "And who is ready to face a fellow omo Oba (Emperor/Pharaoh) Alare in a fight?" "Oba (Emperor/Pharaoh) Ogboroganda!" "Oba ni ta o!" ("The Emperor/Pharaoh Ogboroganda!") "That is outside!"

Then the Oba (king) Oshiguwa was very please when he realized that surely it is the Oba (Emperor/Pharaoh) Ogboronganda, who's fame as the best ever of all the Oba Alare's descendant warriors that is outside the wall of Ijebuland. And he ordered

"my entourage which shall consist of some of the best warriors and the chiefs shall approach the invaders warriors' camp."

However, when Olu (Lord) Olugbolu heard of the Oba (King) Oshiguwa and his entourage approaching.

He ordered

"one of Oja (war minister) shall inform my brother the Oba (Emprior/Pharaoh) Ogboronganda that there is now peace, and the Oba of the city with his entourage are coming to greet him and pay him their homage."

Then when the Oba (King) Oshiguwa saw the staff of authority of the Oba (Emperor) Alare being held by a warrior who was standing by the horse of Olu (Lord) Olugbolu, he recognized the Oba (Emperor) Alare's staff of authority base on the oral narration of it. And the Oba (king) Oshiguwa got down from his horse and bow before the staff and all his entourage prostrate before the staff. Then the Oba (king) Oshiguwa look Olu (Lord) Adebolu straight in the eyes, and both of them looked each other all over for some time.

Then Oba (king) Oshiguwa said

"I think you are his brother Olugbolu, tell him that two cows with horns can not drink from the same rounded head calabash, and for the interest of peace and continuity, wish him well for me."

And Oba (king) Oshiguwa get on his horse and rode away very fast, and he said

"Ijebuland meet your Oba ni ta o! (Emepror that is outside)."

Thereafter, Olu (Lord) Olugbolu order

"why are my people afraid?"

Then the people got up and start singing and rejoicing, and Olu (Lord) Olugbolu order the chief warrior close to him

"you go and inform Oba ni ta (Emperor outside) that his people are ready to meet their king."

However, when the Oba (Emperor) Ogboroganda heard, what had happened, he felt pity for the Oba (king) Oshiguwa, and he said

"who can accept the rejection by his people so gracefully like this? How I wish to be able to see this my cousin king, embrace him and kiss him goodbye."

But realizing why this could not be possible the Oba (Emperor) Ogboronganda said,

"yes he is right!" "For sure no two rams shall successfully drink at the same time from the same rounded pot head. Fearwell by cousin the Oba (king)

Oshiguwa, till meet in heaven before our father the Oba (Emperor) Alare, and OLORUN-ELEDUMARE."

So the Oba (Emperor) Ogboronganda, accept the people's peaceful gesture, and he order an Oja (minister)

"tell my brother Olu (Lord) Olugbolu!" "Here come the Oba ni ta o! (The Emperor outside!)."

However, when Olu (Lord) Adebolu received his brother's response which was an indication that all was well, and no more waging of war against their own cousins, with joy he told the to people

"Oba nita bo!" "Oba nita bo o!" ("the Emperor outside is coming!" The Emperor that is outside is coming now!")

So his brother become known by the people as the Obanta (the Emprior outside), since Olu (Lord) Olugbolu who later was given the title of the "Olisa" (Prime Minister) by the Oba (Emperor) Ogboronganda always called his brother jokingly Obanta (Emperor outside).

Then the Oba (Emperor) Ogboronganda rode into the city on a white horse which nobody had ever rode before, and said

"igba tun tun ti de fun wa ni ile Ijebu, pelu alafia, ati ifon kon bele." ("here come a new era of prosperity, and peace for us in the Ijebuland").

However, inside the city all the people came to greet the Oba (Emperor) Ogbornganda, and one of the ladys stood out among them because of her beauty, so the Oba (Emperor) Ogboronganda order

"let this gorgeous lady be brought to the palace for me to talk with her."

And when the Oba (Emperor) Ogborogonda realized that she was the Omooba Obirin (Princess) Winiade, the daughter of the Oba (king) Oshiguwa, he ordered "let her bring the crown on the throne to me so that I shall wear it."

So Omooba Winiade carried the crown with both hands to the Oba Ogboronganda and she kneel down on her two legs, and he took it from her and placed it on his head then he sat down on the throne. Thereafter, Olu Olubolu hand over the staffs of authority of the Oba Alare, and others in the palace to the Oba Ogboronganda, one after the other with his left hand which the Oba Ogborogbanda recieved with his left hand. Then Olu Olubolu went on his left kneel holding his sword with his right hand, and said

"Kabiyesi O!" "Kabiyesi O!" "Kabiyesi O!" ("The Unquestionable one!" "The Unquestionable one!" "The Unquestionable one!")

While he placed his head to the ground before the Oba Ogboronganda, and immediately all the chief warriors of both the Ijebuland and those that came with the Oba Ogboronganda, removed all their swords and charms and prostrates before the Oba Ogboroganda and the Oba Ogboroganda lift his brother Olu Olubolu up immediately and he sat close to him. While all the people, Olus (Lords) and Chiefs are saying

"Kabiyesi O!" "Kabiyesi O!" "Kabiyesi O!" "Alaye luwa Oba wa!" "Da saki re Oba wa!" "Kade pe lori Oba wa!" "Ki bata pe lese Oba wa!" "Igba Odun Odun kan ni o Oba wa!" ("The Unquestionable oh!" "The Unquestionable oh!" "The sole authority here on earth!" "All honor are yours!" "May the Royal Crown remains!" "May the Roya Shoe remain!" "May the Royal Thrown remain forever!")

And they remain prostrating, then the Oba Ogboronganda said

"thank you all get up, sit down, remain cheerful and celerate."

Then the palace clowns start singing the praises, and praising the Oba Ogboronganda's ancestors, and the ancestors of the Ijebus. However, the Oba Ogboroganda raised his left hand, and the singing and dancing stop. And he said "it would be good to give honor to whom honor is due",

then he look at the Olus of the Ijebu-Ode and ordered

"let my brother Olu Olubolu stand before me",

and indicating that he should be on his kneels.

And order

"the leafs of the Royal ordination and appointment shall be plucked from their tress."

Thereafter when the leafs arrived he took off Olu Adebolu's hat and placed the leafs on his head, and he pronounced

"you my brother Olu Olubolu!" "Shall henceforth be the owner of the right and the title of the Olisa (the Prime Minster) Ijebuland"

which means that the Olisa Olubolu is the second in command to the throne. And which is the Chief Prime Minister of the throne of the Oba (Emperor) Ogboronganda.

Then later, he raised his right hand while the dancing and celebration is going on and ordered

"the Olisa, shall inform the Oba (king) Oshiguwa to be ready to migrate to any location of his choice outside of the Ijebuland, and he shall take with him as many people as he want except his daughter Winiade, who shall be my new Queen. It shall be known that the thrones of the Ijebuland, shall become one."

Then the next morning the Oba Oshiguwa choose his entourage and he left the city. However, after a week of preparation, with dancing and singing by the people, young women, and the virgins the marriage ceremonies of the Oba Ogoroganda and the Aya Oba (Queen) Winiade which last for two weeks took place.

The Awujales

The Oba (Emperor) Obanta about 1424

Some days after, the Oba (Emperor) Ogboroganda, now call the Oba Obanta, sat on the Royal throne that was made of an iroko tree (Mohany) which was placed on the floor higher than the rest of the floor in the palace. Then the Oba Obanta, summoned the Otupode who is the leading Otu (the most senior ward administrator) and order,

"get me all the Otus."

Then, the Otupode fell down at the front of the Oba Obanta on the floor with his face looking downward and he said,

"Kabiyesi o!" "Kabiyesi o!" "Kabiyesi o!" "Moje e pe yin o, Kabiyesi!" "Igba ekeji Osa!" "Kabiyesi, Kabiyesi o!" ("The Unquestionable one!" "The Unquestionable one!" "The Unquestionable one!" "I heard that you summoned me so I have come," "the Unquestionable one!" "The second in command to nobody but the gods!" "The Unquestionable!" "The Unquestionable one!")

And the Oba Obanta, responds,

"welcome the Olori Otu (the leading ward administrator) how is your home, your children and wifes?" "Get up yes I summoned you before me."

And the Otupode, rise up, but still not looking the Oba Obanta directly, with his face looking downward, he said

"ka de pe lori o Oba wa!" "Ki bata pe lese Oba wa!" "Kabiyesi o!" "Igba Odun Odun kan ni Oba wa!" ("May the Royal Crown remains!" "The Royal shoes remains!" "The Unquestionable, may your reign be forvever without an end!"),

and he remain standing while the Oba Obanta said

"get the all the Otus (administrators) and organize them to get the work done on the beautification of the palace, and other place in the city with furnitures, and painting of the walls and use the taxes and levies from the villages and towns for the job."

"And make sure that the job shall be completed before the Sere festival."

Then when the Otupode had left his presence, the Oba Obanta order

"I summoned Olubiyi, the Odi-Ile (the mimister for the town) to come to my presence."

And when he got to the Oba Obanta, and after had rendered his greetings as Otupode did, and the Oba Obanta had respond also as he did with the Otupode.

The Oba Obanta said

"are the six Iwarafa!" "The Apero-tutu-Ona!" (the Apenas) and his twelve followers ready for the discussions on calling the youth for the military training, and keeping the town well clean and tidy?"

And Olubiyi, remain standing and not facing up responds

"yes Kabiyesi o!"

Then the Odi-Ile left the presence of the Oba Obanta and walk to another room in the palace compound and told the poeple

"the people shall go into the larger section of the palace and you shall sit according to your royal ranks and duties."

Then he signer to the palace leading attendant to inform the Oba (Emperor) Obanta that the people were ready for the deliberation and discussion on the military training and other issues concerning the welfare of the warriors and the land allocation for them to settle in.

Thereafter, the Oba Obanta, rise up from the throne, while the palace Royal clowns made funny jokes and remarks which were compliments of the Oba Obanta's personalities, praising his ancestors:

"Omo Oduduwa!" "Omo Oba Alare Egypt!" "Omo Olu-Iwa!" "Ma gbe ese re lokan kan" "Kori ko ti erin ba te ate gbe ni laye" "Omo Oduduwa!" "Omo Oba Alare Egypt!" "Omo Olu-Iwa!" ....

Then when the Oba Obanta entered the room where the people were waiting for him, they rise up with their face looking down, and making sure they did not made face contact with him, or looked at his direction as he walk pass them and sit on the Royal throne at the higher floor level of the room. Then, the people sat down at their respective positions in the room and continue with their discussion as the Oba Obanta listens and he only question them for clarification on some issues and advice on some, such as the mode of the training. And also how the boys would be call to duty, their age, which family should be the head of various unites and guides of the town gates. The military campaign to be embarked upon, how many military units should be made ready to defend the city and the different towns and the farms together with the traders that move as caravan. Such discussion would take days before they reached good and final conclusion. However, the Oba Obanta would have to leave the meeting while the people continue with their discussions. Eventually, when the final conclusion was reached, the head of each military unit and groups would be summoned before the Olisa, who then inform the the Oba (Emperor) Obanta, who either modified it, or accept the decisions.

Thereafter some weeks later, Oba Obanta summon the Odi-Ode (the Chief Minister in charge of matters outside Ijebu-Ode city). And after the usual greetings, the Oba Obanta enquired

"how are the affairs of the Oba (King) Oshiguwa?"

And the Odi-Ode responds

"Kabiyesi o!" "The Oba Oshiguwa had settled down far away in a remote land."

And after some excitation and looking downward he add

"but some of the villagers that had attacked the Oba Oshiguwa on his way were killed and some that were captured and been brought to Idi ewon (present Idewon) to be killed for the sacrifice to the gods during the Sere festival."

However, the Oba Obanta was very annoyed on hearing this, and he said

"I cannot imagine a leader of the level of the Oba Oshiguwa being attacked by some ordinary slaves."

Then the Oba (Emperor) Obanta got up from the thrown and ordered,

"the whole family of the people that attacked the Oba (King) Oshiguwa's entourage shall be killed and their home burned down so that the family of these people would not be found and remain among the Ijebu race anymore."

Then the Jaguna called on the warriors and gave them instructions

"kill all the families of the people that attacked the Oba Oshiguwa's entourage and it must be ensured that none of these people's family member shall be allow to escape, otherwise the warrior's family that is responsible for their escape shall be killed for his failure to kill the Obas' enemy."

Then one of the war captain, Ajagun was called before the Oba (Emperor) Obanta, he order

"Ajagun arrange the warriors of your unit and they shall stand guard of the Oba (King) Oshiguwa's settlement and shall ensure the safety of the Oba Oshiguwa, and there shall be a peaceful coexistence of the rest of the towns and villages with that of the Oba Oshiguwa's settlement."

However, some days before the Sere festival, there was a quarrel between some members of the Oba Obanta family which involve the issue of taking their slaves away from their farms to work as servants for the warriors at the war fronts. Then the Oba (Emperor) Obanta summoned Muwaro, who was one of the prosperous women that gives strongly to the war efforts to his palace, and after the usual greetings, the Oba Obanta, said

"you have to be patient on this matter, because you know I shall always ensured that your personal needs are met."

Thereafter the Oba Obanta summoned Olidipe, who is the leader of slave recruiters for war, and he order him.

"Olidipe!" "You shall initialize some of the slaves that were captured for attacking the Oba Oshiguwa, and they shall be given the marks of the palace slaves in their faces and be use to replace the slaves that had been taken away from the farms of my close relatives."

Then Muwaro, thanked the Emperor with the usual greetings, and sing the praise of the Oba (Emperor) Obanta's ancestors and family lineage praises.

And she instructs Olidipe

"bring all the slaves to my house so that I can choose those that I like among them before you distribute the rest to all the other relatives, according to their loyalty and nobility to the Emperor."

Then the Oba Obanta summoned the head of his traditional priests name the Ogi

"let the Ogi fix the day the Sere festival shall be celebrated."

And when the Ogi got to the palace, and after the usual greetings, he consult the Ifa (Oracle), and the Ogi said

"Kabiyesi o!" "Ki ade pe lori Oba wa!" "Ki bata lese Oba wa!" ("the Unquestionable one!" "May the Royal crown remain forever!" "May the Royal shoes remain forever!")

"OLORUN-ELEDUMARE is pleased with the your Royal Majesty for your mercy on the slaves that attack the Oba Oshiguwa, and for not killing them."

And he turn the Opele around on the wooden board, made some binary stroke on the board, while he said some words in the form of poetry which was not very audible and add

"the Sere festival should no more involve the killing of several slaves for the sacrifice anymore to appeal the gods."

This festival marks the beginning of the year, and it is delicated to the worship of Ile (the Earth) in appreciation of all the good things provided for human beings through the mother- earth annually.

Then the Ogi continue with Ifa routine looking concentrated, while the Oba Obanta sitting on the thrown, the Olisa, the Olu (Lord/Princes), some Oba present, and Chiefs where observing him as demostrate the intricacy of the Ifa consultation and add

"the Ifa will require, a slave, lot of fish, rats, and one snail as sacrificial items, on the eve of the celebration."

Then after the Ifa consultation, the Ogi who is also the Chief priest of the Oba Obantan, advice the Oba Obanta to put on the Ina-Iponju (the touch light of adversity). This touch was used to trace the way to the place where the "Inile" (vigil i.e. the ritual of propitiating mother-earth) ceremony would be held. And when the ritual entourage got to the ritual ground, the earth was dug and the ritual materials were drop therein and covered up, then the touch of adversity was extinguished and dropped. And the touch light of prosperity was light up by the Ogi for the Oba Obanta. Thereafter, the light was used to aid the Emperor back to the palace. However, the following day night the Agunrins (who are powerful, but of lower ranked palace attendants) were instructed to pick one of their own who would act as a mock king for one day. Then the Ogi adviced the Oba Obanta to grant the palace royal attendances the royal permission for the commencement of the ceremony. And the Oba Obanta's royal clown made jokes:

"a slave of the Oba Obanta, who is to become a lord for just one day, hope the slaves would live beyond to the day before the gods strike them dead."

Then the clown further praise the Oba Obanta praises, and those of his ancestors, and he said

"Omo (The great grandchild of) the Oba (Emperor) Oduduwa!'

"Omo (The great grandchild of) the Alare of Egypt!"

"Omo (The great grandchild of) the Olu-Iwa!" ...

And he remind the Oba (Emperor) Obanta of the great Nuhabi (Noah see Genesis 6- 9) who always maintain peace and was patients in all issues. So when the Oba Obanta heard all these praises from his clown, he extend his right hand to the chief warrior the Balogun, who signals the beginning of the ceremony.

Then the Ogi ordered

"let the Agunrins line up"

and he consult the Ifa (Oracle), and an attendance was choosen among them who he told

"sit on this fake throne which had been designed for this ceremony, and you shall be the fake king and shall maintain a positive and a gentle posture of a king for the period of the ceremony."

And he instruct

"you the Odis who are also palace attendances of higher grade than the Agunrins shall be given a special recognition by some selected Agunrins (palace courtiers) in various groups. Who shall be dressed in the snow-white loin cloths, and with brass decorations on their ankles. These Agunrins are to be honored and you shall flaunt your wealth, and some of you Agunrins are to act as misers."

And after ensuring that the servant had complied to the instructions the Ogi add

"food and drinks shall be provided in great quantities for the Agunrin's team that are to be honored."

However, at the night fall when the time to pay homage to the "King-For-The-Day" approached, the honorees were told to be carried shoulder high by their fans, and made to go before "The Majesty" (the fake king). Mainwhile the honorees who satisfied their group members with lavish entertainment were given the "red carpet" treatment with the accompanying songs:

"Teete, Oludese n wa - - - Oludese
Teete Oludese n wa ...."

Meaning:

"welcome he, the one with brass decorations on the legs is approaching welcome he, the one with brass decorations on the legs is approaching."

And they continue singing, walking towards Imose Quarters and to the Apebi's court and then the honoree were dismounted and they were allowed to joined the dancing procession. However, the team that had been lavishly feted were easily recognized by the type of grand reception accorded to the honoree by those who support him. But those Agunrins that are miserly towards their supporters were not honored, and the procession continue as group after group continue to approach and pay homage to the Eso, the "One-Day-King" on his throne of honor. The festival made the people in Ijebu-Ode to had merriment, they drank palm wine, eat Ikokore, Eberipo, Obe Egusi elefo with Eba and different types of vegetables and they danced to Gbedu, Omole, Agogo, Iyalu and many different types musical instruments. Different kinds masquerades, and acrobatics dancers entertained the Oba Obanta, the Olias, and the prominent people in the palace and various place in Ijebu-Ode and other cities in Ijebuland.

However three seasons after the Sere festival, about four hours before the Afunpe Oba (the king's flutist) start singing and blows the flute, which was an indication to alert the people when the Oba Obanta, decides to go to his inner chamber which was his sleeping section of the palace. The ladies that were chosen to perform the evening dance and to entertain the king and the prominent people in the city, were dancing, and one of the ladies danced very well and she was so beautiful to the extent that she got the attention of the Oba Obanta. And he order the Olugbode, (the chief in charge of entertainment)

"bring the best lady dancer to my bed chamber after the entertainment for me to talk with her because she had dance to my delight and with her beauty she had found favor in my sight."

Then Olugbode instruct Aka the beautiful lady dancer

"is to be brought to the Oba Obanta chamber after she finish with her dancing."

Then when she got to the Oba Obanta presence the Oba Obanta said to her

"sit down and of which family do you belong?"

She repond kneeling down on her kneels with her two legs before the king "Kabiyesi o!" "Mo yi ika otun o Kabiyesi o!" ("the Unquestionable one!" I lay by my right side the Unquestionable one!")

"Mo yi ika osi o Kabiyesi o!" "Oba wa!" ("I lay by my left side the Unquestionable one!")

"Omo eru yin Odedina ni mi." ("I am the daughter of your loyal subject Odedina.")

Then the Oba Obanta told her "o seun gan arewa obirin mi to dara pupo, osi ku ijo lopo lopo, o si ku ayesi mi pelu, se o ti setan lati di aya Oba?"

("thank you my very beautiful lady, and well done for the excellent dance and your enterainment,

I hope you are prepared to be the king's Queen?")

She with a very delightful smile and excitment as she remain on her kneels responds

"E mi ni kan tan lati di aya Oba, ki ni egbun mi se ti ko le fi aro e jo ijo Oba?"

("What excuse do I have to refuse the king's request and offer?")

"Pelu gbogbo aye mi ati aye mi ni ma fi se ti Oba o Kabiyesi o!"

("I am fully ready and prepared to be of the king's service o king!")

"Mo ti setan lati di aya Oba o Kabiyesi o!"

("I am ready to be the king's Queen o king!")

Now placing her head downward not looking the Oba Obanta in his face

she add

"Kabiyesi o!" "Ki ade pe lori o Oba wa!"

("The unquestionable one!" "May the Royal crown remains o king!")

"Ki bata si pe lese Oba wa o!" "Igba Odun, Odun kan ni Oba wa o!"

("May the Royal shoes remains o king!" "May the king's Reign be forever!")

Then Oba Obanta raised her head up and encouraged her to look at him directly in his face, but with great fear and trembling she obliged to his kind guesture and he left her and he order

"the beautiful lady Aka shall be given the Royal escort to her father's house."

Then a Royal guard place her on one of the kings horse and escort her from the palace to the Odedina's house. And the following morning the Oba Obanta inform his two Oloris (Queens)

"I shall be taking Aka, the daughter of Odedina as my new Queen."

However, the two Queens fell on their kneels and priase the decision of the king saying

"Oba lo ni ilu, ilu lo ni Oba, eyi ti Oba ba se ase gbe ni ("the King is the utmost head of his community and the King's decision is the final").

Then the Oba Obanta, sitting on his throne in the day court summon the Olisa, and after the usual greetings the king inform the Olisa

"I shall take Aka, the daugther of Odedina as my new Queen."

On hearing this the Olisa said

"Kabiyesi o!" "Ki ade pe lori!" "Ki bata pe lese Oba wa!"

"Igba odun odun kan ni Kabiyesi o!"

"It is well for you my brother to enjoy yourself with the beautiful dancer Aka and I am sure she shall delight you with her beauty and charm."

And the Oba Obanta got up from the thrown and sat by his brother side and said

"I hope you will now stop competing with me when it comes to beautiful ladies? because I beat you with this one."

The Olisa shaking his head and he responds

"Just beacause you win for the first time after I had beat you on several beautiful ladies does not mean you are the best when it comes to wooing beautiful ladies."

The Oba Obanta responds

"you should give me my credit when it is due you may be the smooth talker, I got the best one now" and turning his head from side to side, dancing and he add

"I got the dancer Aka! Aka!!" "Let my fast brother go and look for another of her type o."

Then his brother responds

"OK!" "My brother! The lover man!!" "I have more responsibility to take care of than amusing myself because of one beautiful lady dancer!!!"

Then he got up and said

"I have to summorn the chiefs and inform them of my dancing brother's decision of taking the beautiful dancer Aka the daughter of Odedina as a Queen."

However he called the Obas and the chiefs for the meeting, and he inform them about the new Queen. Then after the meeting the chiefs send three chiefs among them to inform Odedina of the King's intention to take his daughter as his Queen. And when the Chiefs got to Odedina's house,

Odedina who was also aware of the reason for their coming to his house said

"Why I am so honored that three very important chiefs in our land should visit my house?"

"And what can I offer you my Lords? Hope you would not mind the little comfort which your humble subject would be able to offer you?

As he was talking Odedina's wifes came out from their rooms and they kneel down on their two kneels and said

"You are all welcome to our house chiefs we are very delighted and honored for such important personalities as you chiefs to come to our house."

Then Aka came out too and she instructs her sibbings and they brought sits for the chiefs to sit under the shade of two trees in the their compound.

However, the chiefs look at Aka and laughing they said

"Eri eniti a tori wa lo ti se ike ati a pon le eyi."

("See the person that made us to come is already showing care for us")

And Odedina said

"Thank you my children for the chairs"

and he told his elderest son

"Odewale!" "You and your brother should run to Ogundele and buy the best pots of Palm wine he has."

Then Odedina's wifes brought water in calabashs for the chiefs and kneeling before them and they said

"here is some fresh cold water from the pot we had gone to the stream very early this morning since we had sense that we are going to have some important visitors today. Because the sign that we observed yesterday when those powerful warriors lead our beautiful daugther Aka home is something unusual. Hope she has not done anything bad? We had trained her very well, and our husband is a very disciplined and honest subject of the Oba ruling houses"

The leading chief said

"Thank you Odedina household!" "We are highly delighted for your hospitability and besides we are the people that have intrude into your house without even anouncing it. And we have come as a very strong deligate of a very important personal in our land to seek an important request from your household and family."

"And as to the enquiry that your beautiful dancer daugther Aka!" "Had done anything bad I am not aware that she had done anything bad to anybody."

Then the wifes said

"if our beautiful daugther had not done anything bad then we assume your coming is of joyful purpose then. Now we can be of peaceful mind and concentrate on providing you the messengers and cheifs all the comforts you will need and deserved while you take your time and tell our husband and our family your reason for coming."

Then Odedina and some of his brothers, sisters together with his uncles and mother enter the compound and they exchange greetings and pleasantry with the chiefs and they are enterained them with Kola nuts and Palm wine which was poured into small calabashs by the palace's attendants for the chiefs and the members of Odedina's household and invited guests.

Then Odedina cleared his throat and said

"Ti omode ba pa eku o to da je, ti o ba pa eja o le da je, sugbon ti o pa aro gidiga, ani oun ti se ikan ila, a si gbe to awon obi re lo. Eyi ni mo fi pe awon ebi mi wa si ile ti emi, ki awon alejo wa ti won je awon Oloye pataki ni ilu wa ati ile Ijebu wa le mo pe emi no ni a won eyan. Ti e ba ma fi ola Oba mu mi lo si tubu, ta bi pelu mu Arewa omo mi Aka lo si tubu pelu awon e ni yan mi a le suru so otun ati si osi."

("When a young child did something of less significant he/she should be able to make decision on it by himself/herself, but whenever, the child had or about to take a big step in life, he/she should know better to consult his parent. For this reason I have invite my mother, uncles and siblings since we suddenly have the most powerful chiefs of our city and of Ijebuland in our house without knowing what is wrong and for the fear that me or my beautiful daugther Aka could be taken away by the king, so that they can me help beg the king or come to our resque.")

Then all the chiefs laugh and said

"well done Odedina!" "We thank you and your household for your hospitability, comfort and the entertainment. We the chiefs are no more small child and we know it is not that essay to just let go our beautiful daugther like that, so we have to take our time and wait for better way and opportunity of letting you know that one of your beautiful daughter shall be taken away from your household very soon."

However, Odedina eldest uncle said

"which one among of you chiefs wants to take our daugher from our home just like that without even taken the proper consultation from her father's family."

The most senior chief responds

"we have not come just to take the very bueatiful Aka away without the proper consultation from her father's family, we are very rooted in the custom and tradition of our land."

Also another chief said

"we cannot disrespect Odedina's family that is the reason we have come to know her family and then put forward our request for her to be part of our family too. And we can assured the family of Odedina that we are very respectable and responsible people in the whole of Ijebuland."

Then Odedina mother said

"we all can see that you are the highest chiefs in the whole Ijebuland and as you men know we mothers are more easy to deal with when it comes to letting our daugther go to another family. So just like the question already asked you chiefs, which of you chiefs want be our family inlaw?"

The most senoir chief responds

"any one of us can be a suitable suitor of your beautiful daughter Aka because the girl is not only beautiful, she is of very good charachter and she can dance very well also. So any one of us will be able to deliver her to the actual place where she belongs."

Odedina responds

"Baba Oloye Arunah!" "Se bi agbalagba ni yin, a ni ta ni ninu eyin Oloye won yi lo fe mu Omo wa Aka kuro ni ile baba e? A sa le wa fi Omo wa Aka fun idile Oloye meta po lekan?"

("Chief Arunah!" "We all observed that you are an elder person, just let us know whose family home are we releasing our daughter Aka for? We know can not give her to three Chiefs' household.")

Then Chief Arunah said

"thank you Odedina!" "Baba Aka!" "You have make a very important observation, which has help us clearified our request. We chiefs here are working on a very high instruction that is above our influence that is why we want you to release your daughter for the three of us or any one of us that you like most."

However, the most eldest man in Odedina household said

"Ese eyin Oloye wa!" "Eku ogbon ati lakaye!" "Awa idile Odedina je ologbon ati oloye eniyan pelu. Gege bi e ti se se alaye ti ye wa, se bi Oloye agba Ijebu ni eyin meteta je? E ti wipe a ku le fun enikan ninu yin ni Omo wa Aka, sugbon e si ti fi ye wa pe, enikeni ti a ba fi Omo wa fun ninu yin, bi enipe a fun gbogbo yin lo ni. To ba je be a je wi pe, eyin Oloye meteta je asoju enikan pataki ni gbogbo agbegbe ilu Ijebu wa yi ni. A wa ebi Odedina a si pe Omo wa Aka jade ni i sin yi ki o wa ba wa yan oju oro yi."

("Thank you the chiefs!" "For your wisdom and explanations!" "We the family of Odedina are also peope of knowledge, we have understand your points we know that you three chiefs are very prominent in the affairs Ijebuland. So by given our daughter Aka to any one of you which is just as given her any of your families is an indication that we are dealing with a higher family that enbrace the whole of Ijebuland. Then we would have to call on our daughter Aka to help us in solving this issue.")

Then Odedina called

"Iya Aka!" "Pe Omo e Aka wa o, a ni oro la ti bere lowo e"

("Aka's mother!" "Pease call your daughter Aka we need her here for some questioning.")

and Aka's mother responds

"Mo ti gbo yin Oko mi Olowo ori ale e lomi, Omo yin Aka ti bo o"

("Yes I have heard you my lovely husband, your daughter Aka is on her way.")

So Aka walk out from the house and kneel down on her kneels with two legs in the front of her father and said

"E mi re o baba mi, mo se tan da yin lo un e bere yin"

("Here I am my father I am ready to answer any of your enquiry")

But the most senior chief said

"A ba arewa lobirin Aka!" "A si ti wa niyin lati aro, baba re si pe e jade osi lo je ipe re be, o si wa si odo awa Oloye metata yi."

("Why did you ignored us three chiefs, beautiful lady Aka!" "Knowing that we have being here since morning because of you, but only answer your father's call instantly.")

And Aka respond

"Ejo o yin baba mi Oloye metata!" "Mo fi se afo ju di si yin rara o, ipe baba mi ati ti awon ebi mi se pataki si mi ni isin yi ni igba ti mo ti ni oko."

("Please my elders and the three chiefs!" "I am not trying to be rude in any way, my father and members of my family are more important to me now that I am not yet married to any family")

Then the Odedina's family leader said

"Thank you my daughter!" "You have demostrate to these chiefs and every body that you are a well trained lady and that your family is very important to you."

And facing the chiefs he add

"you can see that our daughter is not a way ward woman, so we are going to tell her to make her choice of the symbol of authority or identity of the man that had approach her on a matter of affection that she can identify here. So I would want you chiefs to present for her any thing that can help her to remember who the person is."

However, the most senior chief said

"that should be easy since we all have our caps here for her to choose from."

So the chiefs put down their caps the mat and they instruct that any other person that thinks she should choose him to place their caps on the mat. And Odedina's mother said

"Aka my daughter!" "Please do not be afraid or be ashame to make your choice of the symbol or the cap of any person that had made an affectional pass on you that you would want to be your husband."

Then Aka walk to the three chiefs' cap but ignored them and walk pass the mat on the floor and she appoach the staff of authority of the Oba Obanta that was placed at a corner in the compound.

Then the most senoir chiefs said

"yes!" "Your daugther is a well trained child!" "With a good knowledge of our custom and tradition she would be a good wife in the Oba Obanta's palace and we are blessed to have her as one of our Queens."

And all the household of Odedina prostrate before the Oba Obanta's staff of authourity as if it has just arrived. Also the Ajurins begin to praise the Oba Obanta's linage praises:

"Omo Oduduwa!"

"Omo Uku Ogewu!"

"Omo Arunah/Alare!"

"Oba Ogboroganda!"

"Ako-Yebe Yebe-lori-Ogun!"

"Oba Obanta!"

With dancing and singing the Oba Obanta's entourage left the Odedina's family and return to the palace to give their report of marriage proposal introduction.

And after the Chiefs had left his house, Odedina told his wifes,

"my wifes can you see that my daughter Aka!" "Really look like me? She is full of good character and beauty, and our family is now so honor to be part of the Oba Obanta's household."

The senior wife who was the mother of Aka, said

"so you can now realize that she looks like her father!" "But each time you are correcting her whenever she dones some thing wrong, she is always my daughter."

56

Then she ran to her husband's arm and she kneel down at his front and said;

"o se oko mi olowo ori mi!" "Baba omo mi Aka." ("thank you my good husband!" "The father of my daughter Aka.")

The other wife also joined her, and kneel down by her side and said

"my senior!" "So you have forgotten that fathers only accept good report concerning their children, so the good child belongs to the father, but the blame for a bad child is always the mother's fault."

And Odedina, responds

"thank you my good wifes,"

and he look at their faces robing his hand on their faces and smiling he add

"my wifes you shall prepared gifts and take them to Queens in the palace to show them that our daughter Aka shall be willing to support them as the youngest Queen."

Then Odedina dressed up and said

"today is not the day for hunting of animals, I will go to the palace to greet the Oba Obanta."

And laughing, smiling changing his dress over and over he said

"which of this dress shall be OK my wifes for a inlaw of the Royalty of Ijebuland."

The wifes also laughing, while they were examining the cloths and dragged a round shape cain basket with top cover and took many cloths out for him to try on until they reached a concession on one and he said "my life is now changed my wifes!" "Me and my family and extended family are now in wealth, with horses and slaves we shall be blessed as an inlaw of the Royalty of the Obas of Ijebuland."

Then they discussed what the marriage ceremonies would look like and eventually Odedina dressed up and said

"my wifes I am on my way to the palace!" "If any of my friends or any person come to look for me tell them I am on my to the Oba Obanta's palace."

Moreover, laughing and examining him and his dress in admiration the wifes said

"Yes!" "We know your destination the Oba Obanta's palace!" "The new inlaw to the Royalty of the Ijebuland, please while walking majestically be careful not ran on any thing or somebody on your way to the palace, the new inlaw of the Royalty of the Oba Obanta."

So with joy the household of the Odedina celebrate being an inlaw of the Royalty of the Ijebuland.

However, the Oba Obanta order the leading guard

"make ready the Royal horse and summon the Olisa, and inform him that I shall have to take a tour of Ijebu-Ode, to see the progress of work done on the city wall and other works in the city."

Then the Olisa inform the Odi-Ile, (the Chief minister in charge of Ijebu-Ode matters) who arranges for the king's entourage to effect the arrangement for the Oba Obanta tour of the city. So the Oba Obanta inspect the works done by the metal workers at Sinepo, where the work on the Obanta's symbols was going on, and he ordered the guard of his Royal symbols who was also in charge of making the appeasement regarding the symbols

"you shall ensure that the jobs are done to the specifications."

And also Oba Obanta order Afin

"Afin you sall build a big house at Odo-Mowo, now called Idomo, over the symbols of the work of brass casting of my image and those of the Ijebuland Obas after me for the generations after us to see the good work we had done and so that the tradition of our ancestors shall be pass on forever."

However after the Oba Obanta had inspect the farms and he had praised the farmers and their slaves for doing good work. He continue on the tour and when he got to a flat terrain which he like, he called the Olisa, who's horse is following his horse and he said

"how are you doing my brother? Come closer,"

Then when he got to his side. Oba Obanta signaled the entourage to stop, got he down from his horse, and all the warriors instantly did the same.

Then the Oba Obanta order

"a road that leads to another direction shall be cleared here now."

Then after the clearing was done to some distance,

the Oba Obanta order

"let the work to stop."

And when the work had stopped he order

"get the fastest worrior on a horse to ride his horse until I tell him to stop."

So the warrior rode the horse and when he reach some distance Oba Obanta order

"let the trumpet be blown for him to stop."

Then he said

"Let a big stone be place here as a boudary indicator for the land of the Olisa and his followers to build their settlement"

However, the land was named Ile-Isa and it is called Olisa till now

Then Oba Obanta called on Odedina and he said

"Odedina the king's inlaw ride closer with me, why is that the future in-law of the throne of Ijebuland should be distance from me?

And the Oba Obanta look at his side and told the Olias as Odedina was coming closeby on his horse,

"you should not let Odedina be too far away from me, because he might decide to ran away with his beautiful daughter Aka,"

And there was laughter from everybody that heard the funny joke. Then the Oba Obanta's clown start praising the King and making more funny jokes and causing more laugher and joy. And the Oba Obanta drummers and entertainers continue making music, and now the Oba Obanta in very happy mode announced

"the marriage to make Aka my new Queen shall take place at the Osu festival,"

Then he signal the return of the entourage back to the palace.

However, among the entourage was Ayegun, who was a distance cousin of the Oba Oshiguwa. He was a very brave warrior and had been away with his warriors to a distance land, where he was well liked by Igbo, who was a descendant of the Uku, the Oba Ile-Ibini. But Ayegun had plot with his men on how to attack the Oba Obanta. So when he heard that the Oba Obanta wants to make Aka a new Queen, he became very jealous of the Oba Obanta beacuse of his wealth, and his fame among the people of Ijebuland. So Ayegun called on Odejayi, the leader of his warriors and told him

"we shall have to go on a secret journey to the Ile-Ibini to meet Igbo, who we know is also jealous of the Oba Obanta. And we shall inform Igbo, of the Osu festival marriage plan that the Oba Obanta will make Aka as his new Queen."

Odejayi respond

"Since we know of Igbo's previous intention of wanting to have Aka as a wife, whom Igbo had seen before when she had perform her dance. But we are aware that since this cannot be possible, because Ijebuland women are not allowed to marry outside of the Ijebu race. It has been like that since Abraham forbid his descendants not to marry the uncircumcised race."

However, Ayegun being aware of Igbo's desire of wanting to kidnap Aka before, said

"we shall persuade Igbo to join force with our warriors and attack the Oba Obanta. When the Oba Obanta would be on his usual tour of the Ijebulands since, the Oba Obanta would not have most of his strong warriors with him on such journey."

Thereafter, when they got to Ile-Ibini, Ayegun and Igbo agreed on the plot to attack the Oba Obanta entourage and that when the fight is going on, Igbo can look for Aka and kidnap her. And they had a secrete sacrifice which they use a virgin girl as the lamb to appease the gods. Then Ayegun and Odejayi returned back to Ijebu-Ode.

Mainwhile, before the Osu festival, the Olisa adviced the Oba Obanta to have the marriage a day before the Osu festival, which the Oba Obanta accept. Then the marriage was announced to the people of Ijebu-Ode and the news got to all the other towns and villages in the Ijebuland, and the people brought gifts and farm products to the palace. The wives of the Chiefs organized the women to do the cooking, the two Queens instruct Aka to be brought to the palace and they lecture her on the ways of life of a Queen and how to prepare her bedding chamber, and assigned Aka her own maids and male servants, who were eunuch. Then the Queens, including Aka, had their hair-styles done to the custom which distinguished them from the other women. Their dress of which the first wrapper was tied long enough to about the ankle-length. And they use their right hand to lift the wrapper as they walk about. Also they had a small piece of cloth that was thrown on their shoulder after tying the first wrapper called "Ipeji." And they use piece of cloth different from the small piece used by other women called "Iborun" to cover their head. This piece was twisted packed together in a twist form and was placed on their head. The two senior Queens dress was similar to that of Aka except that she had her head covered with white laced cloth, which shall be lifted up her face after the necessary marriage rituals and rites have been done by her bridegroom the Oba Obanta. And her father Odedina brought her before the King on his throne, and announced that,

"from now my daughter Aka!" "Belongs to the Royal house of the throne of Ijebuland."

Then the two Queens took Aka by the hand and present her to their husband the Oba Obanta, who then lifts the white cloth up her face, while the two Queens fell on their kneels at the front of the throne. And the Oba Obanta lift Aka up and she stand at his front and he embarrassed her before the whole people and present her back to his two Queens, who took her with them to the inner court with dancing and singing.

Thereafter, the Oba Obanta step down from his throne and then the palace clown was singing and dancing while he also praise the Oba Obanta and his ancestors. However, the Oba Obanta also dance to the delight of the people, and he told the Olisa to join him, while the Olisa signals to all the Obas, Princes, Princess, Obas, Chiefs and the prominent people in the court to join the dance with the Oba Obanta. The Obas, Princes, Princess, Chiefs now dancing with the Oba Obanta who was in the middle with the Olisa close by the King. And the people in the city continue to dance in every open place, right from the palace, making merry, and drinking. Then different types of Masquerades dancers and entertainers entertain the Oba Obanta and his Queens, together with the Olisa, the Princes, the Obas, the Princess, and the Chiefs at the front of the palace. However the people representing different age-groups came and dance and paid homage to the Oba Obanta. Also many entertainment groups, musical orchestras, magicians from all the Ijebuland and other tribes and ethnics present themselves before the throne to greet the Oba Obanta and his three Queens, and the marriage festivities took place for two weeks.

The Title Awujale about 1426

Some months after the marriage, the Oba Obanta embank on his usual tour of the Ijebuland with his entourage, and this time he went with Aka. Then Ayegun informed Igbo to join force with his warriors and they attack the Oba Obanta entourage from the rear at Isa. However, the Oba Obanta who was about to settle down in one the prominent warrior's house call Ogun, heard of the attack and he order

"get my horse men to follow me, now to put this attack and rebellion to a stop. I shall have to deal with whoever is responsible for such wickedness as this."

Then they met Ayegun, who was at a distance and he cursed the Oba Obanta.

"You thief! Your down fall is today for taken the crown that belongs to the Oba Oshigunwa also known as the Lewu."

And riding his horse backward so as not to far away from his guards he add

"I have come to put an end to your pride and useless magical powers that you have being using to steal away the hearts of the people of the Ijebuland from the Lewu."

Then the Oba Obanta responds

"Ayegun!" "How do you plan defeating me Oba Ogboroganda? Is it with your small bandits of an unorganized men? I thought you are a loyal Ijebu warrior, that is why you're given a place in my military, now see what you have done to yourself, death and destruction."

And Ayegun answered

"we would see, who is going to fall today, because with this small warriors with you, you cannot escape my sword."

Oba Obanta laugh and said

"thanks for your insult, you and your big size warriors shall see that the measure of strength is not in the size of an army and it numbers, but in skills, and the sense of purpose."

Then Ogun become very annoyed because of Ayegun's words and his disrespect of the Oba Obana, and he raise his sword and said,

"what else!" "Do we have to hear again from this bastard, and for the insult on the Oba Obanta and all Ijebuland, let me strike him done."

And Ogun took charge of the fight and he lead his men and the warriors to defeat all the warriors of Ayegun without much resistance, because the big warriors of Ayegun combine with that of the Ile-Ibini warriors under the Igbo, were to weak a match for Ogun warriors that was a single unit in the Oba Obanta's army. Then on the seventh day of the fight, Ogun killed Ayegun and cut off his head which he carried with his left hand and brought it to his house where the Oba Obanta and his brother the Olisa together with other higher ranking military Chiefs were having fun, dancing and being entertained by the musicians, masquerades and female entertainers, while the fight was being handle under the command of Ogun military unit. Then when Ogun arrived with Ayegun's head, and lots of slaves of war, to be presented to the Oba Obanta, the Olisa said

"Ogun! Ogun! The strong warrior of all time! You have had another strong warrior's head to the usual counts of your trophy."

Ogun now prostrating, in the front of the Olisa and responds

"who would I resemble if it not you my father and Lord, the Olisa. I am following your footsteps, and always learning from you my baba."

The Olisa, said

"you understand your lord Oba Obanta!" "Now that he is enjoying himself, with these beautiful women and music, you don't want to disturb him with the issue of this small fish compared with those big warriors' heads, that were countless in numbers we had defeated."

Ogun responds

"thank you my lord!" "The Olisa Ijebu!" "I shall claim the head of this fool Ayegun as mine then"

and he threw the head into a basket at the front of his house, and add

"let me too go and wash away this blood from my body and I would join my lords and the Oba Obanta in the party going on."

Then the Olisa and the Chiefs who had came outside of the house to congratulate Ogun for the victory over Ayegun the Oba Obanta's enemy death returned inside the house and join the Oba Obanta and the party.

As the fight continued, Igbo and his warriors, who had concentrate mainly on locating Aka, break away from the campaign and fought their ways back to Isa in search for where the women and Aka were kept. Then when Igbo saw Aka among the women in another house away from where the party was going on, he kidnapped her. And he and his warriors that were able to kill some of the warriors there, rode away to Igbo-Ibini, and Igbo told them

"we don't have to go to my lord the Oba Ibini with this lady beacuse she can easily be discovered there and this would bring more trouble to the Ibiniland."

But when the report of the killing of people, and the kidnapping of Aka the new Aya Oba (Queen) of the Oba Obanta got to the Oba Obanta, the Oba Obanta became very annoyed, and ordered his warriors

"follow me!" "Not on this earth that my wife or family shall be taken away from me"

and the Oba Obanta fought his way through the warriors of the Uku Oba Ibini descendants, and he order

"search everwhere for Aka, she must be found alive and the person responsible for her kidnapping must be found alive and be brought before me."

Then the search party discovered that Aka had been kidnapped by Igbo who had break away from the warriors of Ibini and took refuge in Igbo-Ibini. When the Oba Obanta heard of the report, He took his horse and rode very fast without waiting for any protocol, in anger to Igbo-Ibini, and his brother the Olisa and the other warriors rode after him. However, the Oba Obanta and his warriors cut off the head of any person that stand on their way to the Igbo-Ibini. Then when the warriors got to the Igbo-Ibini, and the Ibinis seeing what had happened to those that stand on the way of the Ijebu warriors, the Igbo-Ibini people became very afraid and decide that since we cannot resist this Oba and his warriors it would be better to point at he direction of the Igbo warriors' place of taking refuge for them before the whole Igbo-Ibini would be destroyed. Then their warriors stop the resistance and allowed the Oba Obatanta and his warriors to continue with their search. So the Igbo-Ibini Chiefs who had heard of the secret place put up the coverage and ordered

"Let the white cloth to be put up,"

and a warrior leader mount his horse and raise a white flag. Then the Oba Obanta on the advice of his brother the Olisa, stoped the killing, and the Igbo-Ibini Chiefs point at the direction of the place of refuge of Igbo and his warriors. However, the Oba Obanta thanked them, and rode his horse to the direction, and arrows and spears were shot toward the Oba

Obanta and his brother who were at the front of the charging Ijebuland warrior Chiefs, but none of the arrows or spears had any effect on them. Eventually, the Oba Obanta got to a rocky terrain where Igbo and his warriors were camping and he broke into the fence and barricades put in place. Mainwhile the fight was very intense and it was the following day that the Oba Obanta discovered where the women were being held. Then he fought his way to the rocky valley terrain, where Igbo had being fighting, and Oba Obanta, ordered

"no one shall kill Igbo!" "But with my hand shall he die!" "Since he had challenge me in a fight and he thinks he is of my equal for trying to take my wife from me when I am still alive. I order Igbo must be caught! And must brought to me alive for me to kill him with my own hand! Nobody shall ever challenge me or take anything that belongs to me and see the sun again! This is a taboo!"

Then when the Oba Obanta spot Igbo he got down from his horse, and threw his sword into Igbo's horse which struck the horse in it's neck and cut it and made a very deep hole, the horse fell and Igbo jump off the horse on to his foot. And with a long sword in his right hand he ran towards the Oba Obanta, and the Oba Oban said some charms words, and the sword he had thrown which had made the cut on Igbo's horse neck returned back to the Oba Obanta's hand. However, Igbo who had thought he had the upper hand and about to make a cut on the Oba Obanta's arm with the sword in his hand, was surprise, and he said

"no wonder the Oba of the Ijebus is feared! "It is because he is very magical."

Then the Oba Obanta defend himself with his sword and he moved backward as if retreating, only to make a u-turn in the left direction, and thrust his sword on the side of Igbo's stomach. And before Igbo could make an attempt to move the King drag the sword out of him, and trust it into Igbo's heart and push the sword more into him. Now the Olisa who had been very close to his brother Oba Obanta side, rush, tried and prevent the the Oba Obanta from continuing fighting in the battle any more. And he quicky took him away from the fallen body of Igbo and drag out the Oba Obanta's sword, which he held in his left hand, and kneel down with his left leg at the Oba Obanta's front, smiling and he present the sword to his brother. Who took it sword from him and said

"where is my wife?

Then the Olisa turn around and he told the warrior chiefs

"now get the beautiful Aka, before my brother mistake our heads for the Ibinis."

And then the Olisa turn arround to the falling body of Igbo, who was in an agony of pain and screaming and begging for his life to be speared, and the Olisa still smiling, cut off Igbo's head, in one strong stroke with his sword. And he took the head with his left hand holding his sword in the right hand and present the head to the Oba Obanta smiling. And Oba Obanta took the head from him with his left hand and said.

"I will not smile with you until we get our wife Aka who is more important to us that any of this Igbo warriors."

Then the Olisa respond

"at least Oko Iyawo (my husband) you have to appreciate your victory, and that of your warriors too who are always very loyal to you!" "Are you ready to smile my dear brother the Oba Obanta?"

And the Oba Obanta raise the head of Igbo upward, and said

"thank you!" "My always smiling brother!" "How life would have being so difficult for me to live without you. Since we lost our mother, you have been like her to me, see you have gave to me now the head of a man that tried but, failed in his attempt to steal my beautiful Queen Aka! That I love so much from me. A queen that I got not as a result of war, but in the time of peace, which does not always come so much in my life and that of your smiling head."

However, as the Oba Obanta was talking Aya Oba (Queen) Aka walked in to the middle of the people, and she was announced by the Oba Obanta's clown, who made funny jokes and sang the Oba Obanta's praise. And when the Olisa saw her, he signer to the Aya Oba Aka to come, which she did and holding his brother wife's hand, which no other human being would dear attempt, the Olisa said

"here is your trophy of peace the Oba Obanta."

Then the Oba Obanta put down the head of Igbo and embrace the Aya Oba Aka and ask her

"how is your health? Hope no bad mosquitoes had bite you?"

The Queen feeling safe in the arms of her husband the Oba Obanta, start crying and the king begged her holding her hands and he said

"you are now safe with me were you belongs."

Then the Olisa, pointing to the lovers said;

"ewo Oko ati Aya!" "Se eri, eni ti o mo ija ara e ja" ("look at the husband and wife!" "And see the person who knows how fight for his possession.")

However, the Olisa now start calling his brother, Amoja-ile-ja which the be people turn to Awujale meaning the person who knows how to fight and repossess his possession. This have become the title name for the Oba (Emperor) Obanta, and it remains the title for the Oba (Emperor) of the Ijebuland. Thereafter, on their way back, the Olisa, said

"what are you the warriors waiting for there are more to be taking home get the Amoja-ile-ja more spoilts of the war. Then the Ijebuland warriors loot the place for precious stones, gold, silver and arts, more slaves of war, and they took beautiful the women as wives. And the Oba Obanta, said

"The the head of the fool Igbo shall remain in the Aya Oba Aka's possession until we reach Ijebu-Ode were it shall be use for ritual."

However, the entourage continue with the visit to the Ijebuland's towns and villages, and when they got to Ijamo where the Oba Obanta honor the Olisa and Ogun for their courage, and he announce

"when Aka who is now pregnant gives birth, I shall honor the child to mark the sweet I had shed in conquering Igbo."

However, Some month later, the Oba Obanta announced the Osu festival. And on the eve of the festival the Oba Obanta light up a very bright Opa (pole) touch light and it was carried by an Agunrin (palace Minister). Then in the morning of the festival all the people of Ijebuland were told to dress in their best attires and to dance while they pay homage and honor to the images of the gods. Later in the day the Oba Obanta's order

"all the images of the Obas our ancestors shall be brought out in the open at the nights of the festival."

Then all the Princes, the Princess, the Obas from the Olisa, and the Chiefs dressed in their best and they pay homage to the Oba Obanta on his throne. The Ijebuland citizens, the young and the old including the virgins also pay homage to the Oba Obanta. The virgins wore bangles made of brass, aluminum or copper and were in their best outfits. However the Oba Obanta first open the dance floor and he dance to the rhythm of the Royal Gbedu drums and other musical instruments. Then the virgins, wearing the "Lagidigba" (black beads made from palm nut shells), "Iyun" (coral beads), and some other varieties of beads on their waists, and they parade around the dancing arena while the dance was still going on. Thereafter when all the participants had danced, the images of the Obas were taken back to their safe places. And when the dance had got to the end, the young men were told to meet the ladies they have admired, and thus they begin the process of courtship in the Ijebuland.

Obanta last days and eventually become a god about 1429

However, some years after the Igbo war and some more wars, a strange deity with a big red stone eyes in a black apparel stood at the back side of the Oba Obanta's inner court singing a song which nobody understand, and the issue was reported to the Oba Obanta. And when he got to the spot where the deity was, the deity start crying in loud voice. But Oba Obanta recognize the deity, and start to sing the song too, and he said

"why are you here in my palace?"

But the deity beg Oba Obanta and said

"please the Oba Ogboroganda do not cast me into the lower part of the earth!"

"I have been sent by my master the Iku (the Death) to visit you the Oba Ogboroganda because the Iku had failed in several attempts to take your spirit to the land of the dead. So the Iku and it's followers had decide to allow you the mighty warrior you are, the Oba Ogboroganda to stay in a different location away from the people, since the gods and the **OLORUN-ELEDUMARE** (God Almighty) want you to organize your home before going to the land of the death."

Then Oba Obanta said

"I shall accept the proposal with joy and praise to **OLORUN!**" "And my ancestors for being considerate. I thank you **OLORUN-ELEDUMARE!** Oluwa awon Oluwa! Oba awon Oba! (he Lord of the Lords! The King of Kings!). The one that knows all things, the one that has being before and shall ever remain forever! Kabiyesi O! Kabiyesi O! Kabiyesi O! (the Unquestionable one! The Unquestionable one! The Unquestionable one!). Thank you for not taking me away without organizing your people of the Ijebuland and for preventing the issue of leadership disagreement that could have create wars among the Ijebuland."

Then the Obanta order

"I shall released you deity from the spell that held you to this spot, and the spell shall move you deity to the Ile-Ila (big house) in a remote rest place where

I Oba Ogboroganda,
Omo Oduduwa,
Omo Uku Ogewu,
Omo Arunah Alare,
Ako-Yebe Yebe-lori-Ogun
I Awujale

shall take my refuge until I join my ancestors, and **OLORUN-ELEDUMARE**."

However, some days later, the Oba Obanta now known as the Oba Awujale summon the Princes, the Princess, the Olisa, the Obas and Chiefs to carried out some rituals to appease the gods.

Thereafter, the Oba Awujale prounced blessing on the people and he said

"my blessing are for all of you the people of the Ijebuland!" "No war shall be able to overcome you Ijebuland!" "And no trouble shall be big enough that shall overcome you the Ijebuland!" "My Ijebuland shall be a force to be recognize among all the tribes and nations of people."

Then he held his brother the Olisa's hand he said

"my first son Moluwa shall sit on the thrown."

Then he order

"get me the leaves for the anointment of the Oba."

However, when the leaves arrived and still holding the hand of his brother the Olisa he said

"the Olisa!" "And his descendants shall serve the Awujale with respect and loyalty as the head of the Obas in the Ijebuland. And the Olisa shall be the most senior of the of the Awujale's ministers in all the Ijebuland."

And facing the thrown add

"these leaves shall be used for the anointmentment of the Awujale!" "Who shall have the authourity and the right of the inheritance of the linages of the Princes and the Princess of the descendants of the Alare be anionted to the this thrown of the Awujale of the Ijebuland in the presence the Olisa and the Obas of the Ijebuland."

Then he place the leaves on the his brother the Olisa's hand and he said

"you shall not be part of my entourage to the big house for the my onward journey to join our ancestors and **OLORUN-ELEDUMARE!** You shall remain with the Awujale after the call had be made and place these leaves on the Awujale on the thrown of the Ijebuland! Farewall my brother the Olisa Ijebuland! Farewall all the Princes! The Princess! The Obas! and the prominent and the minor Cheifs and my people big and small of the Ijebuland farewall."

However, he order

"the Awujale on the throne and all the Prince and the Princess of the linage that are entitle to the thrown of the Awujale the position of the which shall go around among the linage houses in each succession of the Awujale after joining my ancestors shall not follow me on the entourage. They shall not touch dead body of any person or take part in viewing of a dead body."

Then he proceed on the journey to the Ile-Ila (the big house) and followed by the people except those he had forbide not to follow him. However, on the journey he prounced the Obas and the titles of the Obas of the varoius cities and towns that need to have Obas. And he also appoint various leaders in villages and towns in the Ijebuland. Thereafter, at the big house he dismissed everybody and said

"my beloved son Moluwa!" "Shall be crown the Oba Ijebuland, with the title of 'the Awujale Ijebuland' after I had send my ambassador to the palace."

And he moved to the house at the entrance he add

"I shall remain here and be sending my ambassador call 'Awa' to the Awujale to delivery my request and if there is any issue Awa shall bring it before me to attend to it."

And he continue after the recitation of some charm words which was not very audible

"none of my descendants shall accept the name Obanta!" "I shall not be outside of my community! And the Ijebuland! And by these names shall my descendants be known and be praised:"

"Uku Ogewu"
"Ajogun, Abemesan"
"Ogborogonda"
"Ako-Yebeyebe-lori-Ogun"
"Awujale."

Then the Oba Awujale order

"'Awa' (who become the Alawa of the Ijebu Awa a settlement close to the Ile-Ile) and 'Odo' shall be the message bearers and the intermediaries between me and the Awujale on the thrown of the Ijebuland."

So the Alawa reports the request of the Oba Obanta to his son the Oba Moluwa the Awujale Ijebuland. And the regent, Odo was the person the Awujale sends whatever the Oba Obanta request for and Odo would gave them to Awa who takes them to the Oba Obanta at the Ile-Ila. If the Oba Obanta accept them the Awujale and the people of the Ijebuland were happy but if otherwise, the goods would remain in Odo's house because it is a taboo to take back the things that is meant for the Oba Obanta. So the Oba Obanta remains like that for long time and live as a god.

Ijebuland After The Awujale Oba Obanta about 1470

However, some years had pasted, the Awujale Oba (Emperor) Olofin and some Princes, Princess, the Olisa, Obas and notable Chiefs were being entertained at the palace by the musical groups and lady dancers, then the leading court attendant announced

"I am to inform the Awujale Oba Olofin of the arrival of the Oba Ile-Ibini's ambassadors that seek permission to enter Ijebuland with a message from the Oba Ile-Ibini for the Awujale about the war campaign in Ile-Ibini (Benin land)."

Then the Awujale raised his left hand and the Olisa said

"let the messengers of the Oba Ibini be permitted by the warriors at the border city to enter Ijebuland and Ijebu-Ode in the presence of the Awujale Oba Olofin."

Thereafter, Odewole, the most senior warrior brought the messengers that were from the Oba Ile-Ibini's ambassadors that had sought permission of Awujale Oba Olofin to enter Ijebuland and to the presence of the Olisa to hear their proposal of peace in the market town where a conflict was going on. Mainwhile, after the Olisa had discussed the matter with the Awujale Oba Olofin,

Then the Olisa order

"the Ijebuland military chiefs shall be in a session for discussion on the peace proposal of the Oba Ibini's ambassadors and command the warriors at the gates to allow the safe passage of the Ile-Ibini ambassadors to the palace."

Then, after the ambassadors had talked with the Balogun (the army general) Ijebu, the Ogbonis (warlords) and other war chiefs and an agreement had been reached on the peace terms for the traders at the markets. So Olisa lead the ambassadors before the Awujale Oba Olofin. And after the greetings and salutations and the ambassadors had left. And some weeks after, the Awujale Oba Olofin on the advice of the Olisa and the Balogun order

"the Ijebuland peace ambassadors shall visit the Oba Ibini, and inspect the effect of the peace efforts and the lifes of the Ijebus, the people, Ijebuland trade carravans, the trades in the markets and they shall bring back the report of their observation and evaluation to the palace and to the presence of the Olisa and the Princes and the throne."

Thereafter when the Ijebuland peace ambassadors got to the palace of the Oba Ibini, they met the emissaries of the king of Portugal that were visiting the court in about 1472. But the Ijebuland ambassadors came back feeling disturbed and inform the Awujale Oba Olofin of thier findings. However, the Awujale summoned the leading Ifa (Oracle) priest, who consult Ifa and he said

"the Ifa warn that the strangers whom they call "Oyinbo" (white people) have come to trade with us on our lands and not with we the Ijebuland and the Ibiniland only are they going to engage in their trades. The Ifa lay emphasis to this fact, that their presence should not be allowed in Ijebuland because they would bring evil and strange religion to the land."

Then the Ifa priest look more disturbed and at the same time smile, while he held the Opele with his two hands and recites more incantations and he purse, raised his head and look at the Olisa and he said

"the Ifa also warn that Kabiyesi o! Kabiyesi o! Kabiyesi o! Olu awon Olu, Oba awon Oba, Oba ti o gba i do bale gbogbo Oba! we are to be very patient, be vigilant and the Ijebuland people should be warm we shall trade with the white people with caution and be careful because the trade with the white people would bring prosperity to the Ijebuland trade. And the Awujale Oba Olofin should not prevent trade with this strange people, and should not to allow them to enter or give them a dwelling land in Ijebuland. Ifa emphasized that these strange people have come to steal our slaves and youths, which would be taken to their very far away land in very large and strange ships."

Then the Awujale Oba Olofin asked

"what sacrifice shall be made to appease the gods so as to prevent the evils that these strange people might bring with them?"

Then the Ifa priest turn the Odu Ifa around and held the Opele in his hands and made some request

"Ifa o gbo o Kabiyesi!" "Oba to gba ido bale gbogbo Oba!" "Awujale Oba Olofin bi yin eyin baba me wipe ki ni e tutu tabi ebo ti a le se, lati da owo ewu awon alawo funfun yi duro? Ifa wi o, ma fi dudu pe pupa, jowo ma fi pupa pe funfun o."

("the oracle please respond to the request of the lord of lords and the king of kings, the Awujale Oba (Emperor) Olofin, my ancestors what kind of, or what nature of sacrifice, or what item of sacrifice should be used to appeals the gods. So that the evils that these white people should bring to our lands be prevented.")

Then he smiled and look upward and at the direction of Awujale Oba Olofin, and at the Olisa and he add

"Ifa demand seven strange birds, seven slave of war, and seven different types of animals to be use as the sacrificial items."

Then the Awujale order

"these materials shall be provided for the sacrifice to the gods and our Ijebuland shall know peace and progress at all time and all seasons. No evil of any kind either small or big shall have a place within our lands. We shall be victorious over all obtacles, troubles, evils and our enemies, and wars in Ijebuland both at home and away. Yes I pronounced the blessing and glorious prophesy of progress of all kinds and types to our home and the lives of my people in Ijebuland both at home and outside. So shall it be because the gods of our ancestors have heard me and **OLORUN-ELEDUMARE** that owns every thing both on the earth and the heavens have heard me and accept my prayer and requests."

Then the Awujale Oba Olofin look at the Oduwole and the Olisa and he said

"the seven strange birds, seven slaves of war, and seven different types of animals to be used for the sacrifice shall be provided, and thank you

Oduwole for your good work and the gods and **OLORUN-ELEDUMARE** shall be with you and your household."

However, some months after, the Portuguse Captain Ruyde Sigueira order "we shall have to sail on the Lagoon and investigate the route the Ijebuland ambassadors came from to the Ibini court."

And lieutenant Jossy Santos responds

"yes Captain!" "We shall sail the Lagoon, we need to esterblish more volume of trades with this salvage people chiefs, and king before we loose the opportunity to the Dutch who are now competing with us."

Then some days later the Captain discovered that their ship can sail through the lagoon towards the direction they had noticed that the Ijebuland trade caravans use to the market, were they had fought with the Ibini warriors. However some days after some Ijebu tribes farmers and the Ilaje fiisher men saw a big strange moving object on the lagoon, and they inform their Chiefs and the Warriors, who order

"we call you youths and warriors to fight these strange men on the big object. We have not seen anything as big as this object floating and move this fast on the lagoon before. And the Ifa tells us that we should fight them and resist their entering into our land."

However, the leader of the warrior said

"we have to inform the Ijebu warriors since we are their servant on this land and the Lagoon, so that we will not get into trouble if we failed in our fight of preventing these strange people on this big moving object on the Lagoon."

The most senior chief said

"You have made a very good observation Odekunle. We shall do what the Awujale expect of us for our dwelling on the side of the Lagoon and for being given the authority to fish on this big Lagoon that belongs to the Ijebu. Which is to fight and prevent any intruders from getting into the Lagoon front."

However, Odekunle respond

"we have the duty of informing the Awujale of any intruder on the Lagoon, and I would send some warriors to inform the Balogun Ijebuland of these strange people and their big object moving on the Lagoon."

Mainwhile the fight took about two months and when the report of these strange white people and their ship got to Ijebu-Ode. And the Awujale Oba Olofin order

"the Olisa shall commission the Balogun and the Ijebuland warriors to support the fighters of the waterside of the Ijebuland. And we shall prevent these strange people from entering our land, we shall not allow them on our Lagoon front."

Thereafter, when the Portuguese noticed that they cannot force their way into the jungle and the land of the Ijebuland, because the Ijebu warriors were good marksman, strong with their horse, and also good archers. The Ijebus arrows had poisonous warheads, which rains fire on their ship. Then the Captain gave the order

"retreat and we have to prevent our ship from being sunk by these salvage animals"

Then they got back to their ship and they work and put efforts to put fire out of the ship and left the Ijebuland lagoon. Then Captain Ruyde said

"God knows what kind of animals are these people call "Jebu" are, they are deem strong with these archer and almost burn my ship. Sail back to the Ibini I have to talk with their King or Oba God knows what, the funny way they talk with their funny monkey look."

However, when the Captain got to the palace of the Oba Ibini, who refused to talk to the white people until the Captain gave the Oba and his Chiefs more drinks, guns and gunpowder. Then the Oba told the Captain

"strange white people!" "Shall not approach the Ijebuland as warriors!" "But instead place you goods for sale on the seashore with white flags. And the Ijebus would know that you have come for trade with them and have not come to force you way into their land and you mean peace. The Ijebus only understand trade with other tribes."

Mainwhile, the Oba Ibini also send some of his ambassadors to the Awujale Oba Olofin in Ijebuland, to show him the products which the white people had brought to Ile-Ibini, which includes mirrors, metal items, cloths, gin and more and adviced the Awujale Oba Olofin and his chiefs to trade with the strange white people. However, when the Awujale Oba Obalofin saw their products he like them and also noticed that his people were delighted in the products. Then the Awujale Oba Olofin said

"I thank the trade ambassadors from Ile-Ibini!" "I shall also send the Ijebuland trade ambassadors to Ile-Ibini to observe the trades with these strange people and their products."

Then some days after, the Ijebu trade ambassadors made contact with the white people, and got some of their products in exchange for some oil palm, cocoa, kola nut, beans and more. Then Captain Ruyde gave the leading ambassador two guns as a gift for the Awujale Oba Olofin.

However, the Awujale Oba Olofin received the gifts with delight and order

"the Olisa shall summon the Baloun Ijebuland and the warrior chiefs to come to the court to discourse the nature and terms of trades with the white people."

Thereafter about 4 days of discussion by the Princes, the Olisa, the Obas, the Balogun Ijebu, the chiefs and the warlords. The Awujale Obalofin accept their trade policy and he said "we have to be every careful and must not allow these white men on our soil, and no settlement shall be allow for any white man in Ijebuland."

However, from that day the Ijebuland caravan start trading with the Portuguese and the Dutch. Then the Ijebus serve as the middle men in the trade between the white people and other traders in the interior lands such as the Oyo, Iwo, Owu, Ekitis, Ilorin, Ife, Nupe, Ijesha, Ife, and more. Then the Awujale Oba Olofin, the Princes, the Olisa, the Obas, the Balogun Ijebuland, Chiefs and the Warlords practice with the guns given him by the Portuguese ship Captain and they were pleased with it's effective ability in killing games and they also realized that it was the weapon that killed some of the warriors during the lagoon front fight with the white people. Then the Awujale Oba Olofin order

"we have discover a new tool not only good for hunting, but also to strengthen our military and defense of our land against our enemies. We shall have more of these guns product and supply to our hunters and military Chiefs."

Then the trade relation between Ijebuland grew and the Portuguese want slaves in exchange for guns and other goods. But the Awujale Oba Olofin object to such trade and he said

"we have not forgotten the warning of the Ifa priest!" "It's just like yesterday!" "When he warned us that we have to trade with these strange white people with care, because though the trade would bring prosperity, it would also bring problem, because these evil people would want to take our slaves away from us."

However, instead of trading in slave with the white men, the Awujale order

"Ijebuland traders shall buy slaves from the Oyos, Ekitis, Ijeshas, Iwos, Ile-Ifes, Ilorins, Nupes, and more and sell the slaves to the Ibinis, and the Igbos in exchange for guns that came from the Portuguese. And the Ijebuland traders shall have direct trade relations with the white people with other products except selling of slaves to them."

CHAPTER 3

The British Missionaries and Slave ships about 1553

The British missionaries came with their ship about 1553 and request entrance into Ijebuland which the Awujale Oba Adisa and his Warriors resisted and after fight at the Lagoon front for several months, the British could only trade with the descendants of the Ibinis and that of the Ishekiris at the sea coast which is now called Eko. But the British and the French sailors were able to beat the Portuguese and the Dutch in the fight of gaining the control over Dahomey (Togo and Republic of Benin) and the coastal area of Nigeria. However, the rivalry and the expansionist drive between Dahomey and Oyo create room for the fall of Dahomey and eventually Oyo was able to supply large slaves to the British and French.

However, the British haven got so much slaves brought more ships and cargos to the coastal areas and found settlement in present Calabar, where they were able to introduce the Missionary, which they brought with their ships and export slaves, and other agricultural products such as palm oil, timbers, and more.

The Omoloba Oba Orhogbua was attending to his Chiefs over the issues of war, and the distribution of the slaves captured and other things at his palace in Ile-Ibini when the palace leading courtier announced

"the Omoloba Oba Orhogbua!" "Here come Basil Davidson the Englishman!" "Who has brought some goods, and guns from England to visit the court of Ili-Ibini oh Omoloba."

However, the Chiefs were very please with his products and convince Omoloba Oba Orhogbua that trading with the Englishman people would be better since the Portuguese ship have not being coming regularly anymore, so the Omoloba Oba Orhogbua welcome the guest. Moreover, after many years the introduction of the guns had create problems and also gave the minor tribes such as the Efik in Calabar, and the Ishekiris the ability to break free from the strong hold of the Ibini empire, thus result to more slaves being captured and sold to the British. Then Basil Davidson and his men send message to the Btritish Parliament

"I your humble servant and loyal subject to the court of our Majesty king of England the conqueror of India. Hereby inform the British Lords that the bush men in the Coast of Benin would be easy to be govern if more guns should be made available to be sold to them in exchange for slaves. And we have to cause more conflicts among them by selling more guns to the different tribes which would make them to wage more wars on each other and this would give us the large slaves needed for the plantations in the new world in the America and Brazil.

The Captain Basil Davidson
for the Coast of Benin

However, the British parliament saw their interest in gaining more money for the Royal treasury and the Lords also saw more opportunity in making more money in this report even though it was all about stealing from the innocent people and using Christianity as the pretence for sending ships and guns to the coast.

Then the official communication of Parliament was:

"from the Parliament of the Great Britain, use every means to divide the tribes as possible so as to be able to gain control over their coast, the interior lands, and ensure that the needed money and treasures come to the Royal treasury."

Thereafter, the British arrived with more Missionaries ships and the Catholic missionaries followed and there was more settlement of the white people in Calabar, and more slave merchant ships made Calabar their base. The British not only trade in slaves with the Ibinis, and the Efiks, but also with the Nri traders (the Igbo of Awka and Onitsha), Arochukwu (Abia), and Ohafia traders. And eventually, some descendants of Isekiris join Ijebuland migrants from Epe at the coastal line to form Eko village on an Island call Eko.

White people and slave trades about 1620

"Omoshewa!" "Omoshewa!" "What are you looking at since? And why are you taking so long there? I think someone is there with her, who can be there with her? We came to the stream alone and today is the market day almost all the young girls and the women are now at the Oba market."

Yetunde a girl of about eight years old move through the trees and avoid a large stone which almost tripped her and push away some tree branches as she walk through the rain forest. The cry of birds echoes through the rain forest, but she heard no respond from her senior sister, and she was getting worry and her look was that of sadness and about cry when she noticed her sister Omoshewa who was a beautiful girl of about sixteen years old standing with her back turned in her direction, she moved more faster and at the same time being cautious, until she saw more of her, Omoshewa was holding hand with the young white boy of about eighteen years old they meet at the last Oba market day. And she said

"I think she likes him,"

as she thinks loud

"no wonder Omoshewa could not respond to me! "Baba most not know of this, otherwise we both will be in trouble."

However, when she got to where her sister and the white boy were standing and talking, though they are using more of hand and sign in most of their conversation. Then when her sister realized that she was standing closeby she released her hand from the boy's hand and she said

"meet my friend Daveed (David),"

the boy now facing Yetunde removed his hat with both hands on his chest, repeat the same word

"David,"

and taking slight bow his head he add

"please to meet you."

And Yetunde likes the gesture he made and she points to herself, and said

"Yetunde,"

David repeating over and over

"Yetudi!" "Yetudi!" "Yetudi!" ....

while both girls tried without success in making him call their names properly the way they are accustom to, and when they couldn't made him pronounce their names correctly they gave up.

Then Omoshewa realized that they have to finish the washing of the cloths at the stream, drag her sister along with her as they move away and both sisters waving towards David. And David who was still standing, wondering why was she dragging her away, and after some distance Omoshewa turn back and facing the direction of David repeat the word

"Oba!" "Oba!" "Oba!"

Until he understand that she was telling him they would meet again at the Oba market. Then the two sisters ran back to the stream, laughing and Omoshewa said

"what have you being doing since? I thought by now you would have get the washing done halfway?"

Yetune replied

"I would have being doing all the work when you are there kissing and holding hands with your stranger lover."

Her sister quickly correct her,

"please don't say that!" "We are not kissing, he has not kiss me."

Her sister now enquire of her

"so you would have allow him to kiss you? To put that his strange white face on your face? And his long fingers over your breast?"

But Omoshewa, shout at her to stop her from being silly, said

"are you jealous because he likes to talk with me?

Then turn to the cloths she was washing and add

"Yetunde!" "Yetunde!" "Yetunde!" "please I beg you with the Orise Oke (God in heaven) don't say any of this stupid things to Baba or he would kill me."

However, they continue with their washing and singing, and when they were about finishing, some women with their younger daughters came to the stream and start washing their cloths. Then the women called their names

"Omoshewa!" "Yetunde!" "How is your mother so she has not return from Ode-na with the palm nuts?"

Omoshewa and her sister turned to their direction and kneel down and they answered

"Mama Temi and Mama Openu!" "No she has not, she just left yesterday, she usually takes two Oba market days before she would be back."

Then the two sisters finish their work, and put the calabash containers which contain their wet cloth on their heads and walk home. On their way home, Yetunde move very close to Omoshewa and ask in a low voice

"what do you think Mama Yeni was talking about when she said that the Oyinbo (white people) are taking our people to their place in Calabar?"

Omoshewa, now with worry in her look answered,

"I think she meant that some people in the nearby towns where being kidnapped and sold as slaves to the Oyinbo people."

"Eka Osan, baba Agbede" ("Good afternoon the black smith"),

the two sisters greet a man who they meet as they were getting into the dwelling place in the village. And he respond

"E pele, se Ome Ayeji ni yin?" ("Hello are you the children of Ajeyi?")

The girls respond

"beni baba!" ("yes baba!" which mean father because every elder male old enough to be ones father is call baba)

Then the man said

"greet your father for me when he returns from the farm."

However, when the girls got home, they spread the cloths on the lines made by tieing rope around trees with the rope line between the trees. Then Omoshewa gave instructions to her sister on the cooking of the evening meals and they both get to work on the cooking of the meal and other household stuffs. However, the people were returning from the Oba market and there were shouting and panicking. Some women were crying while some men were talking loud giving instructions to them saying "women!" "And you children!" "Stay within the compounds at night and do not to move about as soon as the evening sun is setting and when the Cockerels crows."

Then Yetunde ran from the backyard which was the back of the house and she called

"Omoshewa!" "Omoshewa!" "Omoshewa!"

She answered her and said

"I heard everything too"

and both of them were very afraid. Yetunde was crying and she said

"nibo ni baba mi wa?" ("where is our father now?") "Hope mama mi (my mother) is safe at the Edewomi farm?"

Omoshewa also more afraid and confused, but trying to caution her sister so as to stop her sister from crying said

"how can I know? We can't go to the farm now to look for baba mi, hope he is safe and come home soon"

"Baba Omoshewa!" "Baba Omoshewa!" ...

Owegbemi calls his brother, while he also gives instructions to his wife, and he said

"woman!" "I told you to stay at home!" "Where are you going now when nobody is safe? Do you want to be taken away, with rope in your neck like chicken or goats? Now you can go if you thinks you are wiser than your husband."

His wife answered

"Baba Ewebo!" "I just want to get the goats and the chickens inside their place before the night falls."

Then he realized that the goats would had wondered away from the compound and he said

"that is good!"

Then he called his eldest son

"Ewebo! "Ewebo!"..

who answered

"yes baba mi!" "I am looking at the backyard for the chicken."

And his father responds

"good!" "Nice boy!" "Leave the chicken for your sisters, follow your mother and make sure that the goats are safely return. I just want to check on my brother if he has return from the farm."

However, while he was talking Omoshewa and Yetunde heard him and they approach his house which was in the same compound. And Omoshewa answered him,

"no baba!" (which she meant "no uncle!") "He is not here!" "We are also waiting for his return from the farm."

Then the uncle said

"good!" "You girls can go to my house and stay there, have you get the animals, your goats and the chicken?"

They respond

"no baba,"

then he instruct them

"now go and look for the animals, secure them and stay with my children and wife."

Thereafter he calls on another relative, moving towards the relative's house in the same compound, to follow him to his brother's farm and look for him. Then the two men armed with cutlass and some charms move away from the compound and away from the dwelling side of the village following a footpath that leads to main path that the villagers take to the place where they cultivate yams, cocoyam, cassava and other plants which they sell the surplus after taken the ones for feeding their family away. However, the two men were talking about the kidnapping that took place in the next three villages away from them. And after they had walk for about 40 minutes, they start making

"hoe!" "hoe!" ...

sound which is the manner to call the attention of someone in the farm in order to locate the person or the part of the farm the person might be because the person on hearing the call would walk towards the direction where the sound comes from. But they did not hear any response. Then they were worried, and Owegbemi said

"this is very strange!" "There are three farmers just about five minutes walk from this big tree."

And his friend responds,

"yes Owegbemi!" "Baba Aperi's farm is close to Edegbemi's farm and I called him from this same Iroko tree (Mahogany) last Oba market when we came to help weed his yam farm after fishing work on your brother's farm. Are you almost ready? Because your farm at Aweko is going to be the next."

However, the two men were talking and failed to notice some men that were hiding in the bush nearby, that were lead by two white men. Then the white men gave the men hiding signal to cover their face, which they complied to. And the white man closer to Owegbemi point his gun upward and shot it. The sound of the gun made Owegbemi and and his companion to ran into the nearby bush and falling down in the process, and before they could recover six men hiding rush out and beat them, covered their head with sacks, put ropes in their necks, drag them to their feet and force them to walk towards the farm hut. Then when they got to the hut they heard the voice of Edegbe, Baba Aperi and other farmers talking in lower voice.

"Asking each other what is it that this strange white men want from us?"

Then when they realized that some people were coming, they got up on their feet. However, the white men leader instructs the black men working for him

"you people should remain on guard and make sure that these slaves must not escape."

And he gave three guns to the men and he add

"do not let them to remove the sacks from their heads and have the hands and the legs of the prisoners tied together."

Then Owegbemi realized that they had been kidnapped cried out

"boda mi!" "boda mi!" ("my brother!" "my brother!")

and he made attempt to crawl toward the direction he heard the voice of the farmers coming from. However, Edegbe recognized his brother's voice, he cried and said

"my brother Edegbe!" "I am finish!" "I am finish!" "You have come to look for me and they have taken you too!" "And put sacks on our heads, ropes on our hands and legs when we are not chicken and goats!"

Then the guards pushed the new prisoners into the hurt and start flogging them with the sticks in their hands shouting instructions "shout up!" "shout up!" "shout up!"

And they shot the guns upwards which caused more fear and panic on the tied men, and they said

"if any of you makes attempt to escape you shall be kill."

Then the tallest of the two white men call on the other white man, whose name was David and he said

"come, we have to go to the villages before these monkeys get to their house safe. We need to get 100 more of them to meet up the cost of our transportation from London."

David now excited thank him and responds

"what a way of making good money!" "We can make more money by kidnapping and selling these people!" "Which is even better than the money I can ever make back in London."

Then the man gave David is hand and he said

"you can call me Smith, I am a sailor with the Royal Ship."

David reponds

"Oh!" "It a pleasure meeting you, my name is David, and I came with the Royal cargo ship last fall."

And Smith ask him

"so you believe in all this missionary stuff?"

David answered him

"kind of! "But not until recently that I realize that the whole mission thing is all a joke, we are send out here to teach these animals how to be civilized enough to understand our language and to be able to make them work for us in order to ship their palm produces and farm products to London for our markets and business."

Smith now smiling and nodding his head as both men continue talking and walk away from the hut, and he said

"yes! "In fact David you got the whole business right!" "There is more money to be made by working together doing this kidnapping and selling them at Calabar, where we have our ships." Then David ask,

"what about these people resisting? I heard that they are savage!" And that they even kill their own for human sacrifice!"

Smith responds

"yes!" "You can be correct!" "They do fight back, then when we have not made these better guns that kill more than their dame guns. They are good with arrows and swords but they cannot stand these weapon of ours. They are no match to any white man, with the type of guns that we have made now. In fact this guns are purposely made to aid our killing them effectively, so you have no need to be afraid of them because we can kill them better with our guns and they are now afraid of us. Unlike before nobody dear come near these beasts."

Then Smith signal to the rest of the black men working for them that were waiting at the nearby forest and they were about eight in numbers and he told the one that understand pidgin English "we dey go into the village to get them people okey. Tell you men to work well if dey wan get better monee, because if we fail like yesterday, them pikin go suffer."

The leader of the men now very afraid said

"we go do am, we go fit do am, so no body pikin go suffer any arm. And the monee wey you get make you give us, so no pikin go suffer master."

Then the black men covered their heads with the sacks which has holes at the spots of their nose, eyes, and mouths. However, the kidnapping entourage continue on their search for people to be kidnap and when there was no luck, they move towards the villages since it now getting dark. However, they were able to ambush some women returning from the nearby stream. Some to wash their cloths and others who had gone to fetch water. Then they hide the women in the bush, and signal the guards who where armed with guns and continue with the raids. Thereafter the white men lead the people kidnap in a straight line walk with rope holding them together on their necks and their legs while they beat them. And forcing them to walk and threating them by shooting guns into the air. Then when they got to the ship which was usually hidden in the sea shore, and making sure none of the villagers knew of their presence there. Then the prisoners still with the sacks over their heads and the ropes was replaced with steel and chains while each of the them were hooked on the deck of the ship as the ship was being sail to Calabar and eventually to the ports in the new world (America) and Brazil.

However, Omoshewa after waiting for the return of her father and uncle from the farm, though she refuse to eat, fell asleep, she and all the villagers were scared because of the sound of gun shots which was at fist very closeby and later faint away. The fear eventually made her to fall asleep, only to wake up from a dream in which she saw her father running while being chased by a white lion and when the lion got to him the face of the lion turn to the face of the white boy she had talked with at the stream and she was shouting

"Davie!" "Davee! "Baba mi!" "Baba!" "Baba mi!" ..

Yetude also woke up and both of them were crying. Then the other people in the house also woke up and they were very afraid, and they cannot put on the lamp, for fear of being discovered, shaking and crying and holding on each other until the Cockerels crow continuously, which was an indication that it is sun rise. However, the whole villager start calling the names of the people that were not found and crying. Then the elders of the villages met at the Oba market center, and discuss the issues that had happened. The most senior elder in the villages got up, try and held his cry and anger, and he said

"please call me Orisegbemi!" "He is the most powerful haberlist in our clan, and he is believe to be the most powerful voodoo man, let him come, consult the gods and tell us what is wrong and why our people are being taken?"

Therefter when Orisegbemi got to the meeting, he greets the elders, and said

"Bale!" ("Mayor!") "And the people of Ilu-Agbe we pray the Orise-Oke (God in Heaven) to protect us from this calamity."

Then he sat on a mat he had brought with him and he placed the gods and the charms on it and start to praise the gods. He raise his head occasionally holding his Ifa tools upward to the right and some time to the left. And the Bale Ayeni praises Orisegbemi's ancestors, However, Orisegbemi, look confused and with anger in his face and voice, said

"the kidnappers' helper!" "Are some men in the next villages of Okenuwe!" "They are the one that are assisting the white men in their evil work of kidnapping."

Then Orisegbemi continue

"Ifa says that caution should be used to get these men because they are being threaten by the white men and if they refuse with the kidnapping their children would be killed!"

Then Bale Ayeni thank him and the rest of the elders also start to praise the ancestors of Orisegbemi, while the voodoo man with the help of his apprentice pack his items and put them in his bag, picked his mat and walk away from the meeting. Then the elders agreed with the hunters in Okenuwe to have a secret meeting and plan how to catch these people helping the white men in their evil work. However, the following day by noon, the messengers of the Bales (Majors) of the villages meet and agreed on the secret way to investigate the matter. At nights the whole men in the villages organize themselves into groups and guards to watch the movement of the people. Mainwhile, the Bale Ayeni also join the men sitting under a big Mahogany tree where the secret meeting of the guards was being coordinated, and it was the center point that all the various units of the guards gave their reports and exchange information of their operations. However, Efosa, a short man in his thirties, who was the leader of the guard assign to Okenuwe and the Bale Ayeni were having conversation and Efosa said

"Bale!" "What shall we do about these white people? Do we fight them at their meeting place? Because they had bought the Odegbemi land and had build houses there where they meet with our women and children."

Bale responds

"yes!" "These white people are teaching our children how to talk their own language and dress in their own ways!" "And we do not understand why they bring trouble to our land."

Efosa responds

"it the fault is the Omoloba Oba Ewuare!" "Who did not want us to fight the white people any more!"

"Efosa!" "You are thinking like a small child!" "The Omoloba did not just make us not fight these white men!" "The white men now have more powerful guns, our cutlass, arrows, and swords are no match to these gun of theirs!"

And the eyes of the Bale Ayeni become red and sweeting all over from the head, as if ready to fight, and add

"We don't know why the Orise-Oke make all things happen my son (which he meant male citizen)."

And Efosa, now more sad and confuse, said

"we have to plant someone in their meeting so as know what is going on there."

Then Bale Ayeni responds

"good thinking my son!" "That we shall do, let me send for the Bale Okungbowa so that we can have this talk before the next Oba market, which is their usual big meeting day."

Then Bale Ayeni called one of the boys playing in the nearby tree and instruct him

"my son!" "Now go to the Bale Okungbowa's house at Okenuwe and tell him that he should see me at the big Mahogany tree at Ilu-Agbe tomorrow at noon."

The boy node his head, indicating that he understand the message, and left for Okenuwe immediately.

"Mr Smith, I was informed by some reliable sources that some people in our community here in the Calabar Mission district were being kidnapped."

"Yes Rev Joseph!" "So do I heard Smith respond"

and he raise his up to face the Reverend and adding

"the issue of getting slaves is also part of the Mission's commitment to the Royal trade here in the Bright of Benin. We have the permission of their so call Chiefs and Oba to trade in these animals as slaves in exchange for guns which they need in order for them to kill each other, and to cause havoc and civil war among their communities."

Another man who had being listening to the conversation said

"Rev Joseph, don't you realize that the reason for sir John Hawkins and other merchants in the London community for investmenting in the Mission work is not about saving any soul or the salvation of some silly going to Heaven? The commitment to the Mission's work is all about making money."

Rev Joseph a round belly, thick build man, with a small cap on the back of his head, who was getting disturbed by what he was hearing said,

"but Captain Davidson!" "By!" "In the Lord Jesus Christ!" "What has the Mission work got to do with kidnapping of the poor people for whom we have brought the Gospel of salvation and the redemption?"

Captain Basil Davidson a tall man with bushy moustache, laugh at the top of his voice and he said

"where do you think the finance for your Mission's salvation and redemption comes from?" "The investment of the Royal vessel have to be protected."

Then Smith add

"Reverend!" "I observed that you are not adequately inform of the purpose of your Mission here. We have to make sure your people teach these monkeys to know how to read and write and some spelling and to be able to speak pidgin so that they can be able to assist us in our work here, and work as general labor for the supply of the materials needed for the factories in London and other cities of Europe, and America."

Then Captain Davidson responds

"Reverend!" "Hope you are not misunderstanding us, the guns and the weapons business have expand so as to make our economy grow, and we have found a good market in these salvages and also by causing enough havoc among themselves with our guns make us to be able to have control over them."

Then Mr. Smith smile and he add

"divide and rule them that is the word and so will it be!" "That is our expedition in this God forsaken Bright of Benin."

Rev Joseph, who was annoyed, but try in holding it, said

"sir!" "But!" "But!"

Then stand up and he add,

"please excuse me gentle men!" "I think I may have to get along for my journey to the Mission house in Okenuwe."

However, as he was about to get out from the room, he met David, who had being standing closeby the door and had listen to the conversation.

"Oh!" "David when are you coming back to Okenuwe? We cannot afford to lose a good hand like you in the God's work going on in the Mission field here in Calabar."

Then David walk with the Reverend father to his chariot and said

"I may have to wait here for some time to see to some business before coming to join the Mission."

Then the Reverend responds

"thanks my good brother in the Lord!" "We shall be praying for your soul,"

and both men made the sign of the cross and part ways.

"My brothers!" "We have to finish this tombo (palm wine) because I have told Iye Ronkie to get us three more fresh ones."

"Oleoke!" "We have to drink very well for the work since we need all the spirit the wine can provide so as to be able to have good focus,"

"yes Odele!" "You always talk sense!" "Since I have know you!" "The master almost get rid of us last time when the work did not go well."

Then after drinking and having merriment at the palm wine tapper's joint, the five men got up and left for their homes. Oleoke a thickly build man in his fifties wearing a rich native woven cloth, who was the leader of the Ibini men that work for the white men in the kidnapping business, was on a path and was wating for a woman whose husband had been kidnapped that was walking towards him who she was very sad, in a deep in thought, and she did not notice Oleoke who was standing on the path she was approaching.

"Akejue!" "What is your problem? I have told you not to think too much about your husband that is missing?" "I have promised many times that I will help you to find him!" "And any where he had gone I can locate him for you and bring him back home."

"You can say that since your wives and children are not missing!" "And you don't have to find any of your own!" "So you can not know what it is like not to see your husband for four years since we have married."

Akejue a round build heavy breast beautiful woman with good hair waving to the taste the season, wearing a colorful buba and rapper local dress begin to cry while Oleoke move closer to her, holding her hands, trying in consoling her and he said

"you know I had asked you to marry me before your parent gave you to Igbeike!." "I can take care of you!" "Have I not said so, many times now, without numbers for you not to cry because he is missing?"

Then Akejue releasing her hand from his and stepping backward away from him said,

"thanks I shall have to discuss the matter with my mother, so that my baba can agree."

"Yes!" "Yes!" "Akejue!" "You are a very thoughtful woman you need to let your baba agree first!" "So I should wait for you a day after Oba market to hear what your baba say?"

"Wait for me at the back of the Iroko tree by sunset I would have finish with my trade so we can talk."

However, after he had watch her walk way noticing that she was rolling her big rounded backside as she walked. He walk in the other direction, looking in all directions so as to make sure that no one was at a hearing distance, he start singing and he said

"yes!" "I got that Igbeike kidnapped!" "He took the most beautiful girl in this Ilu-Agbe away from me and now I can have her back to be mine."

Talking, dancing and singing as he walk away feeling jubilant to his house.

"Yetunde!" "Yetunde!"...

Omoshewa called her sister who had been sitting and talking with some girls of about her age while she attends to the customers at the market. But She was relieved when she saw her talking to the white boy they met at the stream, by the big tree. But Omoshewa had a mix feelings about wanting to talk to with the boy again or not, and she turn back in the other direction toward her mother's stall crying. However, David who had saw her coming toward them initially, only for her to turn the other direction felt bad, but at the same time felt ashamed of himself, thinking I must have hurt her feelings because she is crying, or she had knew that I was involve in the kidnapping of her people? Then when Yetunde saw the look in David's face, she turn arround and saw her sister walking away, crying, she ran to her, comfort her and she said,

"mama mi!" ("our mother!") "Would be back from Ode-na tomorrow."

Then Omoshewa she realized that if she did not stop crying, Yetunde will also join her crying and it would be difficult to make her stop. And also, she was feed up for people coming to comfort them whenever Yetunde crys. So she wipe her face with her rapper and said

"I am not crying because mama mi is not here, you know baba mi (our father) and his brother are still missing,"

Then she immediately add

"yes!" "We don't have to cry anymore because the Bale Ayeni has promised that the village elders would bring them back home."

Thereafter, after the sunset and they have had their meal Omoyele a girl of about Omoshewa's age, and she is Omoshewa's friend, and she a member of the white people's meeting came to visit and to remind them of their promise to follow her to the white people's meeting. However, Yetunde was very happy and excited of going to the meeting, because since the kidnapping day, Omoyele and other members of the meeting have being coming to their house, comforting them with foods, and other gifts. And the white man that always put on a small cap at the back of his head have been very kind to the people in the village, telling them nice things through some people who can talk the white man language. Though Omoshewa likes all things about the white people's meeting, but the thought of seeing David and remembering her dream makes her not to be sure if she wants to go or not. However, when it was time for them to leave for the meeting Omoshewa said

"Yetunde should go because I don't feel like leaving the house."

Then Yetunde became afraid, the thoughts of not seeing her sister overwhelm her and she start crying. So Omoshewa realized what the cry can do, and she agreed to go with them to the meeting.

The white man with the small cap on his head wearing a white apparel welcome them and they sang and danced which made Omoshewa felt at home and gave her a lot of relieve from the thought of her missing father and uncles. Then the white people show them some signs and mention some strange words, and put them in different groups. However, Omoshewa was surprise when she saw Omoyele calling the signs the names that is the same as what the white woman calls them, and she can talk like the white woman. Then she realize that it would be better to understand the white's people language and be able to talk to Davee about her dream.

However, the thought made her to concentrate in learning the English alphabet that she and the other new comer were being introduced to at the Mission house. Thereafter, they were send away with some men holding guns in their hands, who guard them to their houses.

Then Omoshewa thank Omoyele, and she said

"o se ore mi!" "Mo gbadu ibi gan!" "O ti soro bi tiwon o" ("thank you my friend!" "I enjoy my coming here a lot!" "You can talk like the white people now").

"Oh!" "I told you Omoshewa!" "That you will like the meeting!" "See we sing, dance, eat nice foods and learn how to talk English!" "You know with this learning you can go to the big Mission town Calabar and later go the white people place in London?'"

Then Omoshewa try to call the word English, as she said

"hnglis!" "hnglis!"

But her friend correct her

"it is not call like that you have say!" "English!" "English!"

However, after several attempts. Yetunde and the whole group burst into laughter as they went on their different path to their homes, and still being guard by the gun men.

However, some month after, Okeole had married Akejue, but she noticed that her husband had more money than what is normal for a hunter and a trader in animals. So she paid more close attention to his activities. And she noticed that he had an unusual timing in his night business, since the village night guards had made it more difficult for kidnapping around the villages. Then the white men had to move more into the interior toward the Yorubaland where there was more raids and kidnapping because of the continuing fight and civil war there. However, one day two strangers came to look for Oleoke, who did not realized that Akejue had return home from her market trade earlier. And knowing that his other wives were also in the market, he allowed them to have their conversation at the backyard which allowed Akejue to overhead their conversation. And one of the men said

"Okeole!" "You bi we leader for di woki we bi do witi oyibo manu them kinappee worki, you fiti torki to masita Smisth (Smith) to stop treaten kili we pikin o. We fee rane comot to ano oda placi if he no stop the threate, and sefu we don tire of dis kinappen thin o."

The second man whose voice seems familiar said

"you famumile safee!"

But Oleoke became very sad, and looked in every directions and he responds

"mi birothersi!" "Yona no kno whi I abi do thisi supidi kinappee!" "na becosi masita Smisth!" "Wan killi mi pikin dem ani mi farmili!"

Then he look very afraid, pace up and down and add

"mi bin trie e witi no succucess to bi stinieeal themu gunu soteeni!"

"them bi theye gife wee de gunu onini we bi kinappee onni witi themu."

Then the first man moved his legs about and raised his right leg and he hit the ground with it and said,

"wishi kindi lafu bi thisi?" "A bin getii monee!" "A no kuku fi spendi am!" "Becoshi dem ounta washi mani bi choosu to watche foor de kinapper too sef."

Then the second man ask

"Oleoke!" "sebi we bin de guardi?" "We bin exicusi so te di orda gardi bin no catchi we do tisi kinappee tin"

104

However, the conversation continue and Akejue realized the danger she was in, got out of the house from side of the house and quietly walk away to the main compound, shaking and in fear, and she said

"I can't ran away to my father's house!"

However, because the thought of her family being kidnap or killed. So she put on the courage and walk toward the house and she said

"Oku ile!" "Oku ile!" ("Welcome those at home!" "Welcome those at home!")

as she approach the frontage of her husband house. Then Oleoke and his visitors heard her voice and footsteps they got up from their seats and Oleoke said

"it is time for you people to leave because we cannot continue our conversation anymore."

Then Akejue, greets her husband and the visitors as she go on her kneels on the ground. And when she realized that the men are leaving, she protest and said

"why are your visitors leaving so soon? I shall go and get them water from the pot to drink before cooking for them so that they can have strength for their journey."

But the second speaker whom she recognized as Odesetan her husband companion in the village guard, said

"Akejue!" "I know you to be a very good wife!" "Thank you we have to check on our traps at the big forest and it is the elephants hunting season at the North forest, we have to meet with the other hunters, and we have come to discuss these issues with your husband."

Then Okeole said

"let them go to the meeting with the other hunters we can come back and eat the food which you have prepared for us."

Akejue asked to her husband,

"are you also leaving with them, and not going to have your meal?"

Oleoke responds

"yes!" "We shall be back to eat later."

Then she respond

"o da bo o, ma wa ma oje yin sile de yin" ("bye till your return, and your food will be ready then.")

However, after she was sure that they had left the compound, she stay in her room, cry, and she said

"so! it is this wicked man that planned the kidnapping of Igeike?" "The man that I truly love!" And holding the pilow in her hands and close to her chest until she fall asleep.

Moreover, Omoshewa having been member of the Mission for the past ten months, and with her determination to ask David about her dream, had pick some words in English.

"Omsewa!" "You are looking good!" "Oh!"

David realizing that she cannot understand his type of English, change the mode of the conversation and using his hands and he said

"you look good."

And she reponds

"Davee!" "Me no cry!" "No cry little!" "little cry!"

However, David seems very surprise at her improvement in English, and asked

"why cry?"

And she answered

"papa and mama!"

pointing to herself and her sister

"take!" "kenap!" "some bad wite!" "bad!" "bade!"

Then pointing to David and other white people in the Mission house she said

"yu good!" "good yu!" "good!"

And she start crying and her sister together with all the non white people in the meeting were all crying. But, David could not believe that the impact of what he had participate in could have such negative traumatic effects on the life people like this. Mainwhile, since he had spend more time at the Mission without leaving for about two years, he thought loud and he said

"Oh! "I now realized that this people who we thought to be ape and salvages are more human being despact the bad publicity given of them in London and the evil publication in Europe."

Then he walk away, and add

"this people are not animals, they have compassion and their ability to forgive and not show hatred, even when being hurt is far greater than that of the people in London."

And crying, he said

"I am convince that the Mission work is better than the kidnapping and selling them as slaves."

Then Kicking on the scrubs and the grass along his way as he walked to the Mission house and when he met Rev. Joseph. he said

"please Revered can I have a time for a confession?"

The Rev. Joseph responds

"sure!" "There is always joy in heaven for all sinners who confess of their sins."

However, Rev Joseph lead him to the confession place which was a small corner in the building covered with cloth. And inside of it there is a cloth in the middle which prevent the two people from seeing each other. Then Rev. Joseph said,

"my son what is your sin? The Lord is capable of mercy and he shall forgive you."

But David start crying, and Rev. Joseph wait until he was able to recompose himself and said

"when you are ready my son I am listening."

Then David breath in deep and told him of his involvement in the kidnapping. Thereafter, Rev. Joseph said

"my son your sins has been forgiven you, make sure you sin no more."

And he add

"say hay Mary seven time and our Lord payer."

After David had finished with the recitations. Rev. Joseph said

"please David can you wait for me at my office?"

Then David got out form the spot and walk to the Rev. office. And in the office, Rev. Joseph told him

"I had known since that day we met at the Royal trade post in Calabar." And David crying said

"I am soo soory!" "What should I do now!" "I have to do something to help in bring these people back to their home and family."

Rev. Joseph very sad and at the same glad to see his convert changing from his evil ways to the Lord, sat in his chair with a deep breath, and he responds

"David!" "Yes!" "You can redeem yourself by joining the group of petitioners in London and volunteer in the work of stopping the slave trade and the evils in bring weapons to this place just to make these poor souls kill each other. Because of some evil minded individuals who want to make money at any cost and by any means even if it will be by taking advantage of the good work of the Mission, and ridiculing the name of the Lord."

However, after finishing talking, he add

"let pray!" "Our Lord Jesus!" "We pray ye for your mercy and strength in this work of yours in this Mission field in Africa. Thank you Lord for this poor souls that your light has touch, help us in this fight of slave kidnapping and slave trade" "Amen!"

Then both men made the sign of the cross, and David realized that he could talk to the girl and her sister walk towards the people. But Rev. Joseph who was just behind him placed his hand on his shoulder and said

"you don't have to do that,"

and he look straight into his eyes and continue,

"it will cause more trouble for us at the Mission here if you tell them what you have done. My son you can be of more help going to London for the petition work. And telling people there about the evil effects of this bad business of slave trade and how it is affecting the Lord souls here."

David nodding his head with tears in his eyes, said

"thanks Reverend father!" "Thanks Reverend father!" "That I can do!" "So I will go to London with the next ship leaving."

And Rev Joseph responds,

"that is great!" "I have some mails, if you wouldn't mind!" "Please help me deliver them at the saint Patrick's church Mission office in London."

And David follow him to the office and he gave him some envelopes and add.

"May the Lord grant you journey mercy my son,"

Then David walk away of the Mission compound.

Mainwhile, Akejue, had become very weak and lost all hope and interest to live, and cannot eat, her husband tried without success to make her eat. And everybody in the compound also tried to talk to her and ask her what is troubling her, but she would not talk. And after the third day, when she had refused to eat she took the poison for killing rats and she said

"what is good in his life? Why do I have to live with this evil man, who kidnaps everybody and still pretends to be the hero that saves our people against our enemies? I would not be part of this, we all thinks he is saving us and he got the highest warrior chieftaincy title for that effect, but he is the opposite."

However, Oleoke, who had came home earlier to make sure that she could eat, heard everything she had said, but because of fear, shame, and not knowing what to do wait at the other side of the room. Then when she start breathing very heavy, he ran into her room and discovered that she had taken the rat poison on the floor. He carried her and about to take her to the center room, but for fear that she might continue with the kidnapping talk, he left her in her room, ran to the kitchen area. And look for some clay pots, but not so sure of what to look for or what he was looking for, However, some children in the compound were playing and making noise, and he shout at them and said

"Oh!" "Children would you stop playing around!" "you children go out of the compound if you want to play."

Then the children look at him and they were supprise, and they can not understand because it is very unusual of him to make such complain, because normally he always play with them when they play in the compound and always full of jokes. However they left the compound and continue with their play outside. Then he got some palm oil in a calabash, and rush back inside the house, got to her bedside and lift her head up to put the oil in her mouth. While she said,

"you!" "Everybody!" "The Bale!" "Yes Bale!" "You!"

and she breath her last breath. Then Oleoke, shout in loud voice,

"I am finish!" "Yes finish!" "Bale!" "Everybody!" "So she had told some people and even the Bale had known that I am the one!" "the kidnappers there are looking for!"

And he rush out of the compound towards his friend Odesetan's house and at his house he called

"Odesetan!" "Odesetan!"....

The he looked from his window and he saw him. But Odesetan now wondering what could be wrong? Why is Oleoke so restless and calling him like this?

However, he thought he was coming inside the house, but he noticed from the window that he had turned the other direction and walking even now more faster back to the direction of his compound. Then Odesetan called after him

"Oleoke!" "Oleoke!" "Oleoke!" "Can't you wait to talk? What is the matter? You need to slow your pace,"

still walking, half running and trying to catch up with him. However, two women saw them and they said

"what can be wrong with the the two most powerful warriors in our land that they are in hurry like this? Hope they have caught the kidnappers, because we have heard that the people helping the white men are our own men."

Odesetan heard what the women said as he pass them, and when he got to Oleoke's compound, he wait for him in the sitting room because that is the place a visit enter in a house. And after waiting for a while he heard Oleoke's voice as he said

"Oh!" "Akejue!" "Everybody!" "Bale!" ("Mayor!"),

And he heard him breath a very deep breath. Then Odesetan rush into the room where he heard his voice, and saw both husband and wife dead, but he tried to revive his friend using some charms he had in his outer garment pocket, noticing that it may not work. He got out of the room in hurry looked around the sitting room, not able to find what he wants. Then he rush out of the compound, some people were greeting him and praising his ancestors, but he just wave to them, and continue with his fast walk. However, on his way home he said

"what is wrong with me? I should not go back to my house before the Bale and everybody in the village descend on me. Akejue had discovered our kidnapping work and Oleoke had poison her and himself. I would not wait to be caught and disgrace, now the people are shouting my name and those women talking of catching the kidnappers."

Then he look at every direction as he walk to the nearby bush and hang himself on a tree.

However, the news of Akejue and her husband who had taken poison and kill themselves got to the Bale, and they are waiting for the arrival of the herbalist that would carry out the ceremony to appease to the gods because OleOke was the highest warrior title holder in the whole villages around. Thereafter but before the herbalist finish his rituals, a woman ran to the Bale's compound, shouting

"Odesetan!" "Odesetan!" "Odestan hang himself on the tree."

Then the Bale in disbelieved told two warriors to follow the woman's son to the spot. However, The first warrior to get there saw him and he said

"it is true that he is dead!" "And nobody can touch his body because he was the second highest warrior in the land, and the spirit of the dead have to be appeal before the body can be taken down from the tree and buried."

Then when the news of his death got to the Bale Ayeni, he called all the Chiefs and the prominent people in the villages to a meeting at the Oba market. And he said

"my people of Ibini!" "We had not seen this kind of bad omen before in our land!" "The first and the second highest warriors together with one of our daughter died in the same day and they all commit suicide."

Then he ordered

"get me Orisegbemi!' "Let him come and ask the oracle what is wrong and what the gods demand of the villagers."

Thereafter, Orisegbemi consult the gods he looked everybody, breath deep and said

"Koro to je efo ilu efo lo gbe" ("the bacterial that destroys the vegetable, is inside the vegetable.")

Then he adds

"the leaders of the people helping the white men in the kidnapping had taken their own lifes. Akejue kill herself when she discovered that her husband is the kidnapper we have been looking for. And for fear of her parent not being killed or herself bring killed, since she do not know who to trust, and since her husband friend is also involve, so she took her own life."

Then Orisegbemi took his mat, and as he was rising up, he adds

"Bale Ayeni shall provide the necessary thing needed to appeal to the Esu and death because there is war coming, and even more of our people would be taken as slaves to the white man's land."

However, the whole people in the market were silent as the old man in his white rapper dress walked away and his apprentices following him.

CHAPTER 4

Basorun Gaha Influence on Oyo Empire about 1720

"Bale mi!" e wo ni, e jowo e ba mi gbe agba kin le fi joko," ("My husband please help me get a chair so that I can sit down,")

Olabisi the wife of the Osi Balogun (Major General) Gbajumo, told her husband. Haven walk for about 20 munites from their compound to the midwife's home, she became very tired and complained that her water had broken.

"Iya Eweje!" "Ija Eweje!" "Abi e ti wo Iyewu ni? E ha jowo, egba wa o." ("The female herbalist!" "The female herbalist!" "Are you in your inner room? Please help us.") The Osi Balogun Gbajumo said, looking here and there, very worried and standing at the entrance of the house, holding his cap in his hand and sweating. Then he was about to make another call as he held his wife while helping her to seat on a bench at the side of the front of the house, but he said "please take it easy my wife!" "Can you manage and sit down?" "Oh!" "Water!" "Water!" "Please, seat down."

Then a female slave came out from the house and said

"E le O!" "Ha!" "Eyin ni!" "Osi Balogun ati iyawo yin? Iya wa lagbala ni!" ("Hello!" "Ho!" "It is you the 2rd deputy General and your wife? The herbalist woman is at the backyard.")

While she was still talking the herbalist came out from the door entrance, and saw the couple, and the woman in serious child labor. Then she realized that the husband was the Osi Balogun, and she start praising him and singing his ancestors praises as she join in giving his wife the support she needs to get her into the house. However, she place her arm around Olabisi's neck, and support her to walk and she said

"thank you the Osi Balogun, but why are you so much afraid, shacking, and sweating?"

As she walk his wife through the entrance of the house and add

"I shall be able to take good care of my Olabisi, my dear wife of a strong warrior of the Oyo Alafin."

Then she support her inside the child delivery room and let her sat on a bed. And the herbalist start singing the praise to the gods and **OLORUN-ELEDUMARE** (God Almighty). Then she face the Osi Balogun who was a little bit relaxed and she said,

"my Osi Balogun despite all your war experiences and trophys of war you are so much afraid because your wife is in child labor."

But he responds,

"me afraid!" "Where is the fear? I am always capable of the defeat of anything, but just help me make sure that she delivers the baby safe and healthy."

However, the herbalist smile and said

"yes I know you to be a fearless warrior, no pregnant woman that enters this room leaves without a crying baby in her arms."

Then she gave instructions to her two attendants and they left the room and came back with a big calabash in their hands which contain some stuffs she use in the baby delivery work. And she said

"Olabisi!" "The wife of the warrior you shall now have to take the courage as a wife of a warrior, so lie down," as she makes her to lie down on the bed. Then she face him, and said

"the Osi Balogun Alafin Oyo!" "I am not in any position to tell you what to do."

However, the Osi Balogun responds

"Ewo le wa so yi?" "Pase fun ni ti a je!" "Ani ki a ti bi layo, ati ki a gbo oun Iya ati Omo" ("What do mean?" "Who are me to care!" "The most import thing now is the safe delivery of the baby, and for the mother and the child to be safe.")

Then the herbalist said

"Please, may you go and take a seat at the corridor while your child is being deliver."

And he said

"thank you Iya Eweje!"

Then he left the room and follow one of the attendance to a comfortable seat which had been placed there specially for him, to wait. And he continue to praise the herbalist gods and he said

"eni se ti o, ELEDUWA a ma fun yin se" ("may you know no failure, and may God continue to grant you success.")

Then one of the attendants brought him water in a calabash, and he asked her

"is this a good cold water?"

before taking it from her. And she responds

"yes my Lord!" "It is fresh from the cold water pot."

And he took it from her hands as she kneels down at his front and drank it, while she remains on her kneels and she wait until he feels satisfied and he retun the calabash back to her. While she place her head down ward avoiding face contact with him and he said

"thank you, it is a good water, you can stand up now."

However, as she was leaving his presence, the Osi Balogun Gbajumo's warriors rode their horses very aggressively into the compound and asked for their master. And they were taken to the corridor of the house where he sat, and waiting for the message from the herbalist. Then they prostrates on the ground before him, greeting, and praising his ancestors. And he responds

"thank you my children of war, we shall wait to hear the cry of the new born baby before leaving for home."

Then after some few hours the herbalist woman brought a boy covered with white cloth, singing and praising the Osi Balogun's ancestors as she gave the baby to him. And he took the boy with joy and start to praise OLORUN-ELEDUMARE, and his ancestors as he walk to the labor room, congratulate his wife, and he put the baby on her hands. Then he left the house with his warriors on his horse back to his compound and announced the arrival of a new son. The people in the compound start singing his praises, and every person that heard of the news came to the compound to greet him and rejoice with his family. However, the people spread the news through out of all the Oyo towns and villages that

"the wife of the Osi Balogun had given birth to a boy,"

so the people will congratulate one another saying

"congratulations for the new baby boy just added to the Osi Balogun's household, we are on our way to his compound,"

However, some would go as soon as they can to praise him and see the new born baby. Then the Osi Balogun's compound was full of visitors and it continue like that, till the eight day the child was circumcised; that is have a piece of the foreskin that covers the end of the penis, remove by the herbalist woman. And people brought foods, farm products, bags of cowries (money) and more to the compound, as gifts to the mother and her child. The chiefs and important people in Oyo and other places brought gifts and most exceptially bags of money for the Osi Balogun Gbajumo.

The naming Ceremony of the new baby

On the eight day of the boy's birth, as early as the first Cockerel crows the people in the compound start cooking and making preparations. The Osi Balogun provides some big cows, rams and goats. Then the ram of his choice was picked among them and taken to the front of his compound, at the side of a small hole which had being dug by his slave. And the Osi Balogun took a knife from one of his slaves and after saying some prayers in the presences of his friends, family and people slash the throat of the ram, letting it blood drip into a pit. Then the rest of the aminals were killed by the men of the compound. And they use hot water in preparing and for removing the hairs of their skins with knifes and blades and the animals were cut into pieces. Thereafter, the women cook them at the side corner of the compound so as to prevent the smoke of the wood stoves from disturbing people in the compound as the naming ceremony continues throughout the day.

However, the Osi Balogun Gbajumo and Olabisi who was carrying the new boy in her nap as they seat at the front of the people facing the Ifa priest who sat on a mat consulting the Ifa (Oracle). Then the priest ask the Osi Balogun

"what is the name for the boy?"

And the Osi Balogun responds

"Gaha Olalekan Gbajumo!"

However, the Ifa priest repeating the names over and over, as he turns the Ifa items singing and praising OLORUN-ELEDUMARE, and his ancestors. Then he said

"the names are good,"

"there should be a sacrifice for the boy for his future not to be full of trouble and to prevent him from bringing trouble to his father's house and Oyo."

Then the Osi Balogun asked

"when should the sacrifice be done?"

However, the Ifa priest consult the Ifa again, now calling the boy by his first name

"Ifa what type of sacrifice shall be offered to the gods on behalf of Gaha?"

and he responds

"when Gaha is twenty-one days old, he shall be taken to the stream for the sacrifice."

And the priest continue with praising of his ancestors, and when he finish he pick up his mat and tools which he handed over to his apprentice. Then he left the compound, And the people start singing the Osi Balogun's praises and greets the boy's mother and they gave gifts to his parents and everyone calls her Iya Gaha, saying

"the boy shall grow up and be able to live to the expectation of his parent for his name."

However, the compound was full of people, eating, drinking water and palm wine in small calabash, and sitting in their respective groups' circle.

Then after some time the musicians and the drummers start singing, dancers of various types of acrobatics styles, females, virgins with beads in their waists, and necks were entertaining the people. Thereafter, the Osi Balogun and Olabisi were called to come to dance at the front of the musicians, and the praise of the Osi Balogun was sang as they both dance. Then after some minutes the people join them on the dance floor.

Then a week after, one of the Ilaris (palace attendance) form the Alafin of Oyo palace came to the Osi Balogun's compound and he called

"Baba Osi Balogun!" "Baba Osi Balogun!" ("My lord the 2ʳᵈ General!" "My lord the 2ʳᵈ General!") "Where are you my Lord? I am being send to tell you that you are needed urgently at the palace."

as he got into the compund. However, some of the Osi Balogun Gbajumo warriors' almost challenge him, but when they realized that he was an Alafin Ilari, they asked him

"what is wrong?"

And he responds

"I need to talk to the Osi Balogun Gbajumo."

Then a warror told the Osi Balogun

"my Lord the 2ʳᵈ General an Ilari from the palace have a message for my Lord."

And the Osi Balogun responds

"allow the Ilari to come and meet me here at the center room."

Then after the greeting he said,

"good day my lord, your attention is urgently needed at the palace my Lord."

However, the Osi Bogun Gbajumo without looking at him or responds got up from his seat, and a slave brought him his horse which he mount and rode as fast as he can, and followed by his warriors to the palace. When he got there the Basorun (Prime minister) Oyo empire was addressing the warriors. And the Basorun said

"we shall match to join the campaign to stop the Fulani at Ilorin, because the Ilorin warriors have being fighting the Fulani for one month, and they are now advancing toward the walls of Ilorin so there is no time for our delay. We have to go right now before Ilorin falls to the hands of the enemies of the Alafin and Oyo."

However, the morals of the warriors become very high, when they heard the words of the Basorun Oyelesi. Thereafter, the Osi Balogun Gbajumo said

"we have to move and lead our various units. And each army unit must line up under their warrior unit leaders, the foot warriors with their sword, arrows archers and more."

Then the Osi Balogun Gbajumo inspect the leaders as they line up and he release them, as he said

"now go to your warriors and inspect them and make sure they are ready to lay their lives for the glory of the Alafin and Oyo."

However, the army match and the horse men followed them and while the warlords of the various units call commands and instructions. The drummers and singers sang song of the praise of the Alafin ancestors and that of the warlords and prominent warriors of now and the past. Then the Basorun (Prime Minister) called the Are kakanfo (field Marshal) and the Otun Balogun (1st General), the Osi Balogun (2rd General) the Olikoyi (Province Commander) and other warlords to a meeting under a big tree, where they discussed and thereafter they approach their various units. Then the fight was very intense and at the third month of fighting, the Osi Balogun after several success in defends of the Ilorin walls, town, and villages closeby, remembered the sacrifice instruction and he said

"Oh!" "My son Gaha! "My son Gaha!" "What a shame of me!" "I am too busy fighting for Oyo and had forgotten about Gaha's sacrifice and now it more than twenty-one days."

And as he thought about it, he lost concentration and rode his horse away from the war front without given signers for his personal guards to follow him, who were also in the deep fight. However, the Osi Balogun rode away from his side of the battle front, and two Fulani warlords that have being looking for an opportunity to attack him spot him, then they called their guards and attacked the Osi Balogun Gbajumo. Though, he tried to call for the assistance of his guards, but it was too late because the Fulani's were more on him. Then one of the Fulani warlords threw an arrow at him as he was defending himself and fighting the two warriors and another warlord, which hit him at the back. However, he was being hurt because the arrow had poisonous warhead. Then the Osi Balogun Gbajumo shout, and called his guards and rode his horse back towards the Oyo camp. But a Fulani warrior hit his horse at it's side as he try to pass him, then he fell but he quickly got up with the arrow still at his back, saying some charm words and he took out an animal horn from his bag with his left hand and a long sword in his right hand and he fought his way back towards his camp shouting the call of his warriors. Then some of his guards heard him, and he called others and they fought their way to save the Osi Balogun Gbajumo who was fighting with the a Fulani warlord, but he had killed the other Fulani warlord. Then one of the Fulani guards shot an arrow to the Osi Balogun Gbajumo which hit his left shoulder, but still holding his ground he continue to fight the Fulani warlord, while both him and the Fulani warlord had made several cuts on each others' bodies. However, the Osi Balogun trust his sword into the side of the Fulani's horse and he drag the man from the horse to the ground. And before the Fulani could gain his balance, he struck his sword into the Fulani's heart, who fell down on his back while he press down with his sword, then two of the Osi Balogun Gbajumo's guards who had fought their ways to his side assist him to their camp, and they brought some charms from his bag, which was almost turn to pieces. However, the Osi Balogun who was being surrounded by his loyal warriors holding charms and saying things to save him, and after removing the arrows and they had applied band aids. Then the Basorun was called and he attend to the Osi Balogun Gbajumo, who bleeds from every part of his body and the Basorun feeling very sad, shouting the Osi Balogun praise and he ordered

"carry him to his own tent, I shall not loose a General in this battle"

but before they got to the tent the Osi Balogun Gbajumo died. Moreover, when the Basorun saw that he had stop breathing, he rode his horse to highest hill top and he gave the command

"let the warlords hold the position of defense, and blow the trumpet call that a Balogun had fallen in battle."

Then the Fulanis too realized that they had lost two of their chiefs warriors called for retreat. And there was cry of lost warriors at both side of the camps, so the Basorun Oyo call the Chief warriors to give the Osi Balogun his last respect, and seven guns was being shoot seven times into the air. Thereafter, the Oyo warlords starting from the Basorun took their turns in praising the Osi Balogun Gbajumo as he was laid in state. And the following morning the Osi Balogun Gbajumo and other warriors' corpses of important warriors were sent to Oyo town for burials.

Mainwhile, Gaha grew to be a very strong warrior, he was trained in the household of the Basorun who was a relative of his mother. Then Gaha who was a teenager, being stubborn, arrogant, and would not respect the elders. However, one day he went out with his gang, and they raid farms in an Oyo village, and when the farmer saw that the leader of the warriors was the young Basorun boy he said

"e jo wo o!" "Se agbado le fe ni? E lo ka a, se bi ti yin lo ni, Gaha lo ni, ti Basorun na ni a. Eru Gaha omo Basorun ni a."

("please!" "Do you want corn? You can have the whole field, and harvest as much as you want. We are all for you Gaha, the Basorun's nephew. We declare our loyalty for the Basorun.")

But Gaha responds

"stay right there!" "We are not only here for the corn."

Then they stop what they were doing, and being afraid so that Gaha would not kill them. And Gaha add

"you all line up here"

and order one of his men

"bring the rope out!" "I think the rope shall be good in their necks!" "So put it on them and put them in that hut for me."

Then after some thought Gaha said

"who is the owner of this farm?"

And one of them raise up his hand and responds

"I am the owner my Lord,"

and looking down to make sure he avoid eye to eye contact with him, and he add

"the rest are my slaves."

Then Gaha said

"you have to continue with your farm,"

but as the man tried to thank him, Gaha saw his face and said

"Oh!" "It is you Okerejo!" "I have heard a lot about your farm!" "Now you are free, we have to make your farm our base. Take the rope of his neck"

pointing to one of his men who quickly took the rope off Okerejo. Then Gaha smile, and he said "he is a good man!" "And he works hard too, but I heard that you have a farm in Oke Ogun."

And Okereji responds

"Yes my Lord!" "This is my second farm"

Then Gaha looking at his men, laughing and he said

"we only want to scare you!" "We will need you, so you are lucky to have me on your side. You see we need money"

And pointing to his group as he talk, and he add

"you have to tell your slaves to load the corns and other farm produces into our chart and take them to Ede market and bring the money back to me. You are a good man and hardworking so I would not let them sell you and your slaves into the white men slave ship."

Then Gaha men start to sing Gaha's praise and greeting him with praise of his warrior father. Then Okerejo select eight slaves and ordered them

"load the chart with the corn sacks and other farm products and take them to the market as my Lord Gaha had request."

So Gaha continue with this raids in all the villages in Oyo and his reputation for being notorious and mean spread to the extent that his uncle the Basorun Oyelesi was embarrass, because of the complain about Gaha had reach the Alafin (Emperior). Then the Basorun Oyelesi send one of his leading warrior to Gaha to come and see him. However, Gaha was very surprise when he receive the call from his uncle, so he quickly follow the warrrior back home. when he got home the Basorun said

"Gaha!" "Why are you coursing trouble? And now the whole of Oyo is mad with you. I would not want you to bring the Alafin fighters over our family, so you have to leave Oyo to a distance location away from the reach of the Oyo warriors."

Then while the Basorun Oyelesi was talking to him, Olabisi his mother walk into the compound and she was very sad and crying she said

"Gaha!" "Gaha!" "Gaha!" "Why are you making trouble everywhere you go? I am sure you are not going to kill me before my time comes, please hear what my brother tells you to do or do you want the Alafin to bury me alive?"

The fear and sadness in his mother's voice made him to realize the degree of what he had done, and sense the trouble he had got his family into. So he got on his horse and rode it very fast as he couldn away from Oyo and some of his friends followed him.

However, Olabisi became very sick and did not want to eat but always crying. So one day her friend Ikejoke, said

"my friend!" "Why are you always sad and sick like this? If you are not careful you are going to kill yourself because of Gaha, and when you die like this who is going to take care of your other three children?"

Eventually, Olabisi accept to follow her friend to Esugbola, the Esu (Devil) worshipers' priest. And Ikejoke said

"you know when a child becomes so stubborn like Gaha, it is better to offer sacrifice to Esu."

Then after several persuasion they went to the Esu shrine, and as they were about to enter the temple, Ikejoke said

"Olabisi! "Olabisi!" "Olabisi!" "My friend how many times have I call you?"

"Yes!" "Ikejoke!" "What is the matter? You have called me three times, is there any problem?"

"No I have only to warn you that Esu's place is a mysterious place and it is the house situated in middle of three crossroads, please nobody argue with the priest of Esu or any one there, nobody laugh or smile there. The house of Esu is not a place of 'Joy'"

Then Olabisi breath in deep and responds

"you know I am not a child or a stranger to our accestorial spiritual custom, everybody know that you don't expect to have peace in a dwelling that accommodate Esu."

So both women enter the house after passing under some palm tree leaves which was being held by two big trees. At the feet of each tree was a black and white pots in which there were metals which had palm oil poured on them. Inside the middle of the compound, there was a large circle made of stones which had palm oil on them with palm tree leaves, there were human being skulls hanging everywhere, and inside the circle about approximate the middle of it, there were three pots which contain human being heads. The place was so dark except for a pole on which a palm oil lamp hang. Two men wearing black garments with palm tree leaves around their waist were standing without talking. A man walk backward from of one the rooms and approach the center of the circle holding a metal object and stop at the middle of the circle, and the man stood there with his back to the two women and said

"welcome my daughter Olabisi!" "Your problem is now solve you are at the right place to find solution to what is troubling your mind concerning your son Gaha."

"you need to drop the three bags of money for palm oil and eko (corn meal) which is known to be the food of my Lord Esu."

Then Olabisi and Ikejoke drop the bags of money which was under their wrappers. And Esugbola start calling

"Esu!" "Esu!" "Esu!"

And praising the deities of the Esu. Then suddenly there was a loud laughter from the middle of the pots that contain the human being heads as a deity appeared covered by black cloud of smoke. Then Esugbola on his kneels trembling and talking with a shaking voice said,

"thank you for honoring my call my Lord Esu-Odara!" "Onile lorita-meta"! "Enitin yo nibi elekun gbe sun ekun!" ("Devil the wonder being!" "He that has dwelling at the three crossroads!" "You that is deligted and full of joy, while people are face with troubles sorrows, and sadness!.") And Esu said

"Olabisi!" "Why are you being sad when you suppose to be full of joy and happy? Your son Gaha is going to be very rich!" "And become the most powerful, and popular man in Oyo!" "He will live and become old. He shall have fame the one I have given him like no other person in Oyo!" "Your husband Gbajumo!" "Beg me for a son when he couldn't be patient any more because he want a boy, but have many daughters. When the chidren of Adamah are not patient they come to me 'Esu-Odara.' I have to get my reward for making things work for them when there are not being patient! I can make it fast!

Esu now laughing, and it continue

"Your husband not always patient!" "Then he forget to make sacrifice as he was warned, he went to war!" "Which I put in place to make things my way! Olabisi enjoy yourself there is no reason to be sad concerning your son Gaha, you shall have lots of joy! Oyo shall have lot of joy! And be more powerful because of Gaha, you are a woman, that is what you all always want! Money! Happyness! Richess! Let the men be your fools! Use them for your needs and gains! Let them get you money, richess, happyness trick them as long you are a woman that is what you always want from the men fools! I 'Esu-Odara' shall be there for you my women,"

and Esu continue to laugh as it disappers and the dark cloud left too, then Esugbade walk backwards in the same direction he came.

However, the two women now trembling and it appears as if they just wake up from a dream and they realized that they have being holding on to each other for support since, and they gradually start to regain their consciousness walk in fast space out of the compound.

Still speachless Olabisi who was more confused, walk back home speachless and after some minutes walk Ikejoke broke the silence and said

"now you don't have to cry and be worry anymore your son Gaha is a special being, such is the case of children that are specially blessed."

But Olabisi only said

"thank you!"

and both women left at a different path way to thier compounds.

Thereafter, Gaha and his companions became very successful warriors and traders. They continue raiding farmers at villages that are not Oyo major territories, where the influence of the Alafin and the Oyo warlords was not strong. Now They came across a beautiful woman who trades in cloths and very rich, and Gaha became very much in love with her and asked her to marry him. But She said

"I will accept only if you will join us in our trade and be ready to protect me and the others in our trade routes."

And Gaha said

"only for me to be your body guard and you will be mine? That is the easiest thing for me and my men to do."

However, Gaha discovered that there was more money to be made in the trade, which gave him more insight into raiding of the farms and selling the people as slaves to be sold to the white men. Thereafter, Gaha became more rich, powerful, and famous, he had many slaves, and big warriors under him who were competent with the swords, archers, and good horsemen. So whenever there was war between the Oyo villages and the Fulanis and others, Gaha would go to defend the Oyos. Mainwhile, Olabisi who heard of her son fame, begs her brother the Basorun Oyelesi to forgive him and let him come back home. Then after the Basorun Oyelesi had given the matter good thought he said

"I have nothing to loose in Gaha now, the boy have become very popular and I heard he is also he very rich trading in slaves to the white people."

So the Basorun agreed with his sister looking at her while she sat on cain chair at his front in his court room and he add

"yes!" "We have to forgiven him!" "Ta ba fi owo osi ba omo wi asi tun fi ti otun fa mora ni" ("When you give a child purnishement for wrong doing, the punishment is not going to last forever it is for a while.")

And he got from a timber chair, walk towards her and sat by her side and add

"he is also my son!" "I trained him to become a srong warrior and none of my warrioirs have his fame and success."

And both of them with people in the court room talk about Gaha and his stuborn attitudes and his attain might and fame now and they made funny jokes and remarks on the issues affecting Oyo.

Then when the news that the the Basorun Oyelesi had pardon him got to Gaha he became very happy. And he informed all his wifes and warriors

"we are going back to my family in Oyo town."

And also the Alafin that was not happy with him had joined his ancestors. So he eventually returned back to Oyo.

So Gaha became a very succesful warrior, he rised through the ranks and thereafter, he was the Osi Balogun after his uncle the Basorun Oyelesi had died of old age. However, after some time, there was rivalry among the warlords of Oyo over titles and positions. Then the Alafin of Oyo became very sick, Moreover, since he was not favored by some Oyomesi, (Parliament member) that want the Alafin to commit suicide. But Gaha did not like the idea that the Alafin that was favorable to his late uncle the Basorun Oyelesi would have to commit suicide and be treated like that. So he plead with the leaders and the warlords to be in unity, but they had the sick Alafin poisoned, and the Oyomesi could not resolved the mystry of his death. Then the Osi Balogun Gaha became very annoyed and withdraw himself away from Oyo town and stayed in a remote village where he made sacrifice to the gods of his ancestors. However, one day when he had finished his sacrifice, he heard a lound voice and thick cloud filled the room. And Esu (Devil) stood at his front, Gaha was very afraid, panty, while he kneel down. Then Esu said

"why are you not happy!" "It is time for you take charge of the affairs in Oyo."

Then, the Esu took him to the side of a hill and desmostrate to Gaha some margical powers and use some charms which made Gaha turn to different animals of his choices, and Esu laughing louder vanished. So, Gaha saw all the charms and more in three red bags and four wooden mortals, and when he place his legs and hands on the mortals as the Esu had demostrate he turn to Elephant. Also when he turn his eyes round and said

"I am a man!"

And he turn back to a human being. So he demostrates all the powers with the other charms and they work. Then the laughter of Esu become so loud that the whole place shook and the warriors and slaves with him heard it and they trembled and were afriad.

So Gaha return to Oyo with the charms and the mortals. And he made a shrine similar to the one his mother Olabisi and her friend had visited in his compund for Esu which became his main deity.

The Basorun Gaha about 1754

However, the Oyomesi (Parliament) and other important Chiefs and Warlords were in the Alafin (Emperor) palace and they were having the installation process and rituals going on to install Prince Labisi as the next Alafin of Oyo. Then Gaha entered the palace with his warriors, his supporters and the people of Oyo who were mostly youths and that were being opressed by the ruling class of Oyo and the power and influence of the Oyomesi had become so great that all the gains in trades, taxes and levies had being abused and only the people that the Oyomesi likes enjoy the basic things that was meant for everybody. Such that more people ouside of the Oyo town were oppressed and Gaha said

"Oyo is for Oyo people in every place within the Oyo empire, and is not for the Oyomesi to be dictating to us anymore. The people can not coutinue to be living a life of suffering and proverty when the Oyo town people only and the Oyomesi are enjoying plenty and wealth"

Mainwhile, after he finished speaking the people continue to sing and dancing to the drums;

"we don't want the Princes and Kings that continue to take us for granted, taking all the wealth and our properties for themselves and the Oyomesi."

Then Gaha sensing that the people wants him to continue then he got to front of the throne and said

"I am in charge now!" "The people of Oyo are mine now because they support me,"

then he rolls his eyes and he turn to a leopard and the people ran away, but some of the warlords took out their charms, draw out their sword and fought with the beast which killed them and the beast's eyes rolls and it change back to Gaha. And he order

"the King-elect friends who have been rude to me, and their families shall be killed by my warriors."

Then some of Gaha warriors and the palace warriors took the King-elect friends and kill them and their families that day. And Gaha add

"you the palace flute blowers shall be serving me from now on and by the way Oyo have her new Basorun (The Prime Minister) now which is me.

So you flute blowers start blowing your flutes, the drummers and singers line up at my front and you all walk to my compound."

Then he ordered

"What are you Chiefs?" "Or all you Chiefs? if so, now the senior among you must carry me shoulder high, or else you all will loose your titles and compensations."

Then the senior Chiefs reluctantly carried the Osi Balogun Gaha, the self promoted the Basorun Gaha shoulder high as they walk in procession to the his compound.

Then the Basorun Gaha order

"what are you!" "The Oyomesi waiting for? Now follow the procession at the back of the senior Chiefs carrying me shoulder high and you all start singing my praises and that of my ancestors."

And they all compiled instantly,

but as they were get out of the palace, the King elect entourage were coming with musicians and they were going to the palace. And Gaha said

"what an insult!" "Stop the music!" "Stop the music!"

and the music of both side stop. And he add

"you fools pointing to the King elect entourage, if your musician can not see me being carry shoulder high, how about you the King elect can't you see? I don't think you can be my king." And pointing to the drummers and the musicians he add

"you drummers are usefull so join my drummers. You Labisi since you are now a king!" "And there cannot be two kings!" "You have to die!" "So Oyesogo!" "Get the fool king elect a calabash which contains a poison cover with white cloth for him to kill himself."

However, the procession of Gaha continue and he was being carried shoulder high by the most senior members of the Oyomesi and the rest of the Princes, Princess Chiefs, and the poeople followed as they moved from the Alafin Oyo palace to the Gaha's compound. The people of the town and other provinces were all very sad and afraid to talk and more remain in door afraid to get out of their house and compound, only talk in small groups and said

"what kind of thing is this for an Osi Balogun to order the Oyomesi around and demand that he should be carried shoulder high them, killed the Oyo warriors and the most insult and strange of all order, and demand an Alafin to commit suicide. War has enter Oyo! We all are no more save! These evil minded and Esu worshiper Gaha has taken over Oyo"

Then the King took the calabash and the poison in it and commit suicide.

Moreover, the Basorun Gaha became very rich and more powerful in Oyo, and have being leading Oyo warriors to more victories and the Empire expand with more great influences, so the Basorun Gaha took the wifes of the prominent men in Oyo just to provoke them. Then the Oyomesi (Parliament) decided to elect Oduboye as the Alafin becuase the Basorun Gaha was engage in war and not in Oyo to attend to the work of the Alafin. But when Basorun Gaha heard of it, he told his Chief warriors

"we have to go to Oyo and see what the Oyomesi are up to and to confirm if it is true that the Oyomesi are about to appoint an Alafin over me when I am still alive."

However, when he got to Oyo he said

"what a mess!" "And who do you Oyomesi think you are? I and my warriors are fighting in the war front, and you are having good times and about to appoint Alafin over me, now the installation process must stop."

Then Gaha tried to made himself the Alafin, but he could not get it because he did not have the Royal blood in any of his family linage. But eventually, Gaha said "so they will not let me be the Alafin and since I am the most powerful person, I will allow them have their Alafin and hold on the title of the Basorun forever."

So when the Oyomesi realized that Gaha favors the candidatecy of Omo Oba (Prince) Awonbioju, the Oyomesi elect Omo Oba Awonbioju as the Alafin (Emperor) Oyo, thinking Baorun (Prime Minister) Gaha would allow the Alafin Awonbioju to rule.

Thereafter, after the installation of the Alafin Awunbioju to the throne, and when the Basorun Gaha return from a successful military campain, the Basorun Gaha ordered

"the people of Oyo shall line-up the streets to welcome me back from this successful war front."

Then the Basorun Gaha's warriors enforced Basorun Gaha's order and the people were forced to line-up the streets and wellcome the Basorun Gaha. Then the Basorun Gaha ordered

"I demand that all the Chiefs and including the Oyomesi to prostrate for me and greet me as the Alafin Oyo"

So the Cheifs including the Oyomesi were forced to prostrate and greet the Basorun Gaha as if he is the Alafin. Moreover, the Basorun Gaha build his own palace and order all the Chiefs and the Oyomesi to come and pay homage to him. And they all obey him because everybody now fear him since he had killed all his oppositions. Then after some months that the palace had been completed, when the people were making merry and enjoying at the Basorun Gaha's palace the Basorun Gaha told his eldest son

"my eldest son Olaotan!" "You are the head of the millitary Generals in Oyo!" "Do you notice that everyone had come to paid me homage, except the Alafin Awonbioju!" "Now go and tell him to come to my palace to pay his homage also."

So Gaha son, Olaotan went to the Alafin palace and he met the Oyomesi having a meeting, and he said

"you people are so rude! You see me the eldest son of the Basorun Gaha and none of you can greet me."

However, as he was talking the Alafin Awonbioju got into the court where the meeting was taking place. Then all the Cheifs and the Oyomesi except Basorun Gaha son and his guards, prostrates for the Alafin and they said

"Kabiyesi O!" "Kabiyesi O!" "Kabiyesi O!"

So the leading Chief and the Alafin warriors killed six of Gaha guards. Then Olaotan took out a strange black stone from the pocket his dashiki (top garment) and struck it on the ground which instantly turns to two pythons and killed the Chiefs. But the Alafin Awonbioju change to a big strange bird and killed the pythons, and turn back to the Alafin Awonbioju and he said

"Olaotan!" "You are a true son of your father Basorun Gaha, I shall not let your father destroy the city of Oyo and my people of Oyo."

And facing the rest of the Oyomesi and his guards who were already saying different incantations and having various types of weapons of wars in their hands, the Alafin said

"ero!" "Ero!" "Ta ba fe omo loju a ri ran!" "Ero!" "Ero!" ("easy!" "Easy!" "When a child is blown gentle air and its calms the child!" "Easy!" "Easy!") while blowing air with his mouth. Then the Basorun Gaha's warriors who had already encircle Olaotan with their swords and charms in their hands drop their swords and the charms to the floor, and the Alafin's warriors also did the same. Then the Alafin Awonbioju feeling some relief said

"if anybody needs to die because of Basorun Gaha's foolisness let that person be me."

And he face Olaotan pointing to the direction of the palace entrance and add "now Olaotan!", on your way to your compound I shall be there to deal with the arrongance of you and your father. Oyo belongs to me and my forefathers and Gaha can not destroy Oyo."

Then Olaotan surprise on seeing the Alafin Awonbioju's power in actions. But when he regain his full conscience, he point to his guard and said

"you my slaves follow me, we shall go to my father's palace and continue the fight."

But the leading Alafin's guard said

"no Olaotan!" "You have to go alone, none of your slaves shall leave here alive."

Then the Alafin Awonbioju walk into his inner court, his agada made of very rich native wooven cotton swings as he moved in a very fast warrior's movement, the ground shake as he walk in annoyance and returns with some charms, which he put inside his buba pockets under his agada. And he lifts the crown from his head, and put it on the throne while everybody prostrates and shouting

"Kabiyesi o!" "kabeiyesi o!" "kabiyesi o!"

And they sang his praises and that of his ancestors.

Then the Alafin Awonbioju order

"My horse shall be ready"

So with the assisstance of the Ilaris who helped him as he mount the horse and rode it to the Basorun Gaha' compound followed by his guards and warriors.

However, as Olaotan was walking into his father's compound, The Basorun Gaha said

"welcome my son!" "Very well Olaotan!"

And he look at a calabash that contains water which he had his left hand and shaking a small dried melon shell with his right hand with chora beads in both hands wraist, and looking at the water which showed the image of the Alafin Awonbioju as he was riding his horse and he add

"Awonbioju!" "O bo lati wa te ni, o da ebi re ko, eni to fi o je Alafin lo le ebi." ("Awonbioju!" "You coming just to disgrace yourself, and it is not your fault, I should blame myself that made you the Alafin.")

Then the Alafin Awonbioju rode his horse into the Basorun Gaha's compound and said

"Gaha!" "I am here now!" "The slave that have the gut to summon his Lord the Alaffin in disrespect. I have come because I shall not let you destroy Oyo town and the people during my reign."

Then the Basorun laughing responds
"my Lord the Alafin Awonbioju!" "Welcome to my palace!" "I know that my father's household are slaves to that of yours, but you remember that I appoint you as the Alafin!" "So you have the duty to obey me and pay homage to me!" "I am not being rude or asking you what is so difficult!" "Now get down from the horse, go down on your kneels and honor me that is all I demand from you."

And the Basorun walk towards the Alafin Awonbioju and add

"welcome to my palace!" "Can you see that this is the best palace in the whole of Oyo?"

And the Alafin responds as he jump down from the horse,

"I think you are already out of your mind Gaha, for you to be so arrongant to demand.."

But before he finish what he was saying the Basorun rolls his eyes balls and he turn to a lion and it killed the Alafin Awonbioju, Then everybody ran away from the compound and Esu (Devil) laugh in it's usual manner which was so lound.

"Ha!" "Hay!!" "Hay!!!"

And there was very thick dark cloud which covered the palace

Then the lion turn back to the Basorun Gaha, and he said

"you my children and the warriors!" "You go and order the Oyomesi, the Chiefs and all the prominent people in Oyo to come and celebrate my new palace. Now I am in full control of Oyo nobody can tell me not to rule Oyo according to what pleases me."

And he walked to his thrown and sat on it he add

"who ever refuse to come and fails to prostrates before me the Basorun Gaha Oyo, shall be killed and also all the members of his family in all place in Oyo shall be killed."

However, the Basorun palace became the main court in Oyo, and he presides over all issues as the king in his palace. So the Alafin palace became abandon and the Oyomesi also had no more say in the affairs of the Empire. But the Basorun and his children ruled over the Empire.

The end of the Basorun Gaha

The birth of Prince Abiodun

"Eku ewu omo o!" "Omo Oba Obirin Adepeju!" "Bale re wa da, ni bo ni won a lo?" ("Congratulations!" "Princess Adepeju!" "Where is your husband and where had he gone?")

Then the Omo Oba Obirin Adepeju begin to cry, and the herbalist woman was surprise and she said "why are you crying? Your child is very OK and both of you are healthy, so why are you crying?"

But the Omo Oba Obirin Adepeju responds

"bawo ni a se so? Enu wo ni afi bebe pe Omo Omo Alafin Oyo ko leri owo ti o san fun egbebi Omo re?" ("Princess Adepoju responds how will I be able to explain? How do I beg that a grandchild of the king of the Oyo Empire cannot afford to pay the medical bill for the delivery of his child?").

Then the herbalist woman responds

"is it not his fault, that he has no money now, you understand that he has no money, you should endure with him, and love is the most important thing in marriage."

And the Omo Oba Obirin Adepeju responds

"I know that it is not because he is lazy, we are now under this Basorun Gaha the Esu (Devil) servant, who have put all Oyo empire under his yoke."

The herbalist responds

"we shall have to thank OLORUN-ELEDUMARE!" (God Almighty) "For sparing our lives and we shall overcome this Basorun Gaha's yoke and Oyo shall know peace and progress again as it was before, because our ancestors shall not ignore us at this turbulent days which this wicked Basorun Gaha is putting us through."

Then her husband enter and said

"Iya Ipebi!" "E ha ti binu simi bi? Mo ha sure sotun ati sosi ni, mosi ti ri gbogbo owo yin pe, ko da mo si gbi yanyu, asi ni owo to siku ti a o fi ko omo jade" ("The child herbalist are you mad with me now? I have to try as much as I can, and I have the money to pay our bills now and I am also lucky to have enough let for the naming ceremony.")

But the herbalist looking sympathetically at him said

"Kabiyesi o!" "Adegoke!" "Omo Oba Alafin Oyo!" "Oyo kan Alafin kan ni!" ("the unquestionable one!" "Prince Adegoke!" "Of the Oyo Empire!" "The Lord and the owner of Oyo!")

"How can I be ever be mad with you? Who can ever disrespect the Alafin on this earth? The gods shall dealt with the person! We all know how though it is for us now in Oyo, especially you our Lords! "The descendants of the Alafin. OLORUN-ELEDUMARE! Shall give you and your family victory over this Basorun Gaha, the enemy of Oyo."

Then Omo Oba Obirin Adepeju feeling very happy, got up from the bed and held her husband close and said

"thank you my husband!" "My Lord!" "Omo Oba of the Oyo Alafin!" "The son of the Oba that all other Obas prostrates to honor"

and smiling she continue to hold on to him while she praise him and his ancestor, and Omo Oba (Prince) Adegoke looking at his wife in her face and holding her hands responds

"thank you my dear wife!" "We shall overcome this turbulent of the evil joke which the Basorun Gaha!" "Is making us pass through in Oyo. And OLORUN-ELEDUMARE! shall see Oyo through"

and the herbalist woman responds

"ase!" ("amen!")

Then Omo Oba (Prince) Adegoke took the bags of cowries from his pockets and gave them to the herbalist woman. And he said

"Oh!" "I have almost forgotten, here is the money for the delivering of our baby."

But the herbalist responds

"nobody can take money from the Kabiyesi!" (King) "I am always ready to honor the Alafin (Empror of Oyo empire), because the Alafin owns Oyo and everybody."

Then the Omo Oba (Prince) Adegoke and his wife thank her and they left the compound with just two attendance. And the herbalist said,

"me and my household shall be on our way with our gifts for our new Prince."

But Omo Oba Adegoke responds

"we will not want to take gifts from you and anyone in Oyo, because the Basorun Gaha had degree that no gifts, and taxes from anybody shall be paid to the Royal family purse expect to himself and his children."

However, on the eight day after the birth of the Prince, and after he had been circumcised, the Ifa priest said

"what is the name you want to give our Prince?"

and the Ifa priest Adepeju sitting on mat at the front of the Omo Oba Adegoke and Omo Oba Obirin Adepeju who were sitting a timber chair, asked the parent of the boy who's naming ceremony was going on. And the Omo Oba Adegoke responds

"Abiodun Adesogo"

the Ifa priest joke

"the Omo Oba name is not long enough which is very unusual."

However, the priest continue with the Ifa consultation and he said

"Ifa here is the boy's name Abiodun Adesoko, please let us know about the boy's future," then he continue to turn the Ifa tools around flip flop the tools, while he repeats

"Abiodun Adesoko! "Abiodun Adesoko!" "Abiodun Adesoko!"

Then everybody at compound were so silent listening, paying very intensive attention into what the priest was doing. And he look at the boy's parents, smile and said

"the boy is a glorious person that he is going to help Oyo in the most difficult times and situations"

And he look up and around at the people, breath in deep and add

"it okey for now!"

Then all the people present were very happy, singing and praising the boy's father Omo Oba Adegoke and the Royal family of Oyo.

However, then the Ifa priest quietly told

Omo Oba Adegoke

"I will want to have some words with you"

as he pick up his mat and the Ifa tools.

And both men walk to same distance away from the people, and the Ifa priest said

"Abiodun is the Alafin of Oyo that is going to break the yoke of Oyo from the Basorun Gaha."

Then he stop talking and signals to the boy's mother to join them. When she walk to them,

he continue

"Abiodun's reign would solve and break the yoke of Oyo from the hand of the Basorun Gaha, but you the mother will have to warn him to be full of patient and that its only with patient and wisdom that he will be able to do all this things and conquer his enemies,"

and the Ifa priest left for his home. However, one of the Basorun Gaha informat was present at the ceremony, and when he heard the Ifa priest said that the boy Abiodun is going to be successful and help Oyo at her most difficult times, he left the place and said

"the Basorun Gaha should hear this,"

looking sad and hoping the message would bring him more favor from the Basorun Gaha and his sons. Then when the informat got to the Basorun's compound, where there was also a big naming ceremony for the Basorun Gaha grandchild. And the Basorun Gaha personal guard gave him the permission to walk to the Basorun, and he prostrate before him and said

"my Lord the Basorun!" "I was at the compound of that Omo Oba Adegoke!" "He who is having a ceremony and I heard his son is going to solve Oyo problems."

But the Basorun who had taken too much palm wine and cannot concentrate on what he was saying and only pick Omo Oba Adegoke! and solve Oyo problem! signered to the guards to take him away and he said

"thank you very much!" "Go and eat! Drink! Get drunk! Merry and enjoy yourself! I have a good child added to my empire, this is more long years to my reign as the owner of Oyo. Even if they would not crown me the as their Alafin! I am more powerful, rich than all their Princes and Warriors combine."

So when the guards got to his front, he said

"my good friend!" "Have bring an important message as he always does make sure he is well rewarded. Now take care of that Omo Oba Adegoke! Who is the trouble maker! Who wants to solve Oyo problems.

And the guards told the Basorun senior son Olaotan, who reconfirm the story and he said

"give the informant good reward!" "And take care of the trouble maker Adegoke for me now. Oyo belongs to my father the Basorun Gaha! and we his children! I do not know when this trouble makes that call themselves Omo Obas will get that to their foolish heads"

Then some bags of money was given to the informant and some guards were sent to the compound of the Omo Oba Adegoke to kill him.

However, the guards enter the Omo Oba Adegoke compoud when both the boy's mother and father were dancing together to the gungun (talking drum) music and other musical instruments, and they drag the Omo Oba Adegoke to the floor and order

"now prostrate for us!" "You are an Omo Oba!" "And wants to solve Oyo problems!" "How are going to be an Alafin! When the Basorun and his sons and grandson are alive?"

Then the leader of the guard shop the head of the Omo Oba Adegoke off with his machete and throw the head into the crowd. The people cried and ran away from the compound in every directions stepping over each other as they try to escape and killing more people in the process. But the Omo Oba Obirin (Princess) Adepeju escaped with her son and ran away from Oyo town to one of the remote village, and after walking for several days without food, but only eats fruits and leaves whichever taste good, in the forest as she wonders about without any sense of direction. However, one day she was singing praises to OLORUN-ELEDUMARE and praising her Royal ancestors of Oyo Alafin, saying

"o ma she o!" "Ile ola di ile aworo!" "Eni ola ati ayo di eni ti n je eweko lodon!" "Eni ti o gbe ile alayo di eni ti n gbe ni igbe!" "Emi Omo Omo Alafin Oyo!" "Di eni ti ko lara, ti ko si lebi. Eni ti gbogbo eru ati eniyan ma raba ba fun, mo di eni ti bebe ki ojo ma pa. Ati ki orun ma jo eje mi tan!"" ELEDUWA!" "Ni bi lo ju re wa a? Sugbon ni gbo re ju lo, Omo mi Oko mi Olowo ori mi, eri bi o se jo baba re, afi beni po sile."

("Oh!" "What a calamity? A Royal home full of joy and wealth turned to a place of lack and poverty. A person with lots of wealth become extremely poor, and now eats from dumpster and trash. A Royal being accustom to home of luxuries, now dwells in the street corners and in the forest. Me the grandchild of the Alafin Oyo Empire, who have lots of slaves and families, and friends, become destitute. Now homeless without shelter and in the rains and totally damage is my skin with the intensity of the sun. God where is your Mercy! but, in all things when it is good and otherwise,"

then looking at her son on her lap, she add

"my dearest son, my love who is just like his father Oh! what a duplicate of his father!")

Then She sat down tired, without noticing an Ifa priest that had came to the forest to search for some herbs and materials he needs to make some medicine, who had been listening to her as she talks to herself and as she meditates. Then the Ifa priest approached her gently so as not to arose fear in her. And when he got to her side, he said

"yes!" "We have to give thanks to OLORUN-ELEDUMARE in all things!" "When it is good, and when it is otherwise!" "I observe that you're a Royal being of the Alafin Oyo. My name is Gbefaniyi"

and he moved towards her and add

"funfun lele ni awo ti awa!" "Omo Oba e ma beru mo, ko si ewu mo" ("Princess mine is a kind and good type of idol worship practice!" "Please don't be afraid, you will be safe with me.") Then Omo Oba Obirin (Princess) Adepoju, realizing there was a man standing in her front held tight her son, who was covered with her body and tried to ran away. But she remembered the dream she had last night in which she was lost and an Ifa priest in white dress help her and her son. So She breath a deep breath and said

"please what is your name?"

the man in a white cloth said

"Omo Oba Alafin Oyo, Gbefaniyi ni oru ko mi," ("Princess of the Alafin of Oyo my name is Gbefaniyi,")

as he bows and his face not looking directly at her eyes.

Then he help her to her feet still holding tight her son and followed him to his house that was not too far away. However, the Omo Oba Obirin (Princess) Adepeju and her son live in Gbefaniyi's house until Omo Oba (Prince) Abiodun became a young man. And on the advice of Gbefaniyi, Omo Oba Obirin Adepeju agreed to give Omo Oba Abiodun the mark of a Prince and a Royalty of Oyo in his face and body. Then when Omo Oba Abiodun became more than twenty-one years in age, the Ifa priest consult his Ifa and it reveals that it is now safe for the Omo Oba Abiodun to return to Oyo town where OLORUN-ELEDUMARE wants him to belong so as to fulfill his destiny.

Omo Oba (Prince) Abiodun grown up

Moreover, after some years Omo Oba Abiodun had grown up and become well liked by the people in Oyo town, being an easy going person with soft words and of very humble background. Mainwhile whenever he had an encounter with any of Basorun Gaha's guards and warriors, he would always gave them good respects and allowed them to have their ways. Then the Basorun Gaha had become old and haven made his sons the Baloguns, and they were in charge of all the provinces of the Oyo empire. The Basorun Gaha children converts all taxes, revenues and levy to their personal properties to the extents that there was more poverty in the communities of Oyo empire, and the Basorun Gaha himself complains that he cannot get enough money to maintain his large and extravagant life style, which involves lot of money needed to bribe people everywhere.

However, the most senior of the Basorun warriors complain as he address the people "you slaves do not want to pay your taxes?"

and looking at them from front of a table where he sat and add

"Eyin wo, lo ni aya ti e ko fe san owo ori ati isa kole yin pelu? Se e ho ha mo pe Baba Basorun Gaha, ni lo owo ni? ("Who among you people have the courage and boldness to complain that the taxes and levy are too much, so you don't know that the Basorun Gaha needs money now?") But Omo Oba Abiodun who was siting quietly at a corner at the venue of the traders meeting which the Basorun Gaha Ilaris, had called for as an urgent meeting of all the Oyo town traders and their representatives. However, as the meeting was in progress, Olaotan the Basorun Gaga eldest son came in very angry and he said

"bawo ni awon eru mi tin se? Se a ma bebe ki a to gba eto baba mi lowo eyin kini buruku won yi ni?" ("How are my slaves doing? So I have to beg before I can get my father's tax and levy from you worthless people?")

However, Omo Oba Abiodun who sense trouble, and he said to himself

"something has to be done, otherwise Olaotan will start killing and imprison these my people." So he got up and said

"ho!" "My Lord Olaotan!" "The warrior and the true son of the best warrior of Oyo the Basorun Gaha!" "Yes we have to contribute whatever amount you and your father's house demand from us in Oyo."

And he face the rest of the traders and add

"my fellow traders, let us try as much as we can to give the Basorun Gaha the money needed because they are warriors, and we know that it is dangerous to delay warriors when they need money."

So Omo Oba Abiodun put some bags of money on the floor at the front of Olaotan and he personally met with the traders and urge them to bring out the money they have. And the people comply because they realized that Abiodun as an Omo Oba was only trying to prevent the shielding of blood and the killing of people, which was usually the case whenever Olaotan was angry.

The Oba Abiodun the Alafin of Oyo

Thereafter, when the report of what Omo Oba (Prince) Abiodun did got to the Basorun (Prime Minister), he said

"good we now have a fool, and a coward among the Omo Obas of Oyo that we can use to as our puppet Alafin (Emperior) and make him to talk to this slaves for our purpose."

Then Olaotan order the Oyomesi (Parliament Memembers), Omo Oba (Prince) Abiodun, and other important people in Oyo to the palace of the Basorun (Prime Minister) Gaha. And when they were at the palace, the Basorun Gaha sitting on his throne said

"you Oyomesi and this people do not know that you have to greet me? All of you now on your kneels."

Then the Oyomesi and everybody in the palace kneel down except Olaotan and their guards. And the Basorun Gaha after cracking his throught, add.

"I have decided to be nice to Oyo!" "And I have even save you the Oyomesi some trouble of finding a good Alafin (Emperor), which can take the Oyomesi forever."

Then the Basorun Gaha look around and ask Olaotan

"where is the fool!" "That you say is the Omo Oba among them, and what do you call his name?" Olaotan responds

"his name is Omo Oba Abiodun my father,"

and pointing to Omo Oba Abiodun. Then the Basorun Gaha said

"OK!" "you Omo Oba Abiodun!" "See him looking at me with his big eyes balls!"

Annoyed and he shout

"come out here and prostrate before me! before I change my mind and deal with like others"

However, Omo Oba Abiodun who was very surprise and at the same time shaking all over, not knowing what will become of him, and praying

"ELEDUWA!" "ELEDUWA!" "ELEDUWA!" "Let not today be my last day on earth."

And when he was not moving fast enough to the expectation of one the palace guards close to him, the guard him drag him to the front of the throne. Then the Basorun Gaha said

"why are you afraid? You are going to be the Alafin and you are shaking all over, so this what Oyo has turn to? "The Alafin descendants have turn to be weak people, no more brave men among them,"

then Omo Oba Abiodun prostrate before him. And the Basorun Gaha order

"get the leaves require for anointing an Alafin at the back of the compound."

However, as the guard left to get the leaves he said

"I have the tree planted there because I can appoint anybody I choose as the Alafin and kill the person if he cannot do the job as to my taste, so as to appoint another since it is said 'two rams with long horns cannot drink from the same pot'."

Then he turn to his son and add

"you do not need to be their yeye (weak) Alafin (Emperor of Oyo). You will have the title of the Basorun (Prime Minister) after me and your brothers will be the Baloguns (Generals). It is the warlords that are the real leaders and have all the powers just like me. How many Alafin had I appointed and killed?"

His son laughing respond

"I think about four."

Then the guard enter with some leaves in his hand which he gave to Olaotan.

And the Basorun Gaha told Olaotan

"remove the urgly cap form his useless head."

Then the Basorun Gaha took the leaves from Olaotan's hand and place it on Omo Oba Abiodun's head and put the cap on it. And he shout

"Useless Omo Oba Abiodun!" "Or what do you call his name? Get up"

and Omo Oba Abiodun stood up, while the Basorun also stood up and raised Omo Oba Abiodun up. Then Basorun Gaha order

"everbody now prostrate for Omo Oba Abiodun!" "Before I change mind"

then everbody prostrate except him and his son Olaotan. All said

"Kabiyesi o!" "Kabiyesi o!" "Kabiyesi o!"

And the Basorun Gaha said

"congratulations!" "The Alafin Oyo Abiodun!" "You can now order your people to follow you to your palace the Alafin Abiodun."

So Omo Oba Abiodun thank the Basorun Gaha and his son and everybody and he said "we can now go to the palace on the order of the Basorun (Prime Minister) Gaha Oyo."

And he walk away from the Basorun Gaha's palace with the Oyomesi and all the people follow Omo Oba Abiodun to the Oyo palace.

However, when they got to the palace Omo Oba Abiodun was reluctant to seat on the palace throne, then the head of the Oyomesi held his two hands while the rest of Oyomesi prostrate as he lead Omo Oba Abiodun to the throne and made him to seat on it. And the people in the palace prostrate saying

"Kabiyesi o!" "Kabiyesi o!" "Kabiyesi o!'

And they stood up and repeat the process for three times. And Omo Oba Abiodun in tears, crying and he said

"my people!" "my people!" "my people!"

But sill sobbing and looking confused. Then Oyomesi were standing before the Omo Oba Abiodun prayed and the they start the proper process of the installation ceremonies of the Alafin Oyo. However, the ceremonies took several days and each nights Omo Oba Obirin (Princess) Adepeju, the mother the Alafin Abiodun sat with him at the inner court room and told him not to be afraid, and reminds him of what the Ifa priest had predicted about him and always beg him to be patient and to use wisdom in dealing with the Basorun Gaha and the his sons until OLORUN-ELEDUMARE shall grant him victory.

However, after the installation ceremony was over, the Basorun (Prime Minister) Gaha was sitting on his throne in his own palace, and he called his leading guard and said

"go the Alafin's (Emperior's) palace and tell the Alafin Abiodun to come to my palace and pay me homage I believe the ceremony for his installation is now over."

Then when the Basorun Gaha guards got the the Alafin palace, they order "the Basorun Gaha ordered the Alafin Abiodun to follow us to his palace to pay him homage."

Then the Alafin Abiodun got up from the throne took his crown from his head and put it on the throne, but still had a cap on his head and follow them to the Basorun Gaha's palace. When he got to the palace the Alafin Abiodun praise the Basorun Gaha, and praise his ancestors and prostrate before him. But the Basorun Gaha was very surprise, but he kept it to himself, and he said

"Alafin Abiodun!" "Get up and sit by my side, yes you are fit to rule over Oyo" "You shall have to come every time like this to pay me homage."

And he look at the Ilari in charge of the treasury order

"Ojo!" "Bring me 6 heads of cowries for the Alafin Abiodun!" "You see he is a good boy and he knows his place!" "Not like the fools who refuse to respect me and the interest of the people of Oyo!" "The Oyomesi!" ("The parliament!") "Who made themselves the masters of the people of Oyo!" "Yes!

And he become very sad, his eyes balls very red, and about to cry, but he manage to control himself and he continue

"despact the fact that I am his slave!" "And my father's household are not in any way close to look at the dog of the Alafin Oyo lineage in the face. He humble himself and pays me! the Basorun Gaha homage!" "He shall be getting this his allowance every time he comes to pay me homage."

Thereafer, the Basorun Gaha attend to some issues and he was surprise that the Omo Oba Abiodun just sat down without complain, observing everything. However, the Basorun Gaha start boasting of his might, wealth, power and those of his sons whom he had made the Baloguns and warlords in all the towns and villages throughout the Oyo empire. And the Alafin Abiodun did not show any sign of hatred or jealousy towards the Basorun Gaha and his household. Then after some time the Basorun Gaha became feed up in his game, and he told the Alafin Abiodun to leave. But the Alafin Abiobun maintains such a low profile before the Basorun, and always paid him homage every morning. Then the Ilari Ojo, in charge of the treasury who had become fond of the Alafin Abiodun, secretly increace the pay to 10 heads every morning, but the Alafin did not complain for the fear that it might be a set up. Beacuse he had overhead the Basorun Gaha when he was having a discussion with his eldest son Olaotan,

"I am feed up of this Abiodun!" "I thought he is a fool, but he has some wisdom, it now difficult for me to find any fault in him. Which is not good since all this years, it is difficult for me to deal with the way I want and it has prevent me from being able to kill him."

but Olaotan responds

"my father!" "let us just leave him alone he is not a trouble maker, like the rest of them. You know he is also very useful for us, and where do you think we can get some one like him that would be able help us in carrying along this stubborn people?"

Then the Basorun said

"Olaotan!" "Yes!" "I trust you to have good sense, he is useful for us. I am sure you will be able to deal with him and secure this Basorun position as our dynasty if they would not allow us to be the Alafin of Oyo, we shall make their Alafin our puppet."

However, later the Basorun got out from the inner room and noticed that the Alafin was still around and he said,

"Oh!" "You are still waiting, see what a humble person, the Alafin Abiodun Oyo is. Now I release you to go home."

Then the Alafin Abiodun got up from where he sat and walk out of the compound, feeling very sad and disturbed and he got on his horse and rode home, but still maintain his suffering and smiling attitude, greeting and acknowledging the people as they praise him and pay homage to him. And when he got to his palace, and after his usual activities, he order

"I shall be going to the bed chamber because some fever."

And the leader of the Illaris (Palance attendance) announced

"my Lord the Alafin Abiodun!" "Will be going to the bed chamber earlier, because he is down with fever."

Then the Alafin Abiodun told his wife, of his plans and they made a dummy on his bed which appears as him sleeping and he told her

"if the Basorun Gaha send messengers to for me to come to his palace tell them I am down with fever."

However, he disguised and left the palace as an Ifa priest because those were common in the palace. Then he got out of the town gate without any notice, to a town call Akala and into a powerful Chief's house whose name is also Abiodun and still in his disquise. And when he got to the house, he told the him

"I have a personal message for you my Lord that I want you to hear in private."

So the Chief took him to a secret place, and he reveals himself to Chief Abiodun, who was about to start paying him homage falling on the ground, and putting dust on his head and body but he said

"let leave it for another day."

"I have come to you so that we can plan how to free Oyo of the yoke of the Basorun Gaha and his children. The Basorun Gaha have put all the 6,600 towns and villages of the Oyo empire under his evil grip. We have to make strong plans to defeat the Basorun Gaha and his sons and free Oyo from them."

Then, after the plan had been put together Chief Abiodun Adegolu told his wifes and his household

"I have to go on a journey with my visitor and we will be back soon."

And the Chief's wives respond

"very well our husband!" "We shall prepare good meal for you and your visitor to eat when you are back."

Then they left for the house of the Kakanfo (Field Marshal) Oyabi at Ajase, where they finalized their plans and the plot to kill all the children of the Basorun Gaha in a particular day. However, after the plan they send secret communication to all the Omo Oba, the principal Obas, and some Chiefs, in the Oyo county, and a day was fixed for the attack. Then the Alafin Abiodun return back to his palace in Oyo town.

However, the next morning, the Alafin Abiodun went to the Basorun Gaha and paid his usual homage to him.

Thereafter, on the appointed day, the entire group of warriors rose up and killed all of the Basorun Gaha's children and all his relatives. The women in his household that were pregnant were killed, along with his relatives and their embryos were chopped into pieces. Then the Kakanfo Oyabi send his special warriors to lead the attack secretly on the Basorun Gaha children in the various towns and villages. Thereafter the information that the children of the Basorun Gaha had been killed got to him and the Chief Abiodun Adegbolu and then the Kakanfo Oyabi lead the Oyo warriors including Chief Adegbolu to Oyo town. So the leading warrior of the Kakanfo Oyabi, who disguised as a trader, told the guards at the Alafin Abiodun's palace

"I have brought a leather product from Ilorin that is meant for the Basorun Gaha to the Alafin Abiodun who the Basorun Gaha wants to deliver it personally to him."

Then the palace night leading Ilari took the product and the trader to the Alafin Abiodun who was dealing with a land dispute issue invoving a Chief and a warrior in the city of Oyo when the Ilari told the Alafin Abiodun of the traders message.

However, the Alafin Abiodun took the product and he order

"the trader shall leave at once."

Then the Alafin order Chief Oyetola who handles the issues of land in Oyo city to continue with the meeting. But the Ilaris in the palace were all worried, mad and they said

"why is the Alafin Oyo being treated with such a disrespect like this? And it is already night, Kabiyesi o! We will request your permission to go with you, since it is getting late."

But Alafin Abiodun responds

"I am the owner of Oyo!" "And the darkness of Oyo cannot prevent me from protecting Oyo and my people!" "And we all know how the Basorun Gaha thinks, I have to go alone before he get mad and with the pretence that the Alafin, have brought warriors to fight because it is the night and start killing people, he is always looking for a way to kill you my people that is why I have to this alone."

Then the Alafin took the fastest route to the city of Oyo gate, where the trader was hiding at some distance closeby. However, when the warriors at the gate saw that the approaching horse look like the Alafin of Oyo's horse and the rider appears like the Alafin Abiodun, and he was alone they open the gate without asking any question and they thought he was on an evening ride. And The Alafin Abiodun wave to them and they greet him

"Kabiyesi o!" "Good evening!" "hope all is well for the horse ride Kabiyesi!"

However, the trader saw the Alafin Abiodun on his horse and alone, which was part of the plan, and he signaled to others to attack the guards at the gate. So the trader signals like that to other Oyo warriors hiding everywhere for the attacks. Knowing that the guards were only loyal to the Basorun Gaha and his sons, the attackers move very fast and they quietly killed all the guards and the gates warriors and took charge of the gates and the walls as the Alafin Abiodun rode back to his palace. Then inside the city of Oyo and in all the necessaries important posts and positions, the Oyo warriors lead by the Kakanfo Oyabi and Chief Abiodun Adegbolu marched into Oyo. And the Kakanfo Oyabi order

"Now blown the trumpet of the Alafin Abiodun,"

thereafter, when the trumpet was blown the leader of Basorun Gaha's guards who was to stop such attack on the Basorun Gaha was very drunk and he said to the naked women who were dancing for him,

"I believe that trumpet is for that fool Alafin Abiodun that is being blown. Let us continue having fun, by this time tomorrow I shall be having sex with his wives in his bed in order to have him punished."

So the women continue to dance while one them on drum was beating it loud. However, the fight got to the front of guard's compound and one of the leader of the Oyo warriors who also lives in the town said,

"this is the house of Okelere!" "The wicked leader of Basorun Gaha's guards,"

so the people fought their way into the compound and killed all the guards and entered the compound and some nicked women were crying and running out. Then Okelere said

"who are these bastards that are disturbing the enjoyment going on in my house. So I the leading guard to the most powerful man in Oyo can not just enjoy myself?"

Then as Okelere was about to get to the center of the compound, and a warrior attacked him with his sword and cut off his right hand. And said

"this slave who made himself Lord over us!" "We the descendant of the founders of Oyo." Then Okelere who was bleeding beg for his life to be spared, but one of the warriors who had a big axes cut of Okelere's head, and he said "now you can obey the order of your evil master!" "When you meet the Basorun Gaha in hell."

However, The warriors of Oyo had taken the fight to the palace of the Basorun Gaha, and after killing all the guards and his loyal Chiefs throughout the city. But some brave warriors good with the archers and arrows were able to defend the palace for some hours, while the Basorun Gaha who was very old, weak and was not able to run because he was cripple in both legs. But he fought hand to hand with the warriors but he was not able to get to any of the horse, even with his charms the horse where all killed by the order of the Alafin Abiodun who had discovered most of his secrets, when he usually boast of his power and had told the Oyo warriors. Then the Basorun's son Olaotan was able to assist the Basorun Gaha into his charm room which he craw into, and tried without success to stand on the mortals that usually enable him to turn into elephant, because his limbs would not support him. However, he was too weak and was not able to say his charms words Then his son who was very afraid said,

"I have always tell you Baba mi!" (my Father) "To prepare the charm that will make you to remain young forever, but you always keep on postponing the day to make it, now it is too late."

So when Olaotan observed that his father's charm cannot be relied on because his father's memory has failed. He took the charms that he was familiar with, and he became very powerful defending his father and himself, killing more of the Oyo warriors. But the Kakanfo Oyabi order for a lamp and said some charm words and he put the lamp at the front of Olaotan and blew air from his mouth to the lamp then the whole place got into flame burning everthing including Olaotan who shout and he said

"Baba mi (my father) are you just looking as I burn? Baba mi (my father) are you just looking as I burn? ..."

However the Kakanfo was also in the same fire, but not burning and he thrust his sword into Olaotan's heart and he got out of the fire. Then he drag the Basorun Gaha who was also burning outside of the fire to the front of the Basorun's palace where everybody were. So the Kakanfo continue to drag the bulky Basorun Gaha who he tied to his horse on the floor in the street of Oyo to the Alafin Abiodun's palace. Then the poeple in the street said, shouting and throwing stones and things at the Basorun Gaha,

"here is your downfall Gaha, you a descendant of slave in Oyo, but your father found favor and was elevated, you because of your arrogance and wickedness, you have spoilt the name of your father's house. And they continue .... your father found favor and was elevated, you because of your arrogance and wickedness, you have spoilt the name of your father's house..."

Then the Alafin Abiodun was siting on his throne in his palace order

"bring the slave before me."

and when the Basorun Gaha got to his front he shout,

"Basorun Gaha!" "Basorun Gaha!" "See your end now, did you ever think you will ever fall like this? When you are full of arrogance and wickedness and made all Oyo your slaves"

And he look up and at the people and add

"OLORUN-ELEDUMARE!" (the God Almighty) "Reward your father who was a slave and made him a Lord!" "Infact to the Osi Balogun (2rd General) of Oyo army, you his son eventually put your father's good work and name to shame."

However, the Basorun beg and said

"please my Lord!" "The Alafin Abiodun!" "I hnow that you are a man capable of mercy, I beg you for my life! I will be humble if pardon to serve as a slave and I will feed your horse."

But the Oyomesi said

"so you can ask for mercy?, "How many Alafin of Oyo had you killed? And how many people of Oyo had you and your children killed and make their lifes to be miserable?"

And pointing to the Basorun Gaha who's head is now under the Alafin Abiodun's right leg. The Alafin Abiodun said

"it is time for you!" "An ordinary descendant of slave to die and go and meet the Esu (Devil) your master in hell."

Then the kakanfo Oyabi drag Gaha back to his evil palace and the Alafin Abiodun who rode his horse ahead of the rest order

"the posts of his palace shall be put in flame and the evil Gaha shall craw by himself into the flame."

Then when the Basorun Gaha delays in crewing into the fire, the Kakanfo kicked him and some warriors lift him into the flame, and also the Basorun Gaha palace was burn down.

CHAPTER 5

The Fall of Oyo Empire

Alafin Aole 1789

"Kabiyesi o!" "Kabiyesi o!" "Kabiyesi o!" "Iku baba yeye!" "Oba to ju Oba lo..."

The Alafin Oba Aole Arogangan, the king of Oyo empire praises was being render by the palace clown, with drums and singing the Alafin Oba Aole entourage the city of Oyo to examine the damage done to the city by the civil war. Then when the Alafin Aole return to his palace the Oyomesi, the city managers, and the Chiefs discuss on how to raise the money for the repair works of the city. Then the head of the palace guards announced the presence of Omo Oba Afonja from Ilorin. But the Alafin Oba Aole and the Chiefs were surprise that Afonja could come to Oyo form Ilorin without the Alafin Aole summoning him. Then the leading Oyomesi said in low voice

"what is it that bring Afonja to Oyo town? And what an insult on the Alafin Aole for him to come to Oyo town without being summon by the Alafin Aole."

Then the Alafin Aole order

"Omo Oba Afonja shall be allow to come before my presence and to hear what is wrong in Ilorin that made him to come like this."

Then Afonja prostrate and said

"Kabiyesi o!" "Kabiyesi o!" "kabiyesi o!"

and praise the Alafin's ancestors praises. And Alafin responds

"welcome to Oyo town, how are your wifes and childen. Hope there is no serious problem in Ilorin?"

Then Afonja got up and sat on a seat at the front of the Alafin Aole, facing him and they talk about the life in Oyo, and Ilorin. And Afonja said

"this civil unrest and the breaking away of the territories from Oyo is my concern and that made me to come to talk with the Alafin about taking the challenge of the leadership of the Oyo Army as the next Are kakanfo since the Kakanfo Oyabi has pasted."

Then the leading Oyomesi said

"we the Oyomesi would have to talk separately as it is require by the custom and tradition for the appointment of the Are Kakanfo."

However, the Alafin responds

"yes!" "The Oyomesi shall now have a quick session and be ready to give Omo Oba Afonja their conclusion to his request so that he can return to Ilorin."

And the Oyomesi session was announced and all the Chiefs moved to the next court and they discuss the matter. Then after they had left the Alafin said

"thank you for your interest in running of my Army!" "The Kakanfo Oyabi!" "Did a very good job and he unite all the Warlords of Oyo which brought stability and progress for Oyo. The service of everybody is highly appreciated and we shall have to work together to bring back stability to Oyo."

And they had discussions on the Oyo issues and that of Ilorin, then some hours later, the Oyomesi return to the Alafin Aole, and the leading Oyomesi said

"we have found the service of our Omo Oba Afonja! As a warrior to be very good and needed especially in the Ilorin province, but we think it may not be appropriate to dishonor an Omo Oba by making him to take the rank and duty of the Kakanfo! Which is below that of a Royal Omo Oba of Oyo."

But Afonja smile and responds

"yes!" "I had thought about this, but I shall be willing to take the title even though it is lower for me as a Royal Omo Oba, Oyo Army is in confusion right now and since I am the most capable warrior and warlord to be able to bring the much needed glory of Oyo back, I shall take the post."

However, the Alafin Aole sensing that Afonja really wants the title of the Kakanfo so bad, and to avoid more trouble, the Alafin Aole said

"thank you my people!" "For all your efforts on the matter of Oyo! And the needed peace and stability. I shall allow Omo Oba Afonja! From Ilorin to take the post of the Kakanfo Oyo! Since he is a good warrior and a leading warlords. And he had said he does not mind taking a lower title that is lower than that of a Royal Omo Oba."

Then the Oyomesi and everybody prostrate and said

"Kabiyesi o!" "Kabiyesi o!" "Kabiyesi o!"

and the Alafin rise up from his throne and walk to his inner chamber. However some days after the ceremony had been completed and the Kakanfo Afonja have left for Ilorin, the Alafin Aole said to the Oyomesi in a private meeting

"I appreciate your wisdom and the fact that the post of the Kakanfo is not appropraite for Omo Oba Afonja! But since he wants it that bad and in order to prevent further disintegration of the Oyo empire! We have to let him have it and hope he would work hard enough to safe the country."

And after the meeting and when the Oyomesi were on their way out of the palace, the leading Oyomesi told some of the Chiefs

"now that Afonja!" "Have become the Kakanfo! We have more work in our hands because the report of his arrogance and abuses as warlord is too much."

And they disscussed the issue and more as they walk to their home and cities.

However, some years after about 1792, at a market in one of Oyo towns, Alaja-eta a Hausa trader who deals in animal skins, dyes of various types and different types of beautiful crafts made of animal skins got into an augment with two young men, who accused him of teaching the people of Oyo strange religion which could destroy the Oyo traditional religion of Ife and Idol worship. And some warriors who were guards to the Basorun Asamu heard of the agument as they were passing by and they arrest the trader and took his goods. And one the guards saw a book that was covered with nice leather with fine decoration on it and he took it and he said

"I will keep this one for the Basorun Asamu, because he likes leather work with fine decorations like this, which he has lot of them in his possessions."

Thereafter, the Basorun Asamu liked it when he brought it to him and kept it in his prized possessions. Then the Hausa traders report the incident to other Hausa people in their settlement in the Oyo town. So the community headers appoint some delegates to take the matter to the Alafin Aole palace since that was the way of dealing with issues of that nature, and settling of disputes among the various ethics in the Oyo town. Then the Alafin order

"this matter of taking an Hausa property shall be investigated we have to maintain law and order in Oyo."

then after the investigation had been done and he observed that the trader have been wronged.

The Alafin Aole order

"The Hausa goods shall be return back to him and he shall be released and he is to be compensated for the suffering. We just like our ancestors before us have being living in peace with people of other enthics, expectially the Hausas and Notherners in Oyo. It is not at my time that we shall not maintain this good relationship with our neighbors"

Then the palace attendants went to the Basorun guards, collect the Alaja-eta goods and released him. But after Alaja-eta got home with his fellow Hausa men, they discovered that his Koran was not released, and they went back to the Alafin Aole palace to complain. Then the Alafin order

"I have said we must maintain law and order in Oyo so this matter shall be investigated and the koran shall be return to the trader,"

but when the investigation got to the Basorun Asamu and he refuse to let go the Koran. Then the Alafin Aole felt very annoyed and because it was an insult to him for the Basorun Asamu to disrespect him and refuse to obey his wish and command. However, the Alafin Aole summon the Basorun Asamu, and told the Basorun

"I have observed that the Koran belonging to the Malam is still missing, the Koran shall be return to the trader"

but Asamu responds

"Kabiyesi o!" "Kabiyesi o!" "Kabiyesi o!" "We have search every where and nobody know where the Koran is."

But the Alafin Aole who was sure of the investigation report's accuracy and that the enquiry about the Koran indicate that the Basorun Asamu was lying. Then the Alafin was annoyed and he got up from the throne and said

"Is it come to this that my commands cannot be obey in my own capital? Must it be said that I failed to redress the grievance of a stranger in my town? That he appealed to me in vain?"

And he turn to the Basorun Asamu and he points upward he add

"very well then!" "If you cannot find it my father (meaning the deified Sango, who is believed to be deity of thunder storm) shall find the Koran for me."

The god of Sango is reputed to take vengeance on thieves and liars by burning their houses, so the next day lightning struck the Basorun Asamu's house. However, the Basorun Asamu became very annoyed with the Alafin Aole. And the Basorun Asamu was very angry when the people of the town begin to gossip that the Basorun Asamu had stolen the Hausa trader's Koran. And the Songo's deity devotees, went to the palace and asked the permission of the Oyomesi to carry out the ceremony required to appease the Songo, However, the Basorun Asamu paid for the heavy expenses for the ceremony. And the issue made the Basorun Asamu and his supporters to hate the Alafin Aole and blamed him for putting the Prime Minister of the Oyo empire to shame.

Thereafter, some months after, the Owota Lafianun agreed with the Basorun Gaha to allow Jankalawo, who had plot to kill the late Alafin Abiodun to return to the Oyo town and also allowed him to stay in the house of the Owota. Then the late Alafin's wives were angry about this and complained to the Alafin Aole. Though the Alafin initially ignored the issue but when all his wives said to him

"Kabiyesi o!" "Kabiyesi o!" "Kabiyesi o! "You have inherit the late Alafin's wives, his treasures, slaves and throne." "Why not make his cause your cause and his enemies yours as well?" "Why do you allow this Jankalawa to stalk so defiantly about the streets of Oyo."

And they continue to complain always and when the Alafin Aole cannot take it anymore, he order "the Jankalawo shall be arrest and excuted for the offess of attempt to kill the Alafin Abiodun."

However, the Owota's pride was being affected, because he felt it was a disrespect of him that a person in his compound and under his protection should to be summarily executed by the Alafin Aole without a discussion about his offence with him. Then the Basorun Asamu went to the Owota's house on a visit and persuade him to invite the Kakanfo Afonja to Oyo town for a meeting where they can secretly discuss their hatred for the Alafin and plot his downfall. So they met at the set day and they agreed on making plans and opportunity to plot against the Alafin Aole. Then, some years later, the Basorun Asamu had a secret meeting with some of the Oyomesi, at the meeting he and the Kakanfo Afonja had already send some gifts as bribes to them so as to entice their supports. And the Basorun Asamu told the Oyomesi

"you will bring up the issue of fighting the Alafin's enemies!" "At the next meeting with the Alafin Aole!" "And when the discussion is going on, you our Oyomesi should mention that Afonja as a new Kakanfo shall have to take up the campaign against Iwere, which is a fortified place by nature."

However, at the next meeting of the Oyomesi with the Alafin Aole, the members of the Oyomesi that had meeting with the Basorun Afonja, said

"we have to a discussion on identifying the Alafin Aole's enemy and fighting the Alafin's enemy." Then the Alafin Aole said

"I have told you that my enemy is too strongly connected to me because we are the same kith and kin."

Then the war counselor adviced that the last campaign end at Gbeji, so the war should be prosecuted from there."

But the Chiefs that had the secret meeting with the Basorun brought the issue of the Kakanfo Afonja up again, and they adviced "the Kakanfo and his army should be send to Iwere, since the place is fortified by nature because it is on a stiff rocky hill and it is difficult to penetrate by the weapons and horse."

Then the Oyemesi saw sense in it since the most threat to the Alafin Aole was the Kakanfo Afonja, and they agreed to have Afonja attack Iwere, saying

"we will make sure he should not be warn that Iwere is on a rocky stiff hill which is difficult to penetrate, and it would prevent Afonja from defeating Iwere by the expected time of three months, so the Are Kankanfo Afonja will have to commit suicide."

And all the Oyomesi agreed to have the campaign, and the Alafin Aole accept their conclusion. Then the Basorun Asamu was summon to the palace and inform for the campaign against Iwere. So the Basorun Asamu send message to the Kakanfo Afonja to order the Army to fight Iwere. However, the message for the campaign was send to all the Warlords and they all match against Iwere, and the Royal party, consisting the Omo Obas, the Eunuchs, and the principal slaves. Then the Basorun pointing towards Iwere and he said,

"is this the town to be taken on the order of the Alafin Aole?"

The Basorun and the Owota head the troops from the city, the Onikoyi, and the Kakanfo lead the troops from the provinces and they move towards the Royal party. Then the Basorun said

"how can the Royal troops, the Alafin and the Oyomesi send us on this impossible mission? That we shall attack Iwere an impregnable town and is this not products of Oba Ajabo? There is also the Kobis at the Oba Obirin's (Queen's) mother house palace there?"

Then there was army multiny and they join troops of the Onikoyi and the Basorun to attack the Royal party and they kill all of them. Then the whole army camp at the front the Oyo city for forty-two days. But the Alafin send word to the Basorun and the Kakanfo "let them come if they have return from the expedition whether successful or not for interview."

And the Basorun and the Kakanfo send word back that

"the Royal party had been killed because they offend us the warriors."

And the Alafin Aole send his word back that

"very well in any case, the Basorun Asamu and the Kakanfo Afomja shall come to the palace for interview and we can resolve this issue and bring peace back to Oyo."

But after several weeks, and they were still camp at the front of the city, and they could not agree on what to do next, then a warlords said

"we have to carefull because if we go to the palace and meet the Alafin Aole and the Oyomesi, the consequence will be bad for us, we all know that nobody can confront a lion without a consequence."

Then Afonja said

"are we not the warriors of Oyo? And we are now in one accord. Then let us reject the Alafin Aole, and he should face its consequence."

So a warrior slave was giving an empty covered calabash to take it to the Alafin Aole for his head, which was an indication that the Oyo Army had reject him as the Alafin. Thereafter Alafin Aole received the calabash in his inner chamber with some loyal chiefs who were crying. Then the Alafin Aole ordered the head of palace guard to take his children to his mother's house. Then after the children had left, he offered sacrifice to the ancestral gods, and Alafin Aole got out into the palace quadrangle very angry, carrying in his hands a clay bowl dish which contains some charms and three arrows. And he shot one to the North, one to the South, the last one to the West and said the curse words

"My curse be on ye for disloyalty and disobedience, so let your children disobey you. If you send them on an errand let them never return to bring you word again, To all the points I shot my arrow will you be carried as slaves. My curse will carry you to the sea and beyond the seas, slaves will rule over you, and you their master will become slaves."

Then he raise the dish and dash it to the floor which pieces on the ground and he add

"Igba la si a ki so awo, beni ki oro mi o se to! To!" ("a broken calabash can be mended, but not a broken dish; so let my word be-irrevocable!")

Then he took a poison and he died, and after hearing of the death of the Alafin Aole, the camp broke and each of the Chiefs went to their various home.

Are kakanfo Afonja Ilorin about 1793

However, the Are Kakanfo (Field Marshal) Afonja became very influential and powerful warlord in the Oyo empire, and he continue with his ambition which was the throne of the Alafin. Then he was very please that the authority and influence of the Alafin had dinish, so he felt he should build a power base for himself at Ilorin. And he invite a Fulah Moslem priest whose name was Alimi to Ilorin to be his priest. However Alimi like Ilorin and the people of Ilorin who influence him to continue to stay when he felt he want to leave because he cannot stand the atrocity and arrogance of the Kakanfo Afonja. Then Alimi brought his Hausa slaves to work as soldiers and he also invite a rich and powerful Yoruba friend whose name was Solagberu, who stayed at the outskirt of Ilorin. Mainwhile, Afonja like the service which those Hausa rendered and he used them as his warriors and because he could have many of them, he encouraged them to leave their masters and came and work for him as soldiers in his Army. So the Hausa slaves left their masters where they work as barbers, rope makers, cowherds, and more and join the Kakanfo's Army, who protect them against their masters. Then Ilorin became very big, and a thriving town, and Solagberu also brought the Mohammedians (Moslems) from Gbanda,

Kobayi, Agoho, Kuaro and Kobe to his settlement and called the place Oke Suna, which means the quarter of the faithfuls. And Solagberu made them to be separated from their Fulahs or Fulanis who were their co-religionlist.

Thereafter, some years after, the Moslem faith become popular among the Yoruba's of the Oyo country, which the Ijebus call Araoke (very far away people). And this brought about rivalry among the country warlords because they found it more easy to create for themselves sects which gave them more and easy influence on the people with more power and wealth. Their drive to control the larger sect than their rivals lead to fighting, which they called the Jehad or religious war. Then the Jehad further destroyed the unity and peace needed in the Oyo country. Thereafter the Kakanfo soldiers form their brother hood and they called themselves Jama which in a Hausa term was use to distinguish rank and file from their leaders, so as to make them felt belonging to their class of lower ranking warriors in the now big Army of Afonja. However, the Jamas recognized themselves with two rings, one in their right thumb and the other in the third or fourth finger of their left hand, which was called Kender and whenever they greet each other they strike the rings on each other which make a sound.

The Ojo Agunbanbaru about 1796

Meanwhile Ojo Agunbanbaru was talking to some member of his group and he said

"emi Ojo!" "Omo Basorun Gaha!" "Esu to di Oyo mu!" "Nigba aye baba mi Basorun Gaha!" "Oyo lo wa di ro dan ro dan bayi." ("Me Ojo!" "The son of the Basorun Gaha!" "The Devil that sustained the Oyo Empire during the days of my father the Basorun Gaha the Empire cannot be disintegrated and disorganize like this.")

And One of them answered him

"you're always so proud and arrogant like your father, even my uncle that save both of us by hiding us in the Ijebu country where the influence of

the Oyo warriors could not touch us, before he died that is how you will
not listen to him or obey his instructions."

But Ojo responds to his cousin Odewale,

"if we are not of the same household I would have dealt with you long time
ago, and but also because of your words that make sense some times which
makes me to respect you! Now you have to understand that I am the leader
of this group, I have to lead the Oyo warlords back to the glorious days of
our fathers as a family of warlords in the Oyo empire we command respect
and regards among all tribes and place."

The cousin correct him and said

"ma gbagbe pe awon Ijebu le ju awon jagun jagun wa lo o, tori Ile Ijebu aje
ji ki wo o. Obirin Ijebu ko ni fe awa ara Oyo." ("don't forget that the Ijebu
warlords are the strongest because we cannot penetrate the Ijebuland and
none Ijebus are not allowed to stay among the Ijebus. The Ijebu women
are not allow to marry we Oyos.")

Then Ojo responds

"let us leave the Ijebus out of this!" "Since we are not going to attack any of
Ijebuland, villages or towns. We will not be raiding any of their traders and
caravan or their markets, we cannot get into any trouble with the Ijebus.
So you are afraid that we are going to raid among the Ijebus no! No! My
big thinking head cousin."

However, in this manner Ojo and his cousin energize the Oyo youths in
the villages and towns. Then Ojo became a very forceful leader and he raids
many weak people's farms and took their slaves which he sold as slaves to
the Ijebuland traders and caravans for money and other war equipments
such as horses, camels and animals and farm produces since his group did
not have any settlement of their own but move about raiding and stealing
people's farm products and slaves.

Then about 1797, some rebellious warlords with the influence of the Are Kakanfo Afonja, who secretly aid their agitations against the Alafin Adebo attack Oyo towns and villages, and made Gbogun which had earlier fallen their settlement. However, the Alafin Adebo who was also a warrior, but cannot work with the Kalanfo's Army and the Basorun Asamu because of their roles before had made the Oyomesi and the people not to trust them. So the Alafin Adebo decided to lead the small warriors he had at his disposal to deal with the rebels that attack Gbogun their base. But the Kakanfo secretly send his warriors to join the rebel solders and this made them to become stronger and they defeat the Alafin Adebo lead warriors and the Alafin Adebo fall in the process.

However, when Ojo heard of this incident he took up the cause of defending Oyo towns and the remaining towns and villages that were not broken away from the Oyo empire. And he mobilized the youths who wants the glory of the old Oyo back. Then Ojo told his cousin

"we have to avenge the shame brought to our family by killing all of the Basorun Gaha enemies." The cousin Odewale responds

"the Owota!" "Who is parading himself as a powerful warlord eats from Gaha's family money and used the warriors of our fathers and he joined the force that attack us."

So Ojo mobilized his big Army and attacked the Owota and other influential citizens who he and his cousin indentified as Afonja's friends and allies, which were about 100 Chiefs. However, the majority of the youths were behind Ojo, especially since it's was an open fact that the Are Kakanfo Afonja was not interested in the Oyo town affairs, and he was not ready to defend the Oyo empire which had lead to the fall of the Alafin Adebo. Then Ojo send word message to Adegun the Onikoyi and other warlord Chiefs that were the heads of all the Oyo empire province towns

"come to join force with my Army so that we can bring Oyo back to her old glory."

But the Onikoyi who was a seret friend of the Kakanfo was reluctant to agree with the cause. However, after waiting for some months and without response from the Onikoyi and the other Oyo Chiefs. Ojo made a threat openly out of frustration and anger

"I shall dealt with the Onikoyi, and these other warlords after I get my victory over the Kakanfo Afonja in Ilorin."

Thereafter the Onokoyi reluctantly join the Oyo campaign against the Kakanfo, but he secretly send words of encouragement to the Kakanfo Afonja

"you do not have to give up the defend of Ilorin, but defend to the last end until you heard from me, fight to the end."

So the Oyo Army that was full of vigorous youths who were ready to do everything to gain the glory of Oyo back, obeyed Ojo's instructions as they attack some powerful chiefs' towns and villages burring down houses and farms and selling the people as slaves to the Ijebus and the Ibinis and the white people as they move towards Ilorin. Mainwhile some of the people that escaped form the other own tribal identities such as the Egbas, Ekitis, Ijeshas, Modakeke, Ijaiyes and others, and after they had ran away from towns such as Ogidi, Osele and more which were deserted as Ojo Army approach Ilorin.

Then Ojo Army encountered the Afonja and the Ilorin warriors that were full of untrained Hausa warriors who fought blindly without sense of war engagement, but some were good fighters on the horse. However, Ojo warriors with good skillful archers defeat the Afonja warriors and warlords and after several war engagements for three consecutive campaigns. But the Afonja warriors suffered terrible defeats and they retreat to defend the Ilorin town. And since there was no time to build the Ilorin walls and gates which was too late. Then Afonja gave instruction

"the people and my slaves shall make a temporal fortifications with erecting of stockades with locust and sea-butter trees, which shall help us to prevent the attacks on the Ilorin town."

However, after some months of fighting and the Onikoyi obseved that Ojo and his cousin were concentrating on the attack of the Ilorin towns and villages. Then the Onikoyi and some of Afonja friends had a secret meeting with Afonja and they told him

"we are sorry that it has taken this long before we can come to your aid, we have to pretend and follow these young fools that still think we are slaves of their father and uncle the Basorun Gaha, but they have forgotten that 10 seasons 10 Lords is the order of worlds rebellions."

However, Afonja who was happy to see his friend the Onikoyi said

"why do you take so long before you can sum up the courage to see me at my camp? Anyway here is the plan we have to follow in order to defeat this Ojo's big Army."

Then pointing into the dirt floor and using stones and sticks to represent positions and he continues.

"Your warriors shall take the towns and villages where I and my strongest warlords will camp and I will deceive Ojo and his cousin and make them think we are at the other camps which will make them to attack these camps and your warriors can leave without causing any damage to me and my warriors."

And looking at them in the face smiling he add

"But Ojo and his cousin should not be allow to suspect any of your movements."

Then the Onikoyi bend down and rearranged the stones and stick and said

"we shall send your fighters to attack Ojo and his cousin with their slaves, warlords and strong Army at the east side of Ilorin and the south side where they camp now."

Then walking to some good advantage view spot, and look further indicating with his right hand, while the Are Kankanfo and the rest warlords pay close attention to his illustrations and the Onikoyi continue.

"Before one hour match we shall meet them planing to rest that is the reason we are here, we excuse ourselves to go and rest at our camp too. And as the fight goes on we will tell some of our men to say to the warriors that they see the Are Kakanfo Afonja and his strong warlords among the warriors, this will make Ojo and his cousin to have interest in looking for you."

So Afonja who now get the sense said

"I will even have one of my trusted warlord dress his strong warrior with my robe and war garments to make the deception more effective."

Then Afonja embacked on the deception plan as they had agreed and he and the Onikoyi both ride to some distance making sure they can see the camps as the warriors of Afonja secretly attacked the Ojo camp before they ride back to their position as planned. Then the Onikoyi send word to Ojo at his camp

"my Lord!" "We want to make the attack on the Ilorin towns so close their camps so as to cause confusion to Afonja defence plans,"

and Ojo accept the plan while he continue looking for Afonja. Then later his warriors notice the robe and horse that they identified as Afonja and his warlords. So Ojo pursued the warriors but only after fighting them that he discovered they had been drawn into an ambush. And after killing the warriors on the Afonja's horse, he discovered that he was not Afonja.

Thereafter, Afonja and the Onikoyi greet each other goodbye and after watching the effects and the success of their plot, because it has cause panic and confusion in the Ojo camp. Then the Onikoyi order

"the flute is to be blown"

and his Army and other loyal Chiefs left the their camps and went to their towns and villages. However, Afonja watching as they left order his own flute to be blown to attack Ojo camp. The unexpected attack cause more panic among Ojo warriors and they scattered. Then the warlords were killed, Ojo and his cousin's heads are cut off and Afonja and his warlords and lift them up to show to the rest of the Oyo warriors, who were afraid and ran away from their camps and the battle campaign. This incident still make the Ijebus till today to make joke that

"Ijebu ki je Ojo"

which mean that Ijebu people shall never be so foolish and arrogant to behave like Ojo.

The Alafin Maku about 1798

The Kakanfo Afonja was in his palace at Ilorin, where he was hearing a land dispute between a warlord and some farmers, and after the farmers had made their case known without letting the warlord talk, the Are Kakanfo Afonja said

"my warlords have the right to take any land in my country because if not for we the warlords that win wars and protect you farmers and your slaves, there will not be any body living in Ilorin."

But the farmers want to continue talking but Afonja cut them off and he said

"I have made the final decision!" "Let my warlord take the land, and you farmers shall move to another place. There are so many lands any where were you turn in Ilorin that need to be occupied."

However, the worlord who was a Fulani man thanked the Kakanfo, prostrate and left the palace feeling very happy. And the farmers who were already prostrating before the throne also thanked Afonja, praise his ancestors and left the palace feeling very sad and unhappy but pretend as if the judgment was OK to them. However, when the people of Ilorin saw that the power and influence of the Are Kakanfo Afonja over them was so unbearable, they told Alimi

"please our Lord Alimi!" 'We know that you as a priest who as Moslem! you are the only person that the Are Kakanfo Afonja would respect and listen to! Please help us preach to him to be nice to us."

However, Alimi was being giving such regards by Afonja because of his influence over the Jamas who were more than 70 percent soldiers in the Afonja's Army. And Alimi being a priest respects the wish of the people for peace and their coexistence with one another which was contrary to Afonja who was an Are Kakanfo (a Field Marshall) and only interest was to wage war, kill people, exercise control and force over everybody. Then eventually, the Kakanfo Afonja said to the people after several issues that involved complains

"you my people!" "I obsserved that you like Alimi!" "and Alimi you are my priest! And it appears that you would not have stay in Ilorin if not because of your love for Ilorin and my people in Ilorin which I have single handedly build. I have build not only Ilorin but other Yoruba towns, and cities here in the North, while Oyo empire is falling apart, my own country will grow to be the greatest. So Alimi my priest! You can take over the control of the administration of my people's government's issues! While I can be more focus and concentrate on the wars."

Thereafter Alimi became more popular among the people, and he command more respect than Afonja and even among the Yorubas in Iorin. So Alimi settle disputes and also serve as the spiritual leader of the Ilorin country.

However, the victory over Ojo's Army had given the Are Kakanfo Afonja more popularity in the Oyo country, then he match over the Igbonas and defeat them without much resistance. So Afonja feeling more confident in himself said to his warlords

"we have to match against the Iresa for their disloyalty to me and their support to Ojo! And we also have to increase our hold and expand our country by campaign on Iresa! For their failure to send congratulations messages to me for my victory over Ojo."

Mainwhile the Oyomesi (Oyo parliament) members were filling the frustration because of the disunity and breaking apart of the Oyo empire, and they met to find solution to the issues.

And the leader of the Oyomesi address the people at the palace and he said

"my greetings to you all fellow citizens of Oyo!" "We pray the gods of our for fathers and the ancestors of Oyo to help us find solution to this disintegration and civil war that we are facing in Oyo! We have to decide after several attempts without success on the Prince to lead us over the war that is coming."

Then after deliberations they agreed on Omo Oba (Prince) Makua to be crown as the Alafin Oyo. Thereafter, some weeks after the coronation ceremony of the Alafin Makua, they was a rebellion at Iworo and attempts to put it to a stop had become difficult, because all the Warlords found it more easier to made money quicker through raiding of the farmers and selling of their own people to the white men as slaves. And also the Are Kakanfo Afonja was stepping up his effort of his ambition of building an empire with a throne in Ilorin, so he encouraged such rebellion against the Oyomesi and the new Alafin Makua. However, the Basorun Asamu had become a shadow of himself, without influence both in Oyo town and outside. Then the Alafin and Oyomesi haven discussed and consider the facts about the prospect of bringing more warlords to fight the rebellion felt there was no way to work on the issue without the Alafin who was also a warlord, leading the fight himself. Then the Alafin Makua summon the Oyomesi and all the warlords chiefs that were still loyal to him and the Alafin Makua said

"thank you my people!" "Are we going to be looking on this Are Kakanfo Afonja who have being using the power giving to him by Oyo against the Empire? We have to let him know that he shall be loyal to Oyo"

Then the Oyomesi send a word message to the Are Kakanfo Afonja in the name of the Alafin Makua and order him to pay homage to the Alafin Makua with the word

"the New Moon has appeared"

meaning a new king has ascend to throne and there is now going to be a change of attitude from now on. And when the Alafin palace Ilaris (Ministers) got to the Afonja's palace.The kankanfo treat them as a lower ranking slaves and said to them

"why do you have to come to my palace in Ilorin without being summon? Don't you know that Ilorin is no more a province of Oyo Alafin? So you are lucky that you meet with spirit of my mother' ancestors that show mercy, otherwise I shall have you killed for sacrifice to the gods, now you must leave Ilorin before I change my mind."

And he got up from his thrown rolling the horse tail in his hand and add

"since I am an Omo Oba (Royal Prince) of Oyo and nobody recognize me as such, I have now build a country for myself with its capital here in Ilorin town. So tell the Alafin Makua and the Oyomesi hear that the responce is"

"let the New Moon speedily set."

However, when the Ilaris got back to Oyo with the report of the Are Kakanfo Afonja response. Then the Alafin Makua and the Oyomesi realized that they had lost Ilorin.

So the Alafin Makua had no other choice than to call for the small Army which he could mustered. And this consist of few warlords to defend against the rebellion at Iworo then the Alafin Makua personally lead the war campaign himself. But the Oyo Army was not equally well equipped and not good when compared with the soldiers that the rebellious warlords had which were Afonja's warriors. And the Alafin Makua soldiers were defeated and because of the shame, the Alafin Makua took refuge in Iwo which was a province. However, Some Oyomesi members who had sympathy for the Alafin Makua adviced him to return to Oyo town, and they said

"it is not going to be possible to move the government to Iwo town, why do the Alafin remain in Iwo."

Then the Alafin Makua saw sense in what they said, and he return to Oyo town. However, when the Basorun Asamu and the supporters of Afonja heard of it, they told their loyal Chiefs and Warlords to mobilize the people to stay on the street and reject the Alafin by a protest and saying "the Alafin who is not capable of wining wars cannot rule after he was defeated in a war."

And when the Alafin Makua heard of their protest, he took a poison and commit suicide.

The Fulani Rise to Power in Ilorin And

The Fall of the Kakanfo Afonja

Meanwhile, Afonja power had increase and he was aggressively pursuing his ambition of having an Empire. Then his next aggression was against the Epos which had form a military organization and called it Ogo. But the Epos main activities was to raid villages and towns for slaves. And the white slaves traders like them and they said

"we have discover another group that we can encourage with money and guns to fight and make wars so the slaves kidnapping can continue."

However, the civil war momentum was dying, and the white people discovered that a better source for more slaves was through the crumbling of the Oyo empire. And the Kakanfo Afonja became very jealous and suspicious of the group so he enquired from Toyeje who was the Bale of Ogbomoso and the Osi Balogun (2nd General) of the Oyo Army.

"what do you make of these boys in Epo? Do they have any political interest? Because I have heard of rumors that the white people now what to use them"

And Toyeje responds to the Are Kakanfo Afonja

"Oh!" "These Epos boys!" "They are bunch of rascals that are raiding for slaves, without any political or military campaign. Though they are attracting the evil white slave traders that is all, they are just trying to make some money through slave trades."

But the Are Kakanfo Afonja who was not comfortable seeing any group doing the same thing he was known for declared war on the Oyo district. And the Are Kakanfo Afonja campaign attacked several towns and villages, but Iwo and Gbahagaha escaped Afonja total destruction. Thereafter the Are Kakanfo Afonja, felt more secured as the sole power in the kingdom since all the major towns had been subdue, and all the warlords in the Oyo had been killed. But the Jamas were now increase and without any war at hand, then Afonja found it difficult to get them engaged. But they got themselves employed by raiding the farms of all the Ilorin citizens and beyond. However, the Jamas became too confident in the their service to Afonja which gave them protection, since no body could talk to Afonja or complain about his warriors without him condemning that person. A Jama warlord would go to his former master's house and town and made the place his base. If the previous master was nice to him, the master would be protected against the aggression of his fellow Jamas. However, if it the one that was wicked or had treated him bad, the master's house would plundered and such master would lose all his properties.

However, Fagbohun who was the Otun Balogun (1st General) and a friend of the Are Kakanfo Afonja, observed that if the Jamas were not checked, they might attacked the Are Kakanfo Afonja and he told Are Kakanfo Afonja,

"we have to check the excessiveness of these Jamas before they get out of hand."

But the Are Kakanfo Afonja took the warning very personal, feeling who is Fagbohun to tell me that something is wrong with the way I control my warriors. So Are Kakanfo Afonja responds

"I am able to control and organize my warriors, are you not my subordinate in the Army? Do not correct me about the Jamas again."

However, Are Kakanfo Afonja also showed his arrogance toward Solagberu of Oke Suna who Afonja told

"you are invited by my tenant the Alimi to Ilorin so the land of Oke Suna and everything you own are mine, and who are you to tell me how to ran my country?"

So the careless and over sentitive comments of Afonja to Alimi and more people, made them to isolate him.

And incidentally, Afonja discovered that one of his concubines was having secret affair with a Fulani warlord, And he summon the warlord for questioning about the issue, but he disobeyed him. And instead of honoring Afonja, the Fulani would rather take instructions from Alimi. However, when Afonja personal guards went to arrest the Jama, they are beaten up by the Jamas and they said

"we are not Afonja's slaves!" "We only have one master that we listen to, who is Alimi! The priest."

Then Afonja realized the mistake he had made for not listing to the Otun Balogun Fagbohun about the excessiveness of the Jamas. And Are Kakanfo Afonja said

"I shall have to deal with these Jamas!" "And besides their service is no longer reqired to warrant their big numbers which is beyond my supervision."

And he got up from his thrown looking very sad and disturb and he add "also this Alimi now appears to have taken my role as the ruler of my country, so I will have to ask him to leave."

Then he walk back to the thrown, sit down and look at the horse tail in his hand, now looking tired and he appeared as if he feels alone and add

"but let me deal with the Jamas first by sending them away from Ilorin. I will only have to keep small number of their warlords who are loyal to me."

But unknowing that some of the Jamas heard him as he is talking to his loyal Yoruba slaves, and these Jamas told Alimi what Afonja had said. Then Alimi who was already enjoying his position as the judge among the people of Ilorin said

"thank you for this report!" "I will have to take over control of the situation in Ilorin because Afonja arrogance will not enable him to be able to lead this people."

Then Alimi order the Jamas

"you shall keep watch on Afonja's activities and report them to me."

However, some weeks after, Afonja send some of his guards with word message to the Onikoyi and some powerful Chiefs in the Oyo country

"come and help me fight the Jamas warlords which I observed are no more loyal to me before these slaves take over my Ilorin country from me."

But one of the Jamas who had been listening to every of Afonja's conversation with the Yoruba slaves heard the message and inform Alimi, who secretly order

"now arrest of the guards and secretly imprison them so as to prevent them from leaving Ilorin."

Then eventually Afonja discovered what had happen, and he confront Alimi, he was very annoyed, feeling betrayed and he said "you traitor and thief!" "I brought you to Ilorin and made you my priest and now you are trying to seal my throne from me."

But Alimi responds

"I cannot take any of your arrogance anymore and you Afonja have forgotten that I know your secret, you are not an Omo Oba (Prince) there is no any Royal blood of the Alafin (Emperor) Oyo in you. Me and you are relatives, your mother was a slave at the Alafin's palace. You only got the mark of the Omo Oba (Royal Prince) by mistake, and that was why your mother and mine who are cousin were driven out of the palace."

Then Afonja become very angry that the secret he had being preventing from coming out was revealed in the open by Alimi in the present of all his slaves then Afonja order

"get him arrested!"

Then he got up from his thrown and walk to the palace leading guard and shout

"arrest the lier and thief Alimi now."

But the warriors that were loyal to him were very small compared with those Jamas who saw Alimi as their true leader. And the Hausa guards prevent the arrest of Alimi, who escaped. However, Alimi took controls of the Ilorin Army, and majority of the people left Are Kakanfo Afonja for Alimi. Then the Are Kakanfo send word message to Solagberu

"please come and help me afterall we are both Yoruba, see what the Fulanis and the Hausa have done to me, please help him to escape from Ilorin."

But Solagberu send word response back to Afonja saying to Bugaru, Afonja's head slave

"your master has hitherto looked down upon us as his menials and why does he now require our aid?"

However, Are Kakanfo Afonja who realized that he cannot get aid from anywhere, then he attacked the Alimi warriors who had made him prisoner in his own country. But unfortunate, the Are Kakanfo Afonja loyal warriors and slaves were outnumbered by the Jamas and they killed all of the Are Kankanfo Afonja's warlords and warriors. Then Kakanfo Afonja and his personal slave guards that were Yoruba retrieved to the Kakanfo compond, where they fought to the last. And Afonja became tired from the fight and blood was coming out from every part of his body, and the Jamas because of the fear that he might disappear as usual, covered him with darts and tie him upside down on the shafts of spears and shoot arrows at him until he finally died, his house was burnt down and his corpse also burnt to ashes.

Then after Afonja's death, Alimi said to the people

"as a Moslem priest, I believe in Alah's forgiveness, so I will have mercy on Afonja's wives and childen since they have no hand in their father's wickedness."

So he order the rebuild of Afonja's house and told Afonja family to live there. And he told them "it was some misunderstanding that lead to fight between me and your father which cause his death."

Then he made Afonja's children to live in their father's house and they had all his properties and put them under his protection. However, the government of Ilorin is taken over by Alimi and his descendants till today.

CHAPTER 6

The Orile-Egba about 1802

Meanwhile, some years after of the Alafin Aole, the Oyomesi were in disagreement with the Oyo warlords and warriors over the extravagant way of life of the Oyomesi, the Royalties and the corruption in the affairs of the country. There was so much high corruptions, bribing, stealing, and kidnapping of people which were sold to the white people slave traders and taken out by the sea and beyond. And there was a very high poverty in every place in the Oyo provinces. However, the Empire was about to be totally collapse due to the spread of anarchy and rebellions. Then the Alafin Majotu who was just been crown, sat on a timber thrown in his palace that he had insist to be build by placing a very high taxes and levy on the people and traders, and ignoring the high resistance against building it by the people in all the cities, towns, and villages of Oyo. In fact, the people of the provinces were made to take the burden of financing the rich and ostentatious lives of the Royals, the Oyomesi and Chiefs in the falling Empire. And the Alafin Oloris (Queens) took their sits by left side of the throne, at a floor level lower to the throne but above the rest of the people in the palace. And the Alafin Majotu demand of his three wives to be well dressed with their hair beautifully braid in waves or arranged in the good fashion of the day. Then the leading palace Ilari (attendance) was order by the Basorun

"summon Chief Liasbi to the court so as to know what is the issues with the taxes in the Egba." Chief Lisabi was one of the leading warriors of a rebellious groups in some Egba villages of Igbehin, Idoma, Oorun, Gbagura, Oje, and Ijaiye-Maja that was part of Oyo who were not happy with the size of taxes and levy.

Then Lisabi prostrating before the throne, said

"Kabiyesi o!" "Kabiyesi o!" "Kabiyesi o!"

And the Alafin Majotu responds

"welcome Lisabi!" "How are you, your children and wives."

However, still on the ground Lisa responds

"we are fine and the people of Egba send their well wishes also Kabiyesi o."

And the Alafin order

"sit down so that I can hear about this issues of Egbe 'Aaro' And what is in it for Oyo?"

Then Lisabi responds

"thank you Kabiyesi o!" "Ki ade pe lori!" "Ki bata pe lese!" ("the unquestionable o!" "May the Crown remains!" and "Royal shoes remains forever!")

As he rise up and sat down facing the throne. And he continue,

"I am being send to your Royal Majesty! The Alafin Majotu! My Lords the Oyomesi! And the other Chiefs, Warlords, and Warriors of Oyo, by my Lords the Bales, Chiefs and people of Egbas concerning the rising of taxes and levy impose on us which is making our lives to be difficult and uneasy."

Then the leading Oyomesi stand up and said

"Kabiyesi o!" "I advice that we don't listen to this trouble makers' leader and his groups, because they are only trying to cause more confusions in Gbagura, Ijaiye, Oorun and all other small villages and telling these good citizens not to have things to do with Oyo."

And another Oyomesi rise up and said

"Kabiyesi o!" "Why do we have to allow an ingrate like this slave, who call himself Lisabi to continue causing trouble and threaten the stability of Oyo? Because it is not new to everybody in the towns and villages that they have to pay taxes and levy to the treasury of Oyo Alafin which we used in taking care of the expenses of the Palace and Oyo town."

Then another Oyomesi member rise up and said "Kabiyesi o!" "Iku baba yeye!" "Oba to gba idobale Oba!" ("the unquestionable o!" "you that is beyond death!" "King to whom Kings pays homages!")

"we have heard that this slaves are threaten to form their own country and plan to attack the city of Oyo."

Then the Alafin Majotu lift his left hand and pointing to Chief Lisabi. And Chief Lisabi became full of anger and cannot take the insults anymore and he said

"we the people of Gbagura, Ijaiye, Oorun, Oje, and more are not slaves!" "We are part of the descendants of Oranyan!" "Ati pe omo Oduduwa ni wa!, bi ara Oyo, Ila, Ile-Owu...," ("we are descendants of Oduduwa!", "We are equal with the people in Oyo town, Ila, Ile-Owu. ...")

And he moved towards the Oyomesi and add please

"You should hear me!" "We are not planning to wage any war on Oyo Alafin, we are just asking that we should be given equal respect, just like people here in the town of Oyo who pay very little tax and levy, but enjoy more than every place in the whole Oyo empire."

Then the Alafin Majotu got up from his throne very sad and said

"Egbin yi ma a po o, (this insult is too much,) every small villages now want to tell my own town and her people how to rule my Empire. I think what you're telling me Lisabi is that I shall have to ask you when to eat and drink in my house?"

As the Alafin Majotu was stepping down from the throne floor to the next, the leading palace guards arrest Chief Lisabi, while the leader of the Oyomesi got up and order

"take these beads from his neck and hands, omo oko to se bi oloba (this bush man that is claiming being civilized.")

Then after the Alafin Majotu and his Queens had left the palace, the Oyomesi decide to sell Chief Lisabi and his entourage as slaves. But two of Lisabi slaves that had gone on errand for their master were not around when the rest of the people that came to Oyo with Chief Lisabi were arrested, so they escape and inform the people at the town of Ijaiye and Gbagura what had happen to Chief Lisabi and his entourage in Oyo town. Then the members of the Egbe Aaro (Aaro club), had a secret meeting and they decided to investigate the route that the slave wagons which Lisabi and their people would pass. So the leaders of the Egbe Aaro ambush the slave trade wagons and release Chief Lisabi and others and the Lisabi rebel group begin to raid the villages and towns of Oyo selling the people as slaves to the Ijebu caravans at the Ijebu markets in Ipara.

However, Chief Lisabi organized the people in Gbagura, Oorun, Idoma, Igbehin and more secretly and used the money they got from the raids in producing and buying war weapons like swords, archers, horses camels and others from the Ijebu traders. However, the Lisabi Egbe Aaro members grew and become more militants. Then one day Chief Lisabi called the meeting of all the leaders of the Egbe Aaro and said

"we have to take our world in our hand today and free ourselves from this Oyo Ilaris (Ministers) in our towns and villages."

Then the members of the club arm with war weapons were given instructions to secretly kill all the Oyo Ilaris and warlords in their towns and villages mentioned above. And they declare their freedom from Oyo as Orile-Egba with their capital town in Gbagura. However, Chief Lisbia lead the Egba warriors to defend their towns and villages against the Oyo Army whose warlords and warriors had become very weak, reduce in size and strength due to the breaking away of Owus, and the Ekitis, from the Oyo empire.

Now the Egba towns and villages become independent country without a central ruling authority in any individual as Oba or Olu (King or Prince/ Lord), but they have Bales (Majors) of the villages that consist of the Egba territory.

Slave Trade Stoppage Efforts About 1810

Messr. James Adams being slightly build a man in his mid 40s, who worn a buckskin breeches casual attire, sat at the sitting room of his house and called his wife.

"Mary!" "Mary!" "I will be extending line of credit to Messr. Thompson for the business in the Royal Merchant Trading Company in Lagos."

And his wife responds "oh! you mean the business of slave purchase in the Coast of Lagos? I know about the business and there is lot of money to be made in it, you just have to be careful because the business is now risky. Sometimes they run into lost when they are disturb by the weather and most of their cargos are lost overboard if the ship collapse."

And he said

"we in the Liverpool Merchant Banks have Insurance against this lost call 'Freight Insurance Coverage', so whenever such lost happened we have our end of investment protected. And whenever their animals or slaves dies on them, our investment is not lost, we get our money back per every penny lost on each of these animals they carry onboard.

Honey I will be off to the office to take up this deal with Messr. Thompson."

And his wife Mrs. Mary an elegant beautiful lady, in her twenties, who had on a natural figure dress that reveal her shape and enabled seeing the body beneath the clothing. And her visible breasts were shown as part of the classical look, that characterized the breasts in fashion as solely aesthetic and sexual then she walk to him where he sat and responds

"Ok James!" "Be careful out there you know the weather is unpredictable, you sure have your coat? Come let me see your tie,"

and helping him adjust his tie to the taste of the season, and she kiss him goodbye as he open the door of his house. And the driver of the chariot noticed him coming and he got up from his seat, open the door of the chariot for him bowing half way, and he said

"good morning Lord Adams."

But he look up as he open his month revealing his brown teeth, looking at the sky and he responds

"good morning John!" "Hope the horses are doing fine today? "Well clean and feed? I assume it not going to be cold today, Well even if it is, I have a nice suite and the weather shouldn't be any trouble."

John responds

"yes sir, the horses are well clean and they are feeding fine."

He was already sitting on the couch in the chariot as John closed its door and drove away into the street of Liverpool to the office. Then when they got to the Office, John got down, open the door and slightly bow down, removed his hat as Messr. Adams step out of the chariot, and got out into the compound, looked up at the sky again, node his head and he said

"OK!" "Let get into the office and talk to the staff about business"

as he walk into the building. A waiter at the door open the door for him from inside and he said

"good morning Messr. Adams,"

and he answer

"Oh!" "Good morning David!" "How is your wife Doris? Hope she is recovering fine from the cold?"

David a man in his fourties worn breeches, and trousers sewn with a flap in front called a fall front. responds

"yes!" "Sir!" "The Doctor gave her some mixtures of medicines and she seems to be normal now she only has some cough."

Then David extend his hand to take Messr. Adams's bag and also help him remove his top coat and walk behind him as he approach his office door. And his sectary got up from his seat as he walk into the office and said

"good morning Messr. Adams!" "How is Mrs. Mary doing this morning?"

and he responds

"Oh!" "She is just fine as usual, she would not want me to leave the house of course complaining about the weather and cold. But I have to come to the office to see to business as usual and she has to stay at home to spend the money."

Messr. Antony a college educated man about 5feet 4inch tall in an elegant tailor black suite said

"yes!" "Sir!" "that is the job of a good madam to take care of the man and to see to things in the house, making sure the children are well prepared for their daily routines, learn and studies together with being well feed."

Then he followed him to his office, and after David had drop the bag on the table and hang the top coat on a hanger at the corner in the office, check to ensured that the wood was burning fine in the fire place then he sat by the side of the door of the sectary office waiting for when he would be called to deliver message to any member of staff in the office building. However, Anthony wait after Messr. Adams have been sited, and he said

"Sir!" "Your first meeting is with Messr. Thompson about the slave trade finance of the 'Royal Merchant Trading Company' in the Coast of Lagos."

Then Messr. Adams respond

"yes of course!" "I should remember that," "I am sure as a lawyer you have given the financial angle of the deal the necessary look and considerations? You know as a cousin we have to start making good money now because before we realize, all these low class people getting into this slave trade business now will be richer than everybody of the Royal blood in Europe and England."

Then Messr. Anthony sat at the front of his table and said

"we!" "At the legal section!" "And the bookkeeping people had see to it that all the financial details had been thoroughly examined and come up with the financial figure that makes room for good profit for us, and the Insurance aspect had also been taken into adequate considerations."

However, as they were talking David enter the office bow his head slightly and said

"sir!" "Sir Andrew is approaching sir!"

then the heavy footsteps of Sir Andrew was heard by the two men as he walk into the office, and both of them got up to greet him saying

"what a pleasure coming to the office Sir Andrew!" "Hope you are not being disturb in any way by the weather? And how is business in Manchester?

Sir Andrew a tall slim man in his early sixties who won Silk breeches, in a white stockings with hessian boots and appears as if he was dress for the evening or a formal occasions responds

"Oh!" "The weather will always disturb!" "But we have to get use to accommodating the frequent changes in the weather."

Then David brought a pot of tea with three tea cups and sugar, served them the tea and left the room, as they continue talking about the weather.

"You know I am just talking to Anthony about the slave traders in the Coast of Lagos, which the low class people are getting into now and because they are now making so much more money this days and they can afford to buy seats in the Parliament as Ministers of Parliament."

Sir Andrew responds

"yes!" "This is becoming a consign to us now, we cannot depend on taxes and other revenues alone anymore, because these people of low class are getting rich now in this slave trade business."

Then Messr. Adams said

"we have to go into the business like you also, if you are not in a hurry Messr. Thompson will be here by 1 pm for the financial arrangement in the slave trade."

However, Messr. Anthony said

"from the study of the history of the slave business, Britain have being recording some good fortune in the slave trade since the last century. You should realize that our colleges and in particular Oxford has raise a lot of endowment funds and donations from the traders in the slave trade business. Which we have being using in building Libraries, and our banks especially Barclays have gain so big from financing of the slave trading merchants ships, by extending lines of credits to the early cotton manufacturing business in Lancashire hinterland."

"Yes!" "You are correct Anthony!"

Sir Andrew said,

"I have been into the financing of the ship building business for more than 20 years now and the slaves cargos from the Lagos Coast are increasing every day because of their wars against each other."

Messr. Adams said

"we have hand in the promotion of the wars too, since when we discovered that some tribes at the Coast of West of Africa now call Lagos area, are preventing our merchants from getting to their interior land to make discovery and possibly exploitation of the place for Metals, Gold, and Iron in the 17th century. We have being producing the guns for their fighting to continue, and only for us to then realize that they take each other tribes' people as slaves as the price of war which they use in their farms and houses as domestic helps."

Then Messr. Anthony responds

"yes the stubborn tribe is call 'Ijebu'! History even trace them to be warriors from Jerusalem, but we have to agree at the Parliament that nothing of that research work shall be made known to the public and the study have been stop in Oxford and Harvard Universities. The Jebu country King prevent the exploit of the Interior land and their warriors are feared by our men because none of the natives of the other tribes can fight their King who have strong influence on his people and the tribes. But we outsmart the Ijebu by making sure that the other prominent tribe the Yoruba, under their big chief the Alafin of Oyo who did not have strong control over his warriors, is able to get guns for his Army and make sure that the Oyo empire people continue to fight over land. And raiding of each other tribes farms for slaves which they sell to us. We also secretly continue with the policy of making sure their Chiefs are not only bribe with coins from here, and black mail them by kidnapping their children which has been very effective in making them to continue with the kidnapping of their own people as slaves which they sell to us."

Then Sir Andrew said

"we have been benefiting from the proceeds of the slave trades, the West Indices Planters have been building these stately big houses, and their ridiculously extravagant live just like that of Sir William Beckford's Fronthill, Messr. Simpson, Sir Macaulay, Messr. Hawkins, and more like them, fortunes are all from investments in the slave trade business."

Then David walk into the office made a slight bow and said

"Sir!" "Messr. Thompson is here,"

and Messr. Anthony responds

"yes David!" "Let him come in we have been waiting for his arrival."

However, Messr. Thompson a thick body fat man with pot belly won Redingote walk into the office remove his hat as he bow to greet Sir Andrew and said

"good afternoon sir!" "It lovely day meeting your Highness."

Sir Andrew responds

"yes!" "It lovely day of course to see some enthusiastic cousins doing good in this business of slave trade which has a lot of money in it to be made. We would not allow any beggar low class people who are now getting themselves enrich in this trade because, we cannot find a legitimate legislation to prevent the business from accommodating everybody."

Then Messr. Thompson responds

"I can't just take it any more seeing this low class citizens now building big estates everywhere in the West Indices, I have to invest in the transporting of the slaves to the Southern continent where we have larger Plantations for cotton now. The business of cotton is going to be crucial for our Industry, because we have now legislate the investments in the efficient stream engine since the fortune we have gain from the slave business is so huge. It is about 30% to 45% returns in investment."

Then Messr. Anthony said

"yes our earning in Britain alone in the slave business is about £40 Million and this have now been budget in the building of roads, Canals, in Wharves, harbours, for all the new equipments now use by Farmers and the Manufacturers for this year alone."

Messr. Adams said

"you know Andrew, we in the ship building have made a lot of fortunes and the demands for new ships and maintenance of ships has increase and so is our revenue."

Messr. Thompson said

"we are just lucky that the war in this salvage animals countries is continuing among their tribes and we are reaping the investments in the production of more guns and gunpowder which we have been supplying to this place. When the idea first came up to pollute these animals' place with more guns as a solution for them to continue with their wars among their tribes, we thought it is a waste of time and investment, but we feel we just have to concentrate on exploiting their land for mineral resources."

Then Sir Andrew said

"we now realize at last that getting them as slaves is more better resources, because we are looking forward in using these to increase our productivity in cotton in the South of the West Indices, just like the Portuguese are producing more sugar and cotton in Brazil."

Messr. Anthony responds

"the cotton has more demand than wool we export to the European countries, so our factories have been increasing in Manchester, here in Liverpool and the new cities of the New England and we can make more money by producing cotton products for export to the American continent for these slaves, and the Citizens of the West Indices, Europe, Brazil and here in Britain. Since the population is increasing."

However, Messr. Adams said

"here is the Check for the finance for the slave trade investment in the Coast of Lagos, we heard that the land we bought in the place call BadAgric is now yielding it investment at last."

Messr. Thompson responds

"yes!" "We cannot use the land for plantation settlement as we had plan because it is too sandy, and not good soil for farming, but we now build slave holding cells there which is a secret place hidden from these Missionaries and some of the slave trade protesters that are complaining that the Parliament should stop the gun trades and slave trade since it has been abolish in 1807."

Then Messr. Anthony provide the necessary papers to be signed to Messr. Thompson which he sign and the papers authorizing him the funding for buying of more ships and to pay for the slaves he had got at the Badagry slave market to be ship at the Lagos port. And he put the documents in his bag, and said

"these Missionaries are hypocrites, we later realized that their leader Rev. George Whitefield who was believed to a good Evangelist of the Methodist own large investment in slave trades when he died in September, 1770."

Sir Andrew responds

"they are using our funds to carry out their Mission works, living in large houses like Lords and Kings, with large slaves or servants as they want to call them. They own good chariots and the best horses that are well breed all these at the expenses of the Royal Treasury, which resources come from the same slave trade business that they bless because they encourage the sugar factories, the cotton factories and their plantations are Ok by them. But they are condemning the slave trades that is proving the slave workers and all luxury and wealth they are enjoying. The Pope and the Church of England are about the riches Estate in the World now."

Then Sir. Andrew stand up and he said

"I have to meet some pleasure Ladies!" "Hope I am not too late for the party, and hope you all are coming. Especially you that is still a bachelor"

pointing to Messr. Anthony. Then they all walk with him to his chariot and wait as it was been driven away. Then Messr. Thompson shake hands with Adams and Anthony, got into his chariot and it was driven away. And some few hours later, Both Adams and Anthony told the staffs that they were leaving for the party at Sir Andrew's court.

The destruction of Ile-Owu about 1812

However, some years after the death of the Alafin Aole, the Oyo kingdom was in a disorganized condition and more tribal units had break away and acclaimed their independent states. Then the people of Oyo empire cities, towns, and villages that were displayed as refuges as a result of the wars join Owu. Meanwhile, after the Awujale had refused to open the Ijebuland gate to the white people and other non Ijebus, and disallowed the white people from trading in slave on the Ijebuland lagoon. But most of the unlucky ones were sold as slaves to the Ijebus and the rest were sold at the slave market in Badagry to the white people and ship to Europe, America, Brazil and more. Moreover, the Owu youths and warriors had been highly involve in the Alafin war campaigns and they were very proud, stubborn, and brutal warriors. Then the Olu Owu was a parallel authority with Oyo in the Oyo North area, and he was dread by the Oyo warlords and warriors. Then the fall of the Oyo empire create the needed opportunity for the Owu warlords to force their influence on Oyo villages and towns. However, the owu warriors always depend on the use of cutlass, swords, bows, arrows, and they had little use of guns in their war campaigns. Though during the reign of the Alafin Abiodun, the Olu Owu and his warlords were given the mandate to prevent the kidnapping and sales of the citizen of Oyo at the Apomu, the great market town which was under the control of the Awujale Oba (Emperor) Fusegbuwa Ijebuland (Ijebu Country) whose representative at the market was Lugbokun, the Olowu Akipoju who's representative was Lugbaibi, and the Owoni Ile Ife who also had his own representative.

Moreover, the administrative government in Oyo town had fallen and the Alafin Oyo order was no more taken serious by his warlords. So the selling of the people of Oyo as slaves was revived. And Adegun the Onikoyi (Minister of province of Ikoyi), who was the provincial king send a messenger to the Oluwo to put a stop to the kidnapping and selling of the Oyo citizens as slaves. Then the Olowu in attempts of carrying out this order chasten many towns and this result to the destruction of Ikoki, Igbo, Ikire, Iran, Iseyin Odo, and more which were all in the Ife territory. Then the Owoni Ife became very angry because of this and declared war on Owu. Thereafter the Owoni gave the command of the war to his commander-in-chief Singunsin and other war-chiefs who were Okansa, Gbogbo Olu and more and they camp at Dariagbon which was close to Osun and Oba rivers. But the Ifes who were also very good warriors took the war very lightly and they thought a war against Owu would be easy to win, so with war songs and drums they match to the war singing:

"E maha ja a gba
Igbekun la mu a di
Ifa Olowu
E wa la mu a se

meaning

Let us cut ropes
Our captives to blind the Olowu's Ifa
with our corn we'll cook."

But the Owus who thought that they were the super power in the southern regions were annoyed and immediately match out to meet them. The war did not last for long and it was hand to hand battle, in which the Ifes were completely killed, and only about 200 warriors escaped. However, the Oba Iwo in whose province the disaster took place did not admit the Ife warriors that escape into his towns because he of the fear of the Oluwo and did not want the Owu warriors to wage war on his towns and villages. So The humiliated Ife warriors could not return to Ife because of the shame of being defeated in war. Then they eventually stayed at Aunbieye for purpose of recruiting and be able to fight Owu again.

After about five years, about 1812.

However, at Apomu market, a young man from Owu displayed his Aligator pepper in a set of 200 each for sale, and an Ijebu woman came to his stall and priced the Aligator pepper and she said

"good morning papper seller,"

the man responds to her greeting

"good morning ma!" "How is the home, the children and market?"

She responds

"we are all doing fine!" "And how much is the Aligator peppers?"

And pointing to the one in the set of 200 piece each. Then they bargain on the price and eventually, they reach a bargain price and she paid and he help her pack the pepper with some banner leaves which she put in her basket and she lift it on her head and walk to her stall. Then her daughter ran to take the basket from her head as she approach the stall and she took it from her, placed on her own head, and walk with her to the stall. And her brother who had been playing with some girls of about his age at a stall across his mother's stall heard her voice, and he left the place to greet her welcome. Thereafter his mother who was making arrangement for display of the pepper in a set of 10 for sales at a lesser unit price, discovered that the pepper was short by 20 pieces because she could only made 18 sets instead of 20. And she recount it again and again, However, her son who noticed the worry in her look and the usual concentration which was an indication that she was disturb, he asked her "what is wrong mama mi (my mother)?"

And she look worried and responds

"the Aligator peppers were not of the actual numbers that they suppose to be."

Then he count them too, and also another woman closeby her stall came around and the three of the them recount it again, but it was short by 20 pieces. However, the woman that had came to assist in the counting said

"I had a similar experience last market day, but the difference was just 6 pieces,"

also another pepper seller closeby said

"when I observed the same thing last market day, but mine was about 10 pieces shot in count. I thought I had mixed my sales money with some other money."

Then the boy asked

"where did you bought the pepper mama mi, (my mother)?"

And his mother gave a description of the man's stall and him, also the two other women said it was the same stall and man. So the woman said to her son

"Olukoya please don't go there on your own, wait for me"

and she called her daughter

"Olufunke!" "Take charge of the sales, me and your brother Olukoya are going to complain to the man I bought the pepper from that the Aligator is short of 20 pieces."

But the Owu man insist that the pepper were 200 pieces and said

"I count them myself and they were complete."

Then the woman told her son to put the pepper out on the table, and they count it again in presence of the man, but it was short by 20 pieces. And the Owu man became very angry and said

"you and your son have no better things to do that is why you are wasting your time counting and looking for 20 pieces short of Aligator pepper. I am sure you and your son could have taken the twenty pieces away, and now bring me the pepper as short."

Then the woman that said her pepper was also short by 10 pieces at last market day testify to the shortage in the Aligator pepper, and she told the man

"I also noticed the shortage of 10 pieces too last market day when I bought Aligator pepper from you."

Now the other traders closeby join in the argument, and the man said

"you Ijebus!" "Think you are the only people that are smart as traders?"

However, most of the traders at the stall were Owu people, because it was the Owu section of the market. Then the issue got out of hand, and Olukoya felt the Owus were only taking side with the man, because they were all Owus. So Olukoya responds

"we Ijebus are better with trade and we had taken pain to check and noticed that the pepper is short by 20 pieces."

Moreover, the Owu people became mad and one of them slap Olukoya in face, and said

"we Owu!" "Are the first in all things we can not take insult from a small boy even if you are an Ijebu."

And Olukoya also hit him with his fists and he fell. So the Owu traders beat the woman and her son. Then the Owu's market representative call

Lugbaibi who was passing by, asked what happen? And after the Owu traders had explained to him what happen, and he had heard the Ijebu women side. Lugbaibi responds

"what an insult for an Ijebu person to accuse an Owu trader over Aligator pepper shortage. So his words that he was sure that the paper is correct is not enough for you Ijebus to believe him?"

This made the other Ijebu woman to go and report the issue at the Ijebu section of the market. Then Olukoya father heard what had happen to his wife and son, and he rush to the scene and fought with the Owu traders. But Lugbaibi in attempt to scared the Ijebu man draw out his sword which kill the man's wife. So Lugbaibi realized want had happen, ran away from the scene but some Ijebu traders ran after him and the Ijebu traders look for their own market representative at the Apomu market but he was not around. Then when the Ijebu traders caught Lugbaibi they tied him to a tree until the following day. And when the Ijebu market representative Lugbokun came to the market, because when he heard of the incident he immediately came to the market, and he said the matter shall be reported to the Awujale Oba (Emperor) Fusegbuwa. Then some hours later, Lugbokun rode his horse fast to Ijebu-Ode to the Awujale palace. However, the Awujale Oba Fesugbuwa was already expecting Lugbokun and when he got to the throne, and after the greetings, Awujale Oba Fesugbuwa order

"the corpse of the woman shall be brought home and be buried as a warrior."

Then the following month, after the Awujale had wait to hear from the Olowu or some delegates from the Alafin Oyo, and none came. So the Awujale Oba Fusegbuwa became very annoyed and said

"this Oyo people are not wise at all, how can you kill someone and you refuse to even see what is wrong in your action?",

"who shall we deal with among them now, their Oba the Alafin is no more in control, his Empire has crumble, and his word does not carry any weight anymore?"

And the Olisa said as he was prostrating before the Awujale Oba Fusegbuwa

"Kabiyesi o!" Kabiyesi o!" Kabiyesi o!"

"I will advice that Kabiyesi!" "Deals with the Olowu, because the Owus now appears to be the one in control of the Oyo country."

And the Awujale Oba Fusegbuwa responds

"thank you my Olisa!"

Then the Olisa sat down. However, the Awujale Oba Fusegbwa still very angry with the Olowu order

"We shall give them some opportunity to save their Owu and all their Oyos!"

And after some thought he add

"send my word to the Olowu to provide Lugbaibi to my palace for the murder of our daughter, before the Ijebu warriors show him and the Oyos how to behave in a civilize manner."

Then the leading messenger in the palace prostrates as the Awujale began to talk, nodding his head with his face not looking up to avoid looking at the face of the Awujale Oba Fusegbuwa. And he got up after the Awujale had finish talking and signals to the slaves that would follow him on his journey to Ile-Owu. Moreover, the Awujale Oba Fesugbuwa got up with anger in face while everybody prostrate without saying anything as he walked to the inner chamber of the palace.

However, when the Awujale's messengers got to the Olowu palace and he heard the message the Awujale Oba Fusegbuwa had send to him, the Olowu responds

"it is time for Owu to take her place in all things now, as the first in all of all, let the Awujale know that Owu will no more take order from anybody again. And also it was the insult on Owu that result to the accident, let the Ijebus bear it as lost."

Then the Owu youths on hearing of the burst from their Olu lauch attacked on Apomu market and damage Ijebu side of the market and killed some Ijebu traders.

Then when the Olowu response got to the Olisa Dipe, he called on the Balogun, the Apenas, and the Ogbonis, the Olisa was very annoyed, with anger all over in his voice, his eyes balls red, and he said

"we have to take action and make preparation of war plans which we have to present to the Awujale Oba Fusegbuwa and it should be ready before he summon us."

The Apena leader responds

"I have not seen the Awujale Oba Fusegbuwa angry before, I cannot even say kabiyesi last time." The Ogbonis said

"we are ready as soon as we hear the order and the trumpet for war from the palace."

the Balogun who was the most feared said

"the Owu fools!" "Had also attack our markets in Apomu and killed more people, what are we waiting for? The Owu and all Oyo have reach their end, there is nobody that can tell me not make sure that the land of Owu will not be totally destroyed."

However, the Olisa was able to control his emotions as he breath in very deep, and he said

"let us put the anger little bit aside so that we can concentrate on the war plans to be presented to the Awujale Oba Fusegbuwa which is some few hours from now."

Then they deliberate on various alternative models and actions for the war. And the Olisa Dipe summoned the warriors that had gone to spy on the Ile-Owu and the Olowu guards with the various Oyo warlords to give their reports. And after hearing and talking, they conclude that they had what is good enough to be presented to the Awujale. Then the Olisa Dipe got up and said

"I have to meet my Lord!" "Before he tears me to pieces for taking too long,"

and everybody got up with their head not looking at him or his face as he walk away to meet with the Awujale Oba Fusegbuwa. Then after the Olisa Dipe had gone out of sight, the warriors said

"the excess of the Owus have to be put to a stop once and forever."

The leader of the Apena said

"Ijebuland will not tolerant the behavior of the Owus! "And who is Olowu to disobey the order of the Awujale? It is a taboo, even their Alafin would not attempt it. By the time we finish with them, the history of the Owus will be told in the future."

The second-in-command Apena who was more patient than others said

"I urge you my warriors to remain calm and follow the Ijebuland normal protocol before attacking the Owu land."

However, the Awujale Oba Fusegbuwa was in his court with the Omo Obas (Princes), the Olisa, the Obas of Ijebuland and the Balogun Ijebu and the prominent Chiefs, and he sat on his throne feeling very sad as he listens to the various discussions and war plans deliberations. Then the Awujale Oba Fusegbuwa got up from his throne when he cannot stand their deliberation anymore and said

"my anger is great on the Olowu for his disrespect of my person and throne of my ancestors," the moment he rose up, the court also rise and they remain standing, everybody looking down and avoid looking him directly as he talk. While he walked away all them were saying

"Kabiyesi o!" "kabiyesi o!" "kabiyesi o!"

And after he had left the court and out of sight, the Olisa Dipe took control of the meeting and the discussion continue until they reached a final conclusion on the best war plans.

Mainwhile the Owoni Ife was very disturb and annoyed when he heard of the incident at Apomu market. And the Ife chiefs said

"the Olowu and his people have taken their aggressiveness to the limit by attacking the Ijebuland trade."

One of the warlord said

"Owu have step on the tail of the sleeping Lion."

Then the Owoni who saw an opportunity to avenge the insult and the defeat suffered by his Army because of the Owu. Summon his emissaries and send them to Ijebu-Ode and ask the permission of the Awujale Oba Afusegbuwa to support the Ijebuland Army in the campaign against the Owu.

However, the following day after the Olisa Dipe and the Ijebuland warlords had completed the war plans, the Olisa and the warlords present the plans to the Awujale Oba Fusegbuwa for his final approval. The Awujale heard their report, and with sadness in his voice and his stony eyeballs red, and he order

"We shall attack the Ile-Owu and the head of the Olisa Dipe Ijebuland shall be cutoff by me if my mandate for him to command the war, and to destroy Owu completely fails and the Ile-Owu shall be deserted forever."

Then the Olisa Dipe ordered all the warriors to come to camp and assigned the various military units formations under the Ogbonis which some prominent ones were the Kakanfo, also known as the Jagun-Aso, the Lapo Ekun, the Otunsemade of Odo-Esa, the Dagi and more. Thereafter the Ijebus matched upon Owu crossing the Osun river and encamped at Oso farm. Then the Ijebuland warriors with better guns, good marksmen, archers, skillful horse men warriors took Owu by surprise and pushed them backwards towards the Owu land. And the first and the second attacks with better gun fires of the Ijebus and a well planned military formation caused heavy slaughter on the Owu side, that result to lost of 50 of their warlords. However, the attack checked the pride of the Owus who had thought they were the best of all time fighters, because of their usual war success in the Oyo empire military campaigns.

Moreover, the Owus found some courage and lunch ambush and attacks on the Ijebu camps, but they were pushed back to the Owu walls and gates. And the Olisa Dipe rode his horse with guards in places, to a good high hill where he studied the Ile-Owu land, towns and villages. Then he order

"the trumpets for retreat shall be blown"

and called the Ijebuland warlords of the various unit to come under a large tree called the Ogungun, east of the town of Oje. And he shout to the charging warriors and horse men and said

"Moja mo sa la mo akin konjo lo gun!" "Akin konjo to ba moja ti ko mosa iru won ma ba ogun lo ni" ("charging forward, but knowing when to have the wisdom to retreat when necessary is what distinguish a good warrior, otherwise such a warrior falls into ambush.")

However, when the Ife warriors arrived at the camp and there were shout of welcoming them from the retreating Ijebu camps, as they join the warriors waiting for orders from their units' warlords.

Then the Olisa Dipe welcome the Ife prominent military leaders such as Oranmaye, Laboside, Ege and Ogidi while he presides over planning of the strategy to be embarked on in order to destroy the whole of Owu lands, and joking

"we have to ensured that the whole of Ile-Owu is destroyed so that my Lord the Awujale Oba Fusegbuwa would not be able to eat my head in his pot of egusi soap."

And all the warriors respond with laughter and they said

"never!" "It is the head of the Olowu! "That shall entertain the children of Ijebu-Ode at the delight of the Awujale Oba Fusegbuwa."

However, the warlords agreed on the plans and the Olisa Dipe order

"we sall use the caraputs and the archers with fire balls which shall rain onslaught on the Owu towns, while we shall continue to fight our way forward until the walls of the Ile-Owu cities are completely fell."

And he face the Ife commands and said

"we shall send some units of Ife warlords to join Ijebus under the Kakanfo, the Lapo Ekun and Oranmaye which shall strike the cities and towns from the rear, since the Owu warriors are known to hide their strong warriors behind with their women in their farms."

However, after one week of continuous attacks on the walls and gates, together with the head to head fight with the Owu warriors at the surrounding fortified villages and towns of Ile-Owu. The people of Owu begin to panic and there was general confusion, and they start to take refuges at Ibadan. However, some of the Oyo refuges from the North whose homes had been destroyed by the Fulanis, and who were scattered about the provinces, and homeless, without occupations join forces with the Owus. These flock to defend the Owus since they have been allied, with the Oyo warlords in their campaigns of the Oyo empires. Thus this strengthen the Owu morals and made the siege to last for about 7 years. Then in the third year of the fight most of the walls of Ile-Owu had been broken into, and with the sudden increase in the ranks of the Owu war units and formations, the Ijebu warlords order retreat because of rising assults on their warriors. And the Olisa Dipe agreed with the warlords to stop the onslaught on the walls and the rain of arrows which had fire warheads course confusion for their side of the campaign, and because the Owu warriors know their territories and country better. However, the Owu and the Oyo warriors rejoices at this, thinking they had the upper hand and they got out of their hidden camps at nights to reorganize their resistance. But the Ijebus with their allies were able to see them were they hide and continue to rain gun fires and archers on them, their camps and hiding places. Moreover, the siege continue to the 6th year and when the leading gun man of the Owu called the Sakula and most of his warriors were gun down, and this destroyed the moral of the Owu warlords and they order withdrawn of their camps inward and as usual thinking that their other strong warriors should be ready to surprise the Ijebus who would have to match into unexpected continuous gun attacks and guerilla warfare. Then the trumpets from the rear of the Owus, were blown by the Ijebu warriors, which serve as the signal that the Ijebu and Ife at the rear had noticed the hiding places and camps of the Owus as the Owus retreat. Then the Olisa said

"praise to the gods! the ancestors of the Awujale and Ijebuland"

and he praise the ancestors of the Awujale and all Ijebu gods and order

"Blow my trumpets!" "Blow my trumpets!"

which was the signal for the horse men with long arrows that has poisonous warheads to attack all the farms where the Owu warriors were suspected to be hiding and laying in wait for their ambush and to defend of their farms, their women and children. So the Ijebu warriors attacked from the back of the towns, villages and prevent the strong Owu fire arm warlords to be able to do much damage to the Ijebu attacks as they had hope. Then the Owu women and children ran out in panic, and the Ijebu warriors and their allies killed the Owus and the slaughter of Owu warriors continue without stop for the rest of the seventh year. And the Olisa Dipe order

"Make sure the women and children are not killed they shall be saved."

Then the remaining of the Owu people were denied access to their farmland, and it prevent them from getting foods which result to hunger and famine in Ile-Owu and the surrounding towns, and villages. Then the people left and abandon the whole of Owu land which was completely burn down and the farms destroyed by the Ijebuland warriors. Eventually after many days of searching, the Olowu was discovered among the women and children. And he look very tired with gunshot wounds and other cuts from swords all over his body. His wives had discovered him when he had fell after fighting for days and had became very exhausted, since his charms cannot overcome those of the more powerful Ijebuland warriors, and he said

"I have to hid among the women and children and have these gunshot wounds taken care of by the charms and herbs the women had prepared, and I shall be able to mobilize my warriors and find a better way to attack the Ijebus before I die."

But he fell asleep for about two days, and when he woke up all his warlords had be killed and only very few of his warriors were alive, and they were being captured by the slave kidnappers which the Ijebuland warlords and warriors allowed. Then he heard them said

"take away as many as you can so that we can burn down everywhere."

But he tried to get up but the effects of the sleep was so strong because of the charms and herbs the women have prepared. Then the women said to him

"rest first our Lord and husband!" "If you want to have enough strength to kill your enemies."

However, eventually the effect of fire and heat made the women to get out of their hiding place, and he was discovered when the women were crying. And the Ijebu warriors drag the Olowu to his feet, beat him and told him to sing and dance with his wives whom they identified because of their cloths and hair style. And one of the warlords said "this is the foolish man!" "Who cause all this because of his arrogance, now begin to sing and dance the stupid dance."

Then one of the warriors who was a good musician was told to compose a song for the Olowu

and the song he compose was:

"If it were you, would you dance?

If it were you, would you dance?

If it were you to be you that had his town overrun,

Your wife and children taken,

If it were you, would you dance?"

And the warriors said

"let us dance around the fool as he sings and dance, so that he and his wives can have some privacy in the middle singing and dancing."

So the Olowu and his wives were pushed into the middle and made to sing the song and dance, while the warriors also dance circling them.

However, the dance create some excitement and the Olisa Dipe went to see what was exciting his warriors, thinking it was the spirit that the war had came to a victorious end. But when he got there and he saw the Olowu dancing and singing but tired, and begging him to save him from the embarrassment. So the Olisa pity him and his wives and he order

"the Olowu shall stop the dance now"

And when the dance and singing had stop, the Olisa Dipe said

"Akipoju see what have come of you and your stubborn Owu people?"

And the Olisa Dipe order

"the Olowu, his wives and children shall be allow go because they have Royal blood in them, let the gods deal with them."

Then the Olisa Dipe call his warriors to him and said

"this is the order from the Awujale Oba Fusegbuwa!" "Owu shall never be rebuilt and that the wall of Oje which is the nearest town of Ile-Owu shall not extend as far as this Ogungun tree, where we camped."

Then eventually many of the refuges migrate to form part of the Owu community in Ibadan and the present Owu in Egba. And some are in the Ijebuland as the Owu Ijebu and other place. Most that were not lucky were kidnapped and sold as slaves in the slave market in Badagry and ship to America and Brazil.

Then, about 1820, more of the slaves from the coast of Lagos and other present coast of West Africa, were being helped to escape by some white people who did not like the slave trade. And also the British Parliament had been forced to legislate and to provide warships on the Atlantic Ocean to stop the slave ships. However, Rev. J.B. Joseph Wood, and Messr. J.T. Bowen who was an American Baptist, were in a meeting with Rev. Robert Walsh who came as a British Mission delegate to the British Protectorate of Lagos to observe the slave trade business, which was outlaw but the business till continue and the shipment and the cells of slave trade were thriving in Badagry and Lagos port. And Rev. Wood said

"we hope we can do something to try and stop this evil human trafficking and kidnapping here in the interior land close the British Protectorate of Lagos."

Messr. Bowen responds

"the reason we cannot stop the trade is because of lack of will on the side of the American and the British governments to put a stop to this pollution of these tribes with guns. They are the one encouraging and bribing these tribes Chiefs with money and providing them guns so that they can continue to fight each others' tribes and use that excuse to get them slaves by kidnapping the people."

"The Oyo warriors, the Ekitis, Egbas and some Ijebus are encouraged to continue to fight each other and slave raid in farms and villages because of the money given to them by the Royal Merchant Trading Company personals which are making large money in the slave trade."

Then Rev. Robert Walsh said

"but the slave trade is now abolish by the British Parliament?"

Rev. Wood responds

"that is the point!" "But the law is not applicable here!" "May be you can use your good personality and power to help in investigating the reason why the ships are still coming here to trade in slave trade business. It is making our Missionary work looks hypocritical, we are coming as white people to preach to these poor souls and the same ships that brought us are then used to transport slaves back to America, Brazil, and Cuba since the 15th century."

Messr. Bowen said

"if we can wait till around sunset, I will be able to take you to see who the slave trade kidnappers are, when the people will be returning from their farms, trades or the streams where they fetch water which they put in the clay pot on their heads or wash their cloths."

So the three white men went into hiding in one of the villages close to one use as a war camp of the Ibadan warriors. Then the warriors were being lead to the farms of an Ekiti village and raid them in their farms by shooting into the sky and those who tried to resist after been caught alive were shot. Then people were line up and with ropes in their necks and legs when the warriors walk them to the white slave traders. A Chief who was not happy with the money and gifts given them said "this cowries are not enough to bribe the Balogun (General), he would need more and I do not want him to be mad with me."

But Messr. Henry smile and told him through his interpreter

"you should remember that all the other Chiefs have children working for us and they know that to get steady supply of guns, they have to wait until the money comes from the big Chiefs in Britain."

Then he looked their face and add

"if you will not cooperate we would give the guns to the Egbas and the Ekiti tribes. And if that is not enough for your cooperation, your children will be killed."

So when the war-chief heard that their children will be killed he said

"please I understand!" "And tell master that we will cooperate!" "My 10 children are now working and learning how to talk like the white people. I don't want them to die, we will manage this few cowries and gifts, if the white people want more slaves we will go and get them please tell them no killing of our pikin."

Then Rev. Walsh said

"I know this man talking!" "He is Henry!" "He came here as a Missionary he is a good gentleman Christian brother, what has got into him doing this evil kidnapping trade?" "I think I will have to talk him personally now."

But Rev. Wood responds

"please you cannot reveal our secret!" "Because by talking to him you make our lives to be endanger!" "When you hear the reports that some natives killed Missionaries don't you know it is the Missionaries that try to talk to our white men about not to continue with this evil slave trade that end up been killed here?" "So if you want to be save, just keep quiet and pretend that you have not seen or heard anything."

Messr. Bowen said

"that is right Rev. Walsh!" "I should have warmed you that you cannot let any of this white slave traders know that we are spying on them like this, because we are going to be killed. So let wait after the slave traders and the warriors had gone out of sight, then we will go and take care of the wounded warriors."

Then after the white slave traders and the Oyo warriors had gone, they went to the battle field and help the wounded warriors and pray for the dead. And Later when they got to the Mission house, Rev. Walsh said

"I know couple of good Christian Navy Captains that we can enforce the stopping of the slave ships on."

And after their evening meals and prayers they went to bed.

"It is good that you come with us on this assignment Messr. Bowen!" "And it is because of your familiarity with this Coastal area that enable us to see these ships, we have been searching for these ships for months without success."

"Thanks for the compliments Captain T. E. Elliot!" "I have been on the Mission work for more than 10 years and actually I am one of the sailors of the Royal Merchant Trading Company ships then. And I have had my own share of the slave raiding before, but when I met the Lord Jesus Christ through the fellowship of Rev. Wood, then I see the light and have a change of heart. We can't be telling this poor tribes people the good news of Salvation and at the same time be killing them, deceiving and enslaving them just because of our greed for money."

Captain Elliot responds

"thanks be given to the Lord Jesus Christ for his mercy and grace on us and our souls!" "We all have been there!" "I take up this assignment after reading the newspaper and heard the stories told by the slaves that escaped, who are house at the St. Patrick's Mission house in London. And I told my

Command that I will take up the challenge of stopping these slave carrying ships from getting to America, Cuba and Brazil and other Islands."

And Rev. Walsh said

"Messr, Bowen!" "It is your advice which make sense!" "That we should use this slave trading ship call Elisabeth for this search, because they are decisive and think we are one of them in the same slave trading business."

Then the Captain gave the command for the crew

"Let all hands onboard be ready for maneuver of the ship so as to be able to catch up with the ship ahead and the ship shall be made ready to go above 60 knot in order to catch the ship ahead spot from the bridge."

Thereafter he order

"all gunners to be on standby!" "I repeat all gunners to be on standby!" "For possible action if the need be."

Then when the men at the boiler in the engine room in the lower deck gave the signal that the wood had been increase in the amount that will be able to thrust the ship forward. The Captain order

"brace for shock!" "I repeat all hands brace for shock!" "As the ship knot will be increase in knot to above 60 knot."

So the crew and everybody on board held on anything that give them supports and then Captain order

"brace for shock port side!" I repeat all hands brace for shock port side!" "For the starboard maneuvering,"

so the crew and everybody on board move to the left side of the ship and held on the wall and supports on the left side of the ship. As the ship turns in the direction to the right and increase in knot. So When the approaching ship Captain observed the knot of the approaching ship he pressed on the horn of his ship continuously to alert the ship in the same course and said on the speaker

"the ship approaching Elisabeth!" "I demand of you to slow down!" "for Elisabeth to catch up with you."

Then Captain Elliot drove his ship to meet up with the other ship and order

"brace for shock port side!" "I repeat brace for shock port side!"

and thereafter he order

"the ropes and anchor shall be thrown overboard!" "I repeat the ropes and anchor shall be thrown overboard!" "For Elisabeth support so as slow her down and finally stop by the side of the ship."

Then the Other ship Captain and her crew wave to the Captain Elliot who's ship name "Elisabeth" that is written on the side of the ship. However, The other ship's Captain and crews expect the Elisabeth crews to come on board of their ship to tell them what was wrong and why they need their help. But when they observed that Elisabeth was full of the British Royal Naval officers they ran back and inform their Captain whose ship name is Feloz. So Captain Elliot order

"Feloz!" "In the name of the Royal crown of the Queen of Britain!" "Submit yourself for search for slaves on board your ship, otherwise your cargo shall be sink."

Then the crew jump out of the ship overboard and they said

"Captain Jose Barbosa!" "We are going overboard!" "We are not be kill or go to prison for the rest of our lives for your ship."

And the Captain also remove his cap and jump overboard as he said

"Feloz is not my investment and I cannot die because some rich Britons investment."

However, some crew members took their guns and as they were about to shoot towards Elisabeth, the Naval officers shot at them and they drop their guns and fall on deck. Then the Naval Petty officers open the top hatches and got to the lower deck. And when the ship's slave driver heard the slaves making noise because they were scared of the gun shots from the top deck, he beats them but Messr. Bowen who was very closeby him held the scourge at its other end and twist it round the slave driver's neck and suffocate him. Then the leading Petty officer saw him and said to Messr. Bowen

"I guess you a military man also,"

then he let go the slave driver and he extend his hand to shake the Petty office and respond

"yes of course!" "The name is Messr. Bowen,!" "I serve in the United State Army as a Ranger."

And the Naval officer, said "Petty Officer 1st class Edward of the Royal Navy."

However, the two men shook hands and talk about the wars while the rest of the officers arrest the slave driver and other members of the crew that had not escaped. Then Captain Elliot lead Rev. Walsh to the bridge, search and found the ship's activities log book which he read loud and it says:

"the Feloz left the Coast of Africa, with 336 males, 226 females and had been out for seventeen days and she had thrown overboard 55 people."

Then they moved to the lower deck, open the hatchway between the deck and enter the very low space that sat between the decks where the slaves sat between each other's legs, with chains in their necks and hands that were hook to the deck and the ceiling above them, which made it very difficult for them to be able to lay down or even change their position both day or night. And when the Captain examine them, they had different form of marks on them just like the one for branding of sheep which indicates their owners, under their breasts or on their arms. Then Messr. Bowen said "this marks are impressed under their breast and arms with red hot iron for the identity of their owner."

However, when Rev. Walsh look down more closely on the people they perceived some form of sympathy and kindness in his eyes that they had not seen for a long time, and they begin to shout for help and clapping their hands. Some of the women were very excited and held their hand up and try to get up to their feet, but kneel down because the ceiling which was about 3 feet high was too low. The place was air and light tight, and the space between the deck was about 16 to 18 feet. The first space was crammed with the women and girls and the other was filled with the men and the boys. It house 226 in a space of 288 square feet. The female space accommodates 336 of them in 800 square feet. The heat in these place was so great with very offensive odor. Then the Captain order

"the prisoners shall be allow on the deck for them to get fresh air and water which I believe is like a luxury to them now."

Then when the hatches were open, the 517 people of all ages, sexes, some are children, old men and women, all in total nudity, were scrambling out together to taste fresh air and water.

"They came swarming up like bees from the aperture of a hive till the whole deck was crowded and covered from stern to stern." Some children were lying on the space where others had left and they were in terrible dying state. Also some people who were feeling that they don't care as to life or death, and they were all carried out and placed on the top deck by the Officers because they cannot walk by themselves. So when the water was brought for these people the extent of their suffering became reveal, because they rush at the same time like maniacs toward the water. Thereafter, the ship sail peacefully back to Lagos and the Naval Officers lead the former slaves to the Mission house in Lagos C.M.S. compound, where they were house in the Royal Military compound which was under the control of the Governor of the British Protectorate of Lagos.

The Abolition of Slavery In 1833

However, Captain Timothy Elliot, Rev. Robert Walsh and the Royal Naval Officers return back to Britain, and they continue to organize supports of the people in the streets of Liverpool, Manchester, London and other place in Britain and her Colonies. The debate became very intensive in the British Parliament to Abolish Slavery, but many of the slave traders family members, their children and wives were being kidnap by the supporters of the anti slavery and they were made to pay big ransoms to get them. Mainwhile Sir Andrew and his cousins told the British Members of Parliament

"things have now change!" "The commoners are even getting richer more through this slave trades!" "And the study done by the Royal academy, shows that the trade of Britain will be better off with or without the slave trade because we will need the tribal people in their home countries as workers for our factories and Industries raw materials in Manchester city, Liverpool, London and others in Europe."

Messr. Anthony said

"the study also show that there was no more need for slaves on the sugar cane and cotton plantations because we would now have to create a working class citizens in our cities both here in Britain and other European cities and in the United State of America New England."

Thus the Majority of the Members of Parliament vote for the abolition of slavery in Britain and all her colonies in 1833. And they was great joy in the streets of London, Manchester, Liverpool and other cities, then the black people that had being hiding and living in fears were free and able to walk about both at night and days in the streets of the cities and towns in Britain and the Colonies.

CHAPTER 7

The Disintegration of Orile-Egba and the Owiwi war about 1833

However, after the Owu war, Ipara an Ijebu town which had become a town where the Ijebus and the Oyo traders and caravans met and trade as the biggest market in all the countries. All goods and products such as yams, corns, tealeaves, cocoa, slaves, goats, sheep, horse, camels, palm oil products and produce, gun and more were bought and sold at Ipara town and markets.

Meanwhile, there was an Egba man call Esodoye from Itoku, and he trades in tealeaves, yams, cassavas, and timbers. Also he was very rich and he want to buy some of the Owu people captured during the war as his domestic slaves. Moreso, some of the Oyo warlords brought slaves for him and they said

"here are the slaves!" "We got them at the raids in the last Owu war!" "How many of them do you have money for?"

Adelaku who was one of the Oyo warriors, and he was a leader of the slave trader ask Esodoye. Who responds

"my friend!" "I have explain to you that I am new to this buying and selling of slave. I only need them to assist me on my farm, we are now bless with very good land in Itoku."

Then Adelakun said

"good do you have enough food stuffs for the warriors at Oke Ibadan? You know we Warriors that were displaced from Oyo towns and villages of Owu and we have to eat, since we don't have pleasure in farming now you can take as many of these slaves of our hands."

Esodoye now looking very delighted and laughing and said

"if that is the case, my friend!" "You can come over to see the food stuffs that I have. I am sure these yams, cassavas, peppers, tomatoes and more can be useful and help your companions and we can work out an arrangement for more foods supply from my farms base on the numbers of the extra slaves which this one may not cover their price."

Then Adelakun who was very excited and happy signals to one his warriors, who followed him to go and inspect the 18 wagons which Esodoye wants to show them. Then Esodoye lead them to the bush and after a few minutes' walk, they met some men carrying guns, some sitting on the trees while others were standing at the side of the road. And They all greet Esodoye saying

"welcome our Lord."

And Esodoye answered

"well done all of you!"

And indicate to the men to remove the tree branches and the leaves used in covering of the 18 wagons. However, Adelakun and the other warrior with him, were surprise when they saw the wagons and the foods in them and he said

"just like people's report about you Esodoye!"

Smiling, and he add

"I will also show you that our slaves are well taken care too."

And when they got to where the slaves were kept in a house close to the market, Esodoye said

"I will be able to take all of them expect for the women and children."

But Adelakun responds

"there are more women and children!" "Since most of the men died fighting."

Then Esodoye ask

"why can't you sell the women and the children to the white slave traders?"

Adelaku answered

"who wants do this business with those thives? They only want the men and few women and no children, and besides they might not give the cowries or nice white people's things in return for our slaves."

"Yes Adelakun!" "You are correct!" "We at the farms now have to train some of our able body slaves as guards and warriors to fight these white men slaves raiders and their men."

And Adelakun said

"you know that these evil white people have no regards and respect for anybody they even kidnap awon Oloye (Chiefs), awon Omo Oba Obirin (Princess) ati awo Omo Oba (and Princes) pe lu gbogbo ebi (with a whole family) in their house and sell them as slaves."

Then Esodoye nodding his head said

"very soon we shall have to come together and do something about them by getting rid of them from our lands."

And after taking a deep breath he add

"I will take all of them."

Then after deliberation between Esodoye and Adelakun and the other warrior, they agreed on the form of payment for the extra 800 slaves which the food Esodoye cannot pay for.

Then, Esodoye call Ogunsola the leader of his slaves, who was also in charge of the guards and he answered,

"yes my Lord!"

As he jump down from the tree where he stand watch, ran to meet Esodoye and prostrate before him. And Esodoye said

"we have to quickly take these new slaves to Itoku and we must be very careful so as not to lose them to the white slave raiders and their men."

Then Ogunsola nodding his head, got up and gave instructions to the guards and they all got into work. The slaves were line up with rope in their necks and legs while they walk into the wagons that were driven by horses to Itokun which is one of the new Egba towns.

Thereafter, at Itokun after some years, Esodoye called Ogunsola, who join him and his 3 wives as they sat under a tree at the front of his house and he said

"my wives!" "I purposely call you to this meeting so as to be a witness to what I am about to do."

And looking at Ogunsola who was prostrating on the floor in his front, he add

"get up and sit down on this chair,"

and after Ogunsola had sat down, he continue talking and said

"I am very impressed with your service to me and my household!" "You have been very loyal to me. The farm is doing well and the guards under your supervision are having many success. So I have decided to grant you, your slave wife and children freedom. Now you can have your own business and family. But I would want you to continue working for me, doing the work of supervising the farm work and the guards. For business you will have five slaves working for you on the land of your choice close to my farm, and you are free to buy more slaves and increase the size of your farm as far as your strength allows you."

Then after he finish talking, Ogunsola, full of tears of joy fell down at the front of Esodoye crying and thank him. Ogunsola's wife who usually works in Esodoye's house as house help, heard her husband crying, and she rush out, worried and standing by the door-way of house back door. And the youngest of the three wives, who was also crying and whose name was Olasunbo called her

"Onabumi!" "our husband has just grant your husband, you and your children freedom."

And Onabumi ran to her husband side and join him as he was thanking Esodoye.

Then a week after, Esodoye invites prominent people in Itokun and other towns and villages to his house when the freedom celebration for Ogunsola, his wife and children was taking place.

However, some years after the ceremony, Olaronke one of Esodoye's daughter came to Ogunsola's house which was in the same Esodoye's compound to inform Ogundoyin, the first son of Ogunsola that he would have to lead the guards and the caravan to the market at Ikereku, because her mother had gone to another market. And since Ogunsola family had gain their freedom, Ogunsola's wife have being following Olaronke's mother to the market selling her own products. And Ogundoyin was about to leave the house to join the guards at the farm, but when he saw Olaronke approaching the house knowing that he was the only person at home, he wait to know what message she had to give. And Ogundoyin also approached her as she was about to enter the house, and greet her

"welcome madam!"

while he had his head facing the floor. Olaronke smiling asked

"are your brothers at home?"

And he answered

"no they are at the farm,"

then she said

"good!" "I have told you that any time we are together you should stop showing any of the stupid courtesy as if we are not of equal age."

But Ogunsola still remain in the same posture, said

"I have to!" "Because I don't want trouble."

Then she stood by his side holding his hand while using the other hand to raise his head upward and responds

"with me you cannot get into any trouble."

And when their face met, they both start smiling, holding hands, she lead him into his room and close the door. Then they were talking while lying down on the bed. However, she asked

"so you don't like me anymore? You have being avoiding me since five years ago when I touched the slave sign on your face and your chest and asked you what is it for? Because I don't know then and besides, since none of my brothers have such thing on their face and body."

Ogunsola feeling ashame and embarrassed got up from the bed, and she also got up and stand by his side and try to look straight at his eyes while he avoids her direct look. Then she was about to go towards the door and she said,

"If you don't like talking to me anymore!" "I will know better and start learning how to be able to stop wanting to talk to you alone like this."

So Ogunsola realised what it means and knows he would like to marry her, if he has the opportunity and he said

"it is not that I don't like you!" "But you should understand that!" "That!"

hesitating, and looking at his hands. Then she turn back, put her finger on his lip and held on to him very close while her head was placed on his chest and both of them remain standing like this for some minutes without saying anything. Then she lay down on the bed, drag him to her side, and she lay on top of him while he was on his back. With both of their chests beating very fast and breathing heavily, she closed her eyes while her hand move to his face, still not looking at her face directly, so as to avoid looking at the top of her blouse which was revealing her beautiful breasts. She continue moving her hand on his face until it touch his lips allowing her fingers to rub on his lips and mouth, and sucking on her fingers. She said

"I know you still like me!" "Because I always see how you look at me!" "And most of these times whenever I noticed that you're looking at my backside, which I like to roll very well when I walk pass you."

He breath very deep feeling more embarrassed and also more encouraged to look at the wide opening in her blouse which was falling and rising very fast revealing more of her huge breasts. And thinking these are the most beautiful breast he had ever seen, more beautiful and smell nice than those of the women he work with at the farm. Then he noticed that she was sweating and the smell of her pomade attracts him more, and he enquired

"do you what me to open the window? "It is hot in here and you are sweating"

But she responds

"Oh!" "Thank you!" "I know you're a very lovely man!" "And you will be able to take good care of me and our children."

And she look at his face and add

"let us be careful!" "I will take care of the heat by removing my blouse and you can remove your buba (top dress) too or are you shy? I am sure you have seen lot of nicked women because I cannot trust you, at your age of 18. I am sure all the women you work with will like to enjoy this your strong penis."

Then she Looks down the spot where his penis is, as she sat down on the bed removing her buba and the inner wear that was used to prevent her breast from being too expose. So he feels more relaxed smiling, as he looked her breast, and answered

"these are more beautiful and nice."

And they both lay down and more closer and facing each other, as he rob on her breasts with both hands and rolling his tongue on the tip of her nipple, while she put her hand into his pant and took out his penis, which she held, feeling it's heat in her grip and the purse of the blood flowing through it's vains as she rob and stroke the crown of his penis. Then it becoming more and more longer, bigger and harder to her delight and surprise. Then both of them became more excited and happy, instantly he remove his pant, while she open her wrapper which was tie around her waist revealing her hairy virginal. Then she noticed that he looks at her virginal, and she got up from the bed and walk away to the other room where she knew the cool water pot was. She draw water into a big round calabash, and return back into the room with it, walking nicked enjoying his steady look at her face, her breast, and following his look through her rounded backside. Then she gave the calabash to him, let him drank the water and said,

"drink my love!" "Before I drink!" "So that you can stop sweating."

Moreover, he took the calabash from her hand as she went on her kneels at his front, looking at her face, her breast, and down to see her virginal, but she raised his head with her hand and said

"please concentrate on your drink!"

Smiling and enjoying the attentions and his big eyeballs looking at her body and she add

"before water runs through a different direction!" "I am here and my body is all yours to enjoy, so drink first."

So he drank the water and handover the calabash to her, and after she had drank too and asked him

"do you wants more water?"

But he responds

"no thank you!" "My beautiful Olaronke!"

Hearing him called her name in his thick baritone voice, made her to be more hunger for his lips on hers. So she lie down with her mouth on his and they kiss, moving her hand through his chest, down to her soft hairy virginal rubbing her fingers about it's edge and on top of it. While he also robs on her breasts, and now feeling her nipples tip getting bigger and harder as she draw herself up and placing her breast to his mouth. Then feeling the hunger and excitements he rolls his tongue on her breast. And she gives the sound of joy and excitement and held his hand and gently move it through her stomach down into her virginal. As his hand was feeling her virginal which was so hot and wet, she locate his very hot and long penis and after playing with it, and wondering how she would feels like if it is in her virginal. And Imagining the jokes she heard her mother made with her friends about big penis in their virginals, she held his penis, made him to lie on top of her and guard his penis into her virginal. So both of them feeling the hot sensation of each other and enjoying it while he continue the penetration of his penis into her until he was able to get through. Initially, feeling the pain around his penis while she shout in excitement and joy as his penis drill deeper and deeper as he continue to have sex with her.

Meanwhile, Commander Forbes a British naval officer and Mr.Beecroft, Her Britannic Majesty consul for the Bright of Benin and Biafra were in a meeting with some sailors, Missionaries and merchants from Europe and America. And Forbes said

"as regards to the commodities that are cargo going with my ships under my command, I give the assurance we shall be able to ensure that they sail save on the Atlantic to the ports in America and Brazil."

And Mr Beecroft said

"there should not be any cause for our business transactions to fail, since the people in the interior towns and villages continue fighting and killing each other, the kidnapping of slaves shall continue."

Mr. Smith said

"we have been in this business for some years now and the expectation on us by our partners to supply cargo of slaves for the sugarcane plantations and cotton plantations in America and Brazil are still very high and we shall ensure that these merchandize get to them because we pay a lots pounds in taxes and levy to the Royal treasury."

Then Mr. Johnny Thompson responds

"I shall have to agree with you Mr. Smith, the demand for this salvage slaves is extremely high and the Royal treasury taxes and levy are increasing, so where is the justification for us to stop this business of slave trade?"

But Rev D. Hinderer said

"we have to understand that the people of Britain have summit their desire to see the end of this slave trade business to stop and what is going on here makes mockery of our missionary works among this poor people."

Mr. Beecroft responds

"sorry Reverend!" "My assignment is clear!" "As a trade representative of the Royal Merchant Trade Post here!" "My work is to ensure that the guns, warfare merchandise and other products from the factories in Europe, America are sold to these people and also let the materials needed for our factories get there. We have to ensure that the money we need in Europe and America for the development of our country and the economy of our towns and cities are made here, and beside that we have to create employment for people which reqiures getting of the raw materials from this place. We sell guns to these people as factions and encourage them to fight each other. And in exchange for our guns and gun powders we raid their farms and villages for slaves."

And Commander Forbes said

"we don't have to raise any military force now to help in stoping the fight. We cannot help their high Chiefs now who are asking for help to stop the supply of guns to the factions which is what we had planned and encouraged, it makes it easy to get more slaves through the raiding for slaves as they continue their civil war and rebels."

Then he look at the face of others as if seeking their supports and add

"the position and policy from the high command and parliament is to continue with the raids and civil wars, until the needed number of slaves for the cotton and sugarcane plantations in America and Brazil and other new Islands like Cuba are met. So we have to continue with the supply of the guns and gunpowder inorder for us to get our slaves. And I have to comply you understand Reverend?"

Then looking at a big clock that he took out of his jacket, he said

"Oh!" "I almost late!" "It is about time for my meeting this fools' chiefs."

And he got up from his seat and add

"may I excuse myself gentle men for another meeting?"

As he took his hat from the desk, and walk away from the room.

However, at Oke Ibadan, some white men were at a meeting with some warriors which includes Adelakun, Opeagbe, Oluoyo, Abidogun, Apasa, and more. The leader of the white men said,

"thank you gentlemen!" "We are giving you the assurance that our guns and gunpowder will be ready and we can double our supplies as soon as we get the slaves that we had told you we need. And please don't forget we want more of healthy men and women, no children."

Another white men said

"you people can keep the children in your farms, let them eat better food so when they are grown up as boys or girls we will have them."

Then after the interpreter had finish talking, the warriors discussed among themselves and made their warrior shout

"Muso!" "Muso!" "Muso!"

as they left the meeting. But the most senior warriors stayed to conclude the meeting with the white men.

However, after the meeting, the warriors told Adelakun

"inform Esodoye!" "That we are not going to be able to supply him any slave for now!" "But he shall continue to supply us the same amount of food for the Warriors as he has been doing until we shall be able to meet up with the demand of slaves for the white men, and let him know that we will have more guns and gunpowder for him too."

But Adelakun responds

"we cannot just stop giving him slaves like that and expect him and his slaves to have the strength to work!" "He also sell these slaves at other markets and use the money that he gets to provide for his household and his people."

But the other warriors told Adelakun

"tell him that it only going to be for few years!" "When the ship of these white people have make two turns because we all know that this is how this evil white people do their business."

Then Adelakun left the meeting in annoyance for his house. However, some days after the meeting, The Balogun (General) of the Oyo Army, called Adelakun to his house for a meeting. And after Adelakun had greet him the Balogun said

"please my child!" "I will advise you to tell your friend Esodoye!" "To take the condition that these other warriors have offer. I have told them that it is wrong not to honor an agreement they already made with Esodoye, but they want the guns and the gunpowder so bad that their ability to reason is now being blocked. I have to follow what they now want, we are in time of you younger generation. The white people have come with their guns and turn everything upside down. People don't cooperate with each other anymore, since it easy to kill anybody with a gun."

So Adelakun saw the danger he was in if he continues to resist the interest of his mates because just like the Balogun was warning him, with gun no amount of charm a warrior has eventually he will fall to the power of the white man's gun. So Adelakun prostrate and thanked the Balogun and he said,

"Thank you baba (Lord) Balogun!" "For your fatherly wisdom and the advice!" "I will carefully talk to Esodoye and I pray that the gods will be with me when I will be talking with him."

Then the Balogun was so impressed with Adelakun and he order

"get give me the my emblem of duty"

which is an object that is a personal emblem of his rank as Balogun Oyo

And one of his slaves brought the object and he handed it over to Adelakun with his left and said some charm words as he did so and said

"here is a symbol of my personality as the Balogun Oyo take it I increase you in charm today"

So Adelakun recieved it from his left hand with his left as he prostrates at his front and said

"thank you baba Balogun Oyo!" "We shall remain under your good leadership and command for more years."

Then he got up and left for his house.

However, the following day Adelakun left Ibadan for Itoku with some warriors to inform his friend of the new position of trade. And when they got to Esodoye's farm, Esodoye had been informed that Adelakun was on his way with some warriors by Ogunsola. So Esodoye invite Adelakun and his companion to meet him at the front of his house, and signals Ogunsola and his son Ogundoyin to remain with them as he listen to the visitors. However, Adelakun was reluctant to talk, Then Osun who was the next senior warrior, said

"thank you Esodoye!" "We appreciate the business we have been having with you, but things will have to change for now, because we realize that we need to get more guns from these white people. And everyone know that most of our people are being taken as slaves by these evil white people and they have being transporting to them to their country beyond the sea."

But Adelakun made attempt to talk, and Osun indicate that he should not worry, and add

"my Lord!" "We understand that it may be difficult for you to explain the message to your friend."

Then facing Esodoye he continue,

"the whole Oke Ibadan Warriors want you to continue with the supply of the food as usual, but we may not be able to give you any slave or money until we get enough guns, which we are prepared to share some with you."

However, Esodoye look very sad and confused, but he did not say anything. Then he look at his friend's face and then at Ogunsola, who knew his master very well, and Ogunsola said to the Warriors

"my master!" "Will like to have a word with me in private."

Then Esodoye feeling very angry got up and walk to his house and Ogunsola and his son followed him. And when they were inside the house Esodoye said

"thank you Ogunsola for the wisdom in getting him away from the meeting when you noticed that I am very angry."

Then as they were talking Adelakun who also had excuse himself got inside the house. And Esodoye asked

"who is that man?" "Is he not a junior warrior to you? And why he is so disrespectful of you?" Adelakun responds

"yes!" "This is the way Oyo has turn to now!" "There is no more respect among the ranks."

"I had tried without success to explain to them that it is wrong not to honor the trade agreement with you but they would not listen to me."

And he look very sad, breath in heavily, looking downward and add

"the Balogun cannot even talk to them because they will not listen to him,"

then he brought out a charm which was an emblem of the Balogun's rank and continue "look here is the Balogun Oyo emblem which he gave to me as a bribe so that I can talk to you"

and show it to Esodoye as his prove of resisting the warriors trade decision. Then there was a silence, which was broken by Adelakun, when he breath in deep and said in a sad tone,

"we will have to agree to their demand for now!"

looking his friend's face, and his guards' face, he continue

"until we can find a way out."

Then Esodoye put himself together and follow his friend out of the house. And when they had sat down, he said

"though your request will be very hard because I have to feed my family, and also I have other responsibility in our community here in Itokun which requires some money. But since the Balogun Oyo had personally send my friend to let me know the importance of this issues, I have no choice but to accept your conditions for now."

Then the warriors got up praising the Balogun Oyo and told Ogunsola

"what are you waiting for?" "Are you not just a slave in this place?" "Now lead the way to where the foods are and start loading them."

Then Ogunsola gave his son the the look of calm down, while Esodoye and Adelaku got up and walk to the side Ogunsola and told him in a lower voice

"please take the insult as it is is coming from us."

But Ogunsola said

"who I am to complain?"

And he order the slaves to load the foods to the warriors' wagons and after the loading was done. Adelakun excuse himself from his friend and follow his warrior companions.

Warlords at Oke Ibadan

However, the warriors morals became very high when the foods got to Oke Ibadan. Then the senior warriors had a meeting and conclude that the Balogun Oyo should sanction it that they have to divide themselves into units to raid the Egba towns and villages for the needed slaves, since their communities had no walls and it can be easy to penetrate without much resistance. Then the Balogun Oyo agreed with their decision and they choose chief Fadeyi, and chief Agbeni, to meet with some Ijebu warriors who had refused to return back to the Ijebuland after the Owu war. And had join the slave raiding Oyo warriors, and had made Ibadan which was a farm village of the Ijebus as their new settlement. Moreover, on their way to a Ijebu Chief call Kalejaiye's house where the meeting would be held, they made jokes about their houses. But in actual fact none of this warriors had build the house by themselves, they usually occupy any house abandon as a result of war which the owner had left. Then when they got to the house they said

"Kalejaiye!" "Your house look better now!" "It appears you have being taking good care of it."

And he responds

"yes!" "It is better when compared with when I moved in!" "The lazy owner left it uncared for."

Another warrior joke,

"what do you expect of the foolish owner of the house?" "Since he have to spend most of his time at the farm, and his wives gone to the market doing buying and selling."

Then chief Fadeyi said

"I wonder why some fools get into these business of farming, selling, cassava, yams, tomatoes, when we can go and raid as much as we want and sell their products and the farmers themselves as slaves."

However, after almost everyone excepted for the meeting were present, Bankole said

"we thank you Kalejaiye!" "For allowing us in your house, and hopefully after the next war all of us will be able to claim houses for ourselves. We are here to invite you and other Ijebus here in Ibadan that have interest in the raid and to display of the Egbas from their new towns and villages. The Maye Ife who commands the most respect among us now in Oke Ibadan, had agreed with the white people to supply them with slaves in exchange for guns and gunpowder." Then Kalejaiye responds

"I was also at the meeting, but we have to let Amiobo, Osunlalu, Oguada, Arowosanle and some others who are not here now to know of this."

Then Bankole said

"we also come to know if you the Ijebus that have being part of our raids at other place will want to be part of this, because we heard that the Awujale Oba Sotejoye had order that the place close to Abeokuta to shall be raid."

Then Fadeyi asked

"what is the reason the Ijebus do not want war against Abeokuta and her surrounding villages and towns?"

And Arowosanle responds

"it is because of Igbore!" "which is a land first settled by Asa Omo Oba Obirin (a Princess) of the Awujale Oba Jadiara Agbolaganju who invite an Ijebu warrior Afota Modi as her husband."

Then the Ijebu warriors said

"we can join the raids!" "We only have to be careful and make sure that nobody attack Igbore and the villages close to her which we call Abeokuta because of the big rock."

And Kalejaiye said

"but the new settlements of the Egbas we can attack, and we will have to send word message to the Ijebuland villages and towns that are close to the Egbas that we will not attack them, but we are only after the Egbas because they support the Owus in the Owu war."

However, the whole warriors agreed and they said

"this the best reason to make the attack on the Egbas, and since some Owus have even settle among them and we think the Awujale Oba Sotojoye will see that we are after the Owus also."

Thereafter, there was a conflict between Idomapa and Gbagura over land territorial limit and the Maye Ife took side with Oluwole the Bale Idomapa and the following week he called the Oke Ibadan warriors and told them

"I had talk with Oluwole about our support for Idomapa, and we will join their camp and fight against the Gbagura. And since Oluwole is a weak worrior we shall take control of the conflict and turn it to war against the Egbas."

However, on the day set for the attack at Gbagura, the Bale Oluwole order his slaves

"begin the construction of the public building close to the disputed territorial limit, since we have the support of the Oke Ibadan warriors and some powerful Ijebus nobody can stand on our way and from preventing us from using the land."

Then when some of warriors arrived he order

"you warriors shall stand guard over the territorial land, and we shall be ready to defend the land we have the Oke Ibadan warriors and some Ijebu warriors here already around to help us to fight and drive away these Egbas that are now taking our land. And we can now look forward to getting more lands for our farms."

And the villagers respond

"so that is why we have being seeing some strange warriors in our markets and our farms?"

However, The Bale of Gbagura was at home and talking to some chiefs about the disputed territory, when some men entered his house angry and said

"we have to fight and drive this Idomapa people from our land,"

and they prostrate and greet the Bale and the Chiefs. Then the Bale said

"we know that we may have to fight to drive them out of the land, but we have to talk with Bale Oluwole and the Chiefs of Idomapa before going to war."

One of the men said

we had talk with their chiefs before and they insult us that we have to go back to our Bale who would inform us that Idomapa has power over Gbagura."

Then the Bale Gbagura was annoyed and he said

"Oh no!" "They are making mistake!" "Our grandparents were the owner of this land they were the one that farm on this land, before the Idomapa."

Also another man entered the house and said

"war!" "War!" "has come!" "What are we waiting for Bale?"

he prostrates in the front of the Bale, he got up and continue,

"the Bale Oluwole is constructing on the land!" "And he had told the Idomapas to attack us on our own land. Also we have seen some Ijebu warriors talking of attacking the Egba."

Moreso, another man said

"Bale!" "the Oke Ibadan warriors are also around and they are ready to attack us!" "We heard them boasting that now is the opportunity to sell the Egbas to the white people as slaves."

However, the Bale Gbagura order

"Now the warriors shall be prepare for the war and also some of the warriors shall go to investigate the activities of the Idomapa people and bring report."

Thereafter, the people came back the following day and they said

"the Bale!" "The Idomapa people are ready to attack us. And some Ijebu slave raiders are around also, and they had brought with them the Maye Ife, the notorious Ife warrior who is the head of the Oke Ibadan slave raiders also."

Then the Bale thank them and said

"we have to fight to our last to defend our land. This is our land which our ancsetors had farm in before them."

And he looked very sad and with anger in his voice he order

"send this word to all the other Bales and chiefs of Egba villages of what is happening and to tell the people to desert the villages so that they will not become victims of slave raid."

Then the town and village announcers goes about the various market places, villages centers, and cross roads beating a big metal gong and shouting at the top of their voices:

"Ke re o!" "Ke re o!" "Ke re o!" "Bale Gbagura ni ki so fun yin, ti Omode ati Agba o!" ti Okunrin ati Obirin, Olile ati Alejo! Pe awon Ole, Janduku, Ako li lile, ati Aje loju Olile, ati Ako eli leru ta fun Oyinbo, awon Jagun Jagun Oke Ibadan ti ko ogun wo ilu o. Ki Olile gbe ile o, ki eni keni ma se re odo ati lati lo da oko ni a koko yin si igba di e o. Se mo yi re, tabi mo o wi re o?"

"Please listen all!" "Please listen all!" "Please listen all!" "This is a special announcement of an order from the Bale Gbagura that every body and including strangers also shall remain at their homes and no one shall not go to the market, the stream, and the farm for some time now. The Oke Ibadan warriors who are our enemies, theives, and white people slave kidnappers have wage war on us, hope you all understand the announcement?"

And the people would respond

"Owi re o, ati gbo o!" ("Yes, we understand the announcement!")

So the Gbagura warriors reinforced from Ika, Owe, Ikija, Iwoko, Oja and more in the defense of Oorun, because Idomapa is under Oorun territory. Then the Idomapa warriors launched attack on Oorun, and after continuous fighting for about four years, their guns and the gunpowder was low and they can not get supply from the white traders, and they were afraid to talk to the Ijebus, thinking they were part of the conspiracy to destroy them and their villages. Meanwhile The Awujale Oba Sotejoye join his ancestors after about one year on the throne. And it took some time to finish the installation ceremony of Awujale Oba Afesojoye Anikilaya, who continued with the stands of the Awujale Oba Sotejoye and ordered all Ijebu warriors to return back to Ijebuland. But Chief Kalejaiye called the Ijebu Chiefs who were part of the slave raiders who were Amoibo, Osunlalu, Ogunade, Arowosanle and more to a meeting and after the discussions they agreed not to return back to their Ijebuland homes, and they said "we will form our own Ijebu community and have a parallel government in our own settlement which will be just like in Ijebu-Ode, we will have our Awujale, Olisa, Ogeni Oja, Egbo and more because there is plenty of money to be made in raiding for slaves and selling them to the white traders. The white people will support us and give us guns and gunpowder, since we are Ijebu men we can outsmart these Oyo people, because they don't have the sense of unity in anything they do."

So they agreed to continue with their attack on the Egbas and offered a slave as sacrificed to the gods, and also initiate each other by drinking the blood of the lamb which they mixed with their own blood with the believe that none of then can break away or informed the people in the Ijebuland of their plans and actions. Then those Ijebu worriors join force with the Maye Ife who lead the Oke Ibadan warriors and they raid Egba villages. However, the Ijebu slave raiding warriors appeared to be more successful in the raids and the war so it made the Egbas to hate the Ijebus. Moreover the Egba people that were captured were sold to the white traders who ship them to America and Brazil as slaves. Thereafer, after the third year, the Awujale Oba Afesojoye Anikilaya noticed that those few warriors were giving the Ijebuland bad reputation and he summoned his Chiefs to his palace of which the Olisa, the Ogbeni Oja, the Egbo, the Apenas, and the Ogbonis were present and he said

"I know that our custom does not usually allow a father to curse his child, not to talk of the Awujale to curse his Warriors. But this Kalejaiye, have lead Amoibo, Osunlalu, Oguade, Arowosanle and some others to attack the Egbas. And the report says that they are now planning to have a parallel authority of the Awujale of their own."

Then the Olisa and everybody prostrates before the throne saying

"Kabiyesi o!" "Kabiyesi o!" "Kabiyesi o!" "Agbedo!" "Ewo, oro koro, ni ayeyi ko, ewo ewo ewo ni. Ko gbodo je be ni aye ta wa yi ko" ("the Unquestionable one!" "The Unquestionable one!" "The Unquestionable one!" "It is impossible!" "And not in on this earth, it can never happen, it is impossible.")

Then the Awujale Oba (Emperor) Afesojoye got up from the throne and order

"the leader of the guards!" "Get me two calabash with top lids and a calabash with water in it. And you shall prepare a special herbal concoction containing some dried and fresh leaves and seven traditional eggs, seven flywhisk (Ajubara) which shall be left for seven days for potency."

Then after the flywhisk was remove and the Awujale Oba Afesojye recite some incantation on it. And he took it close his eyes and threw the eggs to the bush. After some time, he called one of the palace attendants, whose name was Irenwon and order

"Irenwon now place the flywhisk on your shoulder and run to the bush and pick up the eggs thrown there earlier."

And Irenwon did as he was told, but as he was running, the flywhisk fell off, and the eggs had been broken and scattered everywhere, so Irenwon cannot get them. Then Irenwon return to the palace, prostrate before the thrown and report

"Kabiyesi o!" "Kabiyesi o!" "Kabiyesi o!" "The flywhisk had fell off and the eggs are scattered, and I cannot get them Kabiyesi."

Then the Awujale Oba Afesojoye said

"good!" "So shall it be!"

And he continue with these curse words:

"....an egg that is flung into bush never finds its way back again;

that '.... the flywhisk perishes while being thrown around....

and that

'...this shall be the portion of the insurgent

of warriors forging Egba territory."

However, the following day those Ijebu warriors who were feeling more superior to the rest of the raiding warriors, blew their trumpet and order

"you Oke Ibadan warriors shall join our camp because our side of the campaign is recording better success. And we have to be in charge from now on."

Then Maye Ife called the Oke Ibadan warriors aside and told them

"let the Ijebus make it their own fight, the whole blame shall be on them in future."

Another warrior said

"after all we are getting the slaves which we need for the white traders."

Chief fadeyi said

"why are we even arguing about who is to lead the war? Okunrin ri ejo Obirin pa, ewo ni iyato nibe? Sebi ki ejo sa ti ku ni? (A male see a snake, and a woman kill it what difference does it make about who kill it, in as much the snake die?")

And the warriors became glad and they said

"we don't have to worry over which faction leads the campaign, in as much we get the slaves that we need for the white slave traders."

Then Maye Ife told the Ijebu warriors

"we are ready to work under your command, and with Chief Kalejaiye as the leader."

However, as the discussion about the planning for the war was going on, and one of the Ijebu warrior who just join them whose name was Oresanya start boasting to his friends and he said

"I have a personal issue to attend to at Itoku where my friend farm is, and he had promise me his beautiful daughter whose name is Olaronke to be given to my son Amawo."

Then he looked angry and continue

"but since Amawo is not discipline, I will just go there and take the girl for myself before this war get over to Itoku."

However, Amowo was standing a few distance to his father and heard what he had just said. Then Amawo called some of his friends whose father had horses and told them what his father said, and they become very excited, and said

"we now have a slave mine for ourselves."

One of the them said

"what are we waiting for? Let us go right now to the farm."

But the boy whose father was the leader of their group responds,

"we cannot ride away on the horse now otherwise some of my father's slaves who are guards will noticed and join us and everything will belong to him and his friends."

However, incidentally, Adelakun who had lost interest in the Egba raiding and the war, was standing not too far from the boys and overheard them. Then he said to himself,

"I have being thinking of how to save my friend from this trouble,"

and looking at the poeple closeby to ensure that none of them were paying any attention on him and heard what he had just said, he add

"thank you the gods!" "I have to ride to Esodoye's farm before these boys get there to warn him and help him."

So he quietly walk away to his horse and rode his horse away and pick up the speed after he had got clear of sight.

However, Ogunsola and his son signaled to the guards not to attack the coming horse because he had seen him from afar and recognized him from the top of the tree where he stand watch. Then when he got to the farm Ogunsola welcome him, he and his son followed him to the compound and he told Esodoye what he heard.

Then Ogunsola gives the order to the guards

"be ready for attack on the farm,"

and instructs

"the secret hiding place be dig now."

Meanwhile, earlier some of the slave raider warriors who had followed Adelakun to Esodoye farm before, saw him riding very fast to the farm, so they decide to raid the farm after Adelakun had left. Moreso, they send word message to Amawo about the farm because there were lot of slaves working in the farm and that the owner of the farm was very rich. When the slave they send got to Amawo who was drinking palm wine, with his friends but refuse to leave the wine, but told

"the slave whatever you want to tell me say it here I am not leaving this good palm wine."

So when the slave told them the message, the young warriors said

"surely the gods have given us this slave mine"

And as they were about to discuss what do next, the trumpet for the war to advance was blown. However, they followed the slave to where his master was, then Amawo said "since we know that some of farm guards have guns so let us attack some of our warlords and get their guns and those they have in the reserve place."

Then they made the attack got the guns and went to Esodoye's farm.

Meanwhile, at Itoku Esodoye was inform of the approaching warriors that were very large in numbers, and some carrying guns. And Esodoye became very angry and would not listen to Adelakun who warn him not to expose himself to gun shot. But Esodoye refused to listen and remain standing and saying some charm words and he held a charm in his left hand and a gun in his right hand. However, the attacking warriors had succeed in killing most of the farm's guards because they did not have guns and horses. But Ogunsola who was on the tree was able to kill a lot of the warriors on the horse and his son had been quietly keeping the slaves, his brothers, mother and people in the compound in the secret hiding places. Then Adelakun who had fought his way to where Ogundoyin was join him in keeping the people in the farm save. And as the fight continue, other Oke Ibadan warriors who heard the sound of gun shots came to the farm and join the fight, so with more warriors on the farm, Ogunsola was shot at from more directions, which his charms cannot help him on, so he fell from the tree and broke his neck. But Ogundoyin saw his father fell, and as he was about to get to him, then he saw about five Warriors on him, and he close his eyes as they shot him dead. And he said to himself

"oh!" "My father a brave warrior!" "We shall meet again."

However, Esodoye who had being moving from place to place, and had succeed in killing many of the Oke Ibadan warriors because his charm made him to be invisible to most of the warriors. But Amawo who had some powerful charm also, was able to spot him as he moves, so he fired shot at him saying some charm words, and Esodoye fell, and Adelakun who had been following his friends moves said

"I will not let you kill yourself my good friend."

And killing more of his own warriors while hiding himself behind trees and shrubs saw when his friend fell, so he quickly ran to him and drag him into a safe spot and said some charm words and working on his wounds. Then as the night approaches some Oke Ibadan with archers that has fire on their heads, shut at the houses and they start burning. So the slaves start getting panicking, crying and running out from their hiding places. But Adelakun who was able to see better gun down almost all the warriors with archers. Meanwhile, Amawo was able to take the slaves running about, and he ordered some of his friends

"you get the slaves alive!" "We came here not to engage in fight for land disputs!" "So get as many slaves as we can to make our futunes."

And they were able to discovered where they were hiding, but Amawo keep on seraching for the girl his father talked about hoping to find because his father said she was very beautiful. However, Ogundoyin who was also looking at Esodoye's house and hoping he can get they before it burn down thinking he had to save Olaronke, so he ran from tree to tree until hc got to the house and quietly calling

"Olaronke!" "Olaronke!" "Olaronke!" .....

and the names of other people in the house. But Olaronke who had luckily got out of the house before it got burn down noticed Ogundoyin as he ran from tree to tree, so she hid herself behind a big tree which was surrounded by lot of big grass. And in order to signal Ogundoyin, she took a bead on her waist and threw it towards his direction. Moreso, Ogundoyin saw the bead and moved towards it, but before he could get to where Olaronke was hiding, she was carried by Amawo who was also well charm and having being picking the slaves as they ran away from their hiding to his friends, he had saw Olaronke and also heard when Ogundoyin called the names and he took her to the wagon waiting. Then Olaronke called

"Ogundoyin!" "Ogundoyin!" "Ogundoyin!" ... "Help me!" "Ogundoyin!" ... "Help me!" "I have been kidnap!" "Ogundoyin!" ... "Help me!"

Then Ogundoyin ran out of the house, picked the bead and put it in his pocket, without even care if he was being shot at, ran toward the direction where he heard her voice. And he noticed that some slaves were been put in wagons and driven by horses, then he ran after the wagons. And with his hand in his bubba pocket he took out a charm saying some words as he ran and then he start running faster than what was normal for a human being as he continue to say the charm words. Eventually, he got to the wagon in which Olaronke was, climb it and sat on the top of it.

However, the effect of the Awujale's incantation and curse start working on the Ijebu warriors and other warriors attacking the Egbas. Then the Ijebu warriors were fighting with the Oke Ibadan warriors and they killed each other. And the Egba warriors who were closeby saw that the Oke Ibadan warriors were running away from their hiding places and camps, and they also saw that they had killed each other and all the Ijebu warriors were dead and their heads cut off, so they called their warriors and ran after the retreating Oke Ibadan warriors and killed some of them, while very few escaped.

Mainwhile as the horses with the wagons were running very fast, Amawo who was not a good horseman fell off his horse, and the wagon ran over him, drag him along to a very long distance and his head was broken into piece. So this slow down the horse at the front, and enabled Ogundoyin to jump on it and control it. Then Ogundoyin kicked off the the horse rider who was looking backward to see what had happen to Amawo from his horse. And he was able to slow done the horse he was riding which eventually stop, and the other horses also stop when the first one had stop. So he got down from the horse and open the wagons and release the prisoners. Moreover, holding Olaronke hand in his as they hid in the bush, and some Egba warriors who had witness what had happened from a distance came to their rescue and house them.

Meanwhile, Adelakun took his friend inside one of the house that was not completely burnt, and use a knife which he put on a fire to remove the gun residues form his body, and applied a cloth put in hot water on all the gunshot wounds and continue to give him palm oil to drink and said his charm words until he open his eyes and start crying. Thereafter, the following morning Ogundoyin walked with Olaronke who was holding his hand and refused to let go of him with some slaves into the farm. And

255

they picked their walk trying not to walk on dead bodies and meet up with Adelakun who welcome them with tears and laughter, and wiping off the tears in Ogundoyin's eyes as well. Then Olaronke ran inside the compound calling

"baba mi!" "Mama mi!" "baba mi!" "Mama mi!" .... and the names of her siblings, and others she can remembered and crying. Then Esodoyin open his eyes as he heard his daughter calling, manage with all his strength and said

"Olaronke!" "My beautiful daughter!" "Olaronke!" "My beautiful daughter!" ... "I am alive and I am here."

So she ran to where the voice was coming from, saw him lying on mat at a corner of the house corridor, ran to his arms, crying, and saying

"baba mi!" "Baba mi!" "Thank OLORUN-ELEDUMARE!" "You are not killed!"

looking at him allover and she asked

"where is mama mi and others?

But her father start to cry and both of were crying.

CHAPTER 8

Leadership of the Awujale Oba Afesojoye Anikilaya

However the Egbas realizing that they had gain their victory over the evil Ijebu slave raiders and the Oke Ibadan warriors then most of them return to their villages that are more hidden and also closer. Then they decide to get more guns and gunpowder and their villages heads decided that they would have to fight the Ijebus back when we had acquired enough weapons and big enough.

Thereafter some years later, the Egbas had settled down in few villages and most of them also settled in Ibadan which had become a metropolitan city.

The Owiwi War about 1830

Meanwhile as a result of the fall of the Ibini kingdom (Benin Empire), some of the Ishekiri descendants migrated to the coaster area of the river Niger, where the Lagoon from the boundary of the Ijebuland country meet with the part of Niger delta. And these settlers together with the Ilajes, the Eguns and some Ijebus and more become the inhabitant of Eko Island. And eventually, the British established their trade post there, and Eko become where the British merchants and other European traders and the Missionaries who always came with the British merchant's ships and American made their settlemented. Then and as time goes on Eko become a very important trade post port, Moreso, the Royal Merchant company were able to buy more land from the local Bales. Since the Awujale would not allow their settlement in any of the Ijebuland and would not grant them save passage to the interior land. Thereafter, they bought land from the Bale of the beach by the Eleko thinking the land would be good for settlement, but after several attempts to farm on the land without success, they called the land "bad Agriculture" land which eventually become "BadAgric" and the local people called it "Badagry". However, the chiefs in Badagry, Eko, and became rich dealing in slave trade business, guns, and gunpowder. Eventually, since Badagry was not good for agriculutre the Royal Merchant Company gave the approval for the use Badagry as the land for dealing with slave trade and they said

"it is more remote and will not be easily discovered by the people who are protesting in Europe to stop the slave trade."

However, after some years the Lagoon water by the Eko Island was drenched by the Royal Merchant Trading Company without the approval from the Bale Eko which caused some conflicts and the British government suppress it by using gun to terrorized the people and create a big and active sea port. Then the port served all the coastal areas of present countries of Republic of Benin, Togo, Nigeria, and Cameroun for slave trades and they brought in products from their factories and Missionaries from Europe and return with slaves, and the agricultural products such as palm oil, palm produces, cocoa, timbers, and more to Europe, America continents and Cuba.

Then the British parliament gave the approval to merge all the activities of the Islands in the coastal area of the present Nigeria together and call the place "Lagos" and made it their own territory without fighting any war with the people of the interior since the Royal Merchant Trading Company had succeed in polluting the interior lands except the Ijebuland with guns and had been dividing the people in order to gain access to their lands mostly with the pretence of establishing Missionary works. But the Awujale oba Afesojoye Anikilaya insist that the Ijebuland toll gates at Ipara and other boarder walls of the Ijebuland and the local ports at the Lagoon fronts of the Ijebuland was not accessible to the Europeans, the Americans and their Missionary works.

However, the white people continued their evil slave trade, lies, divide and rule tactics with the aid of guns which they had succeed in terrorizing everywhere except at the Ijebuland where they were not allowed access.

Then the Royal Merchant Trading Posts in Lagos supplied guns and gunpowder to the different tribal warrior leaders, and acting as their military instructors, advising their Olus, Bales, Obas, and the Alafin Oyo except the Awujale Oba (Emperor)

and all the Ijebuland Obas that refused to allowed them in Ijebuland. Actually the Ijebuland followed their Abrahamic (being descendants of Jebusites) nature of closing their wall gates to strangers. So they closed their gates to strangers and non Ijebus. They only allowed trading access to their markets in Ipara and even collect toll gates fees from everybody that are non Ijebus, in fact access for all non Ijebus right from the 16th century non Ijebus cannot enter any of Ijebuland cities, towns and villages and farms without the approval of the Awujale. The Ijebuland has not been conquered by any of the Oyo, Ibini Empire, or any king nor the Awujale have ever prostrates to any Oba, Olu, Bale, or King nor paid homage to nobody. Then there was great pressure by the Royal Merchant Trading Company people to gain access to the Ijebuland, which they cannot because they cannot fight and win any war against the Ijebuland because just with their guns they cannot march the Ijebuland warriors. Additionally, they found it difficult to pollute the Ijebuland with their guns and gunpowder. So the Awujale have been the power broker of all the Obas in all the countries from the 16th century.

After some years, about 1834 Eko has become a big city

"Welcome to Eko!" "You can get down from my canoe now." "Omodele!" "Omodele!"

a canoe transporter calls one of the men that works as helpers and lifters of loads which they usually lift to their heads after rolling an Ojuka (a large cloth roll as a support for their heads) and place the load on it. And he instructs Omodele

"can you take this people to Isale-Eko? (down town of Lagos), They are looking for Olugoke's house."

"Yes I can!"

Omodele responds and look at the men and add

"you are welcome!" "Apo eru melo le ni?" ("How many loads or bags do you have?)

And after they had agreed on the fees he would take, for the loads and for assisting them to the their destination. But Dada Obadina who was the leader of Kiyooku's slaves said

"we are visiting Lagos for the first time."

And add

"oh!" "Thank you we have more than 10 bags which contains cloths and regalina for our Egunguns (Masquerades) call Eyo, which is also call Adimu Orisa (Special diety) of Ijebuland."

Then Omodele responds

"that is good I am familiar with Egugun because I am a descendant of Ojewale, we also have our Egungun call Egunu."

Then Omodele called some boys to help in carry the loads, but Dada Obadina refused them carrying the loads, and said

"my Lord will kill me if he knows I have to give that kind of money to people to carry loads, my fellows are coming with the next canoes."

Omodele supprise open his mount wide for a few seconds and asked

"with more loads?"

Dada Obadina responds

"no!" "Only men and some women and we will be able to carry everything by ourselves."

Then Omodele feeling disappointed, pointing at himself said

"what about me?"

Dada Obadina responds

"you carry mine!" "And get your money for helping us to the house and for the load you carry."

So when they got to the house, chief Olugoke greets the slaves

"welcome!" "You strangers in Eko!" "Hope you were not afraid of the Lagoon?"

And instruct his senior house help

"Jelili show the visitors their living quarters. And take Dada Odadina to the rooms and tell him that Chief Kiooku wants the Eyo Masquerades regalia and the deities materials in the room opposite his own."

Then the two men talk for the rest of the evening until the arrival Chief Olugoke and Chief Kiyooku.

Meanwhile, the following morning after taking their breakfast together at the central part of the house, Chief Olugoke called his son Fadejimi and said

"Fadejimi!" "Fadejimi!" "Fadejimi!" "Bring me the Ayo Olopon."

Then Chief Kiyooku called Dada Obadina and asked

"how is the arrangement for the Eyo regalia? Is everything white and well kept? Make sure the caps are not damaged, make sure the Oparum (Palm tree branch) for the Opanbata is ready. And after I finish with teaching this Lagos people who lacked the courage to drive the 'water goddess' away, as we did in Ijebuland and claim all the land for ourselves how to play Ayo first. Then I will teach him how to make the Opanbata."

And as he was talking Fadejimi brought the 'Opon Ayo' out and placed it on the table they had used for their breakfast. And his father said

"thank you my son!" "Stand by my side!" "And all you people in my household come and see that we Omo Eko (Eko born) are the best in this Ayo Olopon."

Then Kiyooku faced the Opon Ayo and both players arranged the seeds for the game in the four set count on the six rows in each of their side of the Opon (board) and the game begins. And Kiyooku said

"ta ayo fun ope!" "Enu lo ni bi ti aje akara!" ("play game you amateur!" "All he can do is to talk like beans cake eater.")

However, both players showed some concentration counting the seeds and making sure that each set at their side of the board does not create opportunity for his opponent to take the winning seeds as he makes a round by dropping a seed from any of the set of pot at his side of the Opon. while continuing until it ends at his opponent's side with a pot or ports in a row or set, which ends with less than four seeds on a round which is the willing seeds and taking out of the pots by his opponent side of the board. And the men continue making jokes on each other as they play the game. Then the game become more intense after playing several rounds. However, they decide to get up for each side different players to play against each other representing Eko and Ijebuland. So after playing until late in the afternoon, the Eko players gain the upper hand and win the most of the games.

So the following day Kiyooku call Dada Obadina and asked him

"are the Eyo regalia preparations and the Oparun for the Opanbata ready?"

But Dada Obadina responds

"my Lord!" "The regalia is ready, but the Oparun is yet to be ready."

But Kiyooku still in the yesterday game excitement mode, was annoyed, shout, raising his voice and said

"how can you make the Oparun ready? When you were all busy watching the game of Ayo yesterday and had forget that you are just a slave, instead of concentrating on your job. Now you shall not have your usual mean in this house and not only you, with your other lazy fellows too."

Thereafter, some hours later when the Oparun had been brought in to the compound. Kiyooku said

"Olugoke!" "Come and watch how to carve and prepare the Oparun (palm tree branch) for the Opanbata (Eyo Masqurade walking stick)."

Then Kiyooku gave instruction to his slaves on how to make several types of the Opanbatas and also gave instructions to the boys in the compound how to sing, dance to the Eyo Masquerade, and dancing to the drums beats and the Ewi (Poetry or Rap) for the praise of the deity.

However, the song goes;

....

....

chorus:

Eyo O, Aye le Eyo O, Eyo O, Aye le Eyo O, Eyo O, Aye le Eyo O
Eyo bada ni ta to fi golu sere,
Awa ko ni sanwo Olibode odi ile,
Ki le tun gbe owo owo le tun gbe, ki ni mo fi se,
Aso lofi fi ra, Aso ki le ra? Gede Gede Oyinbo,
Etun jale Etun jale Opon Oyinbo,
O sere Olo Oba O sere Olo Oba.........,

....

....

Meanwhile, the excitement of the song and dancing was so great that the palace of the Olu of Eko Oba Oluwole become aware of it. And the Olu of Eko who was talking with some people in his palace heard the sweet melody of the song and the voice of excitements of the people, because more and more people from other compound join in as they heard it and saw the Eyo demonstrations. Then he said

"what has come into my city of Eko that I am not aware of it? Is there a new god in my land that I am not aware of?"

So he ordered his attendant

"go and investigate what is going on and bring me report, no one comes and bring some disturbance to Eko that would not be dealt with."

Then the attendant and some women came back to his palace and told him

"Oh!" "Kabiyesi o!" "Kabiyesi o!" "Kabiyesi o!" "It a good excitment that you would like to see too!" "It is a Masquerade of Ijebuland that is creating the excitement."

However, the report the Olu Oba Oluwole heard excite him too and he send word to Olugoke and Kiyooku

"I shall have to see the Eyo parade during the coming marriage between the Kiyooku son and Olugoke's daugther, which I am aware that Kiyooku has came from one of the Ijebuland towns for."

Thereafter, the marriage ceremony was very successful because of the Eyo Masquerades parade and presentations. And the Oba Oluwole became very much in love with the Masquerades that he requested from Kiyooku for his slaves to take part in the it and also beg for the Masquerades to stay in Eko. And Kiyooku who had thought his slaves would never like to stay in Eko. Said

"I cannot perform the Masquerades all by myself, so I cannot say no but if my slave Dada Obadina agrees to the request of the Oba all is well with me."

But to his surprise Dada Obadina who had been looking for the opportunity to leave the service of Kiyooku, who always use food as punishment for every offence, quickly responds as he prostrate before the Oba Oluwole,

"kabiyesi o!" "Kabiyesi o!" "I will be ready to come to your service as your slave instead of my present master, because I cannot continue serving him without food."

So the slave Dada Obadina and other slaves that took part in the Eyo Masquerade parade were sold to the Oba Oluwole. But the issue of losing his slaves and the Eyo Masquerades caused depression to Kiyooku and he died the next month in Lagos. Moreso, since then the Eyo Masquerades remains in the custodian of the Oba of Lagos as Ijebuland Masquerade, and it is being paraded in Lagos till this day.

However, the Eyo Masquerades and other trades from Ijebuland bring more unity between the people of Ijebuland and Lagos. In fact the people of Ijebuland dominate Eko, Isale-Eko and other areas like Mushin, which the Mushin market that comes from the Ijebu-Imushin which has the same praise:

Oni Imusin Aji lo,

Oni Imusin Alo do ru,

Also Ojota, Ketu, Somolu, Ikorodu, Epe, Ibeju, Leki, Aja, Alapere, and more, are cities of Ijebuland.

The events that lead to the Owiwi war

However, the Eyo Masquerade and trading in slaves have brought prestige and wealth to the Olu of Lagos Oba Oluwole and some other people in Lagos. And Dada Obadina who himself was as a born slave, had became very rich, popular and influential because the Eyo masquerade made people to fear him, and thought that he was a powerful voodoo man. Moreover, the white slave traders saw a very good opportunity in making him their tools for their night slave raids. So he had become a successful slave raider and had large number of slaves.

Then a Lagos Chief name Agoro who had brought some report to Oba Oluwole greets the Oba saying

"Kabiyesi o!" "Kabiyesi o!" "Kabiyesi o!"

prostrates and after exchange of greeting with the Oba, he continue.

"The Ijebuland warriors will not allow us passage through the interior at Ikorodu and other villages in Iperu, Ode-Remo, Isara, Ogere, Ibeju, Leki and more around Epe. Then Oba Oluwole who was very worried and disturbed that the white men had tricked him and other prominent Chiefs into the business of sending people to the interior land to raid for slaves, and they had threaten to kill their wives and children if the raiding stop.

Then one of the Chiefs, was crying, got up and said

"two of my children had been sold as slaves in America because of the last slave raids failed to produce the expected numbers of slaves the white men wants from us."

However, the discussion continue, as Dada Obadina came to the palace and after greeting the Oba and sat down, and One of the Chiefs said

"we can find out from the powerful Eyo Masquerade slave who is now the most successful slaves owner, to tell us the tricks he uses in getting his slaves."

Then Dada Obadina laugh and responds

"I have come to the palace since the opportunity has come for me to fight the Ijebus, for their arrogance and for not giving me the respect which I deserve."

Then the Oba Oluwole said

I heard that the white people had given you a lot of guns and gunpowder to enable you to raid for slaves more."

Dada Obadina responds

"yes!" "Kabiyesi o!" "I can now wage war on the Ijebuland!" "We should remember that the Ijebuland warriors had been destroyed at the war against the Egbas, so now is the time to put a stop to these Ijebuland supremacy and the Awujale Afesojoye telling everybody what to do should stop."

One of the chiefs said

"your word always make sense!" "You are surely very strong and knowledgeable of many things about these mysterious Awujale the Oba of these Ijebuland and his people."

However, the Oba Oluwole who was very jealous about the fame and influence of the Awujale Oba Afesojoye has over all the Obas and warriors everywhere said

"since you do know so much about the Awujale Oba Afesojoye, I bet you can also defeat him for us and since you even have their flamboyant Eyo Masquerades. We think you can defeat the Ijebus for us in Lagos."

Then One of the Chiefs said

"I wonder which wise Oba will leave such powerful Masquerades outside his land without looking for the down fall of his land."

Then Oba Oluwole got up from his throne raise the Irukere (white horse tail) in his hand, rolling it and said pointing to Dada Obadina,

"get up and come before me"

and Obadina went to the throne. Then Oba Oluwole add

"I pronounced you the one to conquer the Awujale and the Ijebuland warriors for us"

and the rest of the people respond

"Asee!" ("So shall it be!")

And with joy and jubinations, dancing to the musical instruments such as the agogo (a hand metal gong), gangan (talking drum), samba and more. And the masquerades of diffenrent types such as the Egunnu, Oro, Agere and more dance. Also the people dance both male and female and young girls with beads on their waist dance before the throne.

Thereafter, the following morning Dada Obadina got more weapons from the white merchants and the warriors of Lagos and Dada Obadina slaves that have being given months of military training by the Royal trade post military advisers and instructors. Join force with the Lagos warriors and they advanced on the Ijebu towns and villages raiding for slaves under the leadership of Dada Obadina. However, the villages and towns of Ijebuland such as Iperu, Isara, Ode-Remo, Ogere, warriors defend themselves gallantly, and after some days of fighting they send messenger to the Awujale Afesojoye Anikilara, who ordered the Olisa Adebote to call the Ogonis and the Apenas to go and defend the Ijebuland towns and villages. Then as the fight continue to being intensified, Obadina realized that the jebuland warriors were not yet finish as he had thought, and that they were very well trained and discipline than his own warriors or Army, and he said

"what kind human being are these Ijebus? That they are not even affected by all our fighting men gun powers."

Then after he saw that almost all the Lagos warriors had fallen and those few left were running away from camp. He order

"we shall have to surrender at this point before we all would be killed by this brutal Ijebuland warriors."

Moreover, when the fight was very close to where he was he shout "the surrender flag is to be carry up for the Ijebu warriors to see"

And he order

"you Oderinde!" "You are the leader of my guards follow me with your warriors to the white men boat and we shall have use it for our escape to the other side of the lagoon before the Ijebuland warriors destroy me"

However, when the boat got to otherside of the Lagoon he order

"where is the white flag? now raise it up for the Ijebuland warriors to see otherwise their boats would be over here before we know it!" "Yes if we surrender quick, the Ijebus would not fight when the opponent have surrender"

Moreso, they wave a white cloth on a stick. And when The Olisa Adebote saw the white flag, he order

"we shall stop our attack!" "the Eko warriors!" "Dada Obadina cowards!" "Have ran away and lucky for them they raise the white flag"

Then when the Olisa get to the palace of the Awujale Oba Afesojoye, he prostrate and said

"Kabiyesi o!" "Kabiyesi o!" "Kabiyesi o!" "I regret to tell you my Lord Kabiyesi that we cannot take the fight to the palace of the Olu Eko because they have beg us with their white flags, which is a bad thing before the gods to continue killing warriors who have surrender."

Thereafter, at Ijebu-Ode the Awujale Oba Afesojoye said

"thank you the Olisa Ijebuland Adebote!"

and he start praising the Olisa and singing the praise of the ancestors of the Ijebuland and all the warriors of Ijebuland. And he add

"you my warriors!"

and he stood up from the thrown and everybody prostrate before him and they were facing the ground and he add

"the Olisa Ijebuland Adebote!" "You have use your wisdom very well and the rest of the fight is now between me and the Olu Eko Oluwole."

Then the Olisa and the Warriors got up and everybody start to praise the ancestors of the Awujale Oba Afesojoye, and when the palace clown start to sing and the drummers start beating war songs. The Awujale Oba Afesojoye (Anikilaja Sa Ogun, Gbegande, Jagun to Gbe li ile to Jagun Eko) got up from his throne and move deep in his spirit as he walked into his inner chamber, and came back with two strange horns in his left hand and on his right hand, he had the big white horse tail and he walked out into the open space in the palace central yard and said

"Olu Eko!" "Olu Eko!" "Olu Eko!" "Oluwole! o" "Now hear my voice!" "And remain under the command of my voice!" "Now thunder!" "Thunderbolts!" "I send you this message, go to the household of the Olu Eko, visit the whole of the household of the Olu Eko and visit the whole of the household, do your work I order you to obey my command."

And instantly, thunderbolts struck, the sky became very dark and lighting appeared in the sky and moved in the direction of Lagos Island and struck the houses in the city of Lagos. Many houses were destroyed in Lagos and the whole of the palace of the Olu Eko and Oba Oluwole was destroyed in fire.

Then the following morning when the whole people in Lagos saw what had happened, and they enquired from their Ifa priests, who were afraid to talk or mention the name of the Awujale Oba Afesojoye, but told the remaining chiefs of Lagos alive and healthy

"we shall have to quickly send the Royal messengers to the Awujale Oba Afesojoye to beg for his forgiveness and request of him to forgive us in Lagos and for his Royal Majesty prayer that the gods shall forgive us and put a stop to the Sango (the god of thunder) from continuing to destroy us and the Eko (Lagos Island)."

However, the Awujale Oba Afesojoye was in his palace with the Olisa Adebote and some chiefs were having discussion about the next Agemo festival celebration, when the palace leading guard announced the request of some Ijebuland chiefs and prominent Ijebuland people who accompany the High delegates from Lagos to see the Awujale Oba Afesojoye. Then the Awujale raised his right hand and the Olisa signaled them to be allow to enter the palace. And when the Awujale Oba Afesojoye saw the High messengers from Eko, the Ijebuland Chiefs and some of the prominent Ijebus who lived in Lagos, and after they had paid homage to the him and they are still prostrating before him, he felt touch and sympathies with them and the predicament of Lagos. Then he order

"you can have your sit!" "I pray to the gods!" "And OLORUN-ELEDUMARE!" "Shall have pity on the household of the Olu Eko!" "So that the work of thunderbolt shall stop its destruction on the Olu Eko's household!"

And immediately the lighting struck, then the Awujale Oba Afesojoye summon the high chiefs of Imeba who were the Lagos emissary to effect his order on the Lagos situation.

Then the following day when the chiefs plead with the Awujale Oba Afesojoye, for the Lagos issue and the palace clown start to praise the Awujale Oba Afesojoye and his ancestors and praising the Nuhabi as a man of peace, the Awujale Oba Afesojoye anger came down and he summoned Chief Abiodun, who was also a priest of the god of thunder (Sango) and ordered

"you shall make a messenger of Agbo, a messenger of Kakanfo, Lapokun, and more and they shall be seven in number. And they shall be call 'Agbade Iko' and I mandate them to the palace of the Olu Eko to embark on administering propitiation rites on the palace and to remove the thunderbolt which I had earlier send and bring it to the palace here in Ijebu-Ode."

So they removed the thunderbolt and it was taken to Ijebu-Ode where it has been kept till date.

From then on, the people of Ijebuland and people in Lagos have become united in all purposes.

The Egbas, Owus, Egbados, settlements in Abeokuta towns and villages

After the Owiwi war and Owu wars about 1836

Meanwhile, the Egbas had not yet settled in Abeokuta but they were ready to move from Ibadan, and other towns and villages to their permanent settlement of their own. However, Chief Sodeke was sitting in his house and talking to some Egba Chiefs and Warlords and he said

"we have to take our destiny into our own hands again just like when we fought for our freedom from the Oyo empire when our leader and father chief Lisabi lead us. We have to put on our courage like brave warriors and show the Ijebus that we are not cowards and weak people."

One of the Chiefs name Oyekumi said

"thank you chief Sodeke!" "And my fellow Egba people present!" "We have been expecting a sitting like this since the last war. And I believe we conclude then that we shall acquire as much weapon of war as we can, and now we have been bless with more than what I don't think other ethnic around us could think of having. And we are ready and up to the task now for the fight with the Ijebuland before they would be able to have another Army. Since all of their warriors had been destroyed and killed in the last war."

However after more contributions from the warlords, Chief Sodeke said

"yes!" "We are ready!" "And with more than enough men of war!" "Because we have had peace which has given us enough time to prepare for the war against Ijebu."

Then Ayejorun laughing and he said

"you can rely on me to help in spying and getting all the informations about the Ijebus' movements, because I know my ways around the Ijebuland's towns and villages."

So Sodeke said to Ayejorun

"thank you! We will want you to guard our men into the towns and villages of the Ijebuland through the secret paths, since we cannot get to the gates and walls of Ijebuland."

Thereafter, on the day that they agreed that the war would begin, Sodeke called the warriors together, and they made sacrifice to their gods and had themselves group into different units under a warlord. Then they went through the secret paths to attacked Remo villages and towns farms, in Makun, Iperu, Ogere, Ode, Ipara, Isara and Ofin and attacked them. Some other small groups also attacked settlement under Ago-Meleki and those under Okun-Owa, up to Ayepe, Imota, Agboru and Ikosi market killing people. Two other divisions of their warriors enter Ijebu-Ode. But before the war started Ayeorun who was a double dealer had secretly sent word to the Ijebuland warlords and told them

"my Ijebuland warrior friends!" "You do not have to worry about the Egba attack for now!" "I would let you know when the attack would begin"

But the Ijebuland warlords called on the people and said

"we know this man call Ayeorun to be double dealer in his trade, we cannot rely on him to tell the truth so it would be better for us to prepared for the war with his Egba people now."

so they evacuate their young children, old women and men from the towns and villages to a secret location by the lagoon and made preparation for sudden attack of the Egbas.

Meanwhile, the Awujale Oba Afesojoye Anikilaya was having a meeting with some traders representatives of some Ijebuland women, when some people from Ijebu-Remo came to the palace crying and said

"Kabiyesi o!" "Kabiyesi o!" "Kabiyesi o!" "Oba wa!" "Ki Ade pe lori Oba!" "Ki bata pe lese Oba!" "Igba Odun Odun kan ni o Oba wa!"

prostrating before the thrown and they continue

"we are from the Ijebu-Remo province Awujale Oba wa o awon Egba ni o, Egba ti ko ogun wo Ile Ijebu o! Awujale o Oba wa egba wa o! (it is the Egbas, oh! Awujale (Emperor) the Egbas have attacked us in Ijebuland, please the Awujale come to our aid!")

Then the Olisa who was in a meeting with the Balogun Ijebu, the Apenas, the Ogbonis and other war-chiefs of the towns and villages that were not under attack and they are already at the palace when the massagers got there and had the message. And the warriors said what is wrong with this Egba people that make them to attack us at our home? We shall show them that Ijebuland is not a place to mess up in."

Then the Awujale Oba Afesojoye quickly order

"the meeting shall be continued by the chief in charge of trades."

And summon the Olisa,

so the Olisa greet the Awujale Oba Afesojoye and present the reports on the war plans put in place by the Balogun Ijebu, the Apenas, Ogbonis and other warlords of Ijebuland. And he said

"some of the details of the plan is that since the attacks are in several place, and the Egbas are already inside the walls, we shall have to trick the them and allow them to to enter more while we will be retreating to Eredo."

And pointing on the ground which have some objects that he used as the model, the Olisa continues

"at Imoye!" "We shall stop them, after they must have shot all their gun powers, and we have observed their strengths, and positions."

Then one of the warrior messengers said

"Kabiyesi o Oba wa!" "The Egbas are using the new type of guns which the white people just supply, since they have been having the white people in their new settlements."

Then the Olisa responds

"In that case, we shall call on our ancestors of Ijebuland and warriors to blind their sense of directions by using the 'Obrin-Ojowu' and the 'Okunrin-Ojowu' (the female and male deities). So that when they shot their guns, they will be shooting to different directions and not at us or our camps or formations."

So the Awujale Oba Afesojoye order

"you my warlords and warriors!" "Shall stay confident!" "And keep hiding at your various assign places, posts and let the deities make them to be more furious and shot all their guns and to almost exhaust their supply of gunpowder before the Olisa shall order the trumpets of attack on this stubborn Egba warriors."

Then the Awujale Oba Afesojoye stood up from his throne, very angry and look upward and face them and he continue,

"I cannot believe the Egbas will be so careless and stupid to pay me back like this. So they think it was by their power or the effort of their guns and the strength of their warriors that made them to be victorious in the last war? I cursed those stubborn warriors so as to prevent the Egba villages and towns not to be destroyed, because of Igbore and Ake in Abeokuta which is our towns and other villages in Abeokuta. So they think they can attack my home, my towns and villages. I shall show them what Ijebu is. As from today and this moment the Egbas shall no longer be able to wage and win any major war again. Their courage as a people shalll not be strong enough for them to come together again to fight, except in minor raiding and violence."

Then the Ijebuland Army match and defend all the villages and towns of Ijebuland, and the Olisa warlords and warriors camp at Eredo and placed the Obirin-Ojowu and the Okurin-Ojowu deities at the middle of the town. However, the Egba Army had came together and decide to continue their massive attack on all the rest of the villages and towns of Ijebuland. Thereafter, when the deities' effects got to them they start shooting their guns upward and at different directions without any coordination and sense of purpose, because their warriors with guns saw the Ijebuland warriors by mirage and they shot at the fake images, while the Ijebuland warriors shot at them and killed them. And they killed them with their archers arrows which had poisonous war head and guns. And most of Egbas had been killed, but Sodeke who also had some charms was able to noticed that the Ijebuland warriors were not affected by their gun powers and most of his warriors had been killed by the Ijebu warriors guns, archers and marks men. Then he said

"we have to quickly find a way of escape since we do not understand what kind of power these Ijebu people are using, that is making all our gun powers not be having any effect on them. We had shot almost all our gunpowder and it has have no effect on them, and they have been killing us."

So the Egbas retreat and they ran away, and the Ijebuland warriors were about to pursue them, but the Olisa order

"blow the trumpet of retreat" "blow the trumpet of retreat"

and the Ijebu warriors stop running after them. And the Olisa said

"the Awujale Oba Afesojoye had told us not to pursue them since they live close to Igbore and Ake in Abeokuta. We don't want to attack our people there too in the process of taking the fight to their new settlement."

Thereafter, when the Olisa and the warriors went back to the palace, and the Awujale thanked them and praise the ancestors of the Ijebuland, and he said "you all my people!" "Did very well for not pursing the stubborn and foolish Egbas!" "To their villages and towns which is close and within Abeokuta that it is our farm lands before and our people live there. And since we have allowed them to settle down close to us, we have to show wisdom and not attack them because he that throws stones in the market should be ready to take care, should the stone wound some members of his own family or his household sustains injury."

Thereafter when the reports of the war effects and damages got the Awujale Oba Afesojoye. He order

"We shall ensure that the people attacked are relocated to the land by the lagoon side and this shall increase the settlements at the Ijebu water side."

However since then the Egbas had not been able to go to a major war on their own but they will have to fight on the side of the Ijebuland.

Mainwhile, the majority of the Egbas settled close to the Ijebus in Ibadan, and the Basorun Oyo Oluyole and the Balogun Oyo who had made Oke Ibadan their settlement always raid the Egba farms at nights for slaves and foods. Then Sodeke made enquiry from the Bale and Olu at Igbore and other villages and towns in Abeokuta,

"can we make here our home settlement, and closeby you since we realized that the place is safe?"

However the land was safe not just because of the big rock call Olumo, but because whenever the Oke Ibadan worriors attacked the place and they tried to starve the people with hunger by cutting of the supply of foods and destroying their farms. But the Igbore and Ake and the area close to her were save because of the Ijebuland Army had being protecting the place from the Oke Ibadan Army and the Dahomy attacks.

So they recieved responds from the Olus and Bales at Igbore and Ake

"Oh yes!" "The lands here which we call Abeokuta are good for farming and save for your people to settle in. We are decsendant of the Awujale and the land closeby Abeokuta is always protected by the Ijebu warriors."

Then Chief Sodeke lead the Egbas to the closeby Ake and Igbore and the place is call Abeokuta and they made Abeokuta their permanent home till date, and eventually more of Oyo towns and villages war refuges also settle at Abeokuta. But some Ijebu youths were not happy to see the Egba warlords living among them at Ipara and Idi Ogungun, so they confront them and an Egba chief name Lamodi who thought he could live in Ipara because it is a market town of the Ijebuland and traders from all places come there to trade said

"since we have pay our toll gate fees I am free to stay in Ipara, and with my voodoo and my guards I should be able to protect myself from anybody."

But after continous trouble from the Ijebu youths, he realized that these youths would bring more trouble for him with the Ijebuland Army. Then told his guards

"we will have to leave Ipara and go to Ibadan because of these stubborn Ijebu youths, which we cannot even beat not to talk of fight with their Army."

Then he moved his warriors from Ipara and Idi Ogungun to Ibadan where most of the Egba people were taking refuge. However, some of these Chiefs: Apati, Ogunbona, Osa, Gbewiri are his followers.

Moreover, Ogundipe who had settled in Abeokuta became a successful blacksmith and he send word message to the Egbas in Ibadan and other place to come and settle in Abeokuta. Meanwhile also in Ibadan, Lamodi who cannot stand the continuous harassments of the Oke Ibadan warlords on them anymore got into argument with them. And he said

"if you fools would not stop harassing my people I would have to do something about it. I have my own voodoo and powers with warriors, how can we be running away from your oppression and now want to attack us here which close to Ibadan, I suppose the settlement allowed you Oyos is at Oke Ibadan."

Then when one of the Oke Ibadan chiefs heard what he said he became mad and ordered

"the Egba homes and farms to be raid, these Egba people met us here in Oke Ibadan, and we think they are under the protection of the Awujale Oba Afesojoye so we let them to stay in Ibadan which is part of Ijebuland where we cannot raid. So who is this one call Lamodi staying outside of the Ibadan close to Oke Ibadan away from the Ijebus and he dear us? We shall make sure that him and his followers serve us as our slaves afterall they are Egbas and here is not Egba-Ile."

However, when Chief Lamodi heard what the Chief said he took his gun and shot him and he died. Moreover, when the Egbas realized that the Chief he had shot was an Ife man they were very afraid, and the Egbas living close to Oke Ibadan outside of Ibadan which is part Ijebuland ran to Abeokuta. But the Ife warriors and the Oke Ibadan warriors pursued them and when they met them at a place close to Abeokuta, they said to them

"we know we cannot attack you here now, but we want Lamodi to come out to face his punishment for the rule of death for death, and we are sure that the Awujale Oba Afesojoye will not be mad with us for this reason."

So Lamodi got out and they shoot him several time until his charm became weak and he died. But the rest of the Egba people continue on their journey to Abeokuta and made home there. Then Abeokuta since 1830s, become the home of the Egba refuges and other Oyo people. And these villages are where they settlemented:

1. **Egba Abeyin:**
   Ake, Ijeun, Kenta, Imo, Igbore and they are under the leadership of the Bale Ake.

2. **Egba Agura:**
   Agura (Gbagura), Ilugun, Ojoho, Ika, and more and they are under the leadership of the Bale of Gbagura.

3. **Egba Oke Ona**: Oko, Ikija, Ikereku, Idomapa, Odo, Podo and they are under the leadership Bale of Osile.

Meanwhile, Chief Sodeke was the main leader that has most influence to bring them together whenever the needs arise. And there was no single individual as their leader such as Olu or Oba, so the warlords of Oke Ibadan and the Alafin made jokes about the Egbas saying

"Egba ko loba gbo won lo se bi oloba"

("the Egbas does not have a central authority such as king or Prince, but all their Bales (Majors) try to make themselves assume the ranks of Oba/ king.")

And Chief Sodeke die in 1844 and the whole Egba and Abeokuta mourn for him as their leader.

Ijebu and Egba Relationship

However, before the death of Chief Sodeke there was always confrontation by some Ijebu youths against the Egbas, because they cannot understand why the Awujale Oba Afesojoye prevent them from attacking the Egbas. Then Chief Sodeke called the Egba youths and told them

"it is not appropriate to make war on your neighbors!" "We and the Ijebus are now one!" "So we should not fight the Ijebuland anymore."

And some warlords said to them

"you young children!" "You know the Ijebuland warriors are not easy to defeat in war."

And Chief Sodeke also add

"since we have taken refuge here in Abeokuta!" "Which have been peaceful because of Igbore, Ake and the villages around cannot be attack by the

Ijebuland warriors, the Dahomy, and the Oke Ibadan warriors raiding for slaves are not allow to attack Abeokuta by the Ijebuland Army so we are safe here."

Then after some years, the Egbas discovered that an Egba man who lived in Ijebuland call Kusoro had been given a chieftaincy title by the Awujale Oba Afesojoye, because of his good conducts among the Ijebuland traders. So Chief Sodeke and other Egba Bales, Chiefs and warlords invite Kusoro and they told him

"we would like to make peace with the Ijebuland, and what can we do to make peace with them and the Awujale Oba Afesojoye?"

Then Chief Kusoro thank them and said

"you have make the right decision because the Awujale Oba Afesojoye! Is a man of peace and honor."

One of the warlord said

"why did the Ijebu warriors attacked us after the Owu war? If the Awujale is a man of peace as you just said"

Another warlord who was younger than the previous one said

"after all, we heard that our fathers defeated the Ijebus before!" "So why can't we come together now and to stop these Ijebus and their Awujale?"

Chief Kusoro laugh and responds

"my young warrior!" "Egba meji ki jara wa ni iyan!" "Afi bawa!" "Ki o gba tami mo gba ti e o!" ("We Egbas have no custom of argument with each other!" "But we put argument to a stop by saying we just have to agree!" "If you will not understand me, I will try and understand you!") Then Sodeke said

"ba wa!" ("yes of course!")

And he look at the warriors face smile and add,

"when we fought them the last time, almost all our warriors were killed by the Ijebu guns and archers arrows which had powerful poison, while we cannot not see the Ijebus shooting at us not to talk of killing them."

Chief Kusoro and everyone in the meeting said

"ba wa!"

Then Chief Kusoro add

"so we have realize that war against the Ijebu is not the solution, but the way out is peace that comes from dialog."

And he smile and look at Chief Sodeke and other elders' face, as if seeking approval before continuing and add

"in that the battle we thought we had won the Ijebuland!" "Was fought by very few Ijebu warriors that attacked us because they were stubborn and refused to obey the order of Awujale Oba Sotejoye who join his ancestors after one year after his coronation. So the next Awujale Oba Afesojoye followed his policy of no attack on Abeokuta because of Igbore is a land first settle on by Asa who was Omo Oba Obirin (Princess) of the Awujale Oba Jadiara Agbolaganju who came from Ijebu-Ode and took a warlord call Afonta Modi as her husband with her. That is the reason we have the Oriki (poetry) of Igbore and Ake:

"Asa ara!"

"Igbore Omo Awujale!"

"Oba Ganju!"

"Jadiara,!"

"Afota Modi."

Then all the people present said

"so that is why they did not followed us to these area!" "During the last war!" "But they blew the trumpets of retreat."

Furthermore Kusoro adds

"we were able to defeat those foolish!" "And disobedient warriors then because the Awujale Oba Afesojoye!" "Had pronounced curse on his warriors that attacked the areas closeby Abeokuta, in which we Egbas settle. So due to that curse those warriors kill themselves, by attacking each other and cut off each other's heads."

Cheif Sodeke said

"no wander we just saw all the heads of the Ijebu warriors' head cut off from their bodies, and the Oke Ibadan warriors were also dead and the rest running away. And we took their guns and ran after them and killed most of them, thinking that our gods had fought for us that day."

Then Chief Kusoro said

"we lost the last battle against the Ijebuland after initially having the upper hand, when the Awujale Oba Afesojoye said he regret that we Egbas attacked him and after then he placed cursed on us that we shall now always lose in any major campaign we go to."

Then the people at the meeting become afraid and said

"what can be done to reverse the curse?"

Chief Sodeke responds

"it will be difficult to reverse the curse of the Awujale, but I appreciate your efforts trying to beg the Awujale Oba Afesojoye on our behalf."

And the chiefs and all the warlords said

"we have to make peace with the Ijebuland and try to beg the Awujale so that the curse can be reverse."

However Chief Sodeke told chief Kusoro

"since you are an Oloye ni Ijebu (an Ijebu Chief), appointed by the Awujale Oba Afesojoye we would like to send you to him that all the Chiefs and people of Egba beg for his pardon and forgiveness for our mistakes."

Thereafter, some months at the Awujale palace the leading palace guard announced

"Kabiyesi o!" "Kabiyesi o!" "Kabiyesi o!" "Oba wa to gba ido bale gbogbo Oba!" "Ka Ade ko pe lori Oba wa!" "Ki Bata ko pe lese Oba wa!" "Igba Odun!" "Odun kan ni o Oba wa!"

while he prostrates and he said

"I announce the presence of Chief Kusoro."

when the Awujale Oba Afesojoye was having a meeting with some warlords. Thereafter the Olisa lead Chief Kusoro and the Egba Chiefs to the thrown and the Awujale Oba Afesojoye received then and they paid homage to him.

And Chief Kusoro said

"Kabiyesi o!" "Kabiyesi o!" "Kabiyesi o!" "Thank you for your love and fatherly role in keeping all of us save in Ijebuland and beyond, including Abeokuta and Ibadan. I have had some serious discussions with my people of Egba and they have send their delegates which is head by Chief Sodeke to come and beg for Royal Majesty forgiveness and pardon and also to pay you homage, because they have realized it is because of your protection that we have been able to stay peacefully in Abeokuta."

Then the Awujale Oba Afesojoye summon awon Omo Oba (the Princes), awon Omo Oba Obirin (the Princess), the Olisa, the Obas, the Balogun Ijebu and other prominent Apenas, the Ogbonis and other Chiefs to be in the meeting at the palace. Thereafter, the Egba delegates were called into the palace and they pay homage to the Awujale and they had discussions with the Olisa and all the Warriors of Ijebuland on issues of war and peace terms, so when they had reach an agreement, and the Olisa present it to the Awujale who pronounced it into law. Then the Awujale Oba Afesojoye said

"thank you Chief Kusoro!" "I am bless to have someone like you as a child.

no Ijebuland warrior or any Ijebu person shall ever disturb your settlements in Abeokuta and the surrounding, including Ibadan and every place where the Ijebu people have settlements."

And laughing, shaking the Orukere (the white horse tail) and add

"from now on the Ijebu and Egbas shall be cousins by the order of the Omo Oba Obirin (Princess) Asa the daughter of the Awujale Oba Jadiara Agbalaganju!"

And he stood up, then imediately everbody prostrate and not looking upward and they said "Kabiyesi o!" "Kabiyesi o!" "Kabiyesi o!" "Alaye Luwa!" "Oba wa Igba Ikeji Orisa!"

And he raised the Irukere up and add

"we Ijebus, Igbore, Ake and other villages in the Abeokuta districts shall have similar three birth marks."

So it becomes official for child born in Abeokuta and other Egbas to have three birth marks on their face just like the Ijebus. However, since then till today Ijebus and Egbas refers to each other as cousins saying "Omo Iye ra a wa" (we are related by of the same Princess).

Egbado Tribes about 1836

Meanwhile, Egbado were part of the Oyo empire and were subjects of the Alafin Oyo, and they were lead by Chief Dekun who called all the

Egbado chiefs, Bales and warriors in Oyo empire to a secret meeting and he said

"thank you all!" "For coming to my house, but before we discuss the main issue let us worship our gods and take a secret vow that everything we say or do will not be reveal to the Alafin Atiba and non-Egbado person."

And all of them said

"we are ready to take the vow, and we are ready to stand as one family to gain our freedom too like Egbas have done."

And one of the Chiefs said

"to tell the Alafin or a non-Egbado of our meeting means death to all of us including the person that even inform the Alafin."

Then Chief Dekun said

"It looks like we are ready to have the vow then and we can be able to fight for our freedom as a family."

Then a ram was killed and everybody in the meeting made a cut in their left hands, and mix their blood with that of the ram and they drank it. Thereafter Chief Dekun said

"the yoke of Oyo is too heavy and we cannot continue to be rule by our cousins and pay for their ostentations way of life, when we find it very difficult to eat regularly and take care of our needs."

And the rest of the people stood up clap their hands and said

"you have said it all!" "you have said it all!"...

and they start praising their ancestors. Then they all sat down had discussion about breaking away from the Oyo empire. And Chief Dekun said "you all know that I am an Olu and I will be leaving for Oke Olu soon."

One of the warriors said

"so it already three years?"

And he add

"you can now enjoy your 10 youngest wives and all your properties in Oke Olu, free of all the problems we will be facing here."

Another warrior said

"so that is a good thing? What about the other wives that he will have to leave behind? I would rather continue living the life of a warrior and can leave any where I want than to been forced to live in Oke Olu."

The the discussion about Oke Olu continue for some time until Chief Dekun said

"thank you all for your sympathy about me and Oke Olu."

Then he wait for their side comments to reduce and he raise his hand and they look at his direction and he continue

"we do not have to be forced to live where we don't want to live, and to take just 10 of our wives and leave the rest. Who can tell awon Omo Oba ati awon Omo Oba Obirin bi won o se ma gbe aye won (the Royal Princes and the Princess what to do?")

And everybody said

"nobody can do that, the person that ever try it will be used to make sacrifice to the gods."

Then they continue to talk and discuss on how to break away from the Oyo empire. However, they decide to kill the Alafin Ilaris taking taxes and levy in their towns and villages. And they all agreed that the revolt should start now, saying

"ti ise ko ba peni a kin pe ise (let get it done now.")

Thereafter they organized themselves on how to get the killing done in Ijana and all towns and villages in Egbado. And the revolution continue for many years until they gain their freedom.

However the war with the Oyo empire Army become too tough for the Egbado and eventually the Oyo Army was able to stop their rebellion, but Chief Dekun was able to escape and he took refuge with the King of Dahomy. In fact about 13000 of the Egbados join him in Dahomy and he became very rich. But after many years Chief Dekun join the slave raiding warriors of Oke Ibadan and on one of the raid, he got into a fight with one of the Oyo warriors who recognized him as one of the rebellious Egbado warriors and report him to the Alafin's guards at Oyo, and he was arrested and taken to the Alafin Atiba palace. Then the Oyomesi charged him as a rebel, a traitor and publicly execute him at a market place.

CHAPTER 9

Founding of Modakeke about 1836

Meanwhile, the Fulani had become the ruler in Ilorin after Afonja's death. Then using Jihad as excuse, they wage wars, campaigns and conquered towns and villages in the Northern part of the Oyo empire. However, the refuges escaped to the Southern part of Oyo, and some settle in Ile-Ife except in Ife town which is the capital town of Ile-Ife, because the people of Ife did not allow them to stay in the town. So they settle in these following places: Moro, Ipetumode, Oduabon, Yakioyo, Ifa-lende, Sope, Waro, Ogi, Apomu and Ikire. Under the protection of the Owoni Ile-Ife, Oba Akinmoyero. And the most prominent of the refuge Chiefs was Chief Asiro who was the Oba of Irawo, and he would always tell the youths

"you my children!" "We shall make peace with the Ife people who are now lording over us because we cannot get into war with the Ife Army, when the Oyo Army are also after us."

So the refuges took jobs as hewers of woods, drawer of water for the Ife people, moreover the Ife youths continued to be restless and want to attack the refuges in their towns and villages saying

"they have to work for us as our slaves, because why do we have to give them land to stay and also protect them from the Alafin warriors for nothing?"

But the Owoni Ife, Oba Akinmoyero ordered his Army

"I demand of the Army to put a stop to the Ife youths' agitations and anyone among them that refused to go home to his parent and stop making trouble shall be put in jail and dealt with."

Thereafter the youths were beaten and put in prison which made most of them go into hiding, and later quietly return home and those in prison were released. Moreso, the Ife youths got into fight with the refuge youths and murder Chief Asirawo, but the refuges elders and the warriors of Ife put a stop to the fight, and they install Asirawo's son, Ojo Akitikori as their leader. Furthermore, some months after, the Ijesa slave raiding warriors start raiding farms in Ile-Ife, and the refuges join force with the warriors of Ile-Ife, and they killed most of them and stand their ground to prevent the raiding. Then, the reigning Owoni Oba Gbegbaaje, become nice to the refuges and the people of Ife also accept them more in their communities and they become friends. But some of the Ife people did not like the refuges getting close to them, arguing that.

"they would become trouble maker later and it is because they made trouble in Oyo that result to their beeing driven away."

Meanwhile, the Ife people killed the Owoni Oba Gbegbaaje, and after the installation ceremony of the Owoni Oba Adegunle, whose mother was from one of the refuges town, and who took precaution against his people killing him by acuminating ammunitions, suppressed the Ife people and killed the murders of his predecessor. Thereafter, the Owoni invite Wingbolu who was the leader of the refuges warriors to his palace to have discussion. Then when Wingbolu got to the palace he greets the Oba saying

"Kabiyesi o!" "Kabiyesi o!" "Kabiyesi o!" "Alaye luwa!" "Oba Ile-Ife!" "Ife Oduduwa!" "Kabiyesi o!"

The Oba Adegunle told him

"sit down and let us discuss how to bring peace to Ile-Ife and bring our people together as one Yoruba people and as cousin whom we are"

And after the discussions they reached a conclusion that the refuges need to have their own separate settlement as one community outside the wall of Ile-Ife under a ruler who would be under the Owoni Oba Adegunle and they shall also have to pay homage to the Owoni. So the Owoni order

"I hereby make a proclamation that the refuges be given a settlement outside the wall of Ife town and confer the title of 'Ogunsuwa' (one whom Ogun (god of war) has blessed with a fortune) on Wingbolu as the leader of the refuges towns and villages in the settlement. And the refuges called the settlement 'Modakeke' (meaning we remain peaceful here),"

and the title of "Ogunsuwa" remains the title of Olu Modakeke. And by 1884 Modakeke population had become 50,000 to 60,000, but Modakeke has not been independent from Ile-Ife.

Ilorin Empire drive and disintegration of the Oyo empire

Prince Atiba about 1840

Prince Atiba was a son of the Alafin Abiodun. His mother fled after his father's death, when he was a child to her own town, because the Alafin had some quarrel with her. Though she was a slave at Gudugbu, which was a small hostage village of the Alafin Oyo. So Alafin Abiodun did not pay much attention to Atiba's mother until one day when her friend from Gudugbu came to visit her, the friend went to the palace and ask for the king's wife, which was very unusual. And the Alafin Abiodun was informed

"Kabiyesi o!" "Kabiyesi o!" "Kabiyesi o!" "There is a strange woman looking for one the Olori (Queens)."

The Alafin Abiodun become curious and order

"let the woman to come before me and tell me what is her business with my Oloris."

Then the woman greets the Oba and she said

"Kabiyesi o!" "Kabiyesi o!" "Kabiyesi o!" "kade pe lori ki bata pe lese Oba!"
"Mo yi ika otun o!" "Mo yi ika osi o!" ("the unquestionable o!", … "Let
the Royal crown remains and Royal shoes remains I lay down by my right
side, and lay down by my left side.")

The Alafin Oba Abiodun responds

"Are you not afraid to come here and enquire for my wife? Suppose I add
yourself to the harem or kill you or sell you?"

She responds

"for my friend's sake I am prepare to undergo any treatment and if your
Majesty make a wife of me, I shall be happy as my friend and we will be
able to see each other every day."

So the Alafin Abiodun was very impress by her courage and allowed her
to stay in the palace with her friend. However, after some months, her
friend became pregnant and the Alafin Abiodun send his wife and her
away to Gudugu and made both of them his representative of a province
and Gudugu become the capital. So the two friends were made the ruler of
the province and the Alafin Abiodun allowed them to visit him regularly.
Meanwhile, there were several Ilaris (Ministers) and a Eunuch working for
the Queen, and the Alafin Abiodun order the Bale of Gudugu to see to the
welfare of the Queen. Then the Queen gave birth to a son and name him
Atiba and also her friend had a son call Onipede. Thereafter, when Prince
Atiba was about 18 years of age, Prince Atiba and his mother return to
Oyo town. Moreover, Prince Atiba become very popular because he was
a good warrior and was successful in military campaigns. However, some
quarrels took place between Prince Atiba and some Princes in Oyo town,
and Prince Atiba made some remarks for which he was misquoted to the
Alafin Aole who became very mad with him. But luckily, his mother was
in the palace and heard the whole thing, so she quickly told her son and
they fled from Oyo town.

Moreoever, after some years Prince Atiba had grown up to be a strong powerful warlord. And he inherits his father's properties and had his attributes of leadership. Meanwhile, he lived with his uncle from his mother side call Akeitan, who trained him in the ways of the warriors. And he had his own slave raiding campaigns, but his uncle adviced him to move away from Oyo so as not to raid them because as a Royal Prince of the Oyo empire it would not be good for him to hurt his own people and make their lives difficult, so Prince Atiba moved to Oja and continue his kidnapping expeditions there. However, he kidnap people of tribes which include the Egbas in the Oke-Ogun districts near Sogaun. Actually, the Egbas were so simple in nature that when Prince Atiba lead an expedition to their villages where he raid and got some people, and he noticed that some warlords had also came to raid for slaves in that area, then he ordered his warriors to follow him and pursued them. But one of his warriors said

"my lord! Are we going to leave this slaves here without putting them in prison?"

But he responds

"they will not escape before we come back,"

but the people captured respond

"we will be here waiting for you our Lord Prince! Until you're back or where can we run away to from an Oyo Prince?"

Then Prince Atiba said

"let us leave my sword here, it belongs to my father and I am sure that every warrior will be able to recognize my father's symbol in it and honor the Alafin,"

then they left the people and pursued the warlords. And when the Warlords saw Prince Atiba and his warriors and also noticed that the way the warrior rides his horse appears like that of Royalty of the Alafin, they said "we have to be careful because this warrior coming looks like an Alafin Prince,"

and they slow down and wait for the rider to catch up with them. Then Prince Atiba order

"you warlords stop right there or all of you shall be in trouble"

and when he got the them he said

"why are you raiding for slaves in my territory? I am Prince Atiba son of the Alafin Abiodun."

Then the Warriors looked more closely at him and saw the mark of the prince of Alafin Oyo in his face and they quickly got down from their horses and said

"Kabiyesi o!" "Kabiyesi o!" "Kabiyesi o!" "Please we do not have the intention of competing with you Kabiyesi!" "We will now tell all our friends that you are around here."

And Prince Atiba responds

"I am not mad with any of you so you can go."

Then Prince Atiba rode his horse in the other direction that he had came and his warriors followed him, while the warlords and their warriors remain on their kneels as they rode away.

And when they got to the place where the people they had been captured were, they were still sitting on the floor. Then Prince Atiba order

"put rope on their necks and legs and walk them to my compound."

So this was the nature of the Egba people, whenever a warlord captured them all he needs to do is to put his cap or sword by the people and whenever any warlord comes to kidnap them they will show him that they had already been taken by anthor warlord, and this is his cap or sword and they will remain there until he comes back. However, Prince Atiba became every successful, more powerful, rich, famous and he commits a lot of acts of violence and extortion with impunity because of his high birth position. Eventually the country was in anarchy and confusion, and Prince Atiba had lawless men that were fugitives who had ran away because they had refused to pay their debts, and slaves who had desert their masters that he raids and made them his slaves. So this made him to become very rich and had slaves that behave like the Jamas in the days of Afonja of Ilorin. In Actual fact, Prince Atiba had the following chiefs as his followers and supporters: Aderinko, Ladejibi, Olumole, Oluwaje, Losa, Oluwaiye, Adefumi, Lakonu, Toki, Maje, Falade and Gbenla. And he also had these slaves who had horses: Eni-d' Olorun (who later become the Apeka), Galajmo, Otelowo and Ogboinu who was his trumpeter.

However, some years later the Ilorin had imposed their Moslem religion on many towns and villages in the Northern part of the Oyo empire. And the people were forced to change their names so as to reflect their Moslem religion by terrorizing them, and killing those who refuse to accept the new religion and also those that refuse to change their names, but the people that resist the Ilorin religion call it "Imo lile", "awon oni imole" (the religion of forceful imposition). Meanwhile, Omo Oba Atiba made a campaign against the Ilorin warriors and he rode his horse through a river when his horse was shot, in his escape, because he could not swim, but his childhood friend Onipede just rode pass him without giving him a helping hand. And Omo Oba Atiba call on him and said

"Onipede!" "Onipede!" ... "Here I am!" "Are you leaving me behind to perish?"

But luckily Omo Oba Atiba's uncle who was closeby saw him as he struggles in the water and offered to help him. But Omo Oba Atiba who was very angry refused his help, but when his uncle called Yusuf who was a good swimmer insist, he accept and Yusuf assist him and his horse to safety on the other side of the river. Then Onipede who was riding the horse bought for him by Atiba made a joking remark when Atiba meet him and he said

"The intrepid warrior that you are, I did not know that a river current could conquer you."

But Atiba showed no sign of being hurt by his action and said no word to him. But he said to himself

"so Onipede has no love for me and he did not even care if I die."

In fact, Onipede continued to enjoy the privilege of being close to Prince Atiba and makes himself to feel more important, he would say whatever he likes and does whatever he wants without even asking or minding if it was Ok with Prince Atiba or not. And he continue to use his relationship with Atiba to influence his own advantage and made all foreigners living in Ago-Oja to be under his own protection and took money from them. He also made the people to give him respects and treatments as a Prince, he would always had a large entourage consisting of large people walking and horsemen everywhere he goes in towns and farms. Also Onipede would order

"everybody shall have to see me before going to the Prince palace."

And made himself of equal status with Prince Atiba, and said

"I am equal and co-partner with Omo Oba Atiba."

But in actual fact, he was not of equal to any of Atiba's war-chief or any of his noble slave. Then eventually after returning from the unsuccessful campaign against Ilorin, Omo Oba Atiba order

"everybody shall work quickly to build a fortify wall against the expected invasion of our enemy Ilorin. We do not want to be exposed and makes it easy for them to attack us suddenly"

So everybody including Atiba's great warlords were digging a trench around the town. But Onipede came to where they were working, being carried shoulder high by his servants and he was making funny jokes. Then Omo Oba became very angry and order

"Onipede!" "Oma ti e go o!" "Ati pe o ni ife awon eniyan ati awa Oyo rara!" "O si ri akiti yan wa nipa rogbo diyan ogun Ilorin. O ya bole ki o mu oko, ko ma gbe koto, ta no fi ara re pe gan? (you are so stupid!" "And foolish!" "And disrespectful of human being!" "And you are not Loyal to Oyo!" "Here we are working to defend against the Ilorin invasion, now get down into the pit and start digging like others, and who are your equal?")

So Onipede who had never done such work before cannot cope, his hands become sore with blister. But when he continues with his arrogance and Atiba cannot stand it anymore he ordered Onipede to be killed.

Thereafter, Omo Oba Atiba become the most powerful person and more powerful than the Alafin and everybody looks up to him as the person to save the country from the yoke of the Ilorin Fulanis. And Omo Oba Atiba told his warlords

"we need to find a way to get rid of this Alafin Oluewu who is not doing anything about this Ilorin invasion of Oyo empire's towns and villages. Or are we going to just fold our hands and sleep until Ilorin makes Oyo her subject?"

Also the people were complaining about the excessive luxurious life of the people at the palace while they were suffering. So Prince Atiba invite the most two powerful war-chiefs in the kingdom who were chief Oluyole in Oke Ibadan and promised him the title of the Basorun (Prime Minister), and Chief Kururmi in Ijaye and promised him the title of the Are Kakanfo. However, the war with Ilorin become very strong and the ancient capital of Oyo (Oyo-Ile) fell to the Ilorin and the Alafin Oluewu was killed. Then the Oyomesi offered the crown to Laguade, who declined it and said

"thank you the Oyomesi!" "And my people of Oyo!" I shall advice that the Alafin position should be offered to the powerful and war spirit minded Prince Atiba of Ago Oja. Prince Atiba will be capable of leading the country to conquer the Ilorin Fulanis and save us."

So Prince Atiba accept the offer as the Alafin and said

"I have accept the Oyo and the Oyomesi with the mandate to lead and safe my people now taking refuges in Saki, Gboho, Kihisi, Ilorin and other places."

Then Prince Lajide, the son of Onsolu and Fabiyi with 32 other messengers entourage were sent by the Oyomesi to invite him to Oyo town the capital. But Prince Atiba said

"you the entourage of the Alafin and the guest shall have to stay in Ago until the end of my coronation and I shall conferred on you Prince Lajide the title of Ona'sokun Ago."

So Ago was taken out the hand of the Bale Ago's family and become the Royal city of the new Oyo empire and no more call Ago-Oja, but Oyo because the Alafin Atiba now resides there. Thereafter the people said "Ago-d'Oyo" (Ago which become Oyo), and is the present city of Oyo. However, Ago-d'Oyo was a very small town in comparison with the ancient city of Oyo (Oyo-Ile). So the Alafin Atiba order

"all the villages and towns of Oyo-Ile and closeby shall be depopulated and their inhabitants be transported to the my new Oyo city."

Then the people of Akeitan, Apara, Idobe, Ajagba, Seke, Gurudu, Jabata, Ojomgbodu and more, the people that are within 10 to 20 miles from Ago were tansported.

"E a se were ki won ma ha fi wa le lo (please hurry up before we will be left behind),"

Adebimpe told her children when the warriors who were to lead them out of their towns to the new capital city were calling on them to come out and be ready to go to the new town. She and the other parents were hurrying and dragging their children out as they walk to the market place. And he Warlord in charge said

"you don't have to be afraid, we have not come to kidnap anybody, we are here following the orders of our new Alafin, Alafin Atiba who wants people in your towns and villages to come and live close to his new palace."

So the people were very happy and the drummers beats the talking drums and the singers sang songs praising the Alafin Atiba and the ancestors of the Alafin Oyo and the gods. Then they march the people to their various new homes making sure they had their goats, chickens, the seeds for planting crops and other animals with them as they left their present home for their new home. However, the Alafin Atiba said

"thank you all my efficient and loyal warriors!" "And my people of Oyo! I also commend your loyalty and patients. You shall be given the location to allow you to live close to the people of the same town and village and to be given the same location to accommodate you under the same Bale or Olu."

Thereafter when the people had been settled in their new towns and villages, the Alafin Atiba summon chief Oluyole in Oke Ibadan and gave him the title of Basorun Oyo, he had promised him. But order him to remain in Oke Ibadan, and he said

"it shall be safe if the Basorun stays in his own city."

However, the Alafin have thought it over that inorder to avoid the situation in which, if there would be conflict between the Alafin and the Basorun, the Basorun who is the second-in-command to the Alafin may not cause trouble for the new city and the Alafin. Also the Alafin Atiba conferred on chief Kurumi in Ijaye the title of the Are-Ona-Kakanfo (the Field Marshal) Oyo he had promised him. Then the Alafin pronounced the following constitutional orders to prevent the collision between the two powerful warlike towns:

1. "That the two towns shall make it their primary aims to defend what is left of the Oyo empire and ensure that they gain back places that have been lost from the provinces to the Ilorin Fulani.
2. That since the last Alafin died in war, the Alafin shall be in charge of all religious, civil and political matters on behave of the nation.

3. That the Oke Ibadan are to protect all the Oyo towns to the North and North-East and has free hand on all Ijesas and Ekitis and Eastern provinces and generally to reduce their subjections.
4. hat Ijayes shall protect all the Oyo of the Western province and to carry on with the operations against Sabes and the disloyal Popos. Additionally, the ancient cities and towns of Ilukan, Saki, Ghoho, containing the remaining citizens of the ancient Oyo and members of the Royal family are not to be placed under the protection of either of these towns, but under the Alafin directive."

Eventually, the Oyo empire had become stable, but the Are Kakanfo Kurumi was a dictator, and he puts to death all chiefs that he thought would become his rivals. But there was a Mohammedan who was a friend of the Balogun Oderinde who live in Oke Ibadan that he respect. However, some powerful men came to Ijaye and they want to make home there, and the Kakanfo tried to make it difficult for them to stay, but the Moslem priest told him

"Are Kakanfo Kurumi!" "Akinkanju okunrin ogun!" "O sa mo pe ore leme ire? Ma gba o ni imoran, pe ki o fi aye fun awon olola ati onisowo pataki ni ilu re yi o. Ki o ma ba je wipe awon alaini ati otosi ni o ma se olori fun nikan. Ati wipe, ki oro aje le fi dagere, ko si le ni ilo siwaju (I will advice you to tolerate other rich and important people in Ijaye so that the province will not be populated by only the poor people and farmers which will not be good for the trade.")

Then Are Kakanfo Kurumi smiling, responds

"Ore mi Imamu Ikewuogo!" "Akewu Gberu!" "O sa mo pe emi re pelu Oderinde ti ba ara wa bo ojo ti pe!" "Koda ori e le wun wi po. Mo gbo alaye re, mi o si ti fi se ogbon, o se o po ore mi ("my good friend the Imam Ikeogo!" "The great Islamic leader!" "Me, Oderinde and you have been friends for some time!" I really appreciate your advice and will make use of it thank you my friend.")

So the Kakanfo allowed them to stay, and Lukusa, Agana, Akiola, Amodu, Lahan and more live in Ijaye. Then the Kakanfo Kurumi ordered "all the taxes and levy are to be brought to my house and it shall go into a separate treasury for my family alone in Ijaye. And I also demand that the gods and the provincial religious ceremonies are to be done only when I am around in Ijaye, or of what purpose will any ceremony be when me the Are Kakanfo is out of Ijaye or at the war front?"

And he told his family after the pronouncement

"you see my sons that is the way to dominate this Oyo people, I want the people to see me as their god, and to dominate their religion practice and make them to look up to me only for solution of their problems."

So the Kakanfo become richer than everybody living in the province.

The Osogbo war against the Ilorin about 1842

Thereafter, the Ilorin Army were in aggressive spirit and they wage in wars against the Oyo country with the aim of destroying her completely, so the Ilorin attack Osogbo which is one of the Oyo province. But the Bale of Osogbo and his warriors after defending themselves for weeks, send message to Oke Ibadan for help. But the Basorun (Prime Minister) initially send few units of the Oyo Army under Obele also call Mobitan, Alade, Abinupagun and some warlords to the battle. However, the Basorun Oluyole who was having a discussion with some people on how to meet some budget cost for the plantation he was working on when the messenger from the war came from Osogbo. Then he send the people away and said

"you have to take care of the works and should make sure that the slaves carry out the work required on the seeds in the nursery beds and transfered them to the next fields after about two seasons."

And after the people had left, the warriors from Osogbo prostrate before him on his throne and they said

"baba Basorun (Lord Prime Minister)!" "The Bale (Mayor) Osogbo send us to tell you that the war situation is getting worst because the Ilorin have brought more warriors to their camp and they are going to launch a full attack by next week."

The Basorun Oluyole responds

"thank you my warriors!" "I shall summon the Balogun Oderinlo and all the warlords to my palace."

Thereafter he told the Balogun Oderinlo and the warlords

"I am going to deal with the Ilorin once and for all, who do they think they are dealing with?" The Balogun (General) said

"the aggression of the Ilorin against Oyo have to be put stop completely otherwise the Fulani will be the Lord over the whole Oyo."

And the Basorun said

"that cannot happen we shall be ready to die than let our chidren to be under the Fulani, which can never happen, not in this our live time."

Then the Balogun order

"the warriors shall go home and be ready the following day to march to Osogbo."

However when they got to Osogbo the Basorun ordered

"the Osogbo warriors shall maintain the central position of the battle, Chief Abitiko and Chief Lajubu shall take the command of the battle by the right wing, and the Balogun with the rest of the Army war-chiefs shall take the left wing."

However, the Ilorin Army launch their attacks from all sides and they said

"Elo ni owo do" ("the fare of the ferry").

Then after the Ilorin camp under the command of Elese was attacked by the Oyo Army and Elese was shot the Ilorin warriors ran away from the camp. But Ali the Ilorin commander-in-chief remain calm and determined, and he ordered for his horse and took control of the rest of his warlords and they surround his horse which made his Army to come back and the regroup. Thereafter he lead his Calvary and they march through the Oyo ranks which enable them to gain some control, and eventually they escape, but the following powerful Ilorin warlords were captured:

1. Jimba the head slave of the Emir of Ilorin.
2. One of the sons of Ali the Commander-in-Chief of Ilorin Army.
3. Chief Lateju
4. Ajikobi the Yoruba Balogun of Ilorin.

Then the first two were released and sent home secretly to Ilorin, for the exchange and the condition of peace. But the other two were Yoruba and they were regarded as traitors to their country and they were taken to Oke Ibadan as distinguish war capture. However, the Basorun sentenced Lateju to death for the allegation that the late Alafin Oluewu was killed in his house and because Oluyole's wives fell into his hands at the end of the expedition. Furthermore, Ajikobi was send to the Alafin Atiba for capital punishment. Meanwhile, the Alafin received the messengers from Oke Ibadan during one of his annual festivals and he ordered his guards to direct their guns on Ajikobi who was gun down, and a lot of people and horses of large numbers were captured from the Ilorin Army. Moreover, the victory over Ilorin at Osogbo form a turning point in the Oyo history because it save the Oyo country from being under Ilorin. But the Alafin Atiba failed to use this opportunity to order his Army to destroy the entire Ilorin Army. He also prefer the capital to remain at Ago because it is closer to the coast and a location that can promote trades.

Ibadan war against Ekiti and Ijesa

However, after some years Oyo had people of younger generation that do not know about the former capital, and it would be difficult to move the capital back to Oyo-Ile without making them abandon their new home with out given then any good reason. And after the war, Ibokun and Ijesa towns which are not too far from Osogbo were attacked by Oke Ibadan and they were taken without much resistance.

Thereafter Atipo and Akinlabi did not return home but they remain in Ijaye permanently. And they become restless warlords, and went on campaigns at the bank of the River Niger on their own and captured Ogodo and Gbajigbo, but the Basorun Oluyole become jealous of their success and popularity. Moreover, the Kakanfo Kurumi was also looking for an excuse and ways to bring accusation against them, and some powerful warlords in Ijaye so as to kill them but eventually, Atipo, Akinlabi and these warlords left Ijaye for Ilorin. Then the Kakanfo invites them to a banquet at Ijaye and killed them which consolidate all the powers in the province under him and he took all their properties. Meanwhile, after some years at Osu which was not far from Ilesa, the capital town of the Ijesa community, the Seriki Ladanu lead an expedition which consist of the Basorun Oluyole and these warlords: Akinsowon, Abipa, Aiyenku and Erinle Sanku. But when the Ijesas heard of their approach they layed an ambush and cut the Seriki's Army in pieces, then the Seriki and all his warlords are killed except Aijenku and Erinle Sanku. Moreover the Oke Ibadan Army attacked Ijesa to avenge the attack and killing of the Seriki and all his warlords. Then the Balogun Oderinlo lead the whole Oke Ibadan Army and they camp at Ede farms for many days, and they launch several attacks on the Ijesas at Osu and everywhere they camp in Iloba. Meanwhile, the fight last for months but the Ijesas eventually vacate their towns, and the Oke Ibadans found the towns and villages empty and they were not able capture the people as slaves. But after some years the Ijesa and Ekiti province become peaceful because there was no war except the Pole war. So, they were safe and there was no attack from the Fulani and their other enemies also. But after some time they start having internal problems which result in asking for external help that lead to their eventual subjugation. However, Aaye and Otun which are the main principal towns in Efon and Ekiti district known as EKITI, witness the first fight because of boundary dispute at Otun. Moreover, Olotun send for help at Oke Ibadan, of which the Balogun Oderinlo send the whole Oke Ibadan Army, and Aaye was attacked. Then the Alaye also send for help from Ilorin, and the Ilorin under General Afunku join their camp. But the Oke Ibadan defeat them and killed General Afunku, and about 100 Ilorin warriors were captured and imprisoned and the rest excaped. Then the Balogun order the farms in Aaye to be destroyed and prevent food from getting to them. So the people who were in the hiding came out because of hunger, and after eating roots of trees, reptiles, and unhealthy things, but the Oke Ibadan camp was full of all kinds of foods. And Balogun said

"how long are we going to remain camping here without getting these people as slaves? You my people when you meet the Ekiti people you should pretend as if you are starving for food and even beg them for food. So that they may think we are also staving for food and we about to die of hunger in our camp so that they would come out of their hiding place"

So the people in his camp to pretend as if they was no food in their camp, which made the Aaye people hiding to come out thinking that the Ibadan warriors should also be weak. And they also build forths upon their town wall and sharp shooters shut at the Oke Ibadan camp which made them to be successful in killing some Oke Ibadan warriors that include Chief Toki Onibudo the Seriki of Oke Ibadan. But eventually, when the hunger become unbearable, Chief Fagbenro the Alaye with his mother risk it and they went to the Oke Ibadan camp to seek for peace. And when the Alaye got to the Oke Ibadan camp he was so surprise that there was much abundant food such as yams, corns, flowers and more in the camp market for sale. And he said

"what do I see?" "And exclaim!" "What about the famine we are told exist in Ibadan camp so that men are reduced to feeding on pounded hey?"

And he bought some food. Then the Balogun received him in a friendly manner and they reach the term of agreement for peace. So they promise to serve the Oke Ibadan, and they were given chief Lajubu with some of his warriors to protect them to Isan. But this was a pretence by the Balogun, because before they got to Isan the whole of Oke Ibadan Army marched against their towns and villages and Lajubu himself gave way for the Oke Ibadans to attack them and raid them for slaves. However, the Oke Ibadan

Army continue with their attack and took Oro, Yapa, Isi and Isan but did not attack their warlords and let them remain. Moreover Itagi warriors stand up to defend themselves and also stop the attack. They hide in the bush and tricked the Oke Ibadan warriors into their towns and villages, as they were raiding for slaves, thereafter the Itagi Army came out and killed them and Chief Lajubu also die among the warlords and warriors killed at their market place. So this campaign open the EKITI country for attack by the Oke Ibadan which continue for many years continuously until the country was completely under the Oke Ibadan.

Oke Ibadan and Ijaye the Batedo war about 1844

Moreover, the Basorun Oluyole felt he should be the Alafin of Oyo, and he said

"the Army have been very successful which is because of my charms and my efficiency as a warlord. I should be able to have the whole of Oyo under my control"

And he was feeling happy and he instructs singers and drummers to sing the following song and the talking drum to say:

"Iba, kuku joba
Mase bi Oba Mo"

meaning

"Be the king at once,
My lord cease acting like a king."

Then he invite some members of the Oyomesi to a big banquet in Oke Ibadan during one of the festivals and told them

"Can you see the success that I have in the my plantations!" "Is it not good if it should be seen all over Oyo?"

Then he took them to one of his farms after the banquet. And when they were walking in the farm he said

"do you all see the success I have in my business here? Is this not good for Oyo-Ile too?"

The Oyomesi members respond

"oh!" "These kind of ideas and inovation will be good for all of Oyo!" "We can invite you to the new Oyo town and to advice the Alafin Atiba on how to get it down."

But when they saw the look of sadness in his face, they get where he was going and they pretend. And said

"Oh!" "You mean Oyo-Ile and under your leadership and reign? That Oyo can get into these kind of success? Yes we will be happy."

The leading Oyomesi said

"what are we waiting for? Let us be on our way to Oyo town and bring the discussion up and convince the Chiefs in the Oyomesi that we need to move to Oyo-Ile. And we are sure the Basorun will know how to do the rest in military way to become the Alafin, since he is the most successful warrior we know now."

And the rest of the Oyomesi said

"yes of course!" "Without the Basorun!" "The peace and the military success we have now would not have been possible. We can work under a successful and a warrior that has alot of business ideas like you as the Alafin Oyo"

However, the Basorun Oluyole become very happy and prepared lots of gifts for each of them, he bid them goodbye and he said,

"I will be expecting progress on our plans. And I will make my plans and war preparation so as to be able to defeat any opposition to our proposal."

But after they had left Oke Ibadan the leader of the Oyomesi said

"thanks to our gods and the ancestors of the Alafin Oyo we could have got ourselves killed today."

The rest of the Oyomesi said

"thank you for being smart and for saving our lives."

One of them said

"who can ever tell the Basorun no and that the Alafin Atiba had degree it that Ago-d'Oyo shall be the capital of the Oyo empire, without him cutting that person's head off?"

Then they said

"we have to let the Alafin Atiba know of this so that he can be careful and we can be protected from the power of the Basorun Oluyole by the Alafin Atiba, afterall he is also a warlord himself."

Another member of the Oyomesi said

"what else did the Basorun wants in this life? He is living as a king, with a very beautiful palace and lots of slaves, and riches What else does he need? Because of his greed for the throne of the Alafin Oyo that does not belongs his linage, he wants to bring war on the empire and put everybody into trouble."

The leading Oyomesi said

"with all we had heard about this Basorun Oluyole and the Are Kakanfo Kurumi both of them because of their greediness and arrogance want to be the Alafin of Oyo at all cost, but people like them will always end in mysterious death and in a bad way."

One of the Oyomesi said

"If they will always die singly it will be better without bringing the whole Oyo empire into war, with troubles and havocs for every citizen of the country."

However after waiting for couple of months and the Basorun did not see any sign nor heard of any argument going on in the city of Oyo about moving to Oyo-Ile, he said to himself

"so these Oyomesi people had deceived me? I will now find a way of tricking the Alafin Atiba by myself to make him invite me to his palace and I will look for means of getting to him personally kill him secretly."

Meanwhile, the Alafin had been warned by the Oyomesi members who came to the Basorun's banquet and they had told the Alafin of the Basorun's evil plans. Then the Basorun send a word message to the Alafin

"let my Lord the Alafin Atiba! Know that I would like to come and see the new Oyo capital, and to pay my homage to Kabiyesi, Iku Baba Yeye."

But the Alafin replied

"thank you the Basorun Oluyole! The new capital is beautiful and I heard that the palace in Oke Ibadan is even bigger and more beautiful than the one in Oyo town. I will be making an entourage of Oke Ibadan, and you shall be able to pay me homage then and also I do not want you to come to Oyo town now."

Thereafter, the Basorun send word message to the Kakanfo Kurumi in Ijaye and with some gifts also to the Oyomesi to convince the Alafin Atiba to return the capital back to Oyo-Ile. But the Kakanfo Kurumi sense that there is something wrong with the Basorun instruction, so he decide to watch the movements of his Warlords and said to himself

"I have to keep away from Oyo town also."

Then he responds to the Basorun's word message

"thank you my Lord the Basorun Oyo!" "I will have to wait for some time before being able to go to Oyo town and deliver your gifts and message to the Oyomesi who will be able to get what you want done."

But after waiting more than two years and the Kakanfo had not gone to Oyo town, the Basorun said

"so this Kakanfo Kurumi descieved also? He shall have to die because even if I succeed in killing the Alafin Atiba this Kakanfo will stand in my way of becoming the Alafin Oyo."

Then the Basorun Oluyole send a word messages to the Kakanfo and every warlords in the provinces of Oyo empire

"I the Basorun Oluyole have heard of some evil plot on the Alafin Atiba, so I command that no one shall have to attack Oyo town unless the Are Kakanfo Kuruni is first attack and killed."

Then the Are Kakanfo Kurumi inform the Alafin Atiba of the evil plan that the Basorun have in mind against the Alafin Atiba and adviced the Alafin Atiba to be careful while dealing with him. Thereafter, the Basorun send word messages for three different times to the Alafin Atiba, saying

"Kabyesi o!" "Kabyesi o!" "Kabyesi o!" "Iku Baba Yeye!" "I want let my Lord to realize the need for capital to be move to Oyo-Ile. And the Alafin Atiba should not forget to fulfill his promise of moving the capital back to the ancient city of Oyo-Ile."

However, on the third time the Alafin Atiba became feed up and he responds

"Tell your master! That if he is ready, let him come on I am ready. As the present Oyo is on the high way to the ancient capital, he should come first and I shall meet him here."

Then the Alafin Atiba called the Oyomesi and the warlords and let them know what is going on, and he said

"we shall have to be prepared for the attack of the Basorun Oluyole because he has been trying to get into confrontation with me for some time now, I think he is interested in my throne."

And as he was talking all the Oyomesi and the people prostrate saying

"Kabiyesi o!" "Kabiyesi o!" "Kabiyesi o!" "Iku baba yeye!" "Oba ti gba idobale Oba. Kade pe lori ki bata pe lese igba odun odun kan ni (the unquestionable, ... the one that has death under his control, the king of kings, may the Royal crown remains and may Royal shoes remains and your reign is forever.")

Then the Alafin Atiba order

"now we shall have to start building the gates of the town and the walls and to prepare Oyo for sudden attack."

He also summon all the powerful voodoo men and Latubosun to prepare and bury charms at all the gates of the city as preventive measure. Then the Oyomesi advice

"Kabiyesi o!" "Kabiyesi o!" "Kabiyesi o!" "We observed that the warriors would need to get guns and gunpowder from Port Novo."

And the Alafin Atiba responds

"Audu Alelo and Kosiju and some Ilaris shall go to Port Novo and buy all the necessary ammunitions for the defence of Oyo town and her surrounding towns and village."

But the Basorun Oluyole had station his warriors close to the capital and instructs them "you are my special wariors on a special asignment you shall be on watch by the capital city Oyo and intercept any ammunitions and weapons going in and out of the capital even if the order is from the Alafin Atiba."

Then when the people Alafin Atiba sent were returning from Port Novo on their way to the capital, the Basorun warriors stop them and said

"what are you carrying? So you don't hear that the Basorun Oluyole had order that nobody shall take any ammunition and weapons of war in and out of the capital city of Oyo?"

The Ilaris of the Alafin said

"you must be very stupid and blind otherwise you will have been able to see that you are talking to the Ilaris and warriors of the Alafin Atiba."

Then the warriors of the Basorun shot them and the bullet made them to scatter and Audu's teeth and his face was damaged, and some of his guards were killed. And the ammunitions they bought was taken from them and the warriors of the Basorun quickly rode their horse to Oke Ibadan. However, when the people that survived the attack got to Oyo town and spread the word that the Basorun warriors had attacked the Alafin Atiba messengers and had taken the ammunitions from them, the people were in panic and they start running into hiding. And when the Oyomesi heard what had happened, they met and conclude that the Oyo town warriors and the remaining warriors in the empire shall fight the Basorun warriors. But the Alafin Atiba said

"we shall not fight and cause havoc because of the foolishness of Oluyole, we should realize that this is what he wants us do and that he is only interested in is my throne and that is why he wants to attack our Army so that Oyo will be destroy since he know he cannot get the crown, but what we shall do is to be patient. With patience we can cook a rock until it melt"

Then everybody prostrate and said

"Kabiyesi o!" "Kabiyesi o!" "Kabiyesi o!" "Thank you for your patience and wisdom."

Thereafter, the Basorun Oluyole was sitting on his throne at his palace in Oke Ibadan thinking loud, and he said

"what kind of Alafin is this Oba Atiba? We all know him to be a very strong warrior, if not even the best and he is not a coward. I have being provoking him now for a long time and with several insults which I know he would never have taken none of them, those days of our going to wars and raiding campaigns."

Then he got up from his throne, put his hand in his pocket, brought out a charm and walk to the central of his palace yard, look everywhere making sure that nobody was closeby and called the leader of his guard and told him

"make sure that no child or woman shall be allow close to where I am standing."

Then he order

"get me a big calabash with water in it and a mirror,"

and he order another guard

"get me a chair."

When everything he had requested for had been done, he order

"all the guards shall move away from the yard now."

Then the Basorun Oluyole start to praise the gods and shacking a small calabash which have dry seeds in it and making some sound as he shakes it. Then he was shaking the small calabash with his right hand while he had some charms in his left hand, And he said some incantations and look into the water in the calabash and he said

"Olugbo owun!" "Olugbo owun!" "Olugbo owun!" "Mo be ni se!" "Iwo Are Ona Kakanfo Kurumi!" "Ma gbo mi kosi fi Oju re sibi, mo pe eleda re ki oju re ati iye okan re ma jemi ni ipe!" "Kakanfo Kurumi o!" "kakanfo Kurumi o!" "Kakanfo Kurumi o!" ..... ("The spiritual world in control of consciousness hear me and come to my aid, you the Field Marshal Kurumi now hear me and let your attention be here. I now command your spirit and your soul to hear my command as I take control of your being Marshal Kurumi Oh!, Marshal Kurumi Oh!, Marshal Kurumi Oh! .....")

Then the mirror start to shack and the calabash also shake slightly and he continue with what he was doing repeating the calling of the kakanfo's name. Suddenly the image of the Kakanfo Kurumi appears, but laughing and said

"Basorun Oluyole!" "I know that you are strong in voodoo, you have forgotten that we learn this evil voodoo from the same court. A kin fi Omo Ore bo Ore (you cannot succeed to make a child of a deity a sacrificial lamb to the same deity,")

laughing and the Image disappeared. The Basorun become more mad, his eyes was so red and his voice very loud and he said

"Kakanfo Kurumi!" "You have escaped!" "Your soul and spirit refuse to be under my control"

Then he walk away from the veranda into his court and he put the charms back into his agada (outer garment) pockets and sat on the throne. Then after thinking for some time while his head rest on the side of the neck support of the timber throne, he ordered the leading guard who with his companion were already standing in their respective positions to return the items he had used at the veranda back to their place. Then the guard left his presence and signals to the guard closeby and instruct him to get some female slaves to get it done, and return back to his former position. And the Basorun said

"yes!" "I know what to do next,"

he summon one of his senior Ilaris

"get some bags of money and some gifts and take them to the Kakanfo Kurumi and tell him that I have not seen him for some time now and I will want him to come to my new palace to see me and you tell him that he has not to come to pay homage to me as the senior officer in the Kingdom. And tell him that I am extending this invitation to all the high ranking war-chiefs in the Oyo country."

And he also called the leading guard and said

"you make sure that my message is sent to all the war-chiefs to come to my palace in Oke Ibadan and pay homage to me, and after that we shall all go to the Alafin palace in Oyo town to pay homage to the Alafin Atiba."

Theafter the Basorun laugh loud and said to himself

"I shall be able to take the advantage of leading the war-chiefs to the Alafin's palace and kill him."

But the Kakanfo replied

"thank again my Lord the Basorun Oyo! Unfortunate I cannot leave Ijaye! Just like you have your own interest and issues to deal with so I have my mine to deal with here in Ijaye."

However, after some time Asu the Areago of Ladejo in Ijaye was accuse of treason by some of Kakanfo's secret informant that the Kakanfo Kurumi had set up to bring the wrong accusations on any Chief he felt that was getting too powerful and popular in Ijaye. But the Kakanfo would not investigate the allegation on him but pronounced that the person shall be expel from Ijaye. So chief Ladejo moved to Fiditi a town located between Oyo town and Ijaye and he rebuild the town because she had been deserted because of war. Then the Kakanfo Kurumi become jealous of Ladejo and he said

"I have to destroy Ladejo completely before I know, he will be rivalry with my children in the future," then the the Kakanfo send 100 of his warriors to destroy Fiditi town. But Asu and the warriors were able to defead themseves and he send word to Oke Ibadan for help so as to prevent the Are Kakanfo from killing him. And when the messenger from Asu got to the Basorun palace in Oke Ibadan, he said

"my Lord Basorun Oyo!" "Asu request your the help and that of the Oke Ibadan warriors to prevent the Kakanfo Kurumi from killing him and destroy the town of Fiditi which he had just rebuild."

The Basorun said

"this is the opportunity I have been waiting for,"

then he order

"the Balogun (General) Oderinlo and Ibikunle the Seriki (District Commander) shall go and make sure that they kidnap in the farms in the villages and the towns in Ijaye and Oyo so as to make their farming to be dangerous there. And I want to use this to cause famine so that the people of Ijaye would become weak."

And he said to himself

"when this had been done the Ijaye warriors and people in Ijaye shall be reduced to hunger and weak before I order attack against Ijaye and Oyo town."

But after several raids on the farms in Ijaye, the Oke Ibadan warriors were defeated by the Kakanfo Kurumi's Army at the Fiditi campaign. Then the Basorun Oluyole put the attack on Ijaye under the command of Seriki Ibikunle while he himself lead the attack on the Oyo farms. Meanwhile at Odogido the Ijaye ambushed and attacked the Seriki's warriors and completely defeat them such that about 140 warlords on horse were caught and killed. But Seriki Ibikunle was lucky and was allowed to escape by some of his friends who secretly help him. Also the Basorun Oluyole campaign on the Oyo farms was unsuccessful because the Alafin Atiba had heard of his evil plans and the villages and towns people had been told to ran away, so when the Basorun warriors got there, they couldn't catch a single person. However the Kakanfo Kurumi killed all the Oke Ibadan warriors he caught and after the third month the Basorun Oluyole heard of what had happened. And he said

"I will wage war against Ijaye and my Army shall meet him at Fiditi."

Then he order

"the bush by the North-Eastern direction to Ijaye shall cleared, for my camp."

Thereafter when the clearing of the bush which took about 5 days for them to camp there. And the Ijaye fight with the Oke Ibadan Army last for two years and both sides record equal success. Meanwhile, the Basorun who had one of his wives who was a powerful voodoo woman went to the war with him and when he heard of the disaster of Odogido, he and his wife Oyainu boast and they said

"if me and my wife are left for the fight we shall be able to take Ijaye by now."

The wife Oyainu also said

"if this war is left for me alone with my Egugun (Masquerade) gods, I will be able take Ijaye." So the warlord of Oke Ibadan felt very bad by the attitudes and arrogance of the Basorun Oluyole towards them and they show no interest toward the campaign. And they said

"we would let the Basorun Oluyole and his powerful wife fight the war by themselves." And eventually both side seek alliance of the Egbas who are now divided, Sodeke and Amoba declared for Ijaye, but Apati being Oluyole's friend and relative declared for Oke Ibadan. Then the Basorun seek alliance of Ogbomoso and the Emir of Ilorin, and the Balogun Ali of Ilorin send him help. The Eastern districts: Apoma, Ikire, Osogbo are all under Oke Ibadan and they join the Oke Ibadan Army. But the Iwo and Ede join the side of Kakanfo Kurumi of Ijaye. However, the war had become the fight of the whole Oyo country's cities and towns against each other. But the Alafin Atiba remain neutral and would not help either side until he was able to come forward as a peace maker between them. Moreover, the Alafin send the emblems of the Sango (god of thunder) with the high priest from Oyo to the Ijaye and the Ijaye camps and said

"what the king on earth may not be able to effect, surely the king from the other world can do, and this unnatural conflict shall now cease."

However Sango's intervention was respected by both sides, and because they were also both tied of the war, they reach peace agreement immediately. And the people of both camps embraced each other, and there was so much joy and tears of joy on both side such that friends, family members and relatives from both side embraced each other crying and they said congratulations for this peace to each other. Then after the war there where some conflicts that involve Oke Ibadan and Ijaye and in fact it was in one of such fight that the Basorun Oluyole when running away from an ambush fell from his horse and sustain internal injury which kept him on his bed for 5 days. Then he called on his respectable warlords and chiefs and said

"you should take care of my household and he died."

But the people were very happy when they heard that he had died and they destroy his house, but before they could burn it down, the Balogun prevent them and order the Agbakin and his warriors to prevent the palace from further damage and from destruction.

Early live of the Basorun Oluyole

Meanwhile, Ogunmola had risen from lower ranks as a private at the beginning of the Basorun Oluyole early administration, Earlier Ogunmola had a single drummer who he would order to sit on the top of a tree, while he would sits on an empty keg of gunpowder and challenge the Basorun to civil war and the drummer would beats the talking drum which say:

"Ogunmola, ija' gboro ni yio pa a dan, dan, dan!
O nyi agba gbiri, gbiri, gbriri!
Omu agbori lowo, O nwo ana Orun yan, yan, yan!"

meaning

("Ogunmola, of a civil fight he shall die for sure, sure, sure!
He keep kegs of powder a rolling, rolling, rolling!
With a jack knife in hand he looking heaven wards steadily, steadily,
steadily!")

Then the Oluyole though, not yet a Basorun but a higher ranking officer,
would send Ogunmola some present and said

"he is hungry, hence he is challenging me to a fight."

The Basorun Oluyole had interest in lots of ventures, and farming, he own
large plantations of different crops, husbandry, and kola nut grooves. He
would often offered human sacrifices in his farms to make the trees to be
fruitful. In fact, one of his wives the mother of his son Owolabi was for
a small offence punished by being used as a sacrificial lamb in his farm.

He would not allow anyone but himself to put on silk velvet which was
very rare then and was very expensive. But allowed only the chiefs to put
on just velvet caps, the Basorun would say

"when the poor people begin to aspire to what they cannot easily avoid to
buy, they would neglect the necessary things they actually need and make
their children and wives suffer."

Moreover, the Basorun had large wives and he would seize any good
looking woman in the street or in the market place and brought her to his
house to become his wife. And there were hundreds of women, that he
did not know by sight that lived in his compound. So when he died the
relatives and husbands of these women rush to his compound and took
their children and their wives away.

CHAPTER 10

Lagos about 1851

Meanwhile, the British Parliament enact a law to allow more exploitation of the British Colonies. And the struggle to gain more Colonies become very intensive among Britain, France, Portugal, Spain, Germany, Dutch and other European countries. However, the fight to gain control of the Coast of Lagos become very strong between the British and France, but eventually Britain was able to gain control of the Bright of Benin and the Coast of Lagos which was pronounced the British Protectorate of Lagos without even going to any war with the Ijebus who were the power that controls the area. Then the British turn the name of the "Royal Merchant Trading Company" to the "British Protectorate of Lagos". Thereafter, they had a meeting with the Chief of Eko and elevate his status to Lord under the British Lordship custom and Eko high Chief which was just a Bale becomes the Olu of Lagos and the Bale of Badagry was place under the Olu of Lagos. Then the land of Badagry which the white people find difficult to cultivate after buying it form the Eleko beach land area Chiefs and the British people called it "BadAgric", and the natives called it in their accents "Badargy". So Lagos expand from the Island to the land surrounding the Lagoon to the main land Musin where the Ijebu-Imusin people established as market for food produce, vegetables and fruits. The Mushin town, Ikorodu, Epe, Agbowa, Ikosi are all Ijebuland which accommodate people from the Interior land who had came to trade and work for the white people's companies and business, that deal in the products from their cities in United States of America New England, Britain, and Europe. Meanwhile the returnee slaves who had came to settle as refuges in Sierra Leone and Free Town were able to traced their origin back to Lagos seaport and they were given home in Lagos Islands, and the Mission community houses in Abeokuta which was an old farm settlement of the Ijebus which the Egbas made their settlement. So the British Parliament realized that the best and only way to gain control of the Interior land and to make the people work for them, was by encouraging the tribes to continue fighting with each other. And they secretly continue with the bribing of the Chiefs and the dimension of the civil wars become very great. However, more slaves were being transported to Cuba, Brazil, and Haiti, which was not wrong by the British Parliament since none of these place were under the control of the Royal Merchant Trading Company.

The White People Assert their Racial Superiority

Moreover, during this period of slave trade, the white people were able to transport more blacks as slaves from the Protectorate of Lagos port to American, Brazil, Cuba, Haiti and the Caribbean Islands. Where they were able to engaged in slave trade in large scale because of their polluting of the Interoir countries land with guns, gunpowder, their fake coinages, counterfeit money and money laundry, expectially in Oyo. Thus this made the white people see themselves as a superior being to the black people. And since then they had succeed in lying to the people of the Interior land who they deceived with the Missionary works that enabled them to bring guns and gunpowder, fake money and only to secretly kidnap the people by the nights and during the wars. However, the white slave traders encouraged the slave raiding warriors to continue waging wars on each other and this enabled them to catch the people as slaves and transport them to these place mentioned above.

Thereafter, when their factories in Britain, Europe, and North America cities especially in New England need raw materials, such as Agricultural products, like coffee, cocoa, tea, palm oils, groundnuts, timbers, and more. And also mineral resources such as iron ore, tin, silver, copper, gold and more and they knew that they do not need much people any more in their plantations in the Southern United States of America. And in their East Coast cities especially in the New England of United States of America that were getting Industrialize in the 1860s so they declared the end to slave trade, which lead to civil war in United States of America. However this was the beginning of the civil war in the countries in the Interior lands close to the British Protectorate of Lagos where the Ijebus had being preventing them from penetrating. Thereafter the white people use guns pollution to intensify the war among the Oyo tribes and they were able to transport large number of the Oyo tribal people as slaves to Brazil, and Cuba. Then the British had the opportunity of getting into the Interior land and began the process of colonization of Oyo, Ekiti, Ijesa, Ilorin, Egba, and some Eastern tribes.

The Ijaye war about 1860

Meanwhile, after the death of the Alafin Atiba, Prince Adelu the prime son (Aremo) became the successor of the Alafin Atiba, because of the new reform rule made by the Oke Ibadan warriors that the children have the right to inherit their parent's properties, and no more old law that make the parent brothers and relatives to inherit their parent's properties. However, this rule became law after the Alafin had accept it and pronounced it as such for the Oyo empire. So the Alafin Atiba adopt its modification that his Aremo also had the right of the inheritance of his father's property and throne, which in this case he would not have to die and be buried with his father the Alafin when he join his ancestors which was the prevailing tradition. And that the Aremo was to be the crown Prince and his successor, only if the Oyomesi reject him for his bad conducts. So Omo Oba Adelu would not have to commit suicide according to the old custom when his father the Alafin Atiba join his ancestors. But the Kakanfo Kurumi refused to accept the new rule, but insist that the Aremo would have to die. Because of this he refused to go to Oyo to pay homage and did not send his congratulations message to Oyo on the Installation of the Alafin Adelu. But the Alafin Adelu tried to make peace with him and said

"the Kakanfo Kurunmi was a commrade of my father during his warlord days, and for this reason I will accomondate his difference in view. And I will have to persuade him to accept the reality of now."

Thereafter, a rich lady name Abu died without a child of her own, and according to the custom her property belongs to the State. However, Ijana where she lived is under Ijaye and since there was a disagreement between the Alafin Adelu and the Kakanfo Kurunmi, the town people do not know what to do with the properties, so they send word message to request the Alafin Ilaris (Messengers) to come and take the properties. And at the same time they send the same kind of message to the Kakanfo, hoping that both parties should know how to to handle the situation. Then the Alafin Adelu send a well equip warlords lead by Akingbehin, that include the Aleyo, the Ona-aka, and the Aremo's Balogun to escort the Ilaris to pick the properties. And the Balogun Kurumi send a warrior unit to attack them. Then the Alafin delegates were attacked by the Ijaye warriors at Apata Mabe near Oke'ho, but they were able to beat their attackers and they also escorts some Oyo traders who were afraid of the Ijaye kidnappers back home. However, the Ijaye warriors attacked them again between Iseyin and Oyo, when the Ijaye warriors pretend that they were from the Alafin and told the traders that

"we are from Oyo and were send by the Alafin to escort you home."

But they open fire on them and the Oyo warriors, so everybody ran away and they were able to captured about 240 traders which include some chiefs whose names were: Aridede, Aleyo, Jigin and more. Then the Alafin Adelu sent request to the Kakanfo Kurumi to release the people. But the Kakanfo refused and said

"I will only release each of them for 10 bags of cowries each."

And the Alafin Adelu sent word message to the Kakanfo saying

"I have claim on you to demand the release these people, for being the king of Yoruba to whom allegiance is due, remember what I did for you in the past. When you sent one Dayiro on an expedition and the people of Saki defeated him and more than 210 of his men were imprison did I not use my authority and influence and obtain the release of them all and send them to you free of charge?"

Despite this the kakanfo refused to release them. However, in order to prevent war with Ijaye, his Majesty sent the Samu (one of the Oyomesi) representing Ijaye to Oke Ibadan to have him to talk with the Kakanfo to release the people. But the Kakanfo Kurumi refused to listen and even chased the Samu when he was on his way to Oke Ibadan, and fortunately, the Samu escaped and return via Iwo.

Then the Alafin Adelu gave the order

"the Oyo people shall go to Ijaye to redeem each of their own relatives."

Thereafter the Alafin decide to punish Ijaye by using the Oke Ibadan. And he send the Ibadan Army 40 slaves, 8 demijohns of beads, with gowns and vest and said

"tell them that I declare war on Ijaye."

However, when the Oke Ibadan warriors heard of Alafin Adelu declaration of war against Ijaye they were very happy, and said

"the town was already placed under a curse by the late Basorun Oluyole! So what are we waiting for? Let us fight and raid their farms for slave now."

But the Balogun Ibikunle in Oke Ibadan did not want to go to war with the Ijaye and he said

"Kurumi is an old man and will soon die, and the Ijayes are our kinsmen. I do not support us waging war on our own, we can find a way around this war."

Then some of the chiefs who opposed him said

"betraying cowardice! We have to go to this war at least to get some slaves which we can sell to the white people"

so as to provoke his anger and to made him agreed to go to war. But the Balogun Ibikunle explained to the warriors "my reason for not wanting to go to war against Ijaye town is because Ijaye is of equal importance like Ibadan. And she is of the same level of military might and skill, it will not make sense to wage war against your own family and blood relations."

But after some time, when the Balogun would not declare war, the common solders tied a cow to his house at night which was an indication that he was a coward, and they also threw stones into his house. So eventually, the Balogun yield to the public opinion and he declared war against Ijaye. Meanwhile, when the Kakanfo Kurumi heard that the Oke Ibadan Army had declared war, he ordered

"now all the young boys and men shall report to camp to be train as a good marksmen, and to be skillful with the bows, arrows and they have to practice every day. We have to patriotic and be ready to die and defend our Ijaye and me your Are Kakanfo."

Then the Kakanfo would amuse himself by singing and dancing to this song:

"A ta opolo ni ipa, o sun ikaka
Gbogbo wa ni yio ku bere."

("A frog kicked and lies on its back
well shall all die by myriads.")

And against the Alafin they sing:

"L' aye Onalu li aro okan le okan
L' aye Kurumi li aro' gba ro' gba
L' aye Adelu ni ipele di tele idi"

("In Onalu's time we used to change of dress
In Kurumi time we used cloths of the time weaving
In Adelu time our best becomes our every days")

Then Kidnappers began to kidnap in the farms and two American Missionaries who had heard of the rumors of war went to search for Mr. J. C. Vaughan in his farm at Ido. But he had escaped back to Ijaye by another route. However, the Missionaries were caught by some boys who brought them to Oke Ibadan on the February 1860, to Rev. D. Hinderer and they said

"white man we have brought you your brothers."

Thereafter the white men went to Abeokuta the following morning. However, after taking the necessary steps to make the Kakanfo Kurumi to see reason for peace, but the Kakanfo refused peace the Balogun Ibikunle said

"Eyin Omo Jama mo fi Ijaye jin o" ("Young men Ijaye is now given on to you.")

And the people respond with

"Muso, Muso" "Muso, Muso" "Muso, Muso",

and they worship Oranyan (deity) and march to war. Then when the Osi Balogun Ogunmola got on his horse and they were singing and the drummers sang:

"Baba mi nre igbo o da ju O! O! O!
Nibi ti Olomo meji yi o ku okan
Nibi ti olomo kan yi o pohora
Iya mi ni nma wa- ki o pada lehin Baba mi
Baba mi ni nma wa- ki o pada lehin Baba mi
Kiniun Onibudo
Iyawo mi to gbe - ki o pada lehin Baba mi
Kiniun Onibudo"

Meaning

("My master is going to the field of the heartless ah! ah! ah!
Where the parent of two will be left with but one

Where the parent of one will be left all forlorn.
Let him whose mother forbids him to come return from following my lord
Let him whose father forbids him to come return from following my lord
The Lion of the Master of the Camps
Let him whose betrothed is of age to be wed return from following my lord
The Lion of the Master of the Camps").
So they march to the war front with the chorus beat by the drummers
"Kiniun Onibudo" "Kiniun Onibudo" ...

Thereafter, the first battle took place at a rocky terrain call Apata Ika (Ika rock) where the Kakanfo's warriors lost terribly and he realized that he was dealing with young generation of Oke Ibadan warriors, who were more aggressive and fearless. So with courage, bravery and his war experience he reorganized his campaign plans and military formations. Then the Kakanfo Kurumi said to himself

"Oh!" "I should not have killed all those warlords!" "And those that I had driven out of Ijaye would have help me in this war."

Then he look very sad and walk tro and fro the front of his camp house and he add

"I will use my war experience and manage to use the warlords loyal to me now and train others."

Then he decide and called the warriors skillful in bows and arrows to take the lead in the defense of Ijaye wall and gates. However, the Egbas join the battle on the side of the Ijaye. Actually, only Sokenu that was against their joining the fight and he complained that it was wrong and said

"after the oath of alliance and friendship we had taken with the Oke Ibadan, it will be a serious breach of faith and even the gods will be against us."

But the other war-chiefs were so mad with Sokenu and they said "what do you know about war? We demand of you to part of this war effort or you shall not be alive when the battle is over."

And Sokenu laugh and rise up to leave the meeting, then the other chiefs and Bales add

"we must not meet you alive on our return you traitor of your fellow Egba interest."

And he responds

"if at all any of you return alive,"

thereafter, he became paralyzed from poison and he died.

The Awujale Oba Afidipotemole Influence

Meanwhile the Awujale Oba Afidipotemole was in his palace in Ijebu-Ode attending to some issues of trade, when a messenger from the Ijaye war told him after the greetings

"Kabiyesi o!" "Kabiyesi o!" "Kabiyesi o!" "The Egba warriors are now in the Ijaye war and they are in the Ijaye camp."

Then the Awujale Oba Afidipotemole summon the Olisa and the warlords of Ijebuland and he said

"we are not part of the Oyo empire and in fact we are not part of the Yoruba, we did not migrate back to Ife (Atlantis) from Egypt and Wadai in Sudan together and they cannot take the war to us, because they know better not to try it. We have never been part of their country and they are never going to be allowed into our gates and country. So let the Egbas follow their own kind in as much our Igbore and Ake farms and villages in Abeokuta are not affected and our trades and Caravans are not disturb, let the Oyo empire continue with their stupidity of fighting over the throne of their Alafin. And as to what I heard Ogunmola said that 'I would dispense with Ijaye first before sparing the time to deal with Ijebu.'"

The Awujale Oba Afidipotemole now angry, stand up and add

"let this word be send to the Oyos who are now settle in Oke Ibadan, come and peel off the hair from my Occiput."

Meanwhile, the Olisa and everybody in the palace prostrate and said

"Kabiyesi o!" "Kabiyesi o!" "Kabiyesi o" "Ki ade pe lori Oba wa!" "Ki bata pe lese Oba wa!" "Oba ti gba Idobale gbogbo Oba!" "Alaye lu'wa" "Igba ekeji OLODUMARE!" "Igba odun odun kan ni o Oba wa!" ("the Unquestionable one!" "The Unquestionable o!" "The Unquestionable o!" "Let the Royal crown remains and Royal shoes remains, the king of Kings your reign remain is forever.")

Then the palace clown and the drummers were singing war songs, and the Awujale Oba Afidipotemole order,

"now go and make blockages and barricades on the Oyo-Oke Ibadan roads and paths, to prevent traffic on these roads."

Then the Olisa got up and order the Balogun Ijebu the Osugbos, the Apenas, the Ogbonis and other warlords to take charge of the Awujale's order and he said

"I am personally responsible for the success of these blockages."

So the blockages were immediately put in place everywhere. However, one prominent Ijebu man name Osinugun Opaso lead the Oyos and Oke Ibadan warriors across Ijebu-Remo to Ikorodu to purchase arms and ammunitions which he sold to the Oyos resident in Oke Ibadan at the battle ground. And when the Awujale Afipotemole heard of what Opaso did he was very mad with him and order

"Arrest Opaso right now and confiscat the ammunitions."

So the Ijebuland warriors attacked the Oke Ibadan war camp and succeed in getting the ammunitions and thereafter, they decide to relax and they said

"we are not at war with this Oyos and we are not in support of the Egbas also so there no reason why we can not enjoy our Palm wine."

And they drank palm wine and even sat down with the Oyo warriors and joking with them as they drank palm wine. But the Oyo people secretly called the Oke Ibadan warriors who fired their guns at the Ijebu warriors when they were sleeping and some of the people that were protesters. So the Ijebu warriors and protesters died at Omi river and they took the ammunition away. Then the Awujale Oba Afidipotemole ordered

"the people of Oyo in Ibadan and Oke Ibadan are to be killed and their properties to be destroyed."

Moreso, the Ijebuland Army carried out the order and the people in Oke Ibadan were captured at the border of Ibadan which made the Oyos to panic and those that escaped plead with the Oke Ibadan Army station at Ijaye that the Ijebus were upon all Oke Ibadan. And the Oyo warriors called for a meeting and they decided to be tricky in their dealing with the Awujale Oba Afidipotemole and his warriors, by pretending to persuade the Ijebus so as to make them to be temporary relax inorder for them to be able to gain more time before dealing the Ijebus. So they took 3 slaves, 3 crowns which were to be taken to the Awujale Oba Afidipotemole palace to seek his forgiveness for the costly jokes made by Ogunmola to the Awujale Oba Afidipotemole. However, these were the names of the people who they send to be presented as sacrificial lambs:

1. Joko-Senu-Mini (Sitting with perfect silence)
2. Ijebukometan (Ijebu does not know deceit)
3. Ogundele, but this name indicates (Ogunmola) would avenge his treatment by the Ijebu after he gets back home. Also those three people had on them a special frankincense and a spell which the Oke Ibadan plan to use in killing the Ijebus and the Awujale. But the Awujale Oba Afidipotemole was able to detect their evil plot and he ordered

"a Royal messenger shall go and tell the Oyo delegate to wait some days at Iperin and to make sure that the spell on them will have become ineffective before they can be allowed in Ijebuland."

Thereafter, eventually when they were allowed to see the Awujale Oba Afidipotemole, they were given a very warm and lavish entertainment,

allowed to present their gifts, permitted to ask for forgiveness and Royal blessing from the Awujale Oba Afidipotemole, who accept their gifts. But when they were about to leave Ijebuland gate at Ipara, the Awujale Oba Afidipotemole send a word message to them that

"if the person who defecates forgets, the person who cleaned up the mess would never forget."

Which means that what Ogunmola said he has not forgotten and he still be expecting Ogunmola to come and attack Ijebuland. Thereafter when the Oyo delegate got to Ijaye and gave the report of the Awujale's response to them they become every worried. So after some days the Olisa ordered

"the warriors shall attack the Osi Balogun (2rd General) Ogunmola warriors at Ijaye and they are to be killed completelly."

But Ogumola was able to escaped and he reinforced at another camp. However, the Ijebuland warriors reasoned among themselves and they said

"we shall have to wait for their war to end so that we would not be drawn to their war."

So Olisa called back the warriors to Ijebuland. Moreover, the Emir of Ilorin also used the opportunity to declared war against Oke Ibadan and he said

"we can now forced them to accept the Koran at all cost."

But there was hunger and starvation in the war camp which the Fulanis cannot endured, so they left and only made raids continuously on the Oyo towns and villages for slaves. However, the Egbas replenished their ammunitions of the Kakanfo Kurumi warriors at Ijaye and they were able to march to war without taking any precaution and hiding from direct gun shots and arrows. But the Kakanfo warned them, but the Egbas insist that they would camp outside the Ijaye wall. However, when the word got to the Balogun Ibikunle that the Egbas were in the Ijaye camp to fight against them, he was unable believe it that the Egbas had came to fight against them after their oath of alliance and he said

"yes!" "They may have come!" "But it must be to negotiate peace between us and the Ijaye."

And again some of the Ibadan warriors brought him the same report that the Egbas had camp with the Ijaye, but he said

"it must be to put an end to the war."

Eventually, when the warriors made a sudden retreat that he realized that the Egbas had launch attack on his Army. But the war-chiefs encouraged one another and they said

"death is better than shame of defeat in war, and humiliation of being made a prisoner."

And the Osi Balogun Ogunmola said

"here is the head is better than here is it face"

adding

"if we cannot resist them here surely we shall not be able to do so at home, If we are driven from this place."

Then he took out his Jack knife and show all his warriors and he said

"It must be victory or -Death."

Thereafter the Oke Ibadan warlords had a meeting and conclude that "we will wait for the Egbas to attack us first."

But the Egbas refused to listen to the advice of the Kakanfo Kurumi who told them

"let them come first and attack you here,"

and thereafter he rode his horse to a spot, look around and add

"but never go after them also!" "never go after them also."

However, the Egbas who were too eager to fight replied

"we have not come here to wait!" "We are warriors too!" "And we have good guns that are about the best and we shall be ready to use them."

So the following morning the Egbas marched out and attacked the Oke Ibadan Army. But the Balogun Ibikunle gave the order that

"no one shall fire a gun until the word for the command to shoot was given. We shall let the Egbas exhaust their gun powder and then we shall answer them with our guns too.'

Then when the Egbas had moved very close and they had been shooting as they matched, but their guns did not do much damage to the Ibadan camp. Thereafter the Balogun Ibikunle said

"Omo Oke Ibadan Egba efi ti won" ("Ibadan boys up at them"),

then the Oke Ibadan warriors rushed out and the fight became intense and it was head to head. Though the Oke Ibadan warriors were initially afraid because the Egbas outnumber them, but they become confident that they can carry the day. And the Osi Balogun Ogunmola rode his horse, inspecting the men as the battle, continuing praising the warriors and mentioning their names as he observed that they were doing excellent job. However, towards the end of the day Abayomi the Bale Ajiye took up the fight as he noticed that the Egbas had left their positions unguarded, so he choose some brave men and they cut through the Egba at the rear with a very loud shout which caused great panic on the Egbas who were caught unaware and killed them almost completely as the Egbas ran away from their camp. But the Kakanfo Kurunmi used his war experience, because he had noticed that the Egbas did not have the military discipline, so he plan against this, then when the Egba formation fell, they ran for retreat, and the Oke Ibadan pursued them, then the Kakanfo ordered his men to intercept the Oke Ibadan warriors. But the Oke Ibadan quickly stop the chase of the Egbas, realizing that the Ijaye warriors were still around so they held their ground. Moreover, the lost by the Egbas made them to be very ashamed by their defeat and blamed it on the Balogun Anoba and they told him

"go to sleep"

which means for him to go and commit suicide. And they said

"instead for you to call for back up of the reserve forces, you gave up and ran away."

Eventually, the Osi Balogun Ogunmola and his warriors were able to capture people as slaves and order that they should be given the Tapa facial marks. And he said

"Emi a so Egba di Tapa" ("the transfer of Egba into Tapa"),

and he ordered

"use the yam peels on the their marks so that they will have thick scars on their faces."

Thereafter the war continued at the Ijaye wall, some Ijaye watchmen that were post on the top of a tall tree near river Ose which give them vintage view of several miles and they were able to announced the approach of the Ibadan warriors. So the battle stayed there for several days until the Ibadan gain control of the river completely and they enter Ijaye and kill thousands of them. However, the Missionaries of the C.M.S. and the

American Baptist at Ijaye help the war victims and the refuges and also sympathizers at home and abroad send foods and products to help in the war recovery efforts. Rev. Adolphes Mann, of C.M.S. and Mr. J.T. Bowen, an American Baptist also help.

Famine

Then the Oke Ibadan make an order to stop food from getting into Ijaye, Oke Ogun towns and villages. And the Osi Balogun Ogunmola who was the leading warrior at Oke Ogun ensured that their farms and markets were destroyed. Thereafter when the people in the cities, towns, and villages around had been completely reduce to hunger by famine, he ordered Ijaye to be evacuated. Eventually, the Kakanfo sons were caught and killed, and his warriors and guards are reduced to few numbers. Also a young woman who was one of his aids, who was always with him in the battle fields, carrys a calabash of charms for the safety and success was wounded in several place of her body and she had become too weak to continue and she died. Then the Kakanfo escaped to his house in a town close to Ijaye. Eventually, after the Ijaye had been completely destroyed and famine had reduced the community the war end. Moreover, the Kakanfo Kurumi died later in old age of broken heart because he realized how he had destroy Ijaye. Then the Osi Balogun Ogunmola return with victory songs and jubilations to Oke Ibadan.

Ijebu and Ogunmola

Thereafter, the Osi Balogun Ogunmola had moved to the next rank in the Oyo Army to become the Otun Balogun (1st General/Major General) Ogunmola. He was very famous and powerful after the Ijaye war, so he felt he was the most powerful warrior around and he said

"who dear challenge me in war? I even challenge the Ijebu in a war."

And he plot for war against the Ijebuland, and instructs his singers and drummers to sing songs:

"Ogunmola Alapa, the husband of Bankelu
He slapped the Akoro in the face,
He challenged Ajero to a duel
with his clenched fist he swing his own,
The Balogun was fighting at Ijaye,
Ogunmola danced thence to gungun drum beats.
The Egba prepare to run away Lagos ward.
Awujale gazes skyward, ready to flee
Alapa would have launched an attack on Lagos
But was stopped by the Lagoon."

So on their way back from the war at Ijaye, he instructs his warriors

"cover my face with cloth so as to prevent me from seeing the rooftops as we will pass through Ibadan to Ijebuland villages which we shall attack and drive them into the Lagoon."

But the Balogun (General) Ibikunle told him

"we shall have to take our rest for some time at home before going to the next war. It is good for our warriors to gain their convidence and be able to focus also,"

So when they got to Oke Ibadan they rest. Thereafter, the Osi Balogun Ogunmola said

"the Ijebus that were in the Oke Ibadan and Ibadan to come for debate with me."

And he ask them

"who among the Ijebuland warriors can stand me in war?"

Then Osinuga Opaso said

"oh!" my Lord Otun Balogun Ogunmola there is no warrior among the Ijebu that can stand you."

Also the following people were his warrior followers: Ogunnupebi, Abinusawa, Agidisanda, Kuyoro, Ole-Oba, and Keke Balogun. But Ogunupebi told him

"there are thousands of men capable of challenging you from any Ijebuland village. Please don not under estimate who Ijebu warriors are, we are the warriors that have never suffered any single war defeat."

Eventually, word got to the Ijebuland Chiefs in the villages and towns close to Ibadand that Otun Balogun Ogunmola was about to attack Ijebuland. Then the Olisa the Obas, the Balogun Ijebu, and chiefs had a meeting with the Awujale Oba Afidipotemole on the issue of war with the Oke Ibadan Army.

The Imakun war

Meanwhile, then the Awujale Oba Afidipotemole sends word message to the Egba after the Ijaye war and he said to them

"I have given to you Imakun which is an Ijebu-Remo town that allowed Osinuga Opaso to use their territory as a passage by the Oyo Army on their way to Ikorodu where they collect arms and ammunitions for the Ijaye war."

However, the Ijebu-Remo Chiefs had plead with the Egbas to help them appeal to the Awujale Oba Afidipotemole to forgive them for their relationship with the Ibadan during the war. But the Egbas realized that they cannot say no to the Awujale Oba Afidipotemole's order and they accept and matched with the Awujale's Army against the Remoland warriors. Then the Remos send to the Oke Ibadan for help. However, when the Oke Ibadan received the message, they quickly accept it and sang this song:

"Nobody can withstand us
Except the hills and the forest, Nobody can withstand us
Except the hills and the forest ...."

Then the Otun Balogun Ogunmola quickly ordered the Army to attack Ijebu towns and villages that were not part of Ijebu-Remo. And the Oke Ibadan camp in these villages: Ipara, Isara, Ode, and Okerekere and divide their war front into two war camps, one under the Balogun Ibikunle which was in Ipara and Ode. And the Otun Balogun Ogunmola to be in charge of Isara. Then the combine forces launch their attack on Imakun and took Ogere. And the Ijebu and Egba Army took the Oke Ibadan Army by surprise such that Ogunmola himself had to escape with luck because the superior gun power of the Ijebu Army was too much for him and his Army. However, Ogunmola became speechless and even when he gots to the Balogun Ibikunle he finds it hard to explain what had happen that made him to lost the battle and his Army defeated just in one week of campaign.

The Oke-Iren War

Then after the defeat of the Oke Ibadan at Isara they quickly camp at a village which is on border of Iperu and they attacked Ikene, Ipara, Irolu. Then the Iperu people ran to the Awujale Oba Afidipotemole and made a strong appeal for forgiveness. Then the Awujale Oba Afidipote, the Olisa together with the Ijebuland Obas and warriors realized and they said

"the Ijebu-Remos who are our cousin had also realized their mistake and had begged for forgiveness so we need to appeal to the Awujale Oba Afidipotemole to forgive them."

And the Awujale Afidipotemole told them

"They shall go and declare their allegiance and submission to me as their Oba and they have to tell the Oke Ibadan Army and Ogumola that they have returned to me as their Lord and father and they do not want the Oke Ibadan camps in the Ijebu-Remo province anymore."

Then the Remos went back to Remo towns and villages where the Oke Ibadan army were camping and told them "thank you!" "We had been mislead by you Otun Balogun Ogunmola please go back to Oke Ibadan, we are still subject of the Awujale Oba Afidipotemole as our Oba and ruler and we want to go back and pay homage to him, so the Oke Ibadan Army should leave Remoland."

Then the Ijebu Army march on Ipara and took the place by surprise such that a single man warrior took down the whole Oke Ibadan warrior unit which consist of Oke Ibadan and Ijebu-Remo warriors. Then the Oyo Army moved their camp to Obu-Igbo near Odo-kisi and when they are sleeping, some warriors among them who were cowards suddenly woke up in a night mare and shouting

"Oyo is here!" "Oyo si here!" "Oyo si here!" ".....

Then the shout caused panic among them in their camp which made the Ijebus to be aware of their camp and attacked them. And the Ijebu Army blew the trumpets of attack on the Oke Ibadan camps and killed most them and the rest ran away. But Ogunmola was again able to escape with the help of his voodoo, though his cap was being destroy with gun shots. However, Mr. Rettford and an American sharp-shooter who also works like a red-cross aid, organized the picking of the wounded soldiers and the warlords. And these Oyo chiefs: Odunjo, the Seriki, Madarikan, the Asaju, Chief Adepo and more were killed and most of the Oyo warriors died when the rest ran away from their camps and the warfront to their home in fear. Thereafter Balogun Ibikunle became ill due to injuries he sustained in the battle and almost all his war-chiefs were killed. So the Ibadan war camp for the first time cannot fight back because all their war-chiefs were shot dead and almost all their warriors were dead because of the war lead by the Olisa Ijebuland, the Balogun Ijebu, the Osugbos, the Apenas, the Ogbonis Ijebu with some few Egba war-cheifs had totally subdue the Balogun Ibikunle, and the Otun Balogun Ogunmola Army. Then the Otun Balogum Ogunmola was the only surving senior war-chief with a very small size Oyo Army which was not capable of war, because the Balogun Ibikunle was sick. The Osi Balogun was killed at Ijaye war, the Seriki, Asaju, and others are all killed at the Iperu war. Eventually,

Osinuga Opaso was capture by the Egbas where was hiding in one of the farms and the Ijebu warriors rescued him and the Olisa order

"the bastard Osinuga Opaso shall die for his sin at Ijebu-Ode so he shall be brought before the thrown of the Awujale Oba Afidipotemole."

Then Opaso was disgressfully shot dead at a big open space in the front of the Awujale Oba Afidipotemole palace for being dishonest and unpatriotic to his town and people.

Towards British Establishment of Colonization Of Nigeria

The Ikorodu War about 1863

However, some of the Ijebuland warriors were called back on their way to the Ijebuland after the war at Iperu, by their war-chief Ogiji. And Chief Ogiji was very angry, his eyes red and with a very loud voice he complain and said

"why did the war end when I was not around? I was sent on an errand to the Ijebu-Remo to protect the traders there. Are you able to get the slaves and the war spoilt for me?"

But the warriors respond

"no our Lord!" "We have to wait for your return as you had instructs us. And we stayed at the houses you left us waiting for your return."

But the Balogun Ijebu Rosanwo was riding behind, and met Chief Ogiji who was still angry and the anger was all over his face. And he was surprise, step down from his horse and asked, because he was his friend,

"what is wrong Ogiji? And why is your face full of anger? The war is over, and the Awujale Oba Afidipotemole had order us to leave the camp and go home."

Then Chief Ogiji asked him

"did you and others get some slaves and the war spoilt?"

And the Balogun responds

"so that is why you are so annoyed?" "We did not have to get slaves besides you have forgotten that the Awujale Oba Afidipotemole had said he gave the slaves and spoilt to the Egbas as compensation. And you know this war is not like the usual war where we take slaves, because we only fought this war to teach the Remos some lesson for disobeying the Awujale's order and to serve as lesson for all Ijebu people not to disobey and also for all of us to learn to stick together as one family."

Then as they were about to leave, the Basorun Egba Somoye call on them and took them to a secret house where the Egbas camped and told them

"my two good friends!" "Thanks to the gods!" "That I am able to see the two of you here before going to the Ijebuland to look for you. I receive a message today from the white slave traders and the Governor of Lagos men in uniform were also among them, and they said they are very disappointed that the war we fought with the Ijebu-Remo did not provide them any slaves!" "And I told them that the Awujale Oba Afidipotemole did not allow us to take his people as slaves, nobody can take an Ijebu person as a slave when an Awujale is on the throne!" "But they gave all these bags of money!" "you can see, they are many more than 50 bags and gifts that we should organize a slave raiding at the markets in Ikorodu area, because the markets and farms there are getting bigger and have a lot of people there now and in the Ikorodu town also."

Then Ogiji said

"that is correct!" "Though the Ikorodu people are Ijebu!" "But we can try and kidnap the Oyos among them at the market in the evening."

However, just as they were talking the white slave traders and the men in uniform came into the compound. And the chiefs exchange greetings with them through their usual interpreter and the slave traders said

"we shall not let the fight extend for long time just two days will be OK, since the two market days is always full of people."

The uniform officers said

"the Governor will be around on the market days so we would be able to come around as if to protect the people. And we will be shooting to send the people away as the fight is going on, then the slave traders will be able to catch as many slaves as possible to the waiting boats and to the secret place the slave ship is located."

Then the Balogun Rosanwo said

"all this bags of money is for us only!" "And not to be share with the Awujale, the Royalties, the Olisa, the Obas and the other Chiefs and in Ijebu and Egba?"

The white slave traders respond

"that is left for you three Chiefs to decide on your own!" "We know you all are smart enough and can figure out how to take care of the money"

then they complete the planning and arrangement for the fight in Ikorodu. And after the white people had left, they decided and said

"we can bring up the following accusations against the Ikorodu!"

1. "They launch attack on Imota and Agbowa and capture them during Iperu war.
2. They also release the people capture at Imakun
3. They release the Oke Ibadan warriors and people capture at the warfront, which should not be because Chief Ogiji was not around who is the senior Chief there."

Then the Basorun Egba Somoye said

"how are we going to let the Awujale Oba Afidipotemole know so we can get more war-chiefs?"

Balogun Rosanwo laugh and responds

"The Awujale Oba Afidipotemole!" "Would never allow slave raiding, not to talk of raiding in Ijebuland."

And Basorun Egba Somoye now supprised and with fear in his voice said

"I should have realized that before getting all these!"

pointing at the bags of money on the floor and he add

"these lot of money!" "Are we going to return them to these evil white slave traders? "Because we can not carry out a slave raid of this nature by just three of us and our warriors and slaves alone."

But the Balogun Ijebu Rosanwo laugh and he responds

"You have forgotten that I am a leader amoug the warlords of Ijebuland!" "I can mobilize some war-chiefs to join forces with our own war-chiefs and since we are not going to destroy the whole of Ikorodu peace, but just the two market days and some farms for the white slave traders to be able to get their slaves that they want to their country."

Chief Ogiji said

"what are these evil white people using our people for in their country?"

The Basorun responds as they were counting and distributing the money and gifts among themselves,

"can you see all this things we buy? From them they want more of the slaves to carry them."

And they continue with the counting and distribution of the money and gifts among themselvies and the war-chiefs that would be involve in the raids.

Eventually, when the fight start the Awujale heard that the Balogun Rosanwo and Chief Ogiji had join with the Egbas to launch attack against the Ikorodu people. Then the Awujale Oba Afidipotemole send a word message quickly to the Basorun Somoye ordering him

"Basorun Egba Somoye!" "Shall go back home with his men and they shall not fight with the Ikorodu because they are my people!" "And I had already compensate the Egbas with the war spoilt of Imagun."

He also ordered

"the Balogun Rosanwo shall leave Ikorodu now and stop the fight because I shalll curse who ever continue with the fight."

But Balogun Rosanwo said to the rest of them

"we would have finished with fight before the messengers and the people return to Ijebu-Ode."

However, just like they had planned it, Governor Glover was nearby the market place, and he heard the gun fight, but his military attaché send the officers to stop them from fighting and the Officers that were working with the slave traders took charge of the command and did as they had planned with the Basorun Egba Somoye. However Balogun Rosanwo ordered the singer and the talking drummer to sing:

"Let Glover shoot his head off

We shall satisfy our desire."

The Egbas also said

"we cannot fight the Imagun war without having slaves to show for it."

So they sing:

"Egba will not fight
Egba will not fight
Egba will not go home empty handed."

But the Balogun of Ikorodu was ready to defend his people and he ordered his singer and drummers to sing:

"It is enough we beg the king
It is enough we beg the king
We offer our Lord in supplication to the slaves of king."

Then the fight began with gun fires, and the Governor military Army quickly came there with some heavy military artillery trying to scared them away and this caused fears and panic among the traders and the people said

"this has not happen before!" "The white people are fighting against us in Ikorodu!"

so the people ran from the market to their home and those in their home ran out. Moreover the White slave traders lead slaves kidnappers and they kidnapped the people and took them as slaves to the boats that were waiting which took them to the ships for journey to Brazil and Cuba. However, the Balogun warriors shot at the Ikorodu Army and the fight became serious and the Balogun Rosanwo warriors and the Basorun Somoye warriors were mostly killed and Chief Ogiji was also shot and he died. Thereafter the Balogun Rosanwo and the Basorun Somoye were evetually captured by the Ikorodu Army with the support of the Awujale Oba Afidipotemole warriors. Then the people were very happy when they captured them and saw all the money they had been bribed by the white people.

CHAPTER 11

Ogedemgbe And The Fall of Ilesa About 1863

Ogedemgbe was a young warrior from Ilesa, who left Ilesa for Oke Ibadan where he became a good warrior under the leadership of Baba Aki, who was also a distinguish warrior. But when the Ijesa rebelled against the Oke Ibadan, Ogedemgbe and other warriors from Ijesaland return to defend their people against Igbajo. However, after the Ijesas were defeated Ogedemgbe was arrested and brought to Oke Ibadan to be executed at the altar of Ogun (the god of war). Then Omole who was also an Ijesa warrior in the Oke Ibadan Army called on Ayibiowu, Odo and others in their group and said

"we have to do something to safe our friend Ogedemgbe from being beheaded at the altar of Ogun tomorrow. He is a good warrior and is about the best in our group, if we lose a war-chief like him we will suffer."

So they agreed to plead with Latoosa who was also Ogbedemgbe's friend and he was the head of the Otun Balogun (1st General) Ogunmola's war boys and he was well liked by everybody. Then Latoosa agreed with them on their plead and talked to the Otun Balogun about Ogbedemgbe that

"he is a good war-lord and leader of warriors that are fighting for the Oke Ibadan, and since we can use him to fight for us we should not kill him."

And the Balogun Ogunmola said

"that it is good!" "You will supervise him and make sure he is not going to bring trouble to my Army?"

Chief Latoosa responds

"yes!" "My Lord Otun Balogun!" "I shall be responsible, and make sure he would not bring trouble to Oyo."

Then the Otun Balogun order

"bring Ogedemgbe before me now."

Then the leading guard in his palace went and removed the chain in Ogedemgbe's neck, hands and legs and walk him to the throne of the Otun Balogun Ogunmola. And Ogedemgbe prostrates at the front of the Otun Balogun Ogunmola, who put his leg on his head and said

"you are lucky today!" "I am with the spirit of my mother who forgives, otherwise your head will have been cut off your body to warship Ogun. Now I am releasing you for Latoosa to work for him, If you fight against my Army again you will be kill."

And he stood up but as Ogedemgbe was about to leave, the Otun Balogun said

"now you have to pay for your sin!" "So as to teach you and others lesson!" "Now get me my sword and hold him down,"

so Ogedemgbe was held by some warriors and he made a cut from the middle of his head to the his face. Then the Otun Balogun left the court and went to his daily worship shrine, where he worship the gods of his ancestors. But the Ifa priest told him

"my Lord the Otun Balogun!" "This Ogedemgbe!" "Is going to be a prominent and popular leader who is going to bring lot of trouble to Oyo and Oke Ibadan."

Then the Otun Balogun order

"now pack the soil of spot of the blood of Ogbedemgbe when his face was cut to be use for the sacrifice so that the Ogedemgbe shall become powerless. I shall not let him have peace of mind and when that is done, we shall see how that foolish destiny of his can be fulfilled."

Then the Otun Balogun in a very furious anger mode shout on top of his voice

"get me the soil now, hurry up, where is that stupid destiny of the stupid boy is going to take place?"

However, Ogedemgbe was told of what happened by some people in the Otun Balogun compound and he escaped with the Ijesa warriors to Ilesa. Thereafter when they got to Ilesa, they plot against Odele who had made all the young men to ran away from Ilesa because of his dictatorship way of ruling. And they fought the Odele Army under the leadership of Ogedemge and eventually the warriors of Odele left him and join Ogedemgbe because he had lose the fight to Ogedemgbe and Odele commit suicide.

Ibadan Under Otun Balogun (1ˢᵗ General) Ogunmola About 1863

However, Otun Balogun Ogunmola was in a meeting with the chiefs and the people of Oke Ibadan, and the singers and the talking drummers were singing his praise

"Kirinun Onibudo!" "Kirinun Onibudo!" ….

Then Otun Balogun Ogunmola said

"since the Balogun (General) Ibikunle had died, the Otun Bale (Assistant Major) Ibadan Sunala was also killed in the Iperu war!" "I am the now the most senior chief in Oke Ibadan!" "And I don't know anybody that can make me to take or accept the title of the Bale (Mayor) Ibadan, because I am not ready to retire yet from warfront. So the only title that I will be please with is the Basorun (Prime Minister) Oyo."

The people and all the Chiefs said

"whatever you want we will support you as our leader."

And Ogunmola add,

"if so what are I am waiting for? Send my senior slave to the Alafin Adelu now to tell the Basorun Gbenla to vacate the title of the Basorun for me because it belongs to me."

Then he got up from his big mahogany seat and looking up and at the people smiling he add

"I know that it is a hereditary title!" "But I insist on having it because of my strength and war sacrifice for the Empire."

So the Ibadan warriors mesengers left for Oyo town and when they got to the palace of the Alafin in Oyo town, the Alafin summon the Basorun Gbenla and the Oyomesi (the Parliament members) and told them what the Otun Balogun Ogunmola's request was. Then the Basorun Gbenla in fear left the palace thinking loud and he said

"my life have end now!" "So I will have to kill myself before this Ogunmola destroy Oyo town because of me!" "I have not offend him!" "But the Alafin Adelu or anybody in Oyo town have not offend him also."

Then the Alafin felt very bad when he heard that the Basorun said he was going to commit suicide and he sent the Oyomesi to him and order

"the Basorun Gbenla!" "Shall not commit suicide!" "I am giving Ogunmola the title of Basorun as an honor!" "For his war achievement and not on merit!" "And for now there is going to be the Basorun Oyo for the empire in the Oyo town, with all the right and privileges of the Basorun and also Ogunmola will be the Basorun Ibadan only."

And the Alafin Adelu add

"since Ogunmola demand for the Basorun's 'chain of office' (represented by the bead in his neck) and the 'Wabi' (a special ornament hide on which only the Basorun sites.)!" "Let Ogunmola have them."

Then the Oyomesi visit the Basorun Gbenla and told him of the Alafin's massage and forbid him not to commit suicide since he was not losing his title and privilege as the Basorun Oyo. And he became happy, and his wives and family celebrate with him and all the people of Oyo praised the Alafin for his wisdom and they also praised the gods of ancestors of the Alafin Oyo.

However, some months after, the Basorun Ogunmola Ibadan send a letter to the Governor of Lagos that he wants the Governor to allow the road construction the government was about to construct to pass from Lagos to Ibadan and Oke Ibadan so as to boast economic of the three big cities because the Awujale Oba Adipotemole refused to allow the white access into Ijebuland except Ibadan that has become a metropolitan city. Then after the road had been constructed, lot of people travelled to their home towns in the Interior land from lagos because of the road. Thereafter, Mr. Philip Jose Meffre, who was a returnee slave together with some Ijesa people traced their home back to Ilesa and there was a great jubilation, merry and parties when the people saw them. Then on their returning back they had a stopover at Ibadan and stayed in the Mission. But some people in Ilesa who were jealous of their popularity send word to the Basorun Ogunmola in Oke Ibadan

"Our Lord!" "Basorun Ogunmola!" "We noticed that Mr. Meffre and his companion were working against Oke Ibadan interest in Ilesa they said Oyo warriors were wrong for the fights." Then the Basorun order

"I summon Mr. Meffre and his companion to my palace"

and when they got to the palace he said

"arrest them on the accusation that they had brought trouble to Ilesa and they were working against the interest of Oke Ibadan," but they denied it and explained

"oh!" our Lord Basorun Ogunmola! We are not warriors, and we only use the opportunity the new road offered to visit our home town."

But the Basorun did not listen to them and had them put in the prison and lucked it up with chains. Then Rev. J. T. Smith, who was the Missionary in charge of the station since Rev. Hinderer was absence, went to the Basorun's palace and plead and he said

"these people are returnee slaves from Brazil, they are good Christians and they have no political interest, just ordinary people who are happy to travel on the new road."

However, the Basorun did not listen to his plead and they remain in the prison.

But incidentally, due to continuous prayer and faith of the Christians in Lord Jesus Christ who is greater than the evil idol worshiping gods of the Basorun. The whole of the Basorun Ogunmola's house was completely burn down, the Basorun himself was just lucky to escaped from the fire. But the section of the house in the compound where the prisoner were did not burn at all and the prisoners were alive and healthy. Then the Basorun became very afraid and said

"surely these men are innocent persons and there is naught else but the interposition of their God. I am not the man to defy the white man's God."

And he quickly released them and sent them to the Mission.

However, when the Ijesa people heard what had happened at Oke Ibadan, they are very annoyed and they attacked Igbajo. Then the Igbajo people sent for the Oke Ibadan Army for help, and the Basorun Ogunmola ordered Osuntoki the Maye and some war-chiefs to defend Igbajo, but the Ijesas defeat them and the town was nearly taken. However, on the 16th December, 1866 the Basorun ordered the Balogun Akere to defend Igbajo. So Akere marched to Igbajo with the Army of Oke Ibadan and they defeat the Ijesas, but the fight continue for many months. Meanwhile, on one day the Oke Ibadan war-chiefs were having a council meeting, and the talk become boring to the Osi Balogun Abayomi who was a young man, so he ordered his warriors to follow him and they took a secret path in the forest to the rear of the Ijesa camp where their war-chiefs were resting and without their guards and look outs and he ordered the attack and the Chiefs were all killed and also the camp was set on fire so the Ijesa warriors were defeated. Then fight was taken to Esa town which was also taken. However, the news of the fight got to Lagos and the Ijesa community in Lagos, and the Ijesas in Lagos begged Governor Glover to intervene on the Basorun Oke Ibadan Ogunmola to stop the attack on Ilesa. So Governor Glover send message to the Basorun Oke Ibadan Ogunmola in Oke Ibadan to stop the attack on Ilesa. And also the Owa Ilesa send demijohns and heavy presents to the Basorun Ogunmola and told him

"we Ilesa people have submit to be under the command of Oke Ibadan because we want peace to remain between us and Oyo."

Then the Basorun Ogunmola called the Balogun Akere and his Army to return back to Oke Ibadan.

However, the Oke Ibadan war-chiefs after they got back home paid tributes in slaves to the Alafin Adelu and the senior warlords also contributes their share to the Basorun Ogunmola according to the custom. And the junior chiefs received their share from their seniors according to their rank and custom. But after some months the Basorun Ogunmola became sick with of small pox, and the Babalawos (Ifa priests) told the warriors to load their guns with bullets and shoot in the direction of Isale Osun district and this was done for several weeks, but there was no solution to the sickness. But on the morning of the 28th February, 1867 the Basorun Oke Ibadan Ogunmola's death was announce with repeated musketry shot. And after two months on the 12th of April, 1867, the Osi Balogun Abayomi died after a few days of sickness. On the 30th April, 1867 the Otun Balogun Tubosun also died. So all the council of war-chiefs that attacked Ilesa were all dead except the Balogun and the Seriki. They were all killed by the spread of small pox which they got by coming into contacts with the white people that had the infections. The small pox epidemic killed lot of people then. before the Vaccine for it was discovered.

Then after the death of the Basorun Oke Ibadan Ogunmola, the Ilesa warriors again rebelled against Oke Ibadan and war was declared. However, the Balogun Oke Ibadan Akere who was the senior Chief refused to distribute the titles to the Chiefs and said

"we shall wait for the war to be over. Then I will be the Bale, and you all can have the titles you deserve,"

but the war-chiefs refused to show interest in the war except Obembe. Meanwhile, when they were at the warfront, the Balogun was able to persuade them with gifts and they agreed to fight. Thereafter the Ijesa made a trench of about of about 10 to 20 feet deep with a drawbridge almost around Ilesa and they make a their stand and defend themselves. but they were defeated at a place which the Oke Ibadan call Fejeboju ("the pool of blood") because of the bloody battle at the place. However, at this place an Ibadan warlord call Ayibiowu command his warriors to attack the Ijesas at Oke Esa road, and the Ijesas defeat him and killed all his warriors and they were all butchered to pieces. But the fight continued and after about 1 year the Ijesa decide to surrender and they negotiate for peace, and they send 400 bags of cowries to the Oke Ibadan camp as submission money. Then when the money got to the Oke Ibadan camp all the chiefs were afraid to touch it because they feared it might have been poisoned. But Obgoriefon said

"Let me die if poisoned!" "I don't mind afterall I am not rich this is the opportunity for to be rich."

So he took the money and this encouraged the rest war-chiefs and they continued with the flight, but eventually the Balogun Akere was killed and the council of the war-chief had a meeting and they decide

"we have to continue with the fight so that it would not appear as if we panic because our leader has died."

And they told the Ijesas

"you had kill the Balogun Akere who was for peace, so the fight will continue."

Then the fight continue on February 15th 1869. However, Orowusi the Asipa became the leader of the Oke Ibadan war-chiefs, but he was not popular among the war-chiefs. However, his son Akeredolu command respect among his peers as their captain. Moreover, Akeredolu and his group discovered that the trench did not cover the whole of Ilesa, but it terminates at the foot of a big rock which was covered by a dense forest. And they also noticed that when it was not battle days only few men were left to guard the entrenchment and the fort which was impregnable and the rest of the Ijesa people were always at home for rest and enjoyment. Then Akeredolu called his group and they went to the rocky terrain, but his father saw him when he was going towards the Ijesa camp area and tried to prevent him from going and he said

"come back!" "Oh come back!" "For so was I bereaved of your elder brother at the Iperu war, when he attempt a feet of valour."

But Akeredolu refused and went off through another direction and making sure that his father did not saw him as he went with his group. So when there were out of the Balogun Akeredolu's sight, they brought out their gun and climbed the rock to the other side and got to the battle field without any resistance. Then the Balogun Akeredolu who was being anxious about the safety of his son, but when he did not know of his where about, he went to the battle ground and the whole Army followed him. And they saw Akeredolu and his group on the other side fighting and they defeat a small guards left there and most of the rest ran away. Moreso, the drawbridges were thrown over the trench to allow his father and his warriors to cross to where they were. Thereafter the trench was filled and the whole of the Ibadan Army were able to pass. However, Ajayi Ogboriefon fought to prominence and he encouraged the soldiers by telling them inspiring words of couragement and he would take out bean seeds from his bag and said "see this is what they are firing now they do not have bullets, come let us get at them."

And this made them to be brave, and he also told them

"Remember the bazaars, the market, what pleasures you often enjoy there, pleasure bordering on crime. Now is the time to atone for them if you will enjoy yourself again with impunity."

However, the Oke Ibadan discovered that the Ilesa were being supplied food and ammunition from Odo, and they blocked the road to Odo. Then Latoosa and Ogboriefon were assigned to block the road. And they fought the Ijesas heavily there and an Ijesa man who was on his way to see his son at the camp saw the Ibadan coming so he hide and witness the whole fight and he was so afraid because they was so much dead body everywhere and he counted about 140 heaps of corpses made when the fight stopped. Then the war-chief told him and others

"the people in the towns and villages should not hear of none of this so as not to cause panic among them which would made them run away and it will be easy for the Oke Ibadan to kidnap them."

Moreover, the Ijesas were able to resist the Oke Ibadan for a lot time because Ogedemgbe lead and encouraged them to fight. But after the hunger and famine become unbearable, and the Ogedemgbe boys called Ipaiye start to behave like the Jamas of Ilorin, because they were going to the people's house taking their foods and animals and eating them. And the people were dying of hunger, on the street and then some families went to the Oke Ibadan camp to surrender to Ajobo the Seriki. Then Ogedemgbe decided to negotiate for peace and he said

"it is better now before all the people we are fighting for died because of hunger which is more painful."

Then he had a meeting with Ogboriefon at the middle of the battle field, and they agreed on the terms of peace. And Ajayi Ogboriefon promised to allow him a safe passage. Thereafter when the peace arrangement had been concluded, Ogedemgbe and his warriors were allowed to leave the battle field through the ranks of the Ibadan formation and they brought valuable beads and cloths to Ajayi to rectified their agreement. Also in the morning of 4th June, 1870 when the Owa Ilesha got to the Oke Ibadan camp and he was given 10 of his wives, and many of his children he could find and also 10 bags of cowries and baskets of kolanuts. And the control of the king of Ibokun (a neighboring Ilesa tributary town) was also given to him. Then the Oke Ibadan Army continued with their fight against Odo, Iperindo, and from Irangan to Ipetu and captured the people as slaves and control of their cash crops. And on the 10th of July, 1863 the Ibadan Army return home victorious.

CHAPTER 12

The 16 years war about 1865

Meanwhile, after the Ijaye war the Ijebus and the Egbas had forbidden ammunition to sold to any of the interior tribes and actually the Oke Ibadan. And now there was some peace, and the trade consist of cloths, salt, rums, gins from the coast in exchange for produce such as palm oil, kernels, cottons, and more from the interior land. Then the late Ogunmola had opened the Oke Igbo road via Ife to Benin for the purpose of getting ammunition. And also the late Alafin Adelu had purchase a large quantity of gunpowder at Port Novo which is half way to Bokofi, but cannot took it no further because of fear of the Ijebus and Egbas might took it from them. Then Are-Ona-Kakanfo Latoosa sent the youngest Mogajis secretly with order

"go and bring the gunpowder the Alafin Adelu had purchased at Port Novo home and be careful not to loose them to the Ijebus"

Then when they had left his palace, he said

"I wish they might encountered the Egbas and the Dahomians who I want them to fight with each other in the process of trying to take the gunpowder from our warriors."

Then the Osi Balogun Ilori and Iyapo the Seriki were sent on the assignment with strict instruction that

"Molest no one, stay clear of Egba territory, go straight by Oke'hu, Igana to Meko; but if any one Molest or interfere with you follow the party home, and we shall come to meet you outside their gate."

And they left Ibadan on the 26th April, 1877 and return back safe on the 21th June without encountering either Egbas, Ijebu or Dahomains and they brought 800kg of gunpowder, some Dane guns, casks of rum and more. Then the next day the all the gunpowder were sent to the Alafin Adelu who took some kegs and sent the rest back to the Oke Ibadan chiefs as presents. Also the king Tofa of Ajase gave four hundred drums of gunpowder to the Oke Ibadan in exchange for their farmlands. But the Egbas were able to discovered it and report it to their chiefs and to the Awujale Oba Afidipotemole. Then the Awujale Oba Afidipotemole sent a word message to the Oke Ibadan Army telling them

"Oke Ibadan have you start your trouble again? You shall have to defend the accusation brought against you by the Egbas, that you had gone to Port Novo to purchase weapons in exchange with the lands close to Abeokuta"

but the Oke Ibadan responds

"we don't care what the consequence would be we had not done any thing bad."

But the Egbas insist

"the Oke Ibadan action was against us and that they are trying to pick fight with us by sending an Army to our backyard."

Then the Awujale order

"the border to Oke Ibadan shall be shut."

Then on the 19th May, 1877 the border was shut. Also the Egbas at the end of a meeting at Sodeke street in Abeokuta said

"we have agreed to close the roads against the people of Oke Ibadan and stop the exportation of salt and foreign goods to them."

Then Ajagunjeun, the Balogun Itoko lead the Caravan to the town gate and they turn the Oke Ibadan back home. However, the Kakanfo (Field

Marshal) Latoosa was jealous of the fames and the military success of the Osi Balogun Ilori who was the son of the late Basorun Ogunmola, and also that of the Seriki Iyapo, who was Ibikunle's son. Then in order to check their power, he set up a military group of his own household and raised some of his slaves to become warlords and made them to command warriors of with the sizes of 400 to 1,000 each. And those warlords were horse riding warriors, and he also stored lot of ammunitions in his compound. Moreover, he also made his eldest son a Mogaji, so as to rival with the other Mogajis in town. Also he made all his sons the head of his personal body guards. However, the other war-chiefs in Oke Ibadan noticed all this and they said

"it appears that the Kakanfo is planning to make members of his family the permanent administrators of Oke Ibadan"

and they agreed with each other to be ready to resist it. Then sometime, later, the Kakanfo told the war-chief

"I am now ready to go on military campaign which I am going with or without any of your support."

Then he called for the meeting of council on the 25th of June, 1877 and he order

"shut the gates against the Egbas, because since the 3rd of June they have been preventing our traders from getting into Abeokuta for trades."

And also he sent this messages to the Ijebus, Ilorins, Ijesas, Ekitis, and Ifes and told them

"here are the reasons for our going to war against the Egbas:

1. We only carryout our loyal duty to the Alafin and bring the Ammunition he had brought in Port Novo home when the Egbas refused to sell us Ammunition.
2. The Egbas close their roads against Oyo and prevent our traders from trading when we have not trespassed on Egba territory.

3. Many of our traders have being kidnapped at Abeokuta and sold into slavery."

But the other Chiefs told him

"Our Lord the Are Kakanfo Latoosa!" "Please let us seek peace rather than war. We are not cowards but if the peace efforts failed then we can go to war."

But the spirit of the Are-Ona-Kakanfo in him would not allowed him to listen to them on the talk of peace all his interest was war. And he responds

"I am Are Kakanfo!" "Or what do people just call me? I have to live to the calling of my duty, which is just to have interested in war and to defend Oyo and her people against her enemy.

So the warlords said

"we understand and agree with you our Lord!" "We do not want to make our wars to be just because to get slaves and the war-glory for ourselves only."

However, the war-chiefs told him

"we cannot wage war against the Egbas without the Ijebus coming to defend them because the Awujale Oba Afidipotemole did not want war in Abeokuta. And also you should realize that the Ijebus have the well advance guns now that is more powerful weapon of good precision which we don't have."

But the Kakanfo laughed and replied

"And with Muzzle-Loading one will I break them."

The Chiefs also respond

"Are Kakanfo!" "You should remember that the elders say 'Ote aladugbo ko dara' ('Warfare between neighbours is a great evil.'")

But the Kakanfo will not listened to them, and he said

"with my charms!" "The spirits!" "And magical powers of the Are-Ona-Kakanfo I am ready to defeat anybody."

Then he walk tro and fro the front of his thrown and rolled the horse tail in his hand and he adds

"I am going to perform a task which God has allotted to me to do, those who say they shall see that I don't accomplish it will not see it done, at it is done it shall be, and when it is finished they shall be no more wars forever in the Oyo country."

Then the meeting end because the other Chiefs felt they are not in the spirit of war and the reason to go to war had not arise. And they told the Kakanfo

"we have to attend the issues of our household for now"

and they left the compound and talking about their war failures as they went to their various home.

Eventually, the Kakanfo called for another council meeting on the 31st July and told the chiefs

"there is no subject of discussion today, but you should go home and prepare for kidnapping expedition at the Egba farm tomorrow morning."

But the Balogun and the other Chiefs refused to go to the expedition, and they said

"we are not ready for such thing now."

And he said

"very well as you are not prepared as you have much time at home as you wish, meantime I go and perhaps by the time I come back then you may be ready."

So the Chiefs reluctantly followed him to attack the Egbas which is duty bond for them by custom to do. And they attacked the Egbas farms on 1st August and captureed Atadi and Alagara and also took the fight to the gates of Abeokuta. Then the Awujale Oba Afidipotemole ordered the Ijebu Army to defend Egbas because of the Oke Ibadan attack on Abeokuta. And also The Awujale Oba Afidipotemole ordered the recall of the Ijebu Agurin (Peace Ambassador to Oke Ibadan) which meant the Ijebu have declared war against the Oke Ibadan. On August 1877, the Ibadan Chiefs though not happy with the war followed the Kakanfo Latoosa to the war but they refused to fight and they said

"we shall only be around at the war camp and let the Kakanfo Latoosa and his slaves with his household do the fighting by themselves."

However the Kakanfo Latoosa frustrates all the young war Chiefs and this made the Seriki Iyapo who was the son of the Basorun Ogunmola to commit suicide. Then after his death all the young warriors of Oke Ibadan vowed not to support the Kakanfo in his war. However, Akintola the brother of Iyapo succed him as the Mogaji of the house of the late Ogunmola, but the Kakanfo broke the power and influence of the household on the Ibadan community. Then, Akintola had to depend on his father's slaves for support of his military might. And the Kakanfo Latoosa continued with the raid of Egbas farms for slaves, but the Ijebus and the Egbs defeat them.

Then on Jan. 17th, 1878 the Kakanfo invite the Modakeke and other towns under the Oyos to join force with the Oke Ibadan Army and attack Ile Ife and defeat Ile Ife. However, when the Awujale Oba Afidipotemole heard of it on October 20, 1881, he became very annoyed, and ordered his Army to go and defend Ile Ife, so on November 16, 1881 the Ijebu Army fought the Oke Ibadan Army at Ile Ife and defeat them. But the Kakanfo said "yes!" "I have get the Ijebus busy fighting elsewhere!" "I will now continue with the fight with the Egbas,"

and ordered the raid on the Egba farms to continue. But the Egbas did not respond to the attacks nor did they defend their villages or farms. So the Kakanfo called the meeting of the Council of Oke Ibadan war-chiefs and said

"since the Egbas in Ake are not ready for war, I shall order to take the fight to Egbas in Osiele before returning back home."

But the rest of the war-chiefs disagred with him and they said:

1. "That we are already exhausted by the days useless exposure
2. That the Osiele is not taken into account before we left home, we have not consult the gods nor offered propitiatory sacrifice as we usually did before attacking a town.
3. That the Osiele from here is too risky and is not advisable because we will leave the rear and base expose to attack by the Egbas should they undertake to attack us by the way of Atadi."

But the Kakanfo who had made up his mind said

"you had better go and reconsider what you intend to do as for me my mind is made up. I am decided, and if there remain only me and my slaves and Aiyikit and Modakeke people with me, I shall take Osiele."

So the Chiefs again reluctantly followed him to the war, but said among them selves secretly

"we are only going to look and not participate in the fight and let the Kakanfo and his family and his slaves to fight the war by themselves."

However, the Kakanfo and his slaves lead the attack on Osiele and they were defeated and about 300 of them were killed or wounded. Then also by the second attack about 220 warriors were also killed, However, the Kakanfo slaves noticed that it was them alone and the Modakekes that engaged in the fights and they also stop being committed to the fight. Then the Modakekes also refused to fight, so now the Kakanfo and his warlords and personal body guards were left committed to the fight, but none of the Oke Ibadan war-chiefs left the warfront so that the Kakanfo cannot accused them of being a coward. So the Kakanfo made to retreat and he told his slaves

"you my slaves I am very disappointed in you. I think you shall always be with on every sides of issues"

Then he sat on his mahorgany chair and look at his loyal warlords face and he consoled himself saying

"there is no one who may not suffer a defeat for even the prophet of God (Mohomet) suffered a defeat."

Meanwhile the Egbas pursued them and killed some of them, then all the Oke Ibadan war-chiefs and the Modakekes return home. However, after some time the Kakanfo tried to make peace with the Ijebuland and he made attempts to make friendship and commerce relationship through the Ijebus in Ibadan and the Ijebu-Remos. But the Awujale Oba Afidipotemole told the Kakanfo

"the Are Kakanfo Latoosa!" "Shall first go make friendly terms with the Egbas!" "The Alafin!" "the Ijesas and the Ifes!" "Then I will see it worthy of any trade relationship, friendship and partnership with you."

So with this responds of the Awujale Oba Afidipotemole the Kakanfo now encouraged the Oke Ibadan war-chiefs to support him and he said

"my warlords and Oyo people!" "Are we going to be ready for the fight againt the Egbas now since the Awujale and the Ijebus are not ready to be friendly with us and we should be prepare because the Ijebus are not easy to be defeated in war"

EKITI REVOLT AND FREEDOM

However, the Ekiti and the Ijesa tribes became very courageous because of their alliance with the Ijebus encouraged them and they were able to break the yokes of the Oyos and Oke Ibadan on them. And the following people: Adeyala, Omo Oba Ila, Fabunmi Oke Imesi, and Odeyale Olajo-Oke form alliance and resist the Oke Ibadan Army dominance of their people. Then they agreed and attacked all the Oyos that were residing peacefully in their towns and they said

"not until we get rid of the Oyos living among us who always tell the Oke Ibadan Army of our war plans and strategy, the Oke Ibadan will always defeat us."

Then they killed the Oyos and some where them were sold as slaves to the Ijebus who used them as their domestic slaves in their farms and houses. Moreover they also killed the Ajeles (Political residents) of Oke Ibadan Chiefs living in their towns and villages. Meanwhile the killing was so intensive that at Ila alone more than 1,000 were killed. Then the Ijesas and the Ekitis moved their ammunitions from Oke Ibadan to Mesin Ipole. Then on the 16th June the Ilorins also joined forces with the Ekitis and Ijesas against the Oyos and Oke Ibadan. Moreover, the king of Ilorin sent words to the Kakanfo that

"If a man's wife desert him and afterward repented and come back to him, is not the husband justified in receiving her back."

And the Kakanfo responds

"yes he is"! "But let the husband beware of what he may contact from the whore."

Actually, this parable is to reflect that the Ekitis had been before under the Fulanis, but later declared for the Oke Ibadan when the Fulanis lost power to the Oke Ibadan. Then the Oyo towns from Ikirun to Iwo and Ife also join force with the Oke Ibadan because that was the only safe route for the Oke Ibadan Army to Benin for ammunition through Oke

Igbo. But the Modakekes were also Oyos and not Ifes, but refused to join the Oke Ibadan coalition because they do not want to be in the same group with the Ifes whom they declared as their strong enemy. Then the "EKITIS" (Alliance) on the 19th August attacked Igbajo being a border town and her residents consist of Oyo people, and other small tribes, but they remain loyal to Oke Ibadan and refused to join the alliance. However, the Kakanfo continued to attack the Egbas inorder to be able to have the route to Porto Novo to get ammunitions. And he made a campaign on Ogatedo and from Meko and he got the Seriki to assist him. Moreover, the King of Ilorin join the Alliance and attacked Ikirun with the aim of destroying the Oyo towns by the river Oba which is close to the Oke Ibadan farms. In fact, they were able to defeat Ikirun, Osogbo, Ede and Iwo and their Villages, but the people of these place had already desert the places. So the Ilorin and the EKITIS could not take any person as slave. However, the alliance of the Ekitis, Ijesas, and Ilorin held their ground and they defend themselves against the Oyo Army.

The Ikirun War Also Known as "The Jaumi War"

Moreover, the Kakanfo Latoosa ordered the Army to march against Ikirun and they worship Oranyan on the 20th October. However, the march to Ikriun was very terrible because it was the raining season, and they lost some men to flood at river Oba and Osun. Then the Balogun Ajayi Ogoriefon lead the fight but the Osi Balogun Ilori who was younger in age with less war experience, was so arrongant and refused to work under his command. Meanwhile, at their camp town one of the Ilori guards went and raid at the market and took the people's properties, and when Ilori heard of it he ordered the soldiers to be brought him and he told his other guards to hold them down, he use his knife to make a cut from their head to their checks. And he said

"this is to teach all of you the lesson!" "This is our town as our camp we are not to steal in our home."

But his Body guards decided not to forgive him for his action, and however, the Akirun the ruler of Ikirun joyfully meet the Balogun and he said

"Ajayi are you come? I am almost done for."

and he responds

"Take courage we are come, your deliverance is at hand."

Then the Balogun Ajayi Ogoriefon had a meeting with the Akirun and the chiefs and he learnt that the allies were at three camps. The Ilorin camp under the command of Ajia are at the North-Eastward close to Ikirun farms, the Ilasare close to the Ilorins under the command of Omo Oba Adeyale Ila and Fabunmi Oke Mesin Command the Ekitis. The Ijesas were under Ayimoro and Ogedemgbe was Eastward. Then the Balogun said

"we have to give our warriors three days to rest before we match to war."

But the Osi Balogun Ilori opposed and said

"the march will be next day we have to there before the allies are aware of our arrival."

And he sit down by a big tree and add

"I am ready to fight if you are not ready,"

but for interest of peace and victory the Balogun accept. Then the Balogun divide the Army into two units, one to be lead by him and to attack the Ilorin and the Ekitis which camp is closeby and is the strongest, and Ilori to lead the fight against the Ijesas camp at the East. But the Osi Balogun Ilori reject the order and said

"the Ilorin and Ekitis lie to the left of us, and I am the commander to the left, to the left therefore I go."

And the Balogun Ajayi Ogoriefon feeling sad and breath in deep, look at the shy then responds

"very good, you can have your own way."

so the Balogun Ajayi Ogoriefon after looking at the warriors over and add

"you should be OK!" "Since you even have the largest warriors, you should be able to have victory with them."

However, the Osi Balogun was so restless, he drank excessively, refused to eat since they had arrived Osogbo. And he order

"get me a bottle of gin, I want the one which is very expensive, we know that expensive ones are the best. So get the good expensive one for me, I shall have to enjoy myself who knows what it is like when we die."

However, it was consider a prestige to drink alcohol, and the more expensive the more admiration you get among the people. Then he mount on his horse and match out of the town by the Ofa gate. And his guards followed him, but he was under the influence of the alcohol and which made him to rode his horse too fast and careless, such that his guards following could not catch up with him. Then, he decided to follow a secret path through the bush so as to launch a surprise attack on the Ilorin from both sides. Since his other warlords lead by the Sariki Akintola had taken the road to the Ilorin camp. Then the Ekitis were surprised when they saw that the Ikirun were marching against them, but after a more closer look they noticed that the Oke Ibadan Army had join them and they report it to their camp. Thereafter Fabunmi and his warriors attacked the Oke Ibadan and defeat them. Moreover, the Osi Balogun Ilori warriors were so surprise when they cannot locate their leader, and Fabumi pursued them to the place where the Osi Balogun Ilori had taken a different direction, and they noticed the Ilori Osi Balogun and his guards, then Fabunmi told his talking drummer to beat the Akintola's war song of

"Kirinun Onibudo," "Kirinun Onibudo" ...

and he send some of his warriors to go and greet them and they should tell them

"you are rather late in coming, but we have almost entered the Ilorin camp, however, you are welcome."

But the warriors did not return because the Ilori's warriors noticed that the rolling of the their talking drum was not perfect and the style and rhythm was also not accurate and they told the Osi of their observation. But the Osi Balogun Ilori only dismissed them and he replied

"what else can it be?" "Is not that Akintola's war-cry Ki-ri-ni-un Oni-budo war-cry Ki-ri-ni-un Oni-budo ...?"

But when he discovered that it was Fabunmi Oke Mesin that have deceived him with the talking drums it was too late. However his guards did not made serious fight and he ran to escape, but because his thinking was affected by the alcohol, he got into the farm and his horse was disturbed and was captured and taken to the Ilorin camp, stripped nicked, and was given a rag to wear. Then some of the slaves that were inprisoned with him said

"now you see what has happen to you falling from riches to rag. Your arrogance and disobedience to the Balogun Ajayi Ogboriefon who is older than you and have more war experience than you has brought us into this mess. I am sure this will teach people like you some lesson that the power and riches they found themselves in control of does not belong to them alone but ELEDUMARE (God Almighty) have make such wealth or power to be in their control for the good and better life of everybody. But because of their greed and arrogance they always abuse their power and position and if care is not taken they will always end up like you now, which is from riches and powers to rags and slave."

Then the Osi Balogun Ilori who was looking downward and was too ashamed to look at their faces crying and he said

"can you my servants please help me!" "To plead to the Ilorin warlords! That I am rich and have very large inheritance from my father!" "And if they can release me I will be nice to you all."

Meanwhile, the Osi Balogun Ilori's warriors that has escaped were able to found their way to the Balogun Ajayi Ogboriefon and they told him what had happened. Then the Balogun order "now my warriors follow me we have to attack the Ilorin and the Ijesa camps, we cannot let them kill the Osi Balogun Ilori."

And they attacked the Ijesas and got into the Ilorin camp so as to rescue the Osi Balogun Ilori. However, some unit of the Ijesa Army who were about to enter into their camp meet them, and the Balogun Ogboriefon ordered attack on them and he said

"Omo Oke Ibadan e gba efi ti won, ema je won o lo -" ("Ibadan boys up and at them let not one escape.")

So the Ijesas who were in panic, and they ran away and The Oyo warriors followed them to their camp and most them were killed. Then the Balogun Ogboriefon said

"you my warriors have learn a good lesson today that you should never disobey the order of your superior and especially elders."

Thereafter, the Balogun Ogboriefon marched Northward to the Ilorin camp where they met about 1,000 strong Ekiti warriors and they attacked them but the Balogun Ogboriefon did not even care about their bullets or if he was shot at or not and he rode his horse straight ahead and he got into the Ilorin camp looking for Ilori and tried to safe him. But the Ilorins heard the drummers of the Balogun and they said

"And who is that again?"

and the Ijesas respond

"it is the Balogun, and they were surprised and said

"any other Balogun besides the one we captured this morning?"

So they fought the Ibadan Army who defeat them and the fight was very tense and lot of the soldiers on both sides died such that the river turn red and it was full of dead bodies. Moreover, the Seriki Akintola who was under the command of the Osi Balogun Ilori who had followed the road to the Ilorin camp, came to the camp. And the Oke Ibadan warriors that were already tied and weak, heard his talking drums beating "Kirinun Onibudo Kirinun Onibudo" and Akintola appeared with his warriors that were still fresh and full of energy to fight, so the Oke Ibadan Army's moral became very high and they followed Akintola as he point his hand in the forward direction and he said

"Awon ta nu? Awon ta l' emba se ta nta?" ("and who are these? who are they with whom are exchanging shots.")

So the warriors followed him and they captured lots of Ijesas and Ilorin warriors as slaves and killed more people. However, all the Osi Balogun warriors captured in the morning were able to escape and they looked for their master. And the Ilorin warlords heard the noise and drums of the Ibadan and they quickly ordered their most priced prisoner of war to be brought out before they escape. Then the Osi Balogun Ilori who had tried to escape by hiding at the back of a big tree, was reported by a woman that he was behind a tree and one of the Ilorin warlord drew out his sword and killed him, and the Ilorin warriors escaped before the Ibadan warriors got to them. So all the three camps of the alliance Army were attacked and destroyed on the same day by the Balogun Ogboriefon and Ikirun was safed.

However, the Ofa people also used the opportunity to break away from the yoke of Ilorin and they damaged the Bridge over the Otin river which made it difficult for the Ilorin Army running away from the war in Ikirun to escape to Ilorin. And most of them in hundreds perished in the river, but the Ilorin Commander-in-chief escaped with some of his favorites wives but most of his warlords were killed or caught. And Omo Oba Adeyala Ila was also killed, but Fabunmi Oke Mesin was able to escape.

However, after the war the Kakanfo tried again to apologies to the Awujale Oba Afidipotemole. But the Awujale and the Ijebus reject the Oke Ibadan Army appology and he said

"we are not move by your pretence of friendship and we have nothing to gain from trade with the Oke Ibadan, who have no major job than to buy ammunition from us which they use in killing their own Oyo people."

Then the Kakanfo plan to attack the Egba farms, but the Awujale Oba Adipotemole order

"the Ijebu Army and the Egba Army shall watch the Oke Ibadan war-chiefs' movements and make sure that the people in the villages by the border of Oke Ibadan are warn whenever the Ibadans make any attempts to raid in their farms or villages for slaves. We shall not allow these good for nothing people who all they do is to kidnap people as slaves and ask for ransom money for them since the slave trade business has been stop by their evil minded white slave trade masters, who are now more."

So all the Ibadan attempts to raid for slave at the Egba farms and villages did not succeed, because they couldn't catch a single person.

The EKITIPARAPOS (CONFEDERATE)

Meanwhile, the Ekitis instead of submitting to the Kakanfo as he had thought, form a bigger alliance which consist of the Ekitis, Ijesas, Efons and other tribes, and they raised a bigger Army and they were ready to the break the yoke off the Oyo empire on them. And they invited Ogedemgbe to come and lead them, who initially refused because of the covenant he had with the Ibadan not to intervene in their war again. But after communicating with the Kakanfo Latotoosa over peace between the Confederate and Oyo, but the Kakanfo did not responds to his word messages because of his arrogance so the Sariki Ogedemgbe to join the Ekitiparapos which was being lead by Fabunmi Oke Mesin. However, the Kakanfo Latotoosa send the Otun Balogun (1st General), and the Osi Balogun (2nd General) to Ofa to defend the province against Ilorin and the Ekerin Balogun (Brigadier) to defend Ikirun against the Ekitiparapos. But the Oba (King) Iwo met them when they arrived with small Army and he said

"what do think you intend to do with this small handful of men?" Don't you realize that the Confederate mean serious business of gaining their freedom finally now and they are a large force."

So the Seriki (Colonel) was sent as a reinforcement to Ikirun, then the Confederate fought with the Oke Ibadan Army and the Oke Ibadans record lost every day, so the Confederate decided and close the roads and the means of communication via Oke Igbo. Then the Lisa Ode Ondo send message to the Kakanfo Latoosa in Oke Ibadan that

"I remain neutral in the fight, and we the Ondos are not involve in the fight."

So the Kakanfo responds

"thank you the Lisa Ode Ondo!" "Please remain neutral and allow us the secret passage to Ibini to buy ammunition and I have sent you some presents,"

and the presents were delivered to the Lisa Ode Ondo by some Oyo slaves.

But the Ijebu-Remos who were traders were not happy with the war blockages because they were not able to trade with the Oke Ibadan which was their major trade partners. So they plead with the Awujale Oba Afidepotemole to effect the opening of the roads. And a Remo Chief name Soderinde the Balogun of the Cavalry told the Kakanfo

"my Lord the Kakanfo Oyo!" "We the Ijebu-Remos beg of you to send some slaves and presents to the Awujale Oba Afidipotemole and to plead with him for peace, because these war blockages have affect our trades with the Oke Ibadan and other Oyo cities and towns."

But the Awujale Oba Afidipotemole took the presents and the slaves, and reject the Remos intermediaries. Then the Kakanfo send some Ijebus who were resident in the Ibadan who were head by Omo Oba Abinusawa that was very influential at Ijebuland to beg the Awujale Oba Afidipotemole to allow friendship terms with the Oke Ibadan, Oyo and the Ijebuland. Then the Awujale Oba Afidipotemole ordered an Agurin (Minister) to go to Aha and give the following speech:

"Why should the Oke Ibadan now desire our friendship? Let them remember the scant courtesy with which they have treated us in the past. When they were going to Ijaye war we remonstrate with them but to no purpose. When we entreated to receive back Ajobo expelled, they utterly refused even to take him home his dead body. When they had difference with Efusetan, Aijenku, Ijapo we interfered on their good offices but we were not listen to. If they are tired of the war and they want peace, let them first arrange with the Egbas, recall their troops from Ofa and from Ikirun, and let the Are go to sleep."

So the Kakanfo realized that the Awujale Oba Afidipotemole and the Ijebus were not ready to negotiate with him and he said

"I cannot stand war with the Ijebuland and the insults of the Awujale Oba Afidipotemole is too much because he is annoyed with me so I should leave him alone before things get out of hand with this too powerful Ijebu Oba."

But the Oke Ibadan Army after fighting for weeks and without a single victory were eventually, able to get a prisoner of war and they question him and he told them

"ha!" "You are not yet fighting against Ogedemgbe but Fabunmi Oke Mesin."

And they asked

"where is Ogedemgbe then?"

He responds

"not yet come."

And they were able to get more information from him about the military formation of the Confederate and that they do not have a very large warriors at the camp closeby. However, the Osi Balogun Akintaro arrived to the warfront from Oke Ibadan with drums and this boast the moral of the Oke Ibadan and they were able to fight the Ekitis on all sides but both sides record equal victories. Then the Confederate invited Ogedemgbe to come and lead them and he eventually join them and said

"it appears that my people are now serious and we ready to gain our freedom from this evil Oyo empire at last. It is unlike before when they had fought just for small time and they would had give up the fight which was the reason the Oke Ibadan Army who are servant of the Alafin Oyo thinks they are unstoppable. And since we have a stable Army that have been fighting for some reasonable time now I will join them at the warfront. freedom for my people at last! At last we are ready to fight for our freedom!" "Freedom!" "Thank you the gods of the Owa Obokun!" "And those of the Ijesas and the Ekitis!" "Freedom at last!"

Then his Army marched to the Ekitiparapos camp with singing and dancing to the gangan (talking drum) beat and the people were lead out of Ilesha.

The Are-Ona-Kakanfo (Field Marsher) Latoosa go to warfront

Thereafter, the Kakanfo Latoosa heard of the report of the warfronts and he was not impressed and when they told him

"our Lord the Are Kakanfo Latoosa!" "Ogedemgbe had not been part of the Ekitiparapo fighting us he is just joining the Ekitiparapos in the warfront."

He responds

"so this war is more difficult than I had thought it will be I better go and take control of things by myself so as to be able to defeat them within just few days, because as an Are-Ona-Kakanfo I have the war spirits in me, and I will always win in battles."

So he ordered his own warlords to march to the warfront and for him to take lead of the fight himself. But his son Sanusi made the war-chiefs very mad when he told his singers to sang this song:

"The expedition that occupied Akere's three years
The war over which Awarun's son have spent six months in vain
But one day will it take Alabi, son of Iyanda Aro
With Silver-Studded hands he'll extricate and bring them home."

Then when the Kakanfo got to the camp he did not congratulate the war-chiefs for job done so far, or called them for the war briefing and plans of strategy to win the war. But Sanusi his son went straight to the camp and ordered the corn field that the war-chiefs had ordered to be plant to be cut down and said

"cut all the corn down now!"

Then he got down from his horse, shouting, kicking and beating the slave warriors and he add

"A ba la jo ti ija ogun yi se pe!" "Ti a si fi se, ta si mi mo si ta si o pelu awon kini won yi!" "To o! Awon Ekiti lo si ba wa fi iga gbaga ("no wounder the war is taking this long!" "And we are here engaged in shoot out with this ordinary Ekitis.")

Then he took a cutlass and cut a long stick and said

"I want all this corn totally cut down. My father the Are Kakanfo Latoosa!" "Is in the war camp now, we are here to fight war!" "And not to farm corn field, and how long are we going to spend just to defeat this Ekitiparapo in war? We did not need it, how long are we going to stay here?"

However, the Kakanfo Latoosa lead the fight the following day and the Ijesa lost the fight because Chief Olubayode was caught and killed so their warriors lost courage and the Oke Ibadan Army pursued them to the gate of Mesin Ipole. But the Ajero saved the situation for the Ekitis, he ordered the defend of the gates and the wall, he defeat the Ibadan warriors, killed their war-chiefs and they retreat. So the Kakanfo Latoosa seeing the kind of defeat he suffered he became ashamed of himself and said

"I am not going to sleep in a house but at the battle field until I win the war."

Though it was wet and cold but when the war-chiefs persuade him to come to the house already prepared for him to sleep and they told him

"it is folly to remain in the battlefield we are all wet and it is still raining. Suppose the Ekitis were to fall upon us in the night it will be all to their advantage, because they will come from their home quite fresh with ammunition dry."

So the Kakanfo responds

"yes!" "I shall go and rest after all I have had my days of war victories before, this little lost should not demoralized me and the Army of Oyo."

But the Ekitiparapos took all the advantages of their position against the Ibadan and used their free access to Ibini for ammunition and prevent them from getting ammunition.

Meanwhile the Ijebuland warriors maintained the road blockages which prevent the Oke Ibadans from getting ammunition and also from trades, and the Egbas continue their road blockages as well. Then the Ekitiparapos were able to buy Long Flintlock guns with large muzzles from Ibini. And eventually, famine was now very high in the Ibadan camps and since they were not allowed move to the nearby farms and villages to get food because most of the farmers in the place had been evacuated. But the corns planted by the war-chiefs had been cut down by Sanusi the Kakanfo son. So the Kakanfo Latoosa moved the camp to Elebolo, and the Ekitiparapos ordered the towns of Mesin Ipole to be vacated and they also moved their own camp to the place where Babalola had three victories for them in the past. So the fight continued and on the 18th May Kupolu the commander of Kakanfo's boby guards was killed, Akintaro the Osi Balogun (1st General) was wounded. On the 1st of June of the Chief was kill, on the 11th of June Ajenigbe the Ekerin (Brigadier) was killed. So the battle at Kiriji recorded more lost on the side of the Oke Ibadan and very little on that of the Ekitiparapos.

The Effect of the Road Blockages/Trade embargos

However, the Oyo country cannot get ammunition and salt they need both at the warfront and for their domestic food preparation. Then the price of salt became very high such that a pound of salt was more than ten shillings. But the poor people cannot avoid salt to cook their meals, so eventually the Ijebus and the Egbas worked out an arrangement that allowed trades with Lagos but though they were also affected by the blockages too because they cannot get slaves from the interior land to work in their farms and their house domestically. Moreover they allowed routes through Ketu and Ejio where they allowed the Port Novo to have a market and also allowed the other parts of the non Oke Ibadan Oyos to trade, they strictly forbid trade in ammunition and only allow cloths, salt and other non war merchandises. Then the situation became so bad in the Oke Ibadan camp and they had less than 100 kegs of gunpowder left which they kept just for emergency escape.

Then in 1880 the fourth war was fight at a town close to Egba district at Berekodo, Oke Tapa, Aiyete, Bako, Gangan, Igbo Osa, Idofin, Idire, Papa, Gbunginu and all these villages were defeated by the Dahomians. And the Oyo empire also lost Ketu, Popo and the Sabe districts to the Dahomians. However, the Derin the Chief of Oke Igbo was now the Oni of Ife elect, and it seem he wants to initiate peace talk, so the Oke Ibadan send him some cloths and some other present so that he could open the road at Oke Igbo, the Ilorin also send him some horses, and the Ekitis send him some presents as well. But the Ijebus and the Egbas insist that the roads shall remain closed. So the Oni told the Oke Ibadan

"I have no power to effect anything on this matter but to be neutral since the Awujale Oba Afidipotemole has insist that the road shall remain close until the you Oke Ibadan and Oyos return back home, leave your camps and let the Ekitiparapos determine their ways of life without the inference from the Oyo."

However, the Ijesas in Lagos purchased a large quantity of ammunitions and sent them to their warriors at their camps to defend their father land

and the young Ijesa men from Lagos went the Ekitiparapos camps and teach them how to use the new Cartridge bullets in the guns. So the powerful guns made the Oke Ibadan to ran away from the battle field because it killed lot of then and the Seriki Akintola was shot in the leg and he fell. But he was able to escaped but his horse was killed and most of the Oke Ibadan and the Oyo warlords had been killed and the Oyo Army had been completely defeated, but because of shame they hid in their camps and refused to leave. Then the British government in Lagos said

"we have to supply the Ekitiparapos weapons because their citizen in Lagos have been convinced by the British Parliament that they want us to advice their Army on the war."

However the British were trying to used the war as an opportunity to further their evil plans of using wars to penetrate into the Interior lands. Which the Ijebus have been preventing, and since the slave trade was no more and they want to exploit the place for the agricultural and mineral materials they need for their industries at Britain and America. However, the Awujale Oba Afidipotemole continued to encourage the Ekitiparapos to hold their ground and fight the Oyos and their Oke Ibadan servants to the end. Then the British Parliament desired to deal with the Ijebus since they now realized that they are the power that could hold and have being controlling the trade and policy of the whole counties in the Interior land. Mainwhile, the Ekitiparapos people in Lagos accept the British government offer to reinforce their Army. And the British changed the outlook of the "Royal Merchant Trading Post Company" to the "British Protectorate of Lagos" to reflects that who is to protect the Interior land trade and peace. And they bought slaves from the Fulanis and Hausas and trained them as their guards. So the white people parade themselves as the one helping the Interior native people to solve their war problem, when actually they were the main trouble because they had been bribing and polluting their Chiefs with bribes and guns so that they could continue to fight and that made it so easy for the white slave kidnapers and slave traders to be able to send the needed slaves to their plantations in the United States of America, Brazil, Cuba, Haiti and other Islands.

Then about June 1881, the Governor of Lagos send another message to the Awujale Oba Afidipotemole to order the opening the road blockages. But the Awujale Oba Afidipotemole was very annoyed and responds

"who do this evil white man think he is? "That he is to be talking to me directly without it coming from his King."

So he ordered the white people messengers

"you shall not to ever come to Ijebuland gates and the messengers of the Lagos government shall not be allowed in Ijebuland and the Interior land again."

Then he look at the Olisa, the Balogun Ijebu and he add

"If not for the Oyos who have not lost their respect!" "You white people would not have being able to enter anywhere in the interior land."

So the governor of Lagos servants and the white people were not allowed to enter into Ijebuland, except Ibadan that had become a metrolipolitan city.

Thereafter the Ekitiparapos also did not allowed the white people, because the Awujale Oba Afidipotemole said

"no white people should be allowed."

However, the Oke Ibadan plans of using the opportunity to get ammunition also failed and the dominance of the Oyo was also broken completely and the Awujale Oba Afidipotemoel used his influence to break the Oyo yoke on the Interior land tribes and the Oke Ibadan Army was defeated and made to be silence forever. Mainwhile the Governor of Lagos adviced the Ekitiparapos to decamp, But the Awujale Oba Afifipotemole said to the Governor messenger

"what an insult!" "That cannot be!" "Is it because the Alafin of Oyo had given you audience, and this makes you feel the Alafin Oyo is the ruler of everybody here?" "The Oyo do not and has never and cannot attempt to stand the Ijebus, so be inform and use your thinking to know who to consult first on the issue of the peace and how to end this war."

Then the Ekitiparapos said to the Governor messenger that

"we are in our country and you come from afar, how can you say we should leave our country?"

and the Oke Ibadan also responds

"nobody say you are to leave!" "We only ask you to retire from the camp into the town of Mesin Ipole behind you to give us the chance to extricate ourselves from the defile through which we must pass. Bitter experience has thought us never to decamp in the face of an enemy, for thus it was in 1865 when we do decamping from Iperu after peace had been made between us and the Egbas and the Ijebus, the Egbas pursue us and brought our retreat dearly. should we repeat the same thing here under the very eyes of the Ekitis it will mean annihilation for us in these ravines and precipices. Retire to the town so put some distance between us, and we will then decamp." But the terms of the negotiation failed. So they the Oke Ibadan send message to the Awujale Oba Afidipotemole and plead that he should order the blockages to stop but The Awujale Oba Afidipotemole refused and he send word to the Oyos

"If you are tired of the war, go home."

But the Oke Ibadan still continued to camp and then attempt to wage war on the Ekitiparapos, on the 26th December and their camp was attacked, but the Oke Ibadan lost the fight again and Belo the son of late Osundira who was well respected as a very brave warlord was gun down and he died.

Then the white people decide to use their divide and rule tactics on the Ijebu warriors, since the Ijebu warriors were in different places fighting. One part was in Oru defending the Ifes against the Oyo warriors who want to get ammunition from Ibini. The other parts was station in the border towns defending the road blockages. So Governor Glover secretly influenced some Ijebuland warriors at the road blockages with bribes and gifts to disobey the Awujale's order and to allowed the road blockage to be open and they should go home. But the Awujale Oba Afidipotemole became aware of it and he insist that the road blockage shall continue.

The Effort For True Reconciliation about 1881

Eventually, after the Dahomian had attacked the Western district of the Oyo empire, and made more threats that we shall

"visit Oyo this coming dry season."

And the people in the district that was already damage by the attack sent message to the Alafin Adeyemi

"Kabiyesi o!" "Kabiyesi o!" "Kabiyesi o!" "Iku Baba Ycye Oba ti gba ido bale Oba!" "we your subject in the Western district have been attacked and been forced to pay taxes and levies to the Dahomy. We will leave to resettle in the Dahomian country if you cannot guaranty our safety any more."

Moreover, the Alafin's Army the Oke Ibadan Army were engaged in war against the Ekitiparapos. So on the 9th of October, 1881 the Alafin request for Rev. D. Olubi who was the head of the Missionaries in the Oyo empire to come with

"any two of his sensible colleague"

and they respond to him, went to Oyo town on 13th and he had a meeting with them and this were the people present at the meeting:

The Olosi who was the Alafin Official aid, The Apeka who was the white men's intermediary with the court. Mr. Jonathan Ojelabi, the most prominent Christian member at Oyo. The Rev. D. Olubi, Mr. J. Okusehide, who was the Catechist at Ibadan. Mr. A.F.Foster, who was the C.M.S. script reader at Iseyin and the Aseyin messenger. However, the Alafin Adeyemi had earlier sent message to the British Government for assistance as follows:

1. "To help in putting end to the war ravaging my Oyo country.
2. To help check the Dahomian aggression on my country."

However the Alafin Adeyemi told the Governor representative at the meeting

"that I had made many efforts to stop the war but they had all failed. So I am looking forward to the cooperation of your Imperial Government for which I have great respect to come and help in this matter. I further assure the Imperial Excellency to undergo any expenses to achieve peace on this matter. Your Excellency shall know that my towns are in great panic now and they are about to scatter because of lack of protection"

in a letter to the Governor in Lagos.

Also he wrote another letter to the Sectary of the C.M.S, and it was address to Rev. J.B. Wood and he request the help of the Mission's the effort toward peace in the Oyo country and he explain

"I had send request to the Governor in Lagos to this effect and I beg your Mission to see to it that the Governor expedite the efforts toward my request for peace."

Moreover, the writer of the letters was the one that was sent to deliver then, and he was instructed to go through Oke Igbo, Ode Ondo and the Mawen country to Lagos so as to avoid the Ijebuland and Egbas who always intercepts messengers from Oyo towns. However, when the Messenger got to the Governor, he was having a meeting with messenger and the representatives of the Oyos, Ijesas and the Ekitis separately, but because there was no more connection between the Interior land and the people in Lagos they knew nothing about the situation there and they cannot relate with the content of the letter. So the Oyo representatives doubt the content of the letter to be from the Alafin Adeyemi and they said

"we do not believe the content of this letter to be real!" "Oyo is the most powerful tribe in the interior so why will the Alafin be the one asking the Governor for help first?"

Then the Governor told the messenger to write the situation of things in the interior land and the reason he believe the people want peace and that he wants the Lagos Government's intervention on the matter to bring peace to the war, and the statement was address as a letter and is dated 28ᵗʰ November, 1883 to the Governor of Lagos. So the Governor after having discussion with representatives, sent his own delegates to the chiefs of the tribes concern and request their true desire for peace and also to verify if the letter was actually from the Alafin Adeyemi. And if so the Alafin should send his Ilari with the Alafin's staff, and these were the delegates:

For

Oyo:

Messr. Simeon D. Kester and Oderinlo Wilson

Ijesas:

Messr. Phillip Jose Meffre and Joseph Hasstrup

So they left with the Alafin's messenger on the 5ᵗʰ January, 1884 with the copy of the Alafin's letter so as to confirm that the letter came from the Alafin Adeyemi. Then the Governor also sent message to the neutral interior Chiefs such as the Chief of Ondo and the Derin of Oke Igbo and told them to send their own messengers to accompany each representatives he had sent.

Thereafter, when the representative got to Oke Igbo, the Derin was very annoy with the messenger of the Alafin and he said

"I doubt the message because the Alafin would not have send such message without consulting with me first, since we at Oke Igbo have being following the instructions and the blockage of the road to prevent the Oke Ibadan from getting the ammunition."

But the Messenger remind the Derin and said

"my Lord the Derin should remenber the message I brought from Rev. Olubi which you admitted was the same message. I am just a messenger and I cannot see the content of the message that had been sealed."

But the Derin refused to hear the messenger anymore and he said

"this whole thing is not making any sense to me anymore let just pray to the gods of our ancestors to help us achieve peace on this matter."

But Mr. J. Haastrup who was one of the Governor's delegates and Akitonde one of Derin's Chiefs told the Derin

"Our Lord the Derin you should try to consider the messenger as a servant of God and since he is a Christian he is not likely to bear false witness."

Then the delegates went on their separate ways to their different destinations. However, the delegate to Oyo were well received and the Alafin Adeyemi who was having a meeting when they arrived. Then later he said

"I confirm his letter that I wrote to the Governor to be genuine, the situation of the Oyo country of which my authority over the Oke Ibadan Army is no more effective to stop the war, and the Ekitiparapos will not want to listen to me too. So I ask for help from the Governor to help bring peace to the my country Oyo."

Thereafter the Alafin Adeyemi wrote a letter and thanked the Governor and confirm his previous letter to be from him and he send an Ilari whose name is Obakosetan with his staff. Moreover, also the Ekitiparapos tribes had received their various delegates and they had send them back to Lagos. So when the delegates got to Oke Ibadan Chief Maye represent the Oke Ibadan Army at the meeting and he explain that

"we have desire for the war to end and we also want an assurance of a safe route to the coast so as to be able trade, which will not cause trouble for us and our neighbors."

Then he looked at the other delegate and he add

"we will prefer the Ikorodu route to Lagos which was freely opened during the time of Governor Glover and we are ready to cooperate with our neighbors for the road to be open and we want the Governor to guaranty security from trouble of the Egbas and the Ijebus."

However, the delegates also received a letter from the Oke Ibadan war-chiefs sent to the Governor which was written by the Alafin Adeyemi messenger which explain

"that the Ijesas are the cause of the war, it is because of their invasion of Ikirun that result to the war. And the Egbas Kidnapped the Oyos and also prevent the Oyos from trading in Abeokuta. But the Ijebus and Ilorins we have no issues with them, and we don't know why the Awujale Oba Afidipotemole makes things difficult for us by taking side with the Ekitiparapos on the war."

So the delegates left for Lagos with the messenger of the Alafin Adeyemi and his Ilaris. However, when they got to Lagos the messenger of the Derin Oke Igbo with his staff and the Osimowe the Chief of the Ondo were already there.

Then they had a meeting with the Governor-General, Sir Samuel Rowe of the Gold Coast, and the Governor of Lagos told the Ilari called Obakosetan to explain what the Alafin want and he said

"my Master present his complement to your Excellency he has sent me to invite your kind interference in the protracted war that has been going on these several years in the interior, in which several lives are being sacrificed yearly. His own effort for the purpose proving abortive and he has been constrained to apply to you as representing a higher power, to enable us to effect peace throughout the land."

The messenger of the Are-Ona-Kakanfo Latoosa of Oke Ibadan said

"the Alafin is our king, and where his representative speaks the Oke Ibadan cannot say otherwise. We abide by what he had said."

Apenidiagba the Owa messenger said

"we have the Oke Ibadan in our duchess now and they should be plucked off."

And the Governor-General replied

"why then did you not eat them off before this time? And why come here to ask this Governor for their interference?"

Then the Ijesa messenger said

"our condition is that unless the Oke Ibadan will guarantee that they will stop making war in the future against the Ijebus, Ekitis, Egbas, Ilorins, we will not agree to peace."

The Seriki Ogedemge messenger said

"I agree with Owa's messenger, we and them are in this war for the same reason, to stop the Oyo from troubling us."

The Ondo messenger said

"we are just interested in peace for all of us."

Then the Governor-General said we have heard all your complain and issues that bring about the war, but we have to consult with our superior on the issue since it involves other countries."

Thereafter the fortnight the Governor-General called the delegates and said

"after the careful consideration of this matter I have my respond in this letter which is as follows:

I have carefully examine the message you gave to me fortnight ago, and I have heard from the Lieut-Governor all that passed in this matter before I came to Lagos.

I appreciate all the action of the King of Oyo in sending to the Governor of Lagos to ask him to send an officer to make peace between the Ibadan and the Ijesas.

I thank the King of Oyo for the compliment he has paid to the English Government in doing this showing that he believes in the honour of the English Government, and he feels confident that an officer of the English Government will deal justly in this matter.

The great Queen whom I serve, Her Most Gracious Majesty the Queen of England and the Empress of India. Has no other wishes than the good wishes towards the entire African people. Her Majesty's instructions to her officers whom she sends to govern this Colony are to promote by all proper means friendship intercourse between those under their rule and the native tribes living near them.

In doing this from time to time her Majesty approved the visiting her officers to many of the tribes neighbouring Lagos.

But Her Majesty has no desire to bring the Interior tribes neighbouring Lagos under the British rules, though the wicked people have said that if the white comes to the interior he want take their country, I tell you publically that my Queen has no wish to take your countries.

As to sending the messenger asked by the King of Oyo, I am quite aware that in sending to ask the Governor to send a massager to Ibadan and Ilesa camps to make peace, the King of Oyo has done a great thing. He has make request that is not be slightly answered.

I have thought over it patiently and very anxiously and what I have is this:

The message given by the Ijesas is not a clear message, They said they want the Ibadans to go away and would make peace on certain conditions, and a part of that condition was that the Ibadan should sign a promise that they will never again make war on any of the allied tribes whether Egba, Ijebu, Ilesa, Ekiti, or Ilorin.

I cannot send an officer to your camp to dictate to you what you shall do there, but I will report all the circumstance to Her Majesty principal officer, and if hereafter the Ibadan should wish to cease from fighting, and agree to such a condition as one of the Queen's may think right, and if her Majesty should direct that one of her officer should visit you to try to find out their conditions, then I will do all in my power to carry out your wish; and although I have found fault with the difficulty in the road, I will even come willingly myself if I am directed to do so

The Queen is very much interested in your welfare, and she wishes our officers to use every right endeavour to increase your prosperity.

Government House, Lagos

April 14th 1882"

Then when the messenger of the Alafin Adeyemi got to Oyo and explained the outcome of the meeting to the Alafin Adeyemi and after the letter from the Governor had been read, the Alafin Adeyemi said

"Let us say in a word the whole thing has collapsed!"

However, the combine forces of Oke Ibadan and Modakeke destroyed Ife town, and when the Awujale Afidipotemole heard of it he was very annoyed and torn his dress to piece and said

"how on earth would anybody in his right mine attack our ancient home?" "Ile Ife is a spiritual home of all of us!" "And I shall not tolerate this at all."

Then he stood up from the thrown and order

"the Army shall march to Oru and assist the Ife Army to defend Ile-Ife."

Thereafter the Ijebuland army launched attack on November 16, 1882 and they defeat the Oke Ibadan and the Modakeke Army. Although some Ife warriors were fighting for the Oke Ibadan Army in the camp at Kriji, but the people of Ile-Ife at home support the Ekitiparapos and they prefer their army fighting to get their freedom from the Oyo empire which was what they desired. Moreover, the Oke Ibadan had desired to attack the Ife earlier, but they held back because of the Modakekes living closeby and some are within the community of Ile-Ife. Mainwhile the events that followed made the Oke Ibadan to look for means to have victory and to be able to capture slaves and also because they need ammunition, did not care and they attacked Ife town.

The Ijebu Peace Effort

Since the Oke Ibadans and the Oyos cannot reach peace, Rev. David Hinderer, who had retired from the Oyo C.M.S. where he had beeen a minister for many years in Oyo, so he sent a letter to the Oyo and Ibadan and other interior tribes living in Lagos and he said

"my fellow believer!" "Of the Gospel of Love, Hope and Peace!" "Through our Lord and Saviour Jesus Christ!" "I am imploring you all as patriots and Christians to see that you achieve peace among your tribes and I also implore you all to put jealousy aside and work as Christians in the interest of peace for your father land."

So the people of these tribes had a meeting and they choose their representatives among their people who lived in Lagos and the representatives met with the Lieut-Governor Alfred Moloney and these following peopple were those appointed for the meeting:

Rev. JAS. Johnson, Pastor of St. Paul's Breadfruit, Messr. Henry Robbin and I.H. Willoughby and they had a meeting with the Governor on 8th December, 1882 and present the following resolution:

"At a meeting of the representative elders of the different tribes, Oyo, Egbas, Ijebus, Ifes Ekitis, Ijesas, Ondos held at the Breadfruit personage on the 7th December in the in reference to the long standing warfare in the Interior, from which both the interior and Lagos had suffered, the following resolution was after a full consideration of the subject is unanimously adopted.

'That this meeting convinced of ex-king Dosumu's influence with the Kings and Chiefs of the Interior, though he no more exercise regal power in Lagos, and this is known everywhere in the Interior, decides that a deputation composed of nominated representation of different tribes be appointed to wait upon him, and to respectively solicit his interference with the King of Jebu and other Kings and Chiefs in the Interior for the peaceable settlement of the Interior difficulty, His Excellency the Governor of Lagos haven been first respectfully informed of it, and the countenance and support of his influence had.'

(Sgd) JAS JOHNSON."

The Governor responds

"that it is in the interest of her Majesty to see that there is peace among the people of the interior. And though the ex-King Dosumu of Lagos nor his Chiefs are allowed to exercise authority in the settlement, but it is in the interest of the people of Lagos to consider their judgment on this matter, the Government will see to do what is best to meet the aim of the community by allowing the ex-King and his Chiefs to the meeting so as to hear their view on this matter."

Then a meeting was held the on the 11th, and King Dosumu said

"I shall thank the people of Lagos representing the various tribes and countries of the interior for their effort in working towards the peace of the land."

The Apena who acts as the spokesman for the king and the rest of the chiefs of Lagos said

"we would like the matter be reported to the Queen, and if they will allow us to talk to the King and Chiefs of Ijebu we shall be willing to do so."

So all the representative said

"yes!" "you are our representatives and our counties and tribes are not part of the Colony of Lagos Govermrnt, so they should go ahead to talk with the Awujale Oba Afidipotemole since it is with his influence we can get this peace talk done in our countries, so that peace would return to our land."

However, Messr. Robbin and Willoughby said

"will have to be careful when it comes to the Ijebus, we remember the trouble we fell into in 1875 during the administration of Governor Dumaresq when we realized that the Ijebu do not want our interaction with the affairs of their country and the Interior people's affairs."

Then Governor Moloney said

"if Dosumu and his Chiefs would be able to use their loyal advantage to influence the matter to bring peace to the country I am confident that Her Majesty's Government would appreciate your effort and it would not be of good interest to involve a different and meddlesome interference in the Interior economy of a government such as Ijebu. I believe that the Alafin's messenger state the fact that 'nothing less than a armed intervention could prevail upon the belligerents to decamp.'

And look at his other white officers and at representatives faces and he add

"the influence of ex-King of Lagos or that of the Awujale of Ijebu-Ode who is unable to put to stop the struggle in his home and not sure if he will be able to guarantee safety for an hour."

The representatives stood up and face him and they said

"what do you white men think you are we the representative of our countries and tribes know that the Awujale Oba Afidipotemole and Ijebuland did not tolerate you in Ijebu. We cannot stand here and you would use this opportunity to make remaks that make the Awujale Oba Adipotemole of your equal, when you are just a representative of your king who is the only equal with the Awujale of the Ijebu."

Then they walked away from the present of the Governor and the meeting. To show their displeasure with him undermining the authority of the Awujale. But Mr. Hinderer sent message to the Governor and he said

"oh Governor!" "The people of the interior are serious about their custom and tradition, just like we do not allow any form of disrespect of her Majesty the Queen of England. They would not want you to disrespect the Majesty the Awujale who is also an Emperor and he is the most influential King that control the trades of the tribes, he can control and call all the tribal Kings and Chiefs together to achieve the needed peace."

However, the representatives resolved and sent the Apena of Lagos to the Awujale Oba Afidipotemole Ijebuland with the objective of putting an end to the war in the Interior. So on 26th of December, 1882, the Apena on the advice of Mr. Hinderer met with the Governor and let him know of the ex-King order to him to represent him and the council to go to the Ijebu for the issue of peace.

However, when the Apena got to the Ijebu port at Ito Ike he heard that there was a riot at Ijebu-Ode, so he did not spend the night at Ijebu-Ode. And the following day, the Awujale grant him audience and he explained to him that

"I heard that a retired Missionary wrote a letter to the representatives of the Interior tribes urging them to work together on achieving peace and they appealled to Oba Dosumu and the council of Lagos with the approval of Governor of Lagos for your Majesty to work on the peace of the land."

So the Awujale Oba Adidipotemole after hearing the Apena, responds

"I shall allow you to go now to the Ijebu camp at Oru and deliver the message to my warlords there."

But the Apena said

"Kabeyesi o!" "I would like to know your mind on this matter Kabiyesi."

The Awujale Oba Afidipotemole said

"it not for me to make my final decision before hearing the advice of my war-chiefs and order relevant Obas and Chiefs in council first."

Then the Awujale Oba Afidipotemole look at the face of the Olisa and some Princes and Obas in the palace and add

"but the right now some of the war-lords and war-chiefs are not happy with me and they are even just leaving the town. You shall meet the Osugbos, the Ipampas, Ilamurins and the Ogboni Odis, I believe some of these warlords are accusing me of being hostile to the Oke Ibadans, after I had agreed with the Obas and Bales of the Ekitiparapos and the Emir of Ilorin and the Alafin of Oyo, before the wars that I shall give them my supports. I had promised to help them to break the yokes of the Oke Ibadan Army from their necks. So now they want me to break my agreement with them because of their sudden desire for peace with the Oke Ibadan war-chiefs and because of the white man wants it, I am an Oba (Emperor) and my word is great."

Then the Apena prostrates and said

"Kabiyesi o, and I should greet you goodbye and I am on my way to Oru and I will bring you the report later Kabiyesi o."

So the Apena Ijebu took the Apena of Lagos to meet with the war-chiefs of Ijebuland at the Ijebu camp in Oru and they were about to leave a meeting but when they saw the Apena they return to their sits. And there were about 320 of the Ogbonis. Then Apena of Lagos told them

"I greet you my Lords and fellow varriors as you are aware the Awujale send me to tell you of my mission as a representative of the Oba of Lagos and the Council on the peace for the war going on to have a discussion so as to come up with a solution for peace."

And they respond

"thank you the Apena of Lagos!" "For coming to visit us at our camp, we also are tired of this war and we are interested in peace we have seen difficult situation now for seven days, and with the Awujale Oba Afidipotemole who will not listen to us that we are not comfortable here and we desired peace with the Oke Ibadan since the war has affect the prosperity of the Ijebu country."

Then the Apena of Lagos was quickly taken to the meeting of the war-chiefs council which was about to end before they would be leaving. And he told them the same thing he had told the other war-chiefs. Then the Balogun said

"Is it customary with you at Lagos to settle quarrel or not?"

And he responds

"yes",

so the Balogun then continued and he said to the chiefs and the people

"what is your opinion of the message of the community of Lagos which the Apena is representing and he is on the mission to solve the war issue and bring peace?"

They respond with a shout of joy

"yes!" "We desire peace and we want to go home"

Then the Balogun said

"for about seven years we have been station in Oru to fight the Army of Oke Ibadan and we are now broke and tired of this war, you can also hear that the people of Oke Ibadan are also tired of war. So we don't think there is a need for the war anymore. Though we do not have issue with the Oke Ibadan, but the Egba is the cause of the war just like we were made go to into Ijaye war in 1860-62. When the Egbas deceived us that two Oyos were fighting them and we went and flog them both, only to know later, when it was already late that the Egbas were the one at fault. The war took us from Ijaye to Oke Kere in the Remo districts, but in actual fact the Oke Ibadan did not had the intention to fight against us. But they had came to defend the Ijebuland against the Egbas, but we join the Egbas and fought the Oke Ibadans. And at the end the war destroyed our Remo districts."

Then he pause, look at the Apena of Lagos as if to demand if the explanation is too much for him to understand, but the Apena of Lagos said

"my Lord the Balogun Ijebu!" "I can take your words and I understand your explanation"

So the Balogun Ijebu continued to narrate different issues that shows how the Ijebus had been drawn into fights by the Egbas

"when had been trying to defend them, the Egbas do not always appreciate our sacrifice of protecting them. You can observe that we are now in this war camp our roads are block from trades. But the Egbas are trading in their market at Erebu and they are enjoying prosperity. And I would want you as the messenger of peace to be free and to help us inform the Awujale Oba Afidipotemole that this is the resolution of the people: We want for the Awujale Oba Afidipotemole to move to his palace from his mother's house. The palace is the official home of the past Awujale which is the place where the people recognize, as the customary throne of the Awujale. And also the Awujale Oba Afidipotemole should stop taking advice from some people but to follow the wish of the people. So the people have given him five days to carry out the people's wish, and also the Awujale Oba Afidipotemole should let the people deal with the Chiefs that have being given him the wrong advice."

Then the Apena thanked them and he said

"I will do what is necessary for peace to reign,"

and he left the meeting. Thereafter he left and went to Lagos and on his way he said "whao!" "So this is the how tough the life of the Awujale is? Sure it is hard dealing different types of heads of which they would hot and cool ones, a leader must be made of peaceful temperament otherwise its trouble?

But before the five days, the Chiefs that the war-chiefs accused left Ijebu-Ode and escaped to Epe which was an Ijebu town. Also The Awujale Oba Afidipotemole left the palace in Ijebu-Ode and said

"I shall not let history to repeat itself on my reign!" "I shall not have to curse my own people I am going to stay in Epe which is my father's home, so that there will peace in Ijebu-Ode."

However, the Oke Ibadan Army Chiefs under Kakanfo Latoosa wrote several letters to the Governor of Lagos begging for help to put an end to the war. But the war continued and as both side record lost and the either side could not decide who to leave the camp first and the modality of breaking their camps. Also life became very hard for the Ekitis also because of feminine since the farmers cannot go to their farms and they were also afraid of being captured by the Oke Ibadan warriors. Then the Ipayes (war boys) were working as robbers in the town of Ilesa, and that of the Ekitis, since the Ajero of Ijero, the Owore of Otun, and Olojude of Ido are all in the war camp town of Mesin Ipole, but the Owa of Ilesa left Ilesa and stay in Ijebu Ere for safety. Also the Awujale Oba Afidipotemole sent his own warriors slaves to Isoya to help Ogunsigun to fight the Modakeke and the Oke Ibadan Army and most of the Modakeke and Oke Ibadan warriors were killed and the rest ran away from their camp.

Rev. J.B. Wood Go To The War Camps

However, Rev. J.B. Wood was the oldest Missionary of the C.M.S. in the Oyo country and he was living at Abeokuta, and he got permission from the Ebgas to go and visit the Mission stations in the Interior. Which were Iseyin, Oyo, and Ibadan, so when he arrived at Ibadan on 24th August,1884 the Oke Ibadan warlords and Chiefs were happy to receive him because he was the white man that the Alafin Adeyemi had been using to relates with the Governor of Lagos. Moreover, he told them that

"I will like to do something about the war peace effort, of which would involve some notable people that would join me in persuading these warlords to decamp."

So Rev. D. Olubi of Ibadan, Mr. Abraham F. Foster, C.M.S. Catechist of Iseyin, the Catechist of Ibadan followed him on 24th to the Oke Ibadan camp. Then they had a meeting with the Kakanfo Latoosa at his reception room, and Rev. Wood told him

"we have come to you to know of your interest on the need for making of peace with the other warlords so that this war can end and we would have to visit the others war camps."

So the Kakanfo Latoosa said

"thank you the white man do you think I am not tired of being in this war front? I had not spend this kind of time like this in a warfront before. The means to end the war is what I strongly desired now too. So I give order for the Maye Oyo to be our spokesman for the Oke Ibadan"

Then the Maye said

"thank you the white man and all of you joining him on this effort to bring this war to an end. I will explain the history of the war to you if you permit me"

after the interpreter had stop talking Rev. J.B. Wood said

"good!" "Of course we we would want to know, that is the reason we had come to your camp"

and the Maye Oyo continued

"the Ekitis and Ijesas made us their protectors and they submit to the Oyo rulership and we help the to break their yoke from the Ilorin and we never had any quarrel with them expect when we help with some internal issues. But the Ijebus are now making them to want to break away from us so they form a Confederate call Ekitiparapos and attacked Oyo territory. So we are here now in the interest of Oyo tribes and fighting their battle and safe guarding our frontier from aggression, and the country from being overrun by the enemy as it they seem determined to do."

But the Rev. said

"that is good!" "Can we request to go and visit the other people's war camp now and later we will have word for you from them?"

So the Oke Ibadan war-chiefs after discussion over it and they said

"it is OK!" "We shall wait for your return, and we want you to carry this flag of truce with you when you go to their camps to show to them that we are done with this war."

Then Rev. Wood and Mr. Foster cross over the Fejeboju stream to the Ekitiparapos camp. But when the Ekiti soldiers saw them coming towards them, they advanced toward them leveling their guns at them. But the Missionaries waved the flag and shout

"don't shoot we are peaceful messenger sent to your commander-in-chief."

So they desist, walk towards them and they also walk toward them, then all of a sudden one of them level his gun at Mr. Wood and he said

"'Ma si yin eyi na (I must first discharge this anyhow"),

which that he let off and the flag was thrown away and they fled precipitately back: Messr. Johnson and Foster, fall down at the top of the Fejebolu hill and rolled down the stream. Mainwhile the Oke Ibadan skirmishers who were watching from the Elebulo hill hasten to their rescue and they dropped in the flight. The whole camp was astir at this incident, and sympathizer poured in on all sides, congratulating Mr. Wood on the providential escape of the Missionaries. And the Missionaries offered thanksgiving to God for his merciful deliverance. Then the Ekitis report what had happened at home and Messrs. Gureje and Apara, who were

Ijesa Christian from Abeokuta who were leader of the rifle corps came to the field the next day to have a look at the men that was fired at and they recognized that they were from Abeokuta and they also saw Rev. Wood in the camp and they report to the Ekiti Obas and Chiefs who all agreed to see Rev. Wood on the battle field, but the Ekitiparapos did not like their proposal for the peace and they said

"we have to fight it to the last of our blood."

But Labirinjo of Lagos told the Ijesas and the Ekitis

"that Mr. Wood is a good Christian and he would do all he can to make sure that there is peace."

So the Ekitiparapos agreed on these terms for peace:

1. "That we claim our independence and would no longer serve the Ibadans.
2. The Owa being the Alafin's younger brother, will still acknowledge him by yearly gift, which not to be taken as tribute but as a token of respect.
3. That we would not carry war into the Oyo territory provided our territories are respected.
4. That we would claim Igbajo, Ada, Otan, and Iresi for the Owa of Ilesa, this places being originally his.
5. That the Ibadans should withdraw from Ofa, handling Ofa over to Ilorin.
6. That Modakeke being Oyos should be remove from Ife soil. And also it shall be our purpose after defeating and driving the Ibadan away to from our territory to fall upon Modakeke and destroy it. Selling the captives to defray the expenses of the war, but out of respect for Mr. Wood we would give up the idea. But Modakeke must be removed.
7. That the exile Awujale be-restated
8. That there be a general lasting peace throughout the country."

Then Rev. Wood and his party return back to Ibadan camp the next day to deliver the peace conditions to them. So after the Ibadan Chiefs meet and discussed they came up with their own terms:

1. "That out of deference to the white man, and in order to achieve peace we agree to grant the Ekitis their independence.
2. The brotherly relationship between the Alafin and the Owa should remain by all means be revived; we have no objection whatever to that, as the Alafin is our Lord and Master.
3. That we agree to respect Ijesa territories provided the Ijesas respect ours.
4. As to Otun, Ada, Iresi, Igbajo, the Owa claim to these places belong to a remote antiquity, and that by tradition only at present they are not subject to the Owa if even they were; and note the inhabitants are not generally Ijesas, but Oyos. It should be left for the people to decide under whom they would be.
5. We objected to removal of Modakeke now, being the key to our own situation, but when the war is over we require at least two years respite from preparation, to remove the town to another site.
6. That if the King of Ofa choose to return to his form allegiance to the Ilorins, that is his own affairs we are protecting Ofa only as a friend, he has never being nor is he now under our. allegiance We are defending Ofa because we do not want to see an Oyo city so historic to be destroyed.
7. As to the King of Ijebu, we have no hands in his dethronement. We only heard the report of it in our camp, we have for years been begging the Ijebus to open the refused. We are only too glad to accept their offer for trade now, how it came about we are not suppose to know, but we cannot hold ourselves responsible for the Awujale's re-statement."

Then the next day Mr.Wood and his party return to the Ekitiparapos camp with the Ibadan replies. After the war-chiefs discussed they came up with this conclusion:

1. "That the four above mention towns be remove at once and go with the Ibadans, the Owa desire them no longer as his subjects

2. That Ofa should be evacuated at once and go with the Ibadans
3. The same with Modakeke"

But Rev. Wood said

"I would like to plead for the sick, the women and children of Modakeke, and she being a big town, to be given more time for their removal."

So the war-chiefs said

"now we grant Modakeke 18 days to move."

Then Rev. Wood and his party returned to the Ibadan camp in the afternoon. And gave them the Ekitiparapos the response. And after the war-chiefs had meet, they said

"we only consider because of our respect for Mr. Wood and we will only remove any of these towns after we have return to Ibadan."

And Rev. Wood and his party return to told the Ekitiparapos. Then they resolve that

"we would move the ultimatum from 18 days to 120 days."

So Rev. Wood and his party returned the following day and told the Ibadan of the change in the ultimatum date. Then the chiefs met and said

"the Ekitiparapos had being dictating the terms of the peace to us, and Hitherto you the Ekitis have been dictating to us, and we have practically accepted all your terms; but now we only have one request to make; as nothing can be done until we reach home, in order to expedite matter let the Ekitiparapos retire from their camp into Mesin behind them -only a mile distant - on the same evening we shall be ready to leave. And we require 15 months at least in which to remove Modakeke, Igbajo, Otan, Iresi, and Ada."

Then on the 18th of October Mr. Wood return to the Ekitiparapos camp and deliver the Ibadan request. The Ekitiparapos response and they said

"we grant 15 months for the removal of the towns and we will never pursue you."

And the Ekitiparapos Commander-in-Chief Ogedemgbe said

"Aja ki ilepa Ekun, Ekun ni won Aja l'awa, Oyinbo maha mu won lo" ("the dog cannot pursue after a leopard, there are leopard and we are but dog white man, do take them away.")

And also the chiefs said

"we are ready to build a temporary house for Mr. Wood and his Companions at the middle of the battle field for them to stay before the Ibadan finish parking away, then we can leave our camp too."

So Mr. Wood return to the Ibadan camp to told them of the Ekitiparapos response the next day. But the Ibadan war-chief response

"we have no objection to the term of temporary house being built and the Ijesa Christian remaining there with the white man (though what effectual guarantee that we prove we fail to see), but we do certainly object to entrap ourselves in a define under their eyes. What the Chiefs may desire is one thing; what the uncontrollable war-boys may do is another. If there are sincere let put a mile between us and themselves, Mesin Ipole is not far. We have accept all their terms, that is our only stipulation we have to make, and this is reasonable."

Then Rev. Wood said to himself and his Companion,

"it evident that it will be difficult to make these people come to terms, so if they cannot agree on this terms now, then it certain that we cannot get them to reach agreement for peace. We should leave them and we pray for God's intervention."

And Rev. Wood and his partner went to the Ekitiparapos and told them of the Ibadan response. They became very annoyed and said

"it is the Oke Ibadan that are not sincere, and we are ready to fight to our last blood."

So Rev. Wood and his Companion left the battle field, then the Ijesas came to the battlefield and fire rockets into the Ibadan camp that night. However, the fight continue when Rev. Wood and the Missionaries left the camp on 17th October, 1884.

Death Of Are-Ona-Kakanfo Latoosa

However, the Kakanfo Latoosa became very depressed after Rev. Wood and his Companion had left and he refused to eat and he can not sleep because his words did not carry respect anymore among the war-chiefs. And the warriors were telling him that he had lost the ability to lead the Oyo Army as a the Are Kakanfo, because no Are-Ona-Kakanfo had ever fail to win a battle after 60 days and is fit to live, eventually, the Kakanfo Latoosa commit suicide but the battlefield continued without even mourning his death. So Ajayi Osungbekun the Seriki became the leader of the Ibadan Army, and eventually they agreed and made him their Balogun. And he said

"I will take the title of the Bale after we get home when this war will be over and hopefully then Akintola the son of late Basorun Ogunmola with become the next Balogun."

The Ife and Modakeke War and Influence of the Ijebu

Meanwhile the battle was very tough for the Oke Ibadan Army under the command of the Seriki Akintola, because the Ekiti was under the influence of the Ijebus warriors who were the Awujale Oba Afidipotemole warriors who lead the Ife Army. And they attacked the Modakeke and the Oke Ibadan Army lead by the Seriki Akintola. Then the Ibadan had to reinforced their warrors for more than two times because they were losing more men every day. However, the Oke Ibadan suffered terrible defeat by the Ijebus. But the Ife Army were encouraged to retreat to the market at Ife and the Modakeke pursued them to the market, while the Oke Ibadan took the fight to Ife Akogun market and the Ijebus came out on the Oke Ibadan and the Modakeke from their hiding places and they killed them with guns and shoot the archer arrows on then. However, as Akintola was running and trying to escape while he was being shoot by the archer shooters he fell from his horse but he was able to escape because of his voodoo which transfered him to a house but many of his war-chiefs and warrior slaves were captured.

However the Balogun Modakeke Adepoju fought like a hero and sacrifice his life for Modakeke town and he encouraged his warriors to press on in defending of the city and while he tried also on working on the repair of the wall, and he was killed by the Ijebu warriors. Then it was reported that Akintola and Adepoju was dead, but Akintola drummer and his cousin Latunji saw him when he was trying to hid and later he got out from the house he had escaped to. Then he was so tired and breathing so heavy and exhausted, and his cousin rode a horse and picked him on the same horse while his drummer beats his war song

"Kirinun Onibudo!" "Kirinun Onibudo!" .....

and he escaped before the Ijebu warriors running toward the horse could reach them. Then one of the Ife warrior closeby tried to drag him from the horse by grabing on his cloth which fell and the Ifes took it from the floor and they sang jubilating song and they carry the cloth up high, as priced item of war.

The British Government Effort To Bring Peace And To End The War In 1886

Then the British Parliament legislate on how to get into the interior land of the Protectorate of Lagos, However, since the need for materials in both agricultural and mineral resource for their factories and Industries had increased. And they said

"we have to enforce our leadership or find whatever means necessary to bring down their strong hold that has been preventing our merchants and people from getting into the interior countries. The Jebu country preventing the British subjects from getting into the Interior counties shall be stop by all possible means. The British Protectorate of Lagos is now separated from the Gold Coast, and hereby constitute a separate Colony and Captain A.C. Moloney is to appointed as the Governor."

Then when Governor Moloney got to Lagos he had a meeting with the staff of the Lagos Colony, and he said

"now we are the British Government Colony of Lagos. As the Governor, my priority is to get the tribes together and make the Ekitiparapos and the Ibadan to decamp. And the war between the Ibadan and the Ofa will have to end also."

Then he face his assistants and continued

"the principal Chiefs of Ijebu, Abeokuta, Ibadan, Ekiti, Oyo and Ilorin will have to be reach out to and a messenger is to be send to them so as to get them on board on the peace mission. The effort made by Rev. J.B. Wood and his colleagues at both camps in 1884 for the work of peace should be mention in the message as well. And they should be told of my intention of coming to have a meeting with each of them, to discuss how to get the solution for peace. Also a letter should be written to the C.M.S. requesting the service of some their Missionaries to go with us on the peace talk with the Obas, and Chiefs of the Interior countries."

However, the content of the letter is:

"Government House
March 18th, 1886.

Sir, - The Venable. Archdeacon Hamiton has most considerately placed your services at my disposal in connection with the satisfying the latest date on the feeling in the direction of the peace obtains between the Ibadan and the Ekitiparapos. You are the most praiseworthy and philanthropic manner come forward to carry out on the subject of my wishes.

They are embodied in the accompany letter address to the Baloguns, Chiefs and the people of Ibadan with whom you say are more intimacy and friendly terms. You will good enough accordingly to consider the contents of such letter as your instructions, and in view of the interviews I have had with you I will have hope to find success as far as it can will attend your endeavours to act as my instruction dictated.

I have, etc,

ALFRED MOLONEY, GOVERNOR."

Then the Governor ordered that similar letters should be written to Rev. Phillips, and all the Obas, and Chiefs of Ijebu, Ibadan, Oyo, Ekiti, Ijesha and Ilorin which was like the one below:

"GOVERNOR MOLONEY TO THE BALOGUNS, CHIEFS, ELDERS AND PEOPLE OF IBADAN

GENTLEMEN - I have the honour to convey that I take this opportunity to announce to you my return on the 8th ult., and my assumption as Governor of the administration of the Government of the Queen's Colony of Lagos.

2. It is a pleasure for me to come again among the people I know and know me, and it is almost needless for me to assure you that, as it has seen in the past so it be in the future, my aim and objective to promote in every legitimate way I can, the general interest and development of West Africa and the peace of the Country.

3. I attach as I am inform you do, to the restoration of peace between you and the countries with which you have unfortunate difference.

4. Entertaining as I have always such a feeling and due appreciation of the value of a general good understanding and friendly relationship in our surrounding, I sincerely invite the entertainment by our neighbours of like sentiment.

5. I am pain to learn that the unfortunate difference which have fruitless, as regards to the country's good, struggled on for years between you and Ijesas and others shall continue. The country and the people are, I gather, tired generally of the miserable and obstructive state of thing, which has done so much mischief, and has been productive of no general benefit; on the contrary there have follow bloodshed, loss of life, devastation, desolation and other miseries.

6. God kindly feeling's love always existed between you and this Colony, may they long continue so; I feel it due to inform you of my return.

7. As regards restoration of tranquility once more to the Country and the interest of contending parties for mediation to be taken by this Government, it may be convenient I should remark that as a matter of course, distinct and unconditional overtures of peace must be made to this Government by all parties concerned; then I may feel myself in a position of being able to send an officer into the Interior with a view to attempt to effect a peace baked upon conditions which we are likely to render lasting one. Each side should know what conditions as far as he is concerned he has to offer, and would most likely to be of duration.

On this part I should be clearly informed.

8. Then it would be well I should be clearly enlightened by each on the nature of the terms of responsibility, as such must rest entirely with the parties carving peace, for the fulfillment of their engagements, if peace be restored each is prepare to offer and accept.

9. ....

17. Both of my messengers may, with the desire and concurrence of the parties concern meet on encamping ground. Wishing you and your

people peace, and your country an early resumption of peaceful occupation on the part of the inhabitants.

I have the honour, etc.,

ALFRED MOLONEY,
GOVERNOR."

Rev. C. Phillips is the one that took similar letter to the Ekitiparapos Chiefs with changes in the paragraphs to substitute the name of Ibadan to Ekiti or Ijesa as the case may be. And also the letters for Ilorin, Ijebu, and Oyo are send through other Governor messenger he assign.

Then Mr. Ajose Johnson left Lagos on the 2rd March, 1886 and he got to Ijebu, and deliver the message orally to the Balogun (General) Ijebu because he was an old friend of the Governor. And he told Ajose to go and deliver the letter to the Awujale Oba Aboki, the Princes, the Olisa, the Obas and Chiefs of Ijebuland.

which was address thus:

"GOVERNOR MOLONEY, C.M.G., TO HIS MAJESTY KING ABOKI AROJOYE AWUJALE OF IJEBU

Government House, Lagos
February 27th, 1886

KING - ....
....
...."

Note the content is the same as that send to the Ibadan above.

However, the Messenger went to the palace of the new Awujale Oba Aboki Arojojoye, because the Awujale Oba Afidipotemole had join the other world. Then the Awujale Oba Aboki sent one of his Agurins (Ministers) to hear the message for him. But the Awujale refused the Governor's messenger from coming before him and complained he should have come to me first before going to the Balogun and not the other way round. So the Balogun went to the palace and explain that the messenger was his friend and this was the reason he came to him first and the Awujale Oba Aboki accept the explanation, and the messenger apologies. Then the Awujale said

"I will not allow this issue to affect the work of peace that ELEDUMARE is doing now."

And he order

"an Agurin shall to go with you the messengers of the war peace effort."

However the Agurin eventually told them that

"the Governor and the Awujale are of the same mind, wishing nothing else but peace."

Then, when they got to Oke Ibadan, the Chiefs were pleased with the Governor's message and they sent him to the Alafin Oyo at Oyo town. And the letter was read to the Alafin, who accept the message with missed feelings and he said

"I shall have to doubt if anything good is going to come from the Governor because my past efforts to make the Government in Lagos do something about the war had failed."

But eventually he response to the Governor with a letter that was written by Mr. Ajose who was order to follow the Ilari call Obakosetan and the Governor's messengers and the Kings envoys go the Ekiti, and Ilesa to the deliver the Governor's similar letter to their Obas and chiefs. And they also reply to Governor and send their representatives and their staff of offices with the Governor messengers. However at the Oke Ibadan and the Ekitiparapos camps, the war-chiefs also send their representatives and the Oke Ibadan war-chiefs said "we will have to fly the flag of truce at the battlefield until we reach the terms of peace since we have up to 6 months for cease fire of peace negotiation."

Then when they saw the Alafin Ilari, they said

"we don't believe the Alafin is ready for peace since he has not send an embasy headed by an Ilari."

And they went on a meeting which consist of the senior warlords and they said

"the absence of the Awujale and Balogun Ijebu envoys and their representatives is not good, we cannot afford to ignore those to whom we are indebted for being able to keep our position at Kiriji to this day, etc."

But after discussion with each other, they agreed to send their messenger with the Governor messengers to Lagos. However, at the battle field both camp messengers came together and put up their flags of truce and exchange greetings. Then the following day, they maintain the friendship and even exchange visit to each other camps. And both side war-chiefs agreed on the Governor's interference, and also accept the Ekiti's peace proposal, that

"the messengers of the Governor should visit the Ilorin camp and induce the Ilorin to agree to the truce, since there was still war going on at Ofa in Ikirun."

However, when they got to Ilorin the Governor messenger tried to get the Balogun Ilorin Karara to send a messenger with him to the battlefield so as to meet with the Balogun Ofa messenger to talk on the peace terms as it was done in the Kiriji camps of the Ekitiparapos and the Oke Ibadan. But Karara refuse, and he said

"the Olofa is a subject of the Emir Ilorin who is my lord and I have no other mission than to win his battle for him and my Country Ilorin."

So Governor messenger realized that the Ilorin had no interest in making peace with the Ofa, because earlier when they met the Emir Ilorin he said

"the matter of peace and war between the Ofa was for the Balogun Ilorin Karara to deal with."

Then when the messengers went back to Ofa, and told the Olofa the response of the Emir and the Balogun Karara, he said

"I know that would be the outcome, so I am not disappointed by their response. We are not slave of the Ilorin as they claimed we are. We are Oyos and our great grandfather settle on this land and later the Ilorin start to make trouble with us when the Oyo empire become disintegrated because of the civil wars. And we have being trying to live in peace with them and even in the past we submit to menial job, working as their domestic help only to see that they want to enslave us. So we now have to stand up for ourselves and fight even if it means to our last blood."

So the Ilorin attacked Ofa the following day and the Governor messengers left Ofa.

The Peace And Resettlement of Modakeke

Thereafter the Governor messengers return to the Ekitiparapos camp on the 16th, and when Ogedemgbe the Seriki Ijesa and the Commander-in-Chief of the Ekitiparapo heard that the Ilorin were not ready for peace with the Ofa. He said

"if the Ilorin would not agree with peace there is no reason why I should not on mine part accept it."

Though the Ibadan Chiefs tried to urge him to act as their in between person in the Ofa and Ilorin, so as to help them to make peace at the battle in Ofa but all the efforts they made to get the Ilorin to agreed failed. So the Ekitiparapo and the Ibadan at Kiriji battlefield discussed and work out a preliminary peace arrangement between them. And they agreed that both sides representatives to be appointed will continued to communicate with each other at the battlefield every morning and bring greeting for each other war-chiefs until both sides finish decamping from the battlefield. So both camps appoint two representatives, and they shake hands with each other, the chiefs and warriors of both sides met and greet each other and talk about their past lives and ask questions about relatives they know and congratulate each other for the peace. Then the Governor messengers called them for breaking of Kolanut as a symbol of ratification and promise of peace made to each other. Then the Governor messengers and the Owa Ilesa greet each other goodbye.

However, on the 24th the Governor messengers got to Modakeke and they went to the battlefield and explain to the Modakeke and the Ife war-chiefs to accept a 6 months cease fire peace term just like it had been done in the Kiriji Camps. And the Modakeke chiefs agreed to accept the peace proposal and they said

"we will only include in the peace terms that the Ifes should stop raiding on our farms."

And the Ife war-chiefs said

"we are OK with the war cease fire arrangement, beacause we are tied of this war that have cost us so much of lifes and furtunes."

Then the Owa messengers, the Alafin's Ilari and the Governor messengers join the hands of the two representatives of both sides in hand shake and they greet each other and talk with each other just like it happened in the Kiriji battlefield. Thereafter on their way back the Governor messengers stop at Ijebu-Ode and inform the Awujale Oba Arojojoye of the peace and cease fire that had been achieved, and he was very pleased with it. Thereafter the Ijebu Chiefs and the war-chiefs were all informed of the cease fire and they express their delight and joy in it. However, the following was the list of the representatives that went to Lagos to have the final rectification of the peace and end of the war.

	Name	Title		Mark	Seal	Date
1	Oba Adesinbo Aboki Arojojoye	Awujale Ijebuland	Ijebuland	X	LS	June 9th 1886
2	Onafowokan Otubunibon	Balogun Ijebu	Ijebuland	X	LS	June 10th 1886
3	Oba Adeyemi	Alafin Oyo	Oyo	X	LS	July 1st 1886
4	Chief Ajaji	Balogun Oke Ibadan	Oyo	X	LS	July 1st 1886
5	Chief Fijabi	Abese Oke Ibadan	Oyo	X	LS	July 1st 1886
6	Chief Fajinbi	Agba-Akin Oke Ibadan	Oyo	X	LS	July 1st 1886
7	Chief Osuntoki	Maye Oke Ibadan	Oyo	X	LS	July 1st 1886
8	Chief Tayo	Otun Bale Oke Ibadan	Ekitiparapo	X	LS	July 7th1886
9	Oba Ogunloye	Owa Ilesa	Ekitiparapo	X	LS	July 2th1886
10	Chief Ogbedemgbe	Seriki Ilesa	Ekitiparapo	X	LS	July 3rd1886
11	Chief OkinBoloye	Owore Otun	Ekitiparapo	X	LS	July 3th1886
12	Chief Odudun	Olujudo	Ile-Ife	X	LS	July 18th1886
13	Oba Derin	Owoni - elect Ile-Ife	Ile-Ife	X	LS	July 14th1886
14	Chief Awotunde	Obalufe Ile-Ife	Ile-Ife	X	LS	July 14th1886
15	Chief Obamuyiwa		Ile-Ife	X	LS	July 14th1886
16	Chief Jojo	Arode Ile-Ife	Ile-Ife	X	LS	July 14th1886
17	Chief Osundulu	Ajariwa Ile-Ife	Ile-Ife	X	LS	July 14th1886
18	Chief Aworinlo	Osrisanore Ile-Ife	Ile-Ife	X	LS	July 14th1886
19	Chief Oye	Balogun Ile-Ife	Ile-Ife	X	LS	July 14th1886
20	Chief Akintola	Obaloran Ile- Ife	Ile-Ife	X	LS	July 14th1886
21	Chief Ogunwole	Ogunsua Modakeke	Modakeke	X	LS	July 16th1886
22	Chief Sowo	Balogun Modakeke	Modakeke	X	LS	July 14th1886
23	Chief Agunleye	Otun Balogun Modakeke	Modakeke	X	LS	July 14th 1886

THE TREATY OF PEACE

Thereafter, the Governor had a meeting with each of the war tribes representative separately, and Obakosetan the envoy of the Alafin Oyo try to raise some objection to the earlier drafted treaty clause of the removal of Modakeke from its present place, but they all told him that the agreement had already been decided and cannot be changed. So the treaty was now signed by the envoys of the Awujale and the Alafin and the messengers of the Obas and chiefs. And here is the content of the treaty:

"Treaty of peace, friendship and commerce between the Majesty Awujale Ijebu, Balogun Ijebu;

The Majesty Alafin Oyo, the Balogun, the Maye, the Abase, the Agba-Akin, the Otun Bale Oke Ibadan;

The Ajero Ijero, the Olujudo Ido, The Seriki Ilesa, The Owoni Ife, the Obalufe, the Obajuwo, the Obalorun, the Ajaruna, the Arode, the Arisanre, the Balogun Ife, the Ogunsuwa Modakeke, the Balogun, and Otun Modakeke.

Whereas the Kings, Chiefs, Baloguns above enumerated parties to this treaty, and to the conditions and article of agreement herein after set forth, profess to be earnestly desirous to put a stop to the devastating war which has for years been waged in their own and adjoining countries, and to secure the blessing of the lasting peace to themselves and their peoples, and have appealed by the envoys and the messengers duly accredited to His Excellency the Governor of the Colony of Lagos and representing Her Most Gracious Majesty the Queen to mediate between them, and arbitrate and to determine such terms and conditions as shall be secure a just and honourable agreed to abide by such arbitration and determination, to do this and their utmost endeavor to carry into effect the terms and conditions so arranged and determined. And whereas the envoys and messengers duly accredited by the aforesaid Kings, Bales, Baloguns, and Chiefs have received in audience by His Excellency and the Governor, and have themselves assented both verbally and in writing to the terms and conditions of peace herein after specified, and have agreed to be bound there-by, and faithfully to observe the same.

Now this is to testify that the Kings, Bales, Baloguns, and the Chiefs aforesaid hereby rectified and conform to the said agreement made and entered by their envoys and messengers for them and on their behalf and solemnly pledge themselves faithfully, loyal and strict to Observe and carry out the following terms and conditions so far as they are individually or collectively concerned:-

1. There shall be peace and between Kings, Bales, Baloguns, and Chiefs, the signatories to this Treaty and their peoples respectively and the Kings, Bales, Baloguns, and Chiefs aforesaid hereby, engage for themselves and their peoples that they will case from fighting and will remain within or retire from their territories as herein provided, and will in all things submit themselves to such directions as may seem necessary or expedient to the Governor of Lagos for better and more effectively securing the object of this Treaty.

2. The Kings, Chiefs and peoples comprising the Ekitiparapo alliance or confederation on to one hand, and the Bales, Baloguns, Chiefs and the people of Ibadan on the other shall respectively retain their independence.

3. The Alafin and Owa shall stand to each other in relation of elder brother to the younger as before when the Ekiti countries were independent.

4. ....

5. In order to preserve peace the town of Modakeke shall be reconstructed on the land lying between the Osun and Oba rivers to the North of it present situation, and such of the people of Modakeke as desire to live under the rule of the Bale and Balogun of Ibadan shall withdraw from the present town to the land mentioned, at such times and in such manner as the Governor his envoy or of the parties principally concerned, and such of the peoples as desire to live with the Ifes shall be permitted to do so but shall remain in the present town of Modakeke, which shall remain territory and under the rule of the King and the Chiefs, who may deal with same as they may think expedient.

6. ....

7. The Kiriji camp shall be broken and the contending parties agree quietly and peaceably without any demonstration to withdraw their armies and their peoples at such time or times in such manner, and by such routes as shall be directed by the Governor, his envoy or messenger after conference with the governments of the parties principally concerned.

8. The signatories engage themselves at or immediately after the signatureof this treaty or at such times as may be directed by the Governor, his envoy or messenger after the conference with the parties principally concerned to withdraw their peoples and warriors and the allies employed or associated with the contending peoples or armies at Modakeke, Isoya, or elsewhere and whereever such allies or people or warriors may be employed in war, or likely to foster or promote war, and further when their peoples, warriors, and allies have been withdrawn, and the camp of Kiriji broken up and disperse to do their utmost by peaceful and friendly means to bring about peace at Ofa.

9. ....

12. As a guarantee of good faith, and for the further and better securing the objects of their Treaty and the faith and strict observance of the terms and conditions thereof, the signatories agree to place in the hand of the Governor his envoy or messenger as when he may determin, such of their leading chiefs as he require as hostage who will continue and remain with him on the battlefield of Kiriji, whilst the armies and people of the respective signatories are dispersing there from, and for and during such time or period as the circumstances or necessities of the case may require, or to give such other or further guarantees as may seem just or expedient to the Governor, his envoy or messenger.

In witness thereof we have hereunto put our hands and the days and dates specified.

The List of Those That Rectify The Peace Treaty

Rev. S. Johnson	The Governor's messenger to the Oyos
Obakosetan	Envoy of the Alafin Oyo
Belewu	Representing the Oyo Nobility
Arinde	Messenger of the Balogun Oke Ibadan
Atere	Representing the Maye Oke Ibadan
Elegbede	Representing Oke Ibadan home authority

Rev. C. Phillips	The Governor's messenger to the Ekitiparapo
Apelidiagba	Messenger of the Owa Ilesa
Olukoni	Messenger of the Owa Ilesa
Fatiye	Messenger of the Owore Otun
Osisalusi	Messenger of the Ajero Ijero
Obasa	Messenger of the Olujudo Ido
Dawudu	Messenger of Ogedemgbe Ilesa
Lomi	Envoy of the Awujale Ijebu
Akinlamu	Messenger of the Osimowe Ondo
Saba	Messenger of the Elders Ondo

Signed, sealed, and delivered in the presence of the undersigned after the terms and condition therein contained had been interpreted and explained by us, or one of us to the respective signatories.

(Signed) SAMUEL JOHNSON, Clerk in Holy order,
    Messenger and Interpreter for the Governor.
(Signed) CHARLES PHILIPS, Clerk in Holy order,
    Messenger and Interpreter for the Governor.
Affix to Treaty, dated 4th day of June 1886."

The Acting-Governor Effort For Peace

After the Treaty had been signed the Governor of Lagos Moloney went to Britain on holiday and the Acting-Governor F. Evans was in charge of the peace mission. So he, Mr. Henry Higgins, the Asst. Col. Secretary and Mr. Oliver Smith, the Queen's Advocate with an escort of 50 Hausa Soldiers which were provided with 50 rounds of ball cartridges for their Martini Henry rifles, a 7-pounder gun a rocket trough with it ammunition. Then they went to the interior to persuade the warring countries Army and their Obas, and Chiefs to break up their camps as they had agreed in the Treaty. However, they left Lagos on the 16th August through Ito Ike which was an Ijebu port to Ijebu-Ode, and they face difficulty with carrying of their loads. The Ijebus refused to let their slaves to carry the loads of the white people. In fact they cannot stand seeing a foreigner in their country. But when the Olisa explained to them that they were here to talk to us on the issues of peace. Then the Ijebuland Princes, Oba and Chiefs, and youths allowed them passage through the gate. But they refused to allow their slaves to carry the white man loads. Saying

"Eni ti o di eru re li o gbe (You that own your load should carry it by yourself). Omo Awujale ko ni Ori eru (We the descendants of the Awujale are no body's slave to carry load.")

Then the Acting-Governor was very surprised and he said

"we have to carry our loads by ourselves? Look we are representative of the Queen of Britain and only come for peace."

But the people would not accept the Governor's explanations and they told him,

"we are superior being in our own right just like you want to believe your Queen is King so is our Awujale is a King. So better for you to send messenger to Oke Ibadan and get people there to help you carry your loads."

Then the Governor sent for people in Oke Ibadan who they paid to help in carrying their loads to Ijebu-Ode and eventually out of Ijebuland. However, the Governor's entourage were well received by the Olisa (Prime Minister) Ijebuland and they were ushered into the Awujale Oba Aboki palace where they were giving a welcome message by one of the palace Agurin (Minister). And each of them were given some presents, and taken to their living quarters. Then the Awujale told the Acting-Governor

"I am also interested in peace, and in fact I had order Ogunsigun the Seriki Ijebu-Igbo to decamp from Isoya but he is being stubborn. However, the Governor's entourage seems to treat the matter so lightly and he said with our peace effort all the war-chiefs will obey orders and they will decamp."

But the Awujale Oba Oboki who is not used to listening to the advice from a foreigner, he was not happy and he told the interpreter who is Mr. Ajose Johnson

"you Ajose shall make sure you inform the Governor to carry out this order,"

and he look very mad, turn his attention to the Olisa and add

"When you reach Modakeke, if these Governor's entourage could not prevail upon Ogunsigun to decamp at once, tell them to kill him, he stained the swords of mightier nations-ambition, jealousy and greed! 'Go home to your villages ..... Those villages and towns with 50,000 to 250,000 souls! And is there any reason why their women should be denied the right and dignity of being their wives?' Men who can control such huge masses of humanity. Capacities which can guide, control, and direct all intricacies of municipal and political machineries of a government, can wage honourable wars for years without external aid or a national debt, bequeathed to posterity might at least be considered as possessing some serious qualities beyond these of children, as they appear to be regarded, and deserving some honourable consideration due to men although they be Negroes. But happily the patronizing language of the letter which discloses so much thinly-veiled contempt, will be lost in translation, and in other respects interpreters may be trusted to make up in tone and expression for what is wanting in style and diction is my slave, and let his followers return in peace."

Then when the entourage got to Oke Ibadan, the Chiefs told the Governor

"we cannot do anything without the order from the Alafin, who is our master and King. So you have to meet him first. If he agrees for us to decamp then we have no choice."

So the Governor's Oke Ibadan messenger left for Oyo town on the 2nd of Sept., 1886. And the Alafin sent an escort that consist of some Ilaris who met them at Fiditi and lead them to Oyo town and lodge them at Apeka's house who was one of the Ilaris. Then they were invited to a state reception as a special quest and they sat with the Omo Obas and Oyo Nobles, under Umbrellas and made to enjoy Royal entertainments and the Alafin Adeyemi present them with presents. And on the 6th of Sept. the Alafin present them the people to help them to carry their loads, who were some King's messagers and they went to the Ibadan camp in Kiriji which they reach on 10th of Sept., 1886. Mainwhile they went to the Ekitiparapos' camp, at the camp Chief Ogedemgbe who had early visit the Governor's messengers at the Ibadan camp, welcome the Balogun Oke Ibadan to his own camp and they all share kola-nuts and drank palm wine as they listen to the Governor's messengers. Then they all agreed on the terms of decamping except on how to make Ilorin camp agree on the same thing for peace, so as to end the war with Ofa. However, on 18th the Ife Chiefs accept the proposal that the Modakekes would be allow 10 months before being remove to a new settlement on the other side of the Osun river, but temporarily they can be allow to stay in Ipetumodu, Oduabon, Moro and other towns. Then on the 21st, they all moved to Modakeke's camp, but the Modakeke Chiefs refuse to make peace with the Ifes. And they reject the proposal for them to move from the land they are and they said

"how strange!" "If we the victorious in the fights with the Ifes, will have to move away for the people we defeat in war. We that should be given more extend time until the dry season when we would have build a new town, and cultivate new fields so that we might not perish for starvation and exposure in the rain."

But the warriors on both sides were not allowed to fight each other, because the fifty Hausa Soldiers were made to line up in two column and separate he two camps at Kiriji, and also the Governor's entourage camp between the warring camps. Then the Governor messengers talk to both camps on several attempts to decide the day to decamp, but on 28th of Sept. both camps begin to evacuate, though it was raining in the morning, and after the rain people came by their thousands on horseback and foot to both camps and the Hausa Soldiers guard the Chiefs and Obas who were signatories of Ijebus, Oyos, Modakekes who are the Peace Treaty representatives and about 200 people present. Also the Seriki Ijesa Ogedemgbe and the chiefs of the Ekitisparapo Army and their signatories of the Treaty also took their seats. The Oke Ibadan chiefs and their representatives also sat on the left side of the Ekitiparapos. The Governor entourage which were accompalied by Capt. Speeding, Rev. S. Johnson and Mr. Willoughby also took their seat. Then after the Treaty and the ratification had been read and translated, the Balogun Oke Ibadan and the Seriki Ijesa sworn friendship with each other. Thereafter, each of the signatories to the ratification of the Treaty were called and they came to the table and sign it, and fixed their seals on the document. However, this is the content of the Proclamation of peace.

"THE PROCLAMATION OF PEACE AND FIRING OF THE CAMPS

The following is the Proclamation of Peace between the Ibadan and the Ekitiparapo at Kiriji -Mesin battlefield on the 23rd September, 1886

Whereas through the friendly mediation of His Excellency the Governor of Lagos and an understanding has been brought about, and a Treaty of peace, friendship, and commerce concluded between the Alafin of Oyo, the bale of Ibadan; the Owa of Ilesa, the Owore of Otun, the Ajero of Ijero, the Olojudo of Ido, the Seriki of Ijesa, the Owoni, the Balogun, the Obalufe, the Obaloran, the Obajio, the Ajaruwa, the Arode, and the Orisanire of Ife; the Ajaruwa, the Ogunsua, the Balogun, and the Otun of Modakeke; And the Awujale and the Balogun of Ijebu.

Now therefore, we special commissioners appoint by His Excellency the Governor of Lagos for the purpose of executing the said treaty in accordance with the provisions thereof, do hereby proclaim, in the name of the signatories of the said Treaty, that peace has this day been established and shall henceforth continue forever between the signatories of the said Treaty and between their respective peoples.

Date at Kiriji-Mesin battlefield this 23rd day of September, 1886.

(Signd)   HENRY HIGGINS: Special

OLIVER SMITH: Commissioner"

Then the mode for the battlefield war camps to be decamp is now being read and the same representative of the Obas, Bales and Chiefs also sign it

"Signed, sealed, and delivered in the presence of
(Signed)   HENRY HIGGINS: Special
Acting Col. Sectary: Commissioners
(Signed)   OLIVER SMITH:
Queen's Advocate:
(Signed)   CHARLES PHILLIPS:
Clerk in Holy Order: Interpreter
(Signed)   SAMUEL JOHNSON: on this
Clerk in Holy Order.": Occasion

Eventually, the camps was evacuated and all the people living in the camp towns and villages moved their domestic effects, and livestock to Ikirun within three days. Then some Oke Ibadan slaves escaped to Ileas and Ekiti towns and villages secretly. However, the Oke Ibadan Chiefs said

"we better go back to Oke Ibadan quickly, because we have seen that just today alone Sanusi, the son of late Kakanfo Latoosa have lost 400 of his slaves, otherwise we all will not have our slaves to take to Oke Ibadan."

So they ordered their loyal guards to keep a watch, on their slaves and prevent them from deserting their masters. On the 25th of Sept. the camp was totally deserted, then on the 26th the Balogun Oke Ibadan and the rest of the Oke Ibadan war-chiefs left the camp and they went to Ikirun. Then when Ogedemgbe heard that the Oke Ibadan war-chiefs had left their camp, he ordered his warriors to leave their own camp also, and they went to Mesin Ipole. However, the Commissioners decide to wait until 28th before they put fire on the camps. Then after both camps had been completely burned down, Chief Ogedemgbe provide about 150 Ekiti people to help the Commissioners to carry their loads to Ilesa and later to Ibadan. Mainwhile, the Balogun Ijebu Ogunsigun ordered his Army to leave their camp since the Modakeke were not ready to follow the Treaty, and they remain in the location of the same settlement. And when they were leaving the people of both Oke Ibadan, Ekiti and Ijesa greet them goodbye and thanked them with songs and musical instruments and there was great jubilations and parties as they moved from village to village and towns to towns on their journey back to Ijebu-Ode. They were given heroic welcome parties in Ijebu-Ode, the people danced and the musician, the women and the youths thanked them for the war and peace at last. The Awujale Oba Aboki and all the Princes, the Olisa, the Obas, and the Chiefs in Ijebuland praised them and gave most of the war-lords and war-chiefs more titles and presents.

CHAPTER 13

Ijebuland War With The British Army about 1892

However, there was a big change in the Ijebuland, people of the other Countries were coming into the Country and the youths were not used to seeing them, and they were complaining to the Princes, the Olisa, the Obas and the Chiefs. But the Awujale Oba Aboki told them

"you shall have to learn how to adapt to these new change of things and the way of life of the people surrounding us now and in every other neighboring countries. Since we had signed the Treaty for Peace and no more war, we shall be ready to accommodate other people who come to our country for trade with us and if eventually living among us, which we have being doing for many years in the Oyo country."

But the youths reject the idea and they said

"Ijebu-Ode, Ajeji ko wo!" ("Ijebu-Ode, no alien to enter!") "Is about to be abolish by the Awujale Oba Aboki!" "And we are not comfortable with this."

Then they had various meeting of the Regbe Regbe (Age grades) and they said

"we the youths own the Ijebuland and it is our future that is at stake, before we know it the white people would be taking our land just the way they are dictating to the Alafin Oyo in his country on what do now. We the Ijebus have never being under any foreign rule and we will not allow any white man to come and be advising the Awujale Oba Aboki on how to rule our country."

Meanwhile, some of the Chiefs told the youths

"it is because the Awujale Oba Aboki and the Balogun Ijebu Onafowokan who had sign the paper of friendship with the people of other countries and white people that this the reason the people are coming into our country. If we do not stop the white people not to enter, they will be in Ijebuland just like they have taken over the Oyo country. So we have to send our delegates to the Awujale Oba Aboki palace and present our case to the Kabiyesi so that he can make a law which will prevent the Oyos and the White people from entering Ijebuland and especially Ijebu-Ode."

However, the Awujale Oba Aboki Arojojoye was in a meeting with the Princes, the Olisa, the Obas, Bales, and Chiefs of Ijebuland and they were having discussions about the issues of the Youth that were not satisfied with the Treaty. When the Youth representatives which was being head by the Awujale's son Omo Oba Adekoya, entered the palace, the Regbe Regbe representatives prostrate before the Awujale Oba Aboki and they said

"Kabiyesi o!" "Kabiyesi o!" "Kabiyesi o!" "Kade pe lori Oba wa!" "Ki bata pe lese Oba wa!" "Igba Odun, Odun kan ni o Kabiyesi o!"("the Unqestionable one!" !" "The Unqestionable one!" "The Unqestionable one!" "May the Royal Crown remains!" "May the Royal shoes remains!" "Our King let your reign remains for ever!").

Then the Awujale Oba Aboki smiles and in joy received them and he said

"my children get up and sit down!" "We know the whole changes in the land and countries is strange to you all now, but later you will understand, so what is your demand my children?"

The spokesman who was Omo Oba Adekoya stood up and said

"Kabiyesi o Oba wa!" "We the Youths of Ijebuland appreciate our father's efforts of peace and the stability of trade with our country Ijebuland and those of the neighboring countries especially the Oyos and the people in Lagos. But we are tired seeing the people of other countries entering our land, we would like the toll gates and fees to continue. We are also afraid because the white people would use the excuse that we are allowing the Oyos to enter our Country and before we realize it, they would want to take our land and slaves from us."

Then the Awujale Oba Aboki thanked them and said

"my children!" "We also have consign on this issues!" "But we shall have to find a way to accommodate change when it become necessary since we had a closer intercourse with the Oyos during the late negotiations for peace- a peace clamoured for and desired by yourselves- you Ijebus have had many of their daughters to be your wives, and they have had children for you. Is it not natural for the parents of these women to visit their daughters and grandchildren? How can you sever the ties of relationship by preventing brothers from visiting sisters, and parents their children? If you will be just and fair, send these women back home with the children born to you, then there will no occasion for any outsiders to enter your Country."

However, the wish of the Youths prevailed and the Olisa with the Obas, Bales, and Chiefs adviced the Awujale

"Kabyesi o!" "Kabyesi o!" "Kabyesi o!" "We would advice Kabyesi to yield to their demand and that whatever they make of their demand its their choice and the youths will live long enough to realize it later, then they will understand that change is only thing we cannot prevent in life." Then the Awujale Oba Aboki ordered that the Olisa to give them their demand. Thereafter the Olisa told the Regbe Regbe representatives

"the Awujale Oba Aboki have granted your request to continue with the toll collections at Ijebuland gates in Ijebu-Igbo, Ijebu-Remo and Ijebu-Ode districts and only allow whoever you feel is safe to enter the Ijebu country."

So Omo Oba Adekoya who was the first son of the Awujale Oba Aboki lead the Youths and they took charge of tolls at the gates and he said

"we have to organize our resistance and prevent the white people from entering our Country and make sure we charge toll at the gates to prevent non traders from entering into Ijebuland."

Then he was happy shaking hands with his friends and collegues and he add

"I will personally go to the Remo district and save the walls and gates there."

However, the Youths organized the work of keeping watch at the gates and the walls of Ijebuland and prevent people they don't trust from entering into Ijebu country. Moreso, One day at the Remo district, a young white Missionary who had earlier entered with some traders, and the Youths detained him and the traders from the Oyo country and other interior land and they were sent to Ijebu-Ode in chains. But, the white man was mainly detained by Omo Oba Adekoya who was very angry when he saw him and he said

"so you white people think you cannot keep to our laws, when we have being respecting your trade rules in your Lagos."

But the white man tried to scared him and by firing a walking-stick gun into the sky, but the Ijebus rush on him and took the stick from the white man before he can load it again. And they drag him into the chariot with the rest of the interior land people to Ijebu-Ode, and they said

"we got one of major enemy now."

However, when the Awujale Oba Aboki heard of the incident, and then when he was passing by on his way through Remo to Ijebu-Ode, he stop at the gate and told the Youths,

"you my children are doing a very good job!" "Preventing your country Ijebuland!" "From the white people which is all I want too. But you will have to know how to separate the evil white slave traders from the white men that are the Missionaries, who are good people and have being helping people in the wars."

Then Awujale Oba Aboki brought some Missionary men both natives and white, with him to a meeting he had with the youths and he told Omo Oba Adekoya and the youths

"now see what the Missionary people look like, so these are the ones that would be allow to enter Ijebu country."

Then the Youths prostrate and thank the Awujale Oba Aboki and they said

"Kabiyesi o!" "Kabiyesi o!" "Kabiyesi o ...... we have observed the difference now and we will only allow the Missionary that look like these people into Ijebuland."

Then they had other discussions on the issues concerning the youths and Ijebuland.

Thereafter some months later, the Ijebus living in Lagos wrote the Awujale Oba Aboki and accused Mr. Ajose Johnson of the offence shown bellow. So the Awujale Oba Aboki order we "shall not allow Mr. Ajose Johnson into Ijebuland for the following offence:

1. That he is longer on the side of peace, but the continuation of the war.
2. That he is building a house for the Alafin Oyo, who is known not to be favourable to peace.
3. That he is supplying the Alafin with arms of precision and ammunition for the Ilorins in order to enable them to wage a successful war against the Oke Ibadans."

However, Mr. Ajose Johnson went to Rev. W.B. George Wesleyan Minister in Lagos and beg him help deny the allegations before the Awujale Oba Aboki and the Balogun Ijebu. Then in March, 1888 Mr. Johnson went to Oru on the advice of Tinubi, the Balogun's son who was also the grandson of the Awujale Oba Aboki, to go and talk with the Awujale Oba Aboki. So he went to Ijebu-Ode and present himself before the Awujale and beg him that the charges are false, but after two days of pleading the Awujale Oba Aboki agreed to allow him to come to the palace. Then the Awujale Oba Aboki said

"Ajose Johnson Is that you? I heard that you are no more for peace but have joined the Alafin in his intrigues."

But Mr. Johnson respond

"Kabiyesi o, not so, my going to Oyo to reside was not my choice, but as an obedient servant I went where they sent me. I am like a rod in the hands of my master, and where I am flung there I must be. Who am I to have a voice of my own in these great political matters? My calling is of a different kind and not Political."

But the Awujale Oba Aboki said

"Don't you say so; your words have gained the ears of Kings and mighty warriors lately; so you cannot think so meanly of yourself. I was so angry that I never intend to see your face anymore, but thanks to the Balogun who vigorously pleaded your cause."

Thereafter he was allowed to pass through Ijebuland and continue on his journey to Lagos by two escorts provided by the Balogun. Then another day at the road blockage at the Remo gate. A Brazilian freed slave who deals in textile trade was returning to Iwo his home town, and he met Omo Oba Adekoya at the gate and he argued and he said

"I cannot pay this amount of toll that I am being charge, and I will have to pass this gate. I am now a free man and I live in Lagos and the white people are the powerful people that are now controlling the country of Oyo and Lagos."

Then Prince Adekoya told him

"go back and make the Alafin and his warriors or the Oke Ibadan Army to fight us so that you can pass through Ijebuland. You are just too foolish not to realize that I am an Omo Oba Ijebuland and even the Alafin Oyo cannot talk to me like this."

Then he face the warriors on patrol and on duty and he order "get him arrested and take all his goods to Ijebu-Ode."

But he beg and said

"please I have beautiful dress, large red silk damask umbrellas which are for Oluiwo and everything are about £800. Please I can pay any amount in fine to be set free."

However, when the Ijebuland Obas, and Chiefs in council heard about his case, they said

"we can have compassion on you. So you can go free and be allowed to pass to Iwo."

But he refused to leave and he said

"I am not ready to leave without my goods what is life worth to me now? I have committed no crime, and I have been utterly ruined. No prospect before me now but utter destitution and beggary! Death is preferable."

Then the Awujale Oba Aboki said

"you are full of arrogance, that is the reason you find yourself in this mess, you think now that you have missed up with the white people, the white people are superior and have power over Ijebu. It may be so among the Oyos where the white people have enter their country and control them there. It is not like that in Ijebuland."

And look at the palace guards and he add

"all right, we will oblige you in this!" "E lo i po o"("Go and kill him,")

then his head was cut off. Moreover after months later, some white people brought their trade to Ibadan and they said to the people at the markets "you people that are dress in this buba and agada dress are inferior being to us and the people that wear English dress and dress in suit, and shirts and trousers."

So the condemnation begin to have effect on the native people and in fact the white were also preventing the selling of the native dress, but allow only the English dress in the market. And they said

"we have to dominate this people and make our culture and way of life to be superior to their own in Lagos and Ibadan."

And when the Ijebu traders saw what was happening they were so annoyed and report it to the people in Ijebuland. Then the Youths in Ijebu-Ode took the matter to the Olisa and the when Awujale Oba Aboki talked with them in his palace, the Awujale Oba Aboki became very annoy and he order

"now get the Oke Ibadan Army and the Ijebu Army and they shall march to Ibadan and Oke Ibadan and get everybody in European dress, either black or white arrested and if you cannot deal with any person, such person shall be send to Lagos."

So Ijebu Army were sent to Ibadan and Oke Ibadan and they enforced the law and some white people, even Missionaries were sent to Lagos for not complying to the Awujale Oba Aboki law. But eventually, after the Governor of Lagos investigate the issue, he sent his envoy to the Awujale Oba Aboki in his palace and he plead

"Oh!" "Your Royal Majesty!" "The Awujale Oba Aboki!" "I the Governor of Lagos sent message not of my own accord but by the Royal Majesty the Queen of England and the Empress of India plead the law be reverse because I have reprimand the white people responsible and such thing would not happen again."

Then the trade in Ibadan markets become friendly again and the people were free to dress the way they want.

Then some weeks after Rev. T. Harding, who was the European Superintendent of the C.M.S. Mission want to pass through Ijebuland to the Interior land, and he was charge £4 before he would be allowed to pass. And the Youths said

"we have our own laws in our Ijebu country just like you white people have your laws in your trades. The Oyo country allowed the white people to enter their country and you caused civil wars and carried their people away and sold them to the slave traders and also kidnap many of them during the wars. We the Ijebus have succeed in preventing the war from continueing and the slave trade have also stop since the Oyos cannot buy guns and gunpowder because of our road blockages. So you white people are now trying to force yourselves into our country, we do not want the war to continue and also we do not want the white people to take our land from us. So please white man pay the toll or go back to Lagos or follow another route to the Oyo country."

Then, Rev. Harding paid the £4 in 1889 to pass through the Ijebuland.

However, some of the peace Treaty was being breached by some Ijesas when they kidnapped about 150 Oyo traders who came to Ekiti Country to trade. But the Oke Ibadan warriors did not fight the Ekitis but only protest and had road blockage. Then the Commissioners who were on their way to Ilorin and were prevented from continuing on their journey, wrote a letter the Owa Ilesa and the Seriki Ilesa Ogedemgbe that they were being detained. Then the Ekitiparapo Obas respond

"who are you? We don't know you; are you Missionary? Why do you trespass on Ijesa soil without first notifying the 4 Kings of the Ekitiparapo?"

Then the Commissioners wrote back and explain

"we had permission to visit the Owa, and though the Oke Bode people did not to allow us. And they refuse to allow to enter, so the Owa provide us people as our guides."

Then Owa and Ogbedemgbe said

"we are sorry for the 10 days detention by the people of Oke Bode."

So after the third day, they had a meeting with the Seriki Ogedemgbe but he refuse to let them go to Ilorin through Mesin and he said

"no road in that path it is full of ditches."

But the Commissioner insist and he said

"I will go with my cook call Mr. Millson the ditches on the path should not be a problem for us."

Then Ogedemgbe refused to let them go and also would not agreed to give them letter to Karara, the Ilorin Army General and he said

"it will only result in misunderstanding with the Ilorin and the Ekitiparapo which I do not want. you Commissioners have to turn back by the way you came through Ikirun to Ibadan."

However, when the Oke Ibadan Chiefs heard of the issue they said

"it is a failure now to get the Commissioners to Ilorin to secure peace for us with the Ilorin, so the fight against Ofa will not stop."

Then they encourage two separate warriors village riots in Ekitiparapo country. However, the Governor of Lagos had a meeting with the commissioners and they were sent with letters to the Awujale Oba Obaki, the Alafin, the Aseyin, the Oluiwo Iwo and the Bale Ogbomoso. The Governor urge these Obas, Olus, and Bales to help in working on ensuring the peace to continue. However, some Ijebus in Lagos who doubt the sincerity of the white went to the Awujale Oba Aboki palace and they said

"Kabiyesi o!" "Kabiyesi o!" "Kabiyesi o!" "We are your children that live in Lagos!" "And we have to advice Kabiyesi not take the white people serious, because we heard them said that our effort is to encourage more fight secretly so as to be able to divide the people of the interior. Since this is the only way we can become relevant in the affairs of the Interior land

and beat the Awujale of Ijebu country who appears to be the Oba more in charge in the Interior countries."

Then the Awujale Oba Aboki said

"thank you my children!" "You are truly Omo Alare!" "I thank the gods of the ancestors of the Awujale and those of the Ijebuland for giving you the wisdom to have come home to protect your fatherland against the evil plans of the white people."

Then he order

"no white man trader from Lagos and other foreign trader shall be allowed to gain access to the Interior land for trade or for any other purpose."

So the law was so strictly enforced that the Olisa said

"you the Ijebuland Army!" "The success of this law depends on me and the Awujale Oba Aboki shall not be angry with me so we have to ensure that no white person and non Ijebu person would be allowed in the interior land."

However, the Balogun Ijebu Onafowokan even refused to grant audience to Mr. Ajose Johnson who was the writer of the Alafin Oyo's letters and the intermediary between the Alafin and the Governor of Lagos, though he was his friend, but for the fear that the Youths would report to the Olisa Ijebuland. But eventually, the Awujale Oba Aboki who was also for peace allowed Ajose and the Commissioners to come to Ijebuland and the palace, to hear what the Governor have to say. Also Ajose exchange communication between the Awujale Oba Aboki and the Alafin Oyo. But the Alafin said

"my complain is about the Oke Ibadan Army, let your Royal Majesty please overlook what had happened in the past. We both are Monarch and we have to work together for the permanent peace."

Then the Awujale Oba Aboki told Ajose

"you shall inform the Alafin Oyo let your Majesty be aware that the major problem is still the white people which you have allowed to gain access to your country. I have encourage the Ekitiparapo and the Ife countries not to further allow this evil white people to have access to their countries as I have not allowed them gain access into mine."

Then also the Alafin beg the Awujale Oba Aboki to help in enforcing the Oke Ibadan Army to obey him and make them to be loyal to him. However, the Youths and the Ijebus in Lagos were determined to prevent the white people from entering Ijebuland and eventually prevent them from entering into the interior land. Meanwhile the blockages against them became very serious and this affect trades in Lagos and the traders in Lagos were complaining because Lagos was very small town on a Island. The main land of Mushin, Ikorodu, and Epe were all part of Ijebuland but are they were under the control of the British Colony, Government of Lagos

The Egbados about 1888

The Egbados were very peaceful tribes and were most loyal subject of the Alafin Ojo. But eventually, after the Fulanis invasion of the Oyo empire, the Egbas conquered the Egbadaos at the battle of Owiwi and by 1888, then they were under Chief Ogundeyi of Iporo Abeokuta which is an Ilaro district that is part of Egba whom they paid tribute to. Mainwhile the Egbados were being attacked by the Dahomians and the Egbas cannot save them from the Dahomian invasions and the annual raids. Then they had a meeting and complained,

"we cannot continue to pay tribute and respect to the Egbas anymore since they cannot protect us from the Dahomians."

Then Chief Falola of Oke Odan said

"let us accept the British Government protection since they have been trying for some years now to make us to be part of the Lagos Government."

Then they appoint some delegates under Chief Falola to go to Lagos and had a meeting with the British Government. And at the meeting their delegates said

"we now feel it would be better to accept your government invitation to be part of Lagos Protectorate Government, since we are being attacked by the Dahomians and the Egbas who are our Lords cannot protect us from them."

So the British Government accept their request and immediately host the British flag in the Egbado district of Ilaro and Oke Odan in 1891. Moreover, the following towns: Ilaro, Oke Odan, Owo, Ijako, Ita kete, Isiyan, Iya Koto, Iwoye, Idogo, Igbeji, Isoto, Itolu, Pahayi, Pokoto, Ijado, Ibese, Ilobi, Erinja, and more were all included in the Egbado Protectorate. Then the Ilaro annexation made the Egbas to protest to the Lagos Government and some Hausa soldiers of the Lagos Army were sent to defend Ilaro. Thereafter the Egbas had series of meeting to discuss the issue of the Lagos government, and Egbas said

"we now agree with the Ijebus that the white people are bad and evil. Their only interest is to sell our people as slaves to their country and now they are planning to get our land from us. We have to join the Ijebu blockage against the white people and prevent trade with Lagos. Then the blockage of trade further destroy business more in Lagos and traders will only open their shops for months without any sales.

However, the British Government annexation of the Egbado from the Egbas and form the Egbado Protectorate, and the Ijebus are now convinced that the white people only interest in the interior land people is to secretly promote wars and take their land from them. Then the resentment of the Ijebu youths against the white people become greater and the Awujale Oba Aboki told the Youths and the Ijebus living in Lagos

"my children!" "We you have done very well in preventing our country from being stolen from us by these greedy white people, but we shall have to be ready to defend ourselves and land against their attack."

Then the Ijebu Army bought guns of the latest sophistication from the French and start preparing for the sudden attack of the British Government.

However, the British people in Britain expressed their displeasure with the Ijebu country blockages of roads and prevention of trades between their traders and the countries in the Interior countries. Then the British Parliament debate it

"that the Ijebu have no trust in our trade and they claim our only interest is to take their countries from them."

Another member said

"they also believe our only interest is that we want to promote our trades above that of the native countries interest. And we are now successful in adding the Egbados Protectorate to our Colony of Lagos. We shall acquire the whole interior land for ourselves before the French make the attempts getting them before us."

Another said

"we are aware that the Ijebus are now trading with the French in ammunitions we don't have to take any chances. And also we shall have to talk with the Ijebu since she is the only country left for us to penetrate, their Awujale and Chiefs are tough people and we don't even know anything about their way of life or culture."

One member said

"the Missionary are not established in their country because they make it difficult for us and any foreigner and even their native neighbours do not know them, because they prevent them from getting into their country as well."

Then the British Parliament vote and conclude:

"that the Ijebu country shall be attack and their wall broken and enforce trade relationship between the Ijebu country and Lagos just like the other neighbouring countries. The road blockage and toll gates shall be stop by the Ijebu Majesty the Awujale of Ijebuland and he shall be compensated for the amount of £800 annually tribute for the toll fees."

Meanwhile Mr. Ajose went to the Ijebuland to interview the people about their preparation and feeling about the war the British have declared againt Ijebuland. And one of the son of the Balogun Ijebu said

"Afi Oyinbo afi Ijebu, dede aiye eru ni won. Ko si Oja ti Oyinbo ta, ti Ijebu ko ta" ("Except the white man and the Ijebu the whole world besides are slaves: there is no market in which a white man may be sold and none where Ijebus may be sold.")

However, the Acting Governor, the Colonial Sectary, and Capt. George Chardin Denton said

"in pursuance of peace with the Ijebu!" "I will propose a visit to the Awujale of Ijebu!" "To talk with him in person in friendly manner and thus I will be able to acquire some knowledge about the Ijebu country."

So he sent word concerning his proposal to the Downing Street for permission, and Her Majesty grant him permission to make the visit. Then he assumed that the Awujale would grant him audience because he had recieved messenge from the Awujale, for him to come. However, he with Oliver Smith, the Queen's Advocate, Thomas Welsh, Esq., a member of the Legislative Council and a Merchant representative, Dr. J.W. Rowland, the Colonial Surgeon, Capt. A.F. Tarbel and Mr. f. Colley-Green of the Hausa force, Mr. Jacob Alesinloye an Ijebu merchant resident at Lagos, and Mr. A.L. Hethersett, the Government Interpreter, with a guard of honour and including the Hausa Band went to Ijebuland. And when they reach Ito Ike, the Ijebus stop them from entering Ijebuland and they said to them

"why are you entering our country with all these people?

The governor interpreter said

439

"the white man say we have come to see the Awujale Oba Aboki, and to talk about peace between our country and your country."

The warrior responds

"If you have come to talk peace with the Awujale Oba Aboki, do you have to come with all these crowd? So you will have to let some them go back before we can allow you into our country. Have you forgotten that we are not under your Government?

But the Governor sent a messenger to the Awujale Oba Aboki

"your Majesty!" "have you forgotten of the permission granted me to visit the Awujale for peace talk and I have ensured that the expenses for the travel had been granted by Her Majesty's Government. And also I will be willing to send home my guard of honour and my attendants so as to reduce the people coming with me to your Majesty country. If it will please your Majesty for me to enter Ijebu country with only few people."

But the Olisa adviced the Awujale Oba Aboki and he said

"Kabiyesi o!" "Kabiyesi o!" "Kabiyesi o!" "My Lord my advice Kabiyesi is not to send his people away since he said he had been granted permission by his Queen before coming on the visit, because we a not dealing with him who is a servant. But we are dealing with him as a representative of his master, the Queen of the white people."

Then the Awujale Oba Aboki gave the order

"the white people and their King representative shall be allowed in Ijebu, but not with a military escort."

So the Governor was allowed to enter the Ijebuland and they got into the land with the Colonial Streamer call Margaret and he went to Ijebu-Ode with his civil attendants only. And the people of Ijebu-Ode were very vigilant throughout and after the Governor and his entourage enter Ijebu-Ode. The Ijebu Army stand guard everywhere and in the palace compound and they were ready to defend the country. However, on the fourth day the Awujale order

"let the Governor to be allowed to come before my present."

Then the Governor was given a sit of honor which the Olisa had provided since he was representing the Queen of his country and he said

"your Majesty!" "The Awujale of Ijebu!" "Her Royal Majesty!" "The Queen send her greetings and the people of Britain and those of her Colony in Lagos also send their greetings. We have come to talk about the issue of trade and peace for both Ijebu and Lagos and the rest of the Interior countries. We have observed and understand now that the Awujale and the people of Ijebu are the most prominent trade partner to talk to and finalize issue of trade in the countries that are neighbouring to the Lagos Colony. So we want the Ijebu country to allow the people of the Interior countries to have free access to the coast by themselves. And to have relationship with the people of Ijebu and that of Lagos. We assure your Majesty and the people of Ijebu that there is great prosperity, more trade and money for the Ijebu country and the neighbouing countries in this relationship. Her Majesty has already approved to pay the Ijebu country the sum of money that is of the equivalent to that your country gets in toll fees on your gates."

After the Governor had finished talking the Awujale Oba Aboki was very annoyed and he call on the Olisa to his side and said

"I make a mistake allowing this fool to come before me only for him to be telling me what to do. I do not think that he and his Queen do have good manner to know that you don't come to another King's country to tell him what to do."

Then the Awujale Oba Aboki got up and the Olisa and every Ijebu people in the Palace prostrates and they said .

"Kabiyesi o!" "Kabiyesi o!" "Kabiyesi o!"

As he walked away from the throne to his inner court. Then the Olisa address the Governor and said

"white man!" "The Awujale Oba Aboki!" "Shall not like to continue the discussion with you instead for Queen to dialogue with the Awujale she sent you here only to come and tell the Awujale what she want. Let her know that Ijebu country is not under the control and will never be under the British Government. Ijebu is different from the rest of the countries where the Queen and her servants can buy them. We are not greedy, all we want is to trade with the countries around us, without losing our land to nobody. It has been since our Ancestors came back from Jebusite, Egypt and Waddai, no foreign power had been able to dominate us, nor has the Awujale ever pay tribute or homage to any King or Lord."

Then the other Obas and Chiefs said

"what an insult!" "On our own land!" "For these arrogant white man to come and try to dictate to the Awujale what he want."

Then the Olisa said

"this is our decision as Ijebu people we don't want to listen to your government dictate anymore and we only want to meet the Yorubas at Oru for trade and the Ijebus will trade with the white people and Lagos people at Ejrin. We do not trust the white people who have no other interest than to take the Interior land for themselves after they had taken the people away as slaves, to enter into our country and the Interior country."

Then the Governor stood up and he said

"I would still like for the Awujale and the Chiefs to have the presents we brought for them."

And the Olisa order

"the Awujale's present shall to be taken, because by our custom no body take away anything that is meant for the Awujale away from him. But as for me, the Obas, and the Chiefs we do not take presents from the Awujale's enemy."

So the Governor said

"this is an insult to Her Royal Majesty!" "To refuse to take her gift to you."

The Olisa responds

"then why don't your Queen!" "And her servants!" "Mind their own business and leave these countries alone, and face only the trade which we gave you get permission for in Lagos coaster area, and stop forcing your Government politics on us."

However, when the Governor return back to Lagos, he sent message back to the home office in Britain, then the Ijebu issue was brought before Her Majesty the Queen and the council of the Colonial affairs advice and said

"I would advice her Royal Majesty that war is be declared on the Ijebu country and to make them to open their country for trade with our merchants."

And the Queen suggest

"we shall have to make sure that we don't damage the government structure of the Majesty the Awujale, and the Ijebuland tradition and custom because the character of the Monarchy looks that of exceptional one and the Awujales of the Ijebu have been holding their ground since history and maintain their Leadership role of the countries in the Interior just as we have maintain our leadership in the affairs of the World. And we shall Ensured that no damage happen to the people of this country also."

Then the Council of Colonial affairs left the Queen palace and declared war on the Ijebu Country.

Thereafter the Governor of Lagos sent for more officers from England, the Gold Coast, and Sierra Leone. And these are the Officers and Soldiers that fought the war against the Ijebu Army in 13th of May 1892:

Colonel Francis C. Scott, C.B. Inspector-General of the Gold Coast Forces, the Commander of the Expedition.

Officers From England

Capt. The Hon. A. S. Hardinge, 1st Battalion Scot Fusiliers
Capt. E.R. Owen, 1st Batt. Lancashire Fusilers
Capt. A.V. Ussher, 1st Batt. Scottish Rifles
Capt. R.L. Brower, 7th Batt. King's Royal Rifles
Capt. J.R.V. Gordon, 15th Hussars
Lieut. C.E. Laurie, Royal Artillery
Lieut. J.F. Davis, 1st Batt. Grenadier Guards

From The Gold Coast

Capt. F.M. Bayley, Assist-Inspector, Gold Coast Colony
Capt. H.D. Larymore, Asst.-Inspector, Gold Coast native Officer Ali, Gold Coast Colony
Mr. Henry Plange, Quartermaster (Acting), Gold Coast Colony.
2 Sergt. Majors, 4 Sergts., 146 N.C.O's and Hausas Soldiers.

From Sierra Leone

Major G.C. Madden
Lieut. C.V.R. Wright
Lieut. E.L. Cowrie
Surgeon Capt. R. Croft
99 N.C.Os and men, 2nrd Batt., W.T. Regiment

Lagos Hausas

Capt. A.F. Tarbet, Asst., -Inspector, Lagos Constabulary
Capt. G.B. A Haddon Smith, Asst., Inspector, Lagos
Sergt. - Majors Dangana and Danksfi
Asst,-Supdts. F. Colley - Green, A. Claud Willoughby pay and Quarter Master W.R. Harding

1580 men rank and file, with 1000 Ibadan Irregular under their own Captain Toyan

However, the British Army war plan was to deceive the Ijebu Army, and after Colonel Francis C. Scott briefing of the Lagos Army by Capt. A.F. Tarbet and Capt. G.B. Haddon Smith said

"it will be difficult to defeat the Jebu on close war contact because they are good marksmen and good with the artillery, sword and archers which usually have poisonous war head."

Capt A.S. Hardinge said

"we heard that they are great warriors just like when they were in Ijebusite and most of their ancestors migrate from Egypt so they have good history of warfare and lot experience as well." Capt. E.R. Owen ask

"are they still excellent with the horse as the marksmen with the archers?"

Then Capt. G.B. Haddone Smith took charge of the briefing and he said

"from our study of the Ijebu warfare, they are still excellent marksmen, good with the horse, but one remarkable thing about their strength is not getting tired in battle and they move very fast in their one and one attack as marksmen. So what we have to do is that we are going to have three camps which would enable us to divide their attention into three places. But two will be active and the third one will be in the shadow to be use for reinforcement if the case may arise because we don't want to under estimate the warriors and Army that have history of no lost in their battles."

Colonel Scott now pointing on the map spread on the table while the rest of the Officers look as he talk said

"We have to first launch our attack at Itu IKe camp in Ehjrin. So that we can draw the attention of the Ijebu Army to these district."

Thereafter he made a circle on the map, and said

"from our camp here in Epe we shall attack the wall of the town in Ijebu-Ode district with the Cannon and rockets. This would enable us to enter their country as conqueror since they have not engage in any war that involve Cannon and rockets attack before."

And he raise his head as if he except someone to say something, and add

"we have the advantage of our streamer boats which is faster than their boats on the Lagoon, so we can move faster than them. Do we follow this plans and is there any question?"

The whole Officers respond

"we understand and already for action sir!"

And he said

"then let go and show the bastard who is the boss."

Then they all left the war briefing and each officer approached their command unit and called the attention of the soldiers to order and form their parade and inspection by the Commandering officer.

Meanwhile, the Balogun (General) Ijebu Onafowokan had already heard of the British Army camp at Ito Ike and he ordered the defence of the Lagoon front cities and towns. Then the archer units and sharp gun shooters were made to man the walls and different places and had being on look out and alert for the invasion. And he ordered the Seriki Kuku to move to Ijebu-Ode to defend the place. Then when the British Army launched their attack at Ito Ike, shooting Cannons and rockets into the forest. The Ijebu Army were initially afraid, but after continuous shooting of the Cannons which mostly burn the forest and killed lot of people in the town and burn houses, the people instead of running away took their charms and they said

"ki lo tu ku? "Ti a ba ma Ku!" "Ka kuku ku ewo ni ti eru!" ("what is left? "If we a going to die let us die why shall we be afraid!") "We Ijebu are not slave to the white and the white will not be able to enslave us alive."

So the Ijebu were able to stand up and defend themselves with their archers and guns which hit the Hausa soldiers which the British were using for their fight. But the Hausas would not follow command and instructions, they only ran after the direction of leading warrior and they were all almost killed by the archers poisonous arrow head weapons and gun shots. Mainwhile the Sergeant will shot

"fall back!" "And stay on column!" "fall back!" "And stay on column!" ...

but they would not listen, and they would not understand the command. But they ran and scatter about, which exposed them and there were more casualty on the side of the British Army than the Ijebus. Then Capt. F. Bayley who was in charge of the Command order

"the Cannon shooting to be stop!" "I repeat stop the cannon shooting now."

And told the Soldiers who were in majority were Hausa and they were only good as guards and watch men and they also lack the ability to listen to instruction and to launch a counter attack on the Ijebus so most of Hausas were killed. Then the British retreat with the loss of some their officers, Major G.C. Madden, Lieut. C.V.R. Wright, most of the Gold Coast Command were killed and the Lagos Hausa Captains was also killed and a lot they were wounded. However, on the side of the Ijebus there were more Civilian killed and lot of houses were burn, and some warriors and war-chiefs were also killed. But the Ijebus pursued the British Army in their retreat and almost start attacking Lagos, but when they saw their people that were crying and protesting. The Balogun said we don't want to kill our own people because of this evil white people. Meanwhile, the Balogun received word that the white people had attack Epe and they were taking the war to Ijebu-Ode. Then he order

"the Army shall go and join the Seriki Ijebu Kuku Force and some of the warlords took the boats to Epe and the battle had move to Ijebu-Ode because the Epe war-chiefs did not have enough warriors to hold the British. Then Colonel Scott who was the commander of the British Army order "we don't want to attack Epe which is going to be part of our city in Lagos Colony. Now we have move to Ijebu-Ode,"

Then at Ijebu-Ode wall the Colonel order

"now the Cannon shall to be shot continuously and ensure we destroy Ijebu-Ode and bring the their king and his chiefs to their arrongant kneels."

So the cannons bombard the wall of Ijebu-Ode and the wall give way and the houses were burn. The poeple were running trying to move more into the interior towns and villages. But the Ijebu Army and people defend the city and the fight took about one year. However, the British find it difficult to penetrate the thick forest of the Ijebuland and both camps suffered almost equal lost. Then the Balogun fought like a hero and he was shot and he fell from his horse. So the Awujale Oba Aboki, the Princes, the Olisa, the Obas, and Chiefs decide

"instead letting the white people destroy and kill the civilian with their Cannon and Rockets, we shall make them to stop the shooting of the Cannons and the Rockets."

So the Seriki Ijebu Kuku got on a white horse, carried a white flag and rode very fast to the middle of the battlefield, waving the flag. So when the British Officers saw the man on the horse with a white flag they order

"now stop shooting the Cannon!" "now stop shooting the Cannon!...."

And the cannon was stop and both sides stop shooting at each other. Then Colonel Scott also got on his horse and drawn his sword and rode toward the middle of battle field. When both war-chiefs met they greet each other and the Colonel realized that the Ijebu man was the Seriki Kuku, who the Ijebu had just recall back home from exile in Ibadan because he was accused of making friendship with the white people. And the Colonel was very happy to see Kuku and called him "Balogun!" "Balogun! ..."

And the Seriki Kuku told him

"the Awujale Oba Aboki will allow the white people to have settlement for trade and the Mission work only and no Military quarters in Ijebu country."

Then Colonel Scott who was also already tired of the war said

"we have not come to take the land from the Ijebu who's people are very difficult to be govern. If not so they would not have to reject a fine war-chief like you."

Then they both sake hands and accept the condition for the war to stop and exchanged their swords, and both of them rode their horses back to their camps. Thereafter the Seriki Kuku went to the Awujale Oba Aboki palace and all the Princes, the Olisa, the Obas and chiefs heard him as he told them his conversation with the white man. However, after the Olisa had inform the Awujale Oba Aboki of the outcome of Kuku's discussion with the white man, the Awujale Oba Aboki order

"the war shall stop and all the war-chiefs and their warriors shall decamp for their homes, cities and towns." "I offer my condolences to all our war heros, and people that were killed in this war. We have fought gallantly, and as usual had not lost our country or crown which had been given us by our ancestors right from Egypt, Ethiopia, Wadai in Suddan and to here the begin of human being land Ife (known as Atlantis). The Army shall remain on their post and protecting the walls and the gates. The war peace agreement of which we are to accomondate the white trade only, which does not involve any land to be given, or allow any white person in Ijebuland for their settlements. Ijebuland is not for sale to any foreigner and we shall maintain the sovereignty of our custom and tradition and we shall look up to the gods of our ancestors to grant us victory in all that we engage in now and in future. Again I congratunates you all my children and my subjects. Ewe so dede we Omo Alare, Ewe so."

Then the British Army went back to Lagos, but left a small unit in Ijebu-Ode to protect the Missionaries and their traders in the Ijebu country.

However, after the war with the British, there was changes in the politics of the Interior land and the Missionary were able to preach and lot of Ijebus became Christians and later Islamic religion also came to Ijebuland. Moreover, because the British were able to get into the Ijebu country, they were able to dominate the interior countries politics. And eventually, the Governor was able to move with his entourage to the Interior countries because the Government that had been able to stand and stop the Ijebus, no other Interior country Obas or Chiefs tried to face the Government in a fight. Then the British Government processed to Ilorin, then the Emir of Ilorin agreed for the war with Ofa to stop and made peace with Oyos on their war with the Ofa. And the Oke Ibadan Army decamp from Ikirun and return to Oke Ibadan. Thereafter, the Governor of Lagos with the Ijebu agreed and they build roads from Epe to Ijebu-Ode, Ijebu-Ode to Ibadan and other roads which promote business and trades between Lagos and the Interior land. Then the British government was able to establish the British Protectorate of the Oyo Country also. And the Egbas also sign agreement of protection with the British, but the Ijebu country remain Independent and refused to be under the British Government.

Acknowlegment

1. The History of the Ijebu, by Moses Botu Okubote (Apena)
2. From CREATION To IJEBU- ODE by Prince (Dr.) Gbolahan Taiwo Adebule
3. The History of theYorubs; from the earliest times to the beginning of the British, by The Rev. Samuel A. Johnson; http://archive.org/stream/historyofyorubas00John#page/6/mode/1up
4. Slave Trade in Nigeria: Encyclopedia, History Nigeria; http://logbaby.com/encyclopedia/ slave-trade-in-nigeria_9329.html
5. The Oyo Empire of Yoruba-Hist; http://www.google.com/search?q=oyo+empire&b.w=...
6. List of rulers of the Yoruba State of Oyo; https//en.wikipedia.org/wiki/list_of_the_Yoruba_ State_of_Oyo
7. PAST AWUJALE; http:// otunkay.wix.com/bokakeye#past-awujales
8. Ijebu History; http://ijrbumn.org/Ijebu_History.html

9. History of Nigeria; http://www.historyworld.net/wrldhis/PlainText Histors.asp?historyid=ad41

10. Britain, Slavery and the trade in enslaved African by Marika Sherwood; http://www.history.ac.uk/ihr/Focus/Slavery/articles/Sherwood.html

11. Race and History Forum by Olomu Eyebira; http://www.raceandhistory.com/cgi-bin/forum/webbs_config.pl?md=read;id=3129

12. HISTORY OF EGBA; https://www.facebook.com/TheYorubaPeople/post/

13. Aboard a Slave Ship, 1829; http://www.eyewithnesshistory.com/slavehip.htm

14. The economic bacis of the slave trade, by Dr. Alan Rice; http://revealinghistories.org.uk/africa-the-arrival-of-europeans-and-the-transatlantic-slave-trade/article/the-economic-basis-of-the-sale-trade.html

15. Enslavement and Industrialisation, by Robin Blackburrn; http://www.bbc.co.uk/history/british/abolition/industrialisation_article_01.shtml

Prince Olugbenga Adegbuyi Moshoodi Emmanuel Orebanwo

Is born in Ijebu-Ode to Princess Adebisi Yusuf a gand daugther of the Royal Majesty Awujale Oba Sotejoye the Paramount Ruler of Ijebuland and the Royal Majesty Awujale Oba Afesojoye Anikilaya the Paramount Ruler of Ijebuland and Mr Babatunde Orebanwo of Erinlu Ijebu-Ode. He has a Bachelors of Science in Quantity Surveying from the Federal University of Technology Akure Nigeria FUTA. And another Bachelors of Science in Electrical Engineering in The University of Texas at Arlington UTA, He is a Java Software Program Developer and He is Veteran of wars with the United State Navy. He has two children Prince Oluseyi Adeshina Ore and Princes Olutosin Adesewa Ore

Printed in the United States
By Bookmasters